FOR MY GRANDCHILDREN,
GLENN, SARAH, IAN, AND JENNA
FOR MY GREAT-GRANDCHILDREN,
ALLYSON, MAIRIN, GRACE, EMMA, MOLLY,
MARGARET, SOPHIA,
AND ALWAYS REMEMBERING GILLIAN

Escaping adversity, she boarded the Greyhound bus as it started to rain and took a seat by the window. With her heart pounding, she pressed her cheek against the glass and watched the raindrops fall. When the bus began to pull away from the station, a silent voice deep inside her cried out—hurry, hurry!

Her story as she tells it is a roller coaster of a read.

CHAPTER 1

I was given the name Kathleen Kelly, but I don't know who I am, and I'm about to leave the only home I've ever known. I stood before her the morning she proclaimed my freedom. She smiled at me—a strange expression coming from the usually stern Sister Renada. I knew her as Mother Renada. Fifty children resided in the old red brick structure known as the orphan home run by the Sisters of Charity. Foster homes eliminated the need for orphanages, remnants of a long-ago era, and as their need was no longer viable for homeless children, they began to close. The one I was about to leave was known throughout the small towns of northern Illinois as Saint Cecelia's Home for Children. It was constructed in the late 1800s, and now in the year 1950, it had served its purpose. Slowly each year, more children were sent to foster care, and the population of the orphanage began to dwindle. I was one of the unlucky ones who had spent my entire eighteen years at the home. On my eighteenth birthday, I was to be given two hundred dollars and sent out alone on my own.

It was a cool fall day, as I stood in Mother Renada's office. All that I owned filled a small bag and one large suitcase.

"Well, Kathleen," I heard her say, "You're a young woman today, and it's your eighteenth birthday, isn't it?" She said it in a patronizing way as if she were speaking to a small child. I was expected to answer this woman the children called Mother. I never liked her, but she was the only 'Mother' I ever knew.

"Yes, Mother, it is," I said, in a voice that didn't portray my true feelings.

She smiled, "Well, you don't have to leave right this minute. The children and the Sisters have a birthday cake waiting in the dining room. They would like to sing happy birthday to you before you go."

I left my belongings in her office and went with her to where the children and Sisters were waiting. The long table was filled with the older children, about thirty in all. I noticed a large cake placed in the middle of the table—probably baked by sister Mary Louise. She was the baker in the home. She offered to teach me to become a baker, but that was when I was fourteen, and she thought I had been fully indoctrinated into becoming a nun. I refused her offer.

I sat at the head of the table, and Sister Renada sat at the other end. Sister Mary Louise lit the candles on the cake, and on her orders they began singing to me. When they finished they waited in anticipation as Sister cut the cake. After everyone finished their treat and said goodbye, I followed Mother Renada back to her office.

With suitcase in hand, I stood there waiting for the two hundred dollars she was to give me. She took her time rummaging through her desk drawer and finally held the crisp twenty-dollar bills and meticulously counted them slowly as if she found it difficult to part with them. I always knew that money mattered more to her than the actual reason for all the donations she received—to have a home for orphaned children. She handed me the money and a slip of paper.

"Kathleen, here is the address of Mrs. Wilkie. She lives on Vicker Street in Clearidge. She agreed to rent you a room in her home until you're settled in your job."

"I have to find work, Mother," I said, feeling frightened at the thought of being on my own for the first time.

"We saved you that worry by acquiring work for you as a secretary for the police department in the town of Arden. The address is written on this paper. It's only a few miles west of Clearidge," she said, smiling. "You've been taught all the necessary skills you'll need."

I thanked her and put the money and the information she had given me into my purse and picked up my suitcase. I offered her my left hand in a gesture of goodbye. She took it and said, "Goodbye, Kathleen, may God be with you."

I turned and walked out of her office into the long dark hall with its highly polished floor. The only sound I heard was the heels of my shoes hitting the floor and echoing against the high ceiling as I walked toward the heavy door, about to step out alone, into the unknown.

Clearidge hadn't been a small town since it was taken over by the city of Chicago sometime in the early 1900s, but people still called the area by its former name. The orphanage had been built while it was still a small town. I just knew the area around it from all the outings we children from the home were taken to through the years. Walking away from the only home I had ever known, I felt a lump in my throat begin to form. I pulled the collar of my coat tight around my neck, as the weather was quite chilly, and walked the four blocks from the orphanage down Archer Avenue until I came to Vicker Street. I turned south and walked several blocks past small frame and clapboard homes with front porches. I took out the slip of paper with the address and looked for 55 Vicker. It was a white frame house with a front porch set far back from the street. I walked up the long walkway, and a small elderly woman appeared at the top of the steps. When I approached her porch, she smiled down at me.

"You must be the girl from the orphan home," she said, greeting me with a friendly smile. I immediately felt the tension in my shoulders ease.

"The Sister called to tell me you were on your way. I'm Anna Wilkie. Come, come in," she said, waving me up the porch and into her home. Once inside, I took in the strong smell of Lysol. Her home appeared immaculate. She showed me to my room, which overlooked the front porch.

"Here, dear, I thought you would like the room looking out at the street," she said. With her home set so far back, there wasn't much I could see of the street. Most of her yard seemed to be in front of the house.

"Thank you, Mrs. Wilkie," I said as I placed my suitcase down.

"You can call me Anna. Well, you look like you could use a good cup of tea—your name is Kathleen?"

"Yes, that was the name that was pinned to me as a newborn when the Sisters found me. I don't know my real last name. The Sisters gave me the name Kelly. They thought it went well with Kathleen like it had a nice ring to it."

"Well, Kathleen, what's in a name? It means nothing. My name of Wilkie was shortened when my father-in-law came from Poland."

She walked me into her kitchen, and I sat at her table. She sat across from me, pouring the tea she had prepared in anticipation of my arrival. She placed a large plate of cookies in the center of the table. I didn't feel like having any, but not to hurt her feelings I managed to take one and place it on my plate.

3

Chasing the Unicorn

"I just had a birthday today," I said, trying to make conversation, and that wasn't easy for me to do, as I was extremely shy.

"Yes, I know, Kathleen. I would think they could have kept you a few extra days past your eighteenth birthday, but it's all about money, isn't it?" she said, with an expression of disdain appearing on her face.

I looked around her kitchen and then gave her my full attention as she began to tell me all about losing her only child in Korea. He was in the Marines, she said, only nineteen when he was sent over. It was the last week of September when she received the news of his death less than four weeks ago. He had been stationed there for at least a year before the first shots were fired in the month of June. Her husband had been deceased for five years. She told me she had her son, her only child, late in her thirties. She talked on and on about him and all the sacrifices she made for him. She appeared to be a sad and lonely woman.

"How did you come to hear about me?" I asked.

"It was Father Walinski, from Saint Anne's parish that mentioned Saint Cecelia's was looking for a place for one of their charges that would be coming of age soon and had to leave the home," she said.

I thanked her and placed my empty cup back on the saucer and excused myself.

"I need to use your bathroom and then unpack," I said.

"Oh, of course you do," she agreed, as she hurried to show me where it was. Once I closed the door, I noticed how everything shined. Not a thing seemed out of place. The towel that hung on a rod appeared unused so when I washed my hands, I took out the Kleenex I had in my skirt pocket and wiped both my hands and the sink. When I returned she led me to the room she had given me.

"There are extra pillows and blankets in the closet," she said, as she opened the closet door to show me. She had emptied it except for a Marine uniform she kept to one side. It was covered in plastic. She shook her head in resignation.

"That's my Gary's uniform. They sent me all his belongings when they shipped his body home for burial. He's buried in Saint Mary's cemetery on Archer Avenue."

She left the room and I quickly closed the door, unpacked my large

4

suitcase and put some of my clothing in the empty dresser drawers. In the closet I hung up the dresses that I had neatly unfolded, along with a coat and jacket. I retrieved my personal articles from my small bag along with the small figurine of a white stallion with a horn sticking out of its forehead. Sister Mary Louise had given it to me when I was six years old after she found me crying when some of the kids made fun of my red hair. I wasn't good at defending myself and sister took me aside and dried my tears. "You come with me," she said, "I have something for you." She held a small figure of a horse with a horn in the middle of its head. She called it a unicorn and then proceeded to tell me a fairy tale about the unicorn. *There once was a princess who lived in a castle very far away, and she was unhappy because she felt quite alone. You see, the king was a busy man and didn't have much time for his daughter and she too didn't have a mother. Her mother had gone to heaven. One day a beautiful white horse with a horn in the middle of its head came into her garden and spoke to her. He noticed how sad she was and he wanted to make her happy, so he offered her a ride and allowed her to climb on his back. During the ride, with the horse running fast and the wind on her face, she felt so happy, but she fell off and the unicorn kept going. She chased after him but she couldn't catch him and the happiness she felt when she was with him was gone. So you see Kathleen, I give you this little unicorn. He represents happiness— keep him with you, always.*

I remembered the entire story as I placed it on the dresser where I could view it. I felt tired and drained of energy after Mrs. Wilkie talked so much about her son. I hoped she would give me some space. I sat on the bed and looked at the slip of paper with the address of the Arden Police Department. I would take the bus in the morning. Kicking off my shoes, I lay back on the chenille bedspread and closed my eyes. My last thoughts were of how frightened and alone I was feeling.

Mrs. Wilkie awakened me when she knocked on my door.

"It's time for supper," she called. I got up to straighten my skirt, then looked in the dresser mirror and combed my hair before I went out to her kitchen where she had set the table and was spooning soup into two bowls.

"Did you have a nice nap, dear?" she asked.

"Yes, I did. Thank you, for letting me sleep."

She looked at me with a sad expression, "I let my Gary sleep whenever he wanted. I always cooked his favorite dishes. This soup is one of them."

I looked into the bowl of dark soup. "What kind is it?" I asked.

"It's Polish soup. It's called blood soup. It was my Gary's favorite," she said, smiling. "If you like it you can have more."

I had all I could do to keep from gagging just looking at it. I took the spoon and put a little on the tip and when I tasted it I knew there was no way I was going to eat a spoonful, let alone the whole bowl. I busied myself buttering a piece of bread, trying to engage her in conversation while thinking of a way to get rid of the soup. I thought of telling her straight out that I couldn't eat it, didn't like it, but something in her demeanor told me she might not take it too well. I sat with the bread in my hand taking tiny bites while holding the spoon in my other hand and listening to her talk on and on about her son. She spoke about all she had done for him and then he went and joined the Marines as soon as he was eighteen. I began to get the picture and understood his escape into the Marines.

When she got up to visit the bathroom, I quickly emptied the bowl into the sink and ran the water to eliminate all traces of the soup. When she returned she noticed the empty bowl.

"Oh, would you like more?" she asked, looking pleased, thinking I had finished the soup. "No, no, I had plenty, thank you. I would like to help you clean up," I said. "Oh, no, that's all right, I do things a certain way."

When she stood at the sink with her back to me, I went to my room. I knew as soon as I made enough money in my new job I would look for another place. I wondered about the position I was to fill and hoped I would be able to do a good job. Knowing it would be work for a police department gave me a good feeling.

The next morning after awakening early, Mrs. Wilkie had a large breakfast waiting for me. She stood in the doorway and wished me good luck as I left to catch the bus to Arden. The bus stopped almost in front of the police station, and I walked to the entrance with my heart pounding. I was nervous; afraid they wouldn't hire me, or after I started working they would fire me, all those thoughts were on my mind. I approached the desk where a big heavy-set sergeant sat manning the phones. Several were ringing as he was barking orders into the mouthpieces of two of them. I stood before him and waited. When he was free he looked over his desk at me.

"Can I help you, Miss?" "Yes, I'm Kathleen Kelly. I came from Saint Cecelia's. I was told you have an opening for a secretary's position."

"Oh, yeah." He turned his head to shout behind him at several cops sitting at their desks. "The new secretary is here!"

One of the policemen came over to me. "Hi, I'm Tim O'Malley." He held his hand out and I took it,

"I'm Kathleen Kelly."

He smiled, "Well, we sure need some help here. The last girl quit to have a baby, so I'm afraid we're pretty backed up with the paper-work."

He explained what my job would be as he led me across the back room. I noticed several cops in the station staring at me as I followed him to what was to be my desk. He turned and announced my name to them. They welcomed me with wide smiles. The desk was a mess, piled high with various papers. Tim looked at the desk and apologized.

"No problem," I said, as I removed my coat, and then sat down placing my purse under the desk.

"He smiled at me, "This needs to be filed in that cabinet over there."

"Oh, sure," I answered. I got right to work, knowing I would have it cleaned up in no time at all. It was what I did for Sister Renada. I took care of several of the Sisters' business affairs. In school I was taught typing and shorthand and they had me working for them since I was in the tenth grade.

My first day on the new job went well and the men were helpful and kind to me. The handsome but tough looking Sergeant Martino at the main desk turned out to be just a big gentle Teddy bear. He treated me like I could have been his daughter—getting me coffee or whatever I needed, telling me he had a daughter my age and how proud he was of her because she was taking college courses at a Junior college. I ended the day tired but happy. When I returned to Mrs. Wilkie, she was interested in hearing all about my first day on the job. I didn't disappoint her. I had no one else to talk to so she heard all about my first day and then all the days after. She never failed to tell me to be careful of men and how they were all the same and not to trust any of them. I would laugh off most of what she said. She cautioned me about being out late and mentioned the murders of two young girls in the area that hadn't been solved yet. I knew about them and figured she intended to scare me into remaining with her each evening. I counted the days until I could save enough money to find another place, knowing it would be another room in someone else's home. I began to feel the need to talk to another person my age. Between the police station and Mrs. Wilkie, I hadn't met another girl I could pal around with.

I spent thanksgiving with Anna Wilkie and her sister Eva, and her family. I felt out of place and couldn't wait for the day to end. The police department was going to hold their annual Christmas party a week before Christmas and would include their entire families. I was looking forward to meeting their wives and children. The occasion would be held in the Elks Lodge in Arden. I was hoping to meet Sergeant Martino's family, especially the daughter he often spoke of. Right after Thanksgiving, the Sergeant surprised me by inviting me to his home to meet his family. He knew I was without a family of my own. He talked it over with his wife, and she insisted I be invited to supper. I couldn't wait to tell Mrs. Wilkie.

I felt I was being disloyal to her and in trying to explain that I had an invitation from one of my co-workers, I had a bad habit of always looking down when I felt the least bit of pressure.

CHAPTER 2

The evening I was to go to Sergeant Martino's home had come and Mrs. Wilkie hovered around asking many questions. When I first informed her of my invitation she didn't seem too pleased. "It's the sergeant at the station. He's a married man, with children my age," I informed her.

"Well, you be careful out there," she said looking worried. "You're not used to the outside world. It's a scary place. They never caught the killer, or killers of the murder of those young women in Clearidge. One was dumped in a field near the railroad tracks and one was found behind the grade school, near the airport."

"I heard about it, but wasn't that many months ago?" I said, thinking the killers might have left the area.

Mrs. Wilkie looked over at me and said, "One can't be too careful these days."

I had mixed feelings about her. As the days went by I became accustomed to her being so attentive to me. I began to feel wanted for the first time in my life. It was a nice feeling—like I belonged to someone and that she really cared about me. Her meddling didn't seem to bother me as much as it did when I first arrived at her home. Thoughts of moving out began to fade away. The Sisters took good care of my physical needs, but I always felt something was missing. I now realized it was the absence of the one person who would love me. After the first month with Mrs. Wilkie, she began letting me help her around the house. She insisted on washing my clothes and made great meals and looked after me the way I imagined a mother would. I managed to tell her that her soup didn't agree with me and to my surprise she wasn't upset at all. She treated me like I imagined she treated her own son. Because I was craving an emotional bond to someone, I didn't rebel, as he must have.

She watched me as I combed my hair and placed a fur headband on and as I was getting into my winter coat, she smiled and came up to adjust the collar for me.

"You be careful, but have a good time. What time do you think you'll be home?" she asked, looking concerned.

"Don't worry Anna, if it's late I'm sure Sergeant Martino will drive me home," I said, reassuring her. For a moment I stood at the door wondering if I should hug her goodbye. This would be the first time I left her home for something other than going to work or shopping. I paused at the door and turned to her and to my surprise she came up and gently kissed me on the cheek.

"I don't mean to scare you and I do want you to have a good time," she said.

"I'll tell you all about it when I get home, if it isn't too late," I assured her.

It was Saturday and the bus was running late. I waited about ten minutes and finally one appeared. When it arrived at the stop where I was to get off, I could see all the Christmas decorations in store windows. The Martinos lived a block off the main bus route so I didn't have far to walk. It was starting to get dark, so I hurried as I walked against the winter wind. I found the address he had given me and the home didn't look much different from Mrs. Wilkie's place. It was a white frame house with a common front porch. I could see the Christmas tree lights sparkling in the window. I was nervous as I rang the bell.

A tall dark-haired girl answered it. Her dark eyes sparkled as she greeted me with a wide smile. "Oh, you must be Kathleen, come in. Dad, Kathleen is here!" she shouted.

All of a sudden it seemed like the whole family rushed to the door to greet me. I was overwhelmed. Sergeant Martino led me into his living room as someone was reaching for my coat before I had a chance to remove it. I took in the entire family that surrounded me. A young boy who looked about six or seven years of age blurted out loudly, "Is she the orphan?"

"Tony, that isn't nice!" his mother said. "She's not an orphan, she works at the station with Daddy." She took my coat and introduced herself. "I'm Lottie," she said, as she introduced the rest of the family. "This is our daughter, Angie." I had guessed when she answered the door that she was the daughter Sergeant Martino often spoke of. "I'm glad to meet you," Angie said. "Dad told me all about you and what a great secretary you are."

The family consisted of four children with Angie being the eldest. The younger siblings were all boys with Tony the youngest. Frank looked about fifteen as did his brother Sal Junior. They all made me feel quite at home. Later, as Lottie was setting the table in their large dining room, I offered to help, but Angie said, "Oh, no, you're our guest tonight." I noticed the table was set for one extra person and wondered if it was for a grandparent who lived in the home, but hadn't made an appearance yet. When the doorbell rang, Tony raced to the door. I was sitting in a living room chair facing the entrance hall and was surprised to see a tall, dark-haired man enter. I felt a rush of blush fill my face as our eyes met. His eyes were dark and penetrating as he smiled at me displaying a perfect set of white teeth. He wasn't the most handsome guy I had ever laid eyes on, but he wasn't bad looking. He appeared to be much older than me.

"Oh, Kathleen, this is Sheriff Dan Robson. Dan, this is Kathleen Kelly," Sergeant Martino said as he introduced us.

"Dan is the top sheriff in Arden," he said, as I stood to greet Dan. We shook hands and he said the usual words like "Happy to meet you, Kathleen."

I replied back, "It's nice to meet you too."

Lottie entered the room and announced that supper was ready, so we followed her to the table. I walked behind her and sat down first, before Dan could be seated, and two of the young boys sat on each side of me. That left the chair across from me empty and Dan took it. I had wished he had taken a place on the same side of the table where he wouldn't have a complete face-to-face view of me. I felt self-conscious sitting across from him and being unable to avoid glancing at him. He stared at me with eyes that seemed to penetrate right through me, or so I thought. He had a kind but intense expression to his face, but he smiled every time our eyes met. I noticed how he would look at my red hair and I felt self conscious about it. The Martino family was very talkative and loud. Their laughter filled the room, distracting Dan from glancing over at me too often. For that I was grateful because I was so painfully shy. I wasn't accustomed to a large boisterous family like the Martinos. Dan joined in with them telling stories and jokes while I remained silent. I didn't have anything to contribute to the conversation. Dan teased me a little bit about my blushing. It was something I couldn't control having a very fair complexion. When there was a lull in the conversation, he looked over at me and said, "You have the bluest eyes— it goes well with your red hair." I was embarrassed and speechless as the children laughed. Finally, all I could say was, "Thank you."

After the meal was over, I was happy that no one said I had come from an orphan home. Sergeant Martino and his wife mentioned what an efficient secretary I was for the police department. Later when we went into the living room, Dan took a seat across from me.

"Do you like your job?" he asked.

"Yes, yes I do," I replied.

"Where do you live?" he asked, and before I could answer, Sergeant Martino started to explain my situation. "She graduated high school and turned eighteen recently and had to leave St. Cecilia's, — you know, the Catholic home for those who don't have any family."

I felt embarrassed, but glad he didn't use the word orphanage. Dan's head rose up as if his interest peeked. He smiled and came over to the sofa where I had been sitting alone. Angie, sitting in a chair across from us filled him in on more than I cared to have him to know.

"She boards with a widow in Clearidge," she informed him.

He looked at me and I thought I saw a hint of pity in his expression, but it soon changed to that of one who began to appear somewhat almost too interested in me. He stared at me without saying anything and it made me uncomfortable until Angie mentioned something about the latest movie she had seen.

"Have you been to the movies lately?" he asked. I shook my head no. "I'd like to take you to one if you'd like and maybe out to dinner afterwards?"

"Oh," was all I managed to say, as Angie blurted out with excitement, "We can double date!" I think she sensed I would feel more comfortable with others along on what would be a first real date. The Sisters were very strict. I wasn't allowed to be with a boy until I was old enough to be on my own. In high school I would watch the girls and boys pairing off together and wished I had a boyfriend of my own. They did allow me to go to my senior prom with a boy they picked from the home that was the same height I was. With both of us at five feet six inches, I had to wear flat ballerina slippers, which were all the rage in 1950.

The evening was coming to an end and it was getting late. I was waiting for Sergeant Martino to offer to drive me home, but Lottie came into the room and asked Dan if he wouldn't mind bringing me home. I became nervous and wished she hadn't done that, but Dan agreed with a reassuring smile that he would make sure to see me safely home.

I followed Lottie to the closet where she retrieved my coat. She sensed I was apprehensive about going with Dan and said, "Kathleen, he's a grown man and the sheriff, you can't be any safer than that."

"How old is he?" I asked. She laughed,

"Old enough to know better. He's around thirty, I think."

I walked back to the living room where Dan waited, and after we said thank you for the supper, and nice evening comments were expressed by both of us, we left. He hurried to open the car door for me and I watched as he walked in front of his 1950 Oldsmobile to get to the driver's side. He was tall. I guessed about six feet tall. I had to admit he was attractive enough, but wasn't sure of his motives for wanting to take me out. I thought he felt sorry for me after hearing I was an orphan. I didn't think he would be interested in an eighteen-year-old kid like me. That is how I felt—like a kid, because I knew very little of how things worked.

He lit a cigarette and then started up the motor. I sat against the passenger door feeling vulnerable and waiting for the ride to end. He was quiet for a few minutes and then he asked me if I knew who my parents were. "No, I don't," I answered. "Oh, that's too bad," he said.

He took a drag on his cigarette and then looked over at me. "How do you like where you're living now?" "I like the lady I board with," I said, and then there was silence. He seemed to be deep in thought and didn't talk much the rest of the way. I pressed my shoulder against the door just waiting for the moment he pulled up in front of Mrs. Wilkie's home. I couldn't wait to get out of his car. When he turned down Vicker Street I began to relax. He slowed down at the curb in front of the house and I opened the door quickly to jump out before he had come to a complete stop. "Thanks for the ride!" I shouted, and as I started up the walk I heard him say, "What's the hurry?"

I pretended not to hear him and hurried up to the porch. I didn't look back and let myself into the house. Mrs. Wilkie had gone to bed as it was close to 1:00 am. I entered my room in the dark and walked over to the window to pull the shade down and that's when I noticed his car was still parked at the curb. Because the street was a longer distance from the house than normal, I couldn't see if he was still at the wheel, but I thought I saw a flicker of light from his cigarette. I pulled the window shade down and turned on the lamp on my nightstand. I sat on my bed in my coat and wondered why he hadn't pulled away. I was afraid to peek out to check if he was still there. I undressed and got ready for bed. I had trouble falling asleep so I got up in the dark to peek between the shade and the window frame. I was relieved to see that his car was gone.

The next morning, on Sunday, I prepared to attend church with Mrs. Wilkie, as I was in the habit of doing ever since I arrived at her home. She was a devout Catholic and never missed Mass. Having been raised in a Catholic orphanage, it never occurred to me to ever miss a service. Mrs. Wilkie drove an old 1941 Ford. I hadn't learned to drive yet and she promised to teach me when I turned twenty-one. I guess she expected me to remain with her forever. As much as I enjoyed her care, I hoped I wouldn't be with her that long. I had dreams of marrying and having a family of my own one-day. At times I thought that day wouldn't come soon enough.

On Monday morning I arrived at work and was surprised to see all the men laughing and greeting me with shouts of, "Did you have a good time Saturday night, Kathleen?" Sergeant Martino smiled and stood up from his desk. "Hey, Kathleen! What did you do to Sheriff Robson? He called yesterday and asked a lot of questions. I think he's real interested in you."

Just then Tim, the young cop who showed me around the first day, shouted, "He's too old for her!" I sat at my desk blushing badly as they kept teasing me. I pretended to be looking at the fresh batch of papers to be typed and filed but they were a blur to me. I was too shy and humiliated to look up from my desk. Tim came over and stood in front of it. I raised my head just enough to view his badge. "Don't let them get to you," he said, sympathetically.

I was attracted to Tim. He was tall and quite handsome with light brown hair and deep brown eyes. I knew he had a crush on me, but I didn't encourage his attention because we worked together. I knew it was a silly reason to discourage him, because I liked him. I smiled nicely and proceeded to attend to my work. He went back to his desk.

Just before quitting time, Tim came up to me. "Can I drive you home tonight, Kathleen?" He asked, looking slightly bashful. He was looking down at the floor.

He reminded me of a little boy I remembered back at the orphanage who always looked that way when anyone spoke to him. I felt Tim was an endearing young man and I couldn't say no. He was close to my age and a new rookie on the police force. He helped with putting my coat on and we left the station with everyone staring including Sergeant Martino, who had a surprised look on his face.

In the car he looked over at me as he drove slowly onto Archer Ave from the parking lot. "Kathleen, would you go on a date with me?" he asked. "I've been thinking of asking you out ever since your first day at the station."

"Yes, yes I would like that." I said it with none of the apprehension I felt when the sheriff asked me out. I was relieved to have a date with him, because it was the excuse I needed to refuse any further interest the sheriff might have in me. I felt comfortable with Tim and I had gotten to know him fairly well after two months of working beside him. He was kind and gentle.

The only facts I had about myself were the words written on the note left with me. I was a newborn baby girl, born on October 10th 1932, named Kathleen, of Irish nationality. Just Kathleen, no last name of course, so the nuns gave me one. I was a foundling that was left on the doorstep of the orphanage.

Tim talked about an older brother who was in the navy, on a ship somewhere in the Pacific. Tim was twenty and his draft number hadn't come up yet but he was worried. He parked the car in front of Mrs. Wilkie's house and we talked about his family, and his fears of being called into the army and I confided in him about the feelings I had about Mrs. Wilkie, and meeting the Sheriff at the Martinos. I didn't mention he asked me out. Tim laughed when I told him that meeting the Sheriff made me feel uncomfortable.

"He's an intense guy devoted to his work and his mother," he said, "She's a widow I think, who some say controls him. Look at him, thirty or over thirty and still single. He practically lives in the Sheriff's office, probably to escape his mother."

I laughed, because at times I felt that way living with Mrs. Wilkie. I looked over at Tim and was seeing him for the first time. When we worked at the station I thought of him as just one of the guys, but he was becoming much more to me.

"So, it's okay for me to pick you up Saturday night then?" he asked.

"Sure, what time?"

"I'll pick you up at six, we can grab a bite to eat and then go to the movies. "Thanks, Kathleen," he said, as he reached over to touch my hand. I smiled at him and he got out of the car and ran around to open the car door for me. I stood at the curb and waved to him as he drove away. I hurried up the walk, because I knew Mrs. Wilkie usually had supper ready the minute I came home. I found her standing at the open door. "Is that one of the Arden policemen? He's good-looking in that uniform, isn't he?" she said.

At times I felt stifled living with her and other times, like when I didn't feel well, and she was very nurturing, I didn't. I was confused and no more than after meeting all the Martinos and Dan, and now getting to know Tim. That evening I gently informed Mrs. Wilkie, I had a date."Oh, you be careful," she said.

I tried to reassure her, "He's the policeman that drove me home. You'll meet him Saturday. He's coming to pick me up at six, so don't plan on supper for me."

"Well one can't be too careful these days," she repeated looking worried.I was annoyed and tried to reassure her."Anna, I'll be with Tim, he's a cop. I can't be any safer than that."

"I know dear, but I worry."

CHAPTER 3

I awoke on Saturday morning to Mrs. Wilkie's phone ringing. I heard her answer it and soon after, she knocked on my door."Kathleen, a phone call for you," she said loudly. I rose up and put on my robe and went to pick up the phone on the hall table."Hello!" I said, with a rather husky morning voice. "Kathleen? It's Dan, Sheriff Dan Remember me?"

"Yes, I remember you," I said, and then there was silence. I waited for him to speak first. I knew what he was going to ask me.

"What are you doing tonight?" he asked. "I would like to take you out, maybe to a movie." I hesitated for a moment and thought of making up some lame excuse to refuse his offer, and then reasoned that he would find out the truth since he worked with the police and came into the station occasionally."I'm sorry, but I have a date tonight," I said.

"Who with?" he asked.

I thought it was nervy of him to ask and really didn't want to answer, but I told him it was with Tim O'Malley. There was a long silence and then he said, "Well, can I call you again sometime?" I didn't want to hurt his feelings by saying no, so I said it would be okay. I regretted it the minute I said it. I knew I should have said no, but I didn't. The few remarks I overheard at the station about him being so devoted to his mother left me with mixed feelings of him being a jerk, or maybe he wasn't a mama's boy, just a kind son and I was judging him too harshly. I wondered how he had my phone number and then realized Sergeant Martino must have given it to him, and it upset me.

When Tim came to pick me up that evening I invited him in to meet Mrs. Wilkie. She greeted him warmly knowing he was one of the policemen I worked with, and she smiled as he took a seat in the parlor. "Have the police ever caught the person who murdered those poor girls?" she asked. Her first question to him shocked me.

Tim laughed and said," No, I'm afraid not, but I'm sure he's long gone from the area. It's been over eight months since any more homicides have taken place around here, and they might not have been by the same person."

"I worry every time Kathleen leaves the house," she said.

"You don't have to worry about that, Mrs. Wilkie," he said, looking up at me as I stood next to where he sat. I felt a little embarrassed over her questioning him. To my relief he stood up and said, "We better get going or we'll be late for the show."

We said our goodbyes and left quickly. On the walk down to his car I apologized for Mrs. Wilkie's questions and manner. "Oh, don't worry about her, she sounds like most mothers when their daughters are going out," he said. I had no idea how most mothers would act since I never had one. Hearing Tim defending Mrs. Wilkie made me feel better.

In the theater he held my hand and I felt safe and comfortable with him. After the movie we stopped for a late supper at a little Italian restaurant. I looked at him across the table and I knew at that moment that I liked him more than I had ever liked any boy. He looked at me in a way that told me he felt the same about me.

I mentioned what meeting Sheriff Dan was like and he laughed, "So, what did you think of the big man, huh? He's tough when it comes to crime, almost driven about some cases to the point that he has gone viciously after people who were later proven innocent."

I knew exactly what Tim meant. I sensed that intensity in Dan's personality. It's what made me uncomfortable when he drove me home from the Martinos. Tim and I talked about the war and how he was worried over what his draft number would be. So far he hadn't been called up and he knew it might be because of the job he held, or maybe they just hadn't gotten to his number yet.

I didn't tell him that Dan asked me out. I knew then I would never date Dan, so there was no need to mention it. The rest of the evening went the way I hoped it would. Tim brought me home and walked me up to the porch. It was still early enough so I asked him in, knowing Mrs. Wilkie would still be up. She came to the door to greet us and seemed pleased to have company.

"Would you like a nice hot cup of coffee or tea on such a cold night like this?" she asked, directing her question to Tim. "That would be nice," he answered, while helping me off with my coat. We sat at her kitchen table and shared the lemon pound cake she baked. The way she looked at Tim surprised me, and then I remembered the picture of her son in uniform always displayed on her fireplace mantel and how there was a little resemblance. Tim was in his police uniform when she first saw him open the car door for me the day he drove me home, so he must have reminded her of her son. She talked about her boy and then asked Tim about his status with the draft. She was very kind to him and that pleased me. She seemed concerned listening to him talk about his situation and the war.

"I will pray for you when I go to mass Sunday," she said. He stood up and thanked her for her prayers and the cake and coffee. "I better go," he said. "You come again," she said, as we went into the living room. She didn't follow us but stayed in the kitchen clearing the table. As Tim put his coat on, I heard her bedroom door close. She wanted to give us a few moments alone before he left. I was grateful for that because it showed how much she approved of him. We stood in front of the door and before I could open it, he leaned against it facing me. He pulled me close to him in a hug and then he let me go a little and looked at me and then he kissed me. I kissed him back and he hugged me even tighter and gave me a long lingering kiss. I felt a rush of feeling I had never felt before. A boy at the orphan home kissed me once when I was fourteen and it wasn't anything like what I felt when Tim kissed me. His kiss was full of passion, but it's what *I* felt that surprised me. It was a deep emotional connection.

"Thanks for a great evening, Kathleen," he said. "Let's do this again, soon."

"I would like that very much."

"Would tomorrow be too soon?" he said laughing.

"Tomorrow is Sunday," I said,

"What would you like to do tomorrow?" "Bowling, how about going bowling? Have you ever bowled Kathleen?"

"No, I'm afraid not, but I'm not afraid to try it."

"Good, then I'll pick you up after lunch."

He kissed me one last time and I watched as he walked down to his car. I wasn't able to fall asleep easily that night because he was all I could think of, and the strange new feelings I was experiencing in his presence. A feeling that was new to me. I had felt quite alone for years and he was filling the void in my life of not feeling wanted and loved by one special person. We dated several times after the bowling date and I knew something special was happening between us.

The Christmas party was a week before Christmas and I was so happy to have Tim as a date to the Elks Lodge. We arrived early and a few of the cops from our station were there, as well as a couple of detectives who worked with the police. I recognized them from the time they would stop in at the station. They had their offices there but were mostly always working in the field investigating crimes of larceny, and whatever else came up—especially murders.

Angie and her boyfriend arrived and she lost no time in introducing him to us. The whole Martino family came into the large room decorated for Christmas. I brought Tim over to them, because they were the only family I knew. The rest of the police brought their families as well, and I met everyone. The band was playing an Irish tune and then they broke into "Jingle Bells". About an hour into the party, Sheriff Dan arrived with his mother. A couple of the cops whispered to Tim, "I guess the only date he could get is his mother," and then they laughed. I held on to Tim's arm when Dan looked over at us, as a way of making sure he knew I was with Tim, but he made no attempt to come over to where we were. I was relieved. His mother was a tall thin woman who walked with her head up in a manner that suggested she felt special holding on to her son's arm, as if she were his date. Finally, after about an hour into the party, he walked over with his mother and introduced her to both Tim and me.

"Oh, so this is the little girl you met at Sergeant Martino's," she said, as she offered her hand to me.

I took it and said, "Glad to meet you Mrs. Robson."

"Oh, it's Mrs. Clarke," she corrected me.

I was confused and said nothing more. I watched them walk back to their table. Tim and I sat with two other young policemen and their girlfriends. "She has a different name than the Sheriff?" I asked.

"I wasn't aware that she did until now," Tim said, sounding surprised. Howard, the cop sitting next to Tim said, with sarcasm,

"Any girl who dates Dan better look out for his mother." "What do you mean?" I asked. "Oh, I heard she has broken up every affair he's had with women years ago and since then no woman has been good enough for him, or to her liking."

Sergeant Martino's daughter walked over to our table with her boy friend, John. She introduced him to everyone and they joined our conversation and again it turned to Sheriff Dan and his mother. Giggles and snickering between the young cops continued at Dan and his mother's expense. Angie seemed annoyed.

"You know, he's really a nice guy who loves his mother. Our family knows him quite well. He's very kind, but of course he comes off rather stringent and cold at times because of all the low life he has to deal with," she said.

After that remark no one mentioned Dan again. I was grateful for that because I liked Angie and didn't want to lose the friendship that had just started between us.

The rest of the evening went well. Everyone knew by then that Tim and I were a couple. When Tim's parents appeared with his sister Barbara, I met the family for the first time. His sister was quite a bit younger than Tim. Mr. and Mrs. O'Malley were quiet people and didn't say much to me. I didn't find them real friendly. Later, after the evening ended and we left the Elks Lodge, Tim explained that Barbara was a foster child that his parents took in when she was three and later adopted when she was twelve.

"They've always wanted a daughter," he said, "and the opportunity to adopt Barbara came, so they did."

"How old is she?" I asked. "Thirteen," he said, and then shook his head a little."Is something wrong?" I asked."Not really, only that she was a model child until the adoption and then she started to rebel. You know, probably regular teenage stuff."

I didn't ask him any more questions. I could see it was something that bothered him. Later that evening when he had taken me home and pulled the car up in front of Mrs. Wilkie's place, we kissed good night.

"You don't mind if I don't come in tonight," he said.

"No, of course not. You don't have to get out of the car and walk me up to the porch," I said, knowing if he did, Mrs. Wilkie might still be up and she might expect him to come inside for another long drawn-out conversation about the war or her son. "It was nice meeting your family," I said.

"I had been meaning to bring you home to meet them at Christmas, but the party came up first. What are your plans for Christmas? Can you join my family for Christmas dinner or does Mrs. Wilkie expect you to be with her?"

"I never gave that a thought," I said, feeling the pressure of being obligated to Mrs. Wilkie. "Tell her we'll spend some of Christmas Eve with her and I have invited you to spend Christmas with my family."

"I'll tell her." He reached over and kissed me again, and then waited until I reached the porch before he drove away.

When I entered the house, Mrs. Wilkie had gone to bed and I was relieved. The next morning I had to bring up the plans Tim and I made for Christmas. I expected her to react a certain way, but she was quiet for awhile and then said, "Well, he's your boyfriend and I guess you should be with him."

"We'll be here Christmas Eve, if you don't have other plans," I said.

"Oh, no, I don't, and I can make us dinner and then you're free to go out if you like. I plan on being with my sister Eva on Christmas. She invited you too, but I'm sure she'll understand that you would want to be with your boyfriend."

I didn't expect that reaction from her and I was happy that she didn't feel I was abandoning her at Christmas. I reached over and gave her a hug, and she smiled.

I was becoming used to Mrs. Wilkie and calling her by her name, Anna, which she preferred, but somehow I wanted to call her a more endearing name. I couldn't think of one other than Auntie. I was too timid to ask her if that would be ok, so I continued to call her Anna.

CHAPTER 4

On Christmas day Tim and I arrived at his home in time for supper. His mother greeted me with a slight smile. She seemed a little distant. The conversation was between both parents discussing Barbara's problems in front of her. They asked me questions about my family. I turned to look at Tim. I was surprised he hadn't told them about me. Before I could answer, Barbara started to confront them on what she perceived as strict rules she disagreed with. Later, after Barbara went to her room, Mrs. O'Malley mentioned the fact that Barbara was a foster child they adopted. They knew nothing of her background and imagined the worst about her parents. "The problems we are having with her are all due to her background," Mrs. O'Malley said. Then looking over at Tim, she continued, "It was a mistake to get involved when we didn't know much about her." With that statement I froze. I realized then why Tim withheld the fact that I was an orphan. The rest of the evening went by with just the conversation about Barbara, and his mother didn't ask me any questions about myself. I was relieved.

January came and went and before I knew it, it was spring of 1951. Another murder occurred in Clearidge, and the war in Korea continued. The cops at the Arden station all talked about the murder, but they weren't invited to help the Chicago police in the investigation. As the war raged on some of the cops were angry with President Truman because he referred to the war as 'Just a police action,' but men were getting killed far from home in a real war. It might not have been another Pearl Harbor, but it was still war. Mrs. Wilkie, a long time Democrat, began to complain to anyone who would listen, that she lost her son in Truman's so-called police action. She was angry and it didn't help her disposition when she talked endlessly about her son. I was tired of hearing about him.

One Saturday night Tim took me to a drive-in movie and we kissed repeatedly, which didn't do much for trying to control ourselves. I was so hungry for affection and so needy, longing to belong to someone, that I would have thrown all caution to the wind, but there wasn't any place to go for privacy, and even if there was, Tim, raised as a

Catholic boy, having attended Catholic high school would have refused to go all the way, and become intimate with me. He said as much when our hormones got the better of us. I admired him for taking that stance and tried to hold back from what I was having difficulty controlling—my neediness for anything that would make me feel wanted and alive. Living devoid of all affection for eighteen years, left me very vunerable. The nuns took good care of our physical needs, but that was all. They frowned on any display of affection between the children themselves, no holding hands for any reason unless we were told to do so when on an outside outing, walking in twos.

There was talk that one of their charges that left the home two years before I did, was not doing so well in the outside world. I would hear the sisters whispering about it after the police came to the home to question Mother Renada. Of course they would never tell any of us children what it was all about, but I was fourteen, and my friend Molly at fifteen were inquisitive, and we would try to listen at a heating vent in one of the bathrooms next to Sister Renada's office. We overheard the word 'prostitute', but wasn't sure what it meant. We would run to the library to look up the word. Molly said she wanted to be loved and thought sex was love. I didn't know what sex was, and didn't have a clue what she was talking about, but she was one of the lucky orphans; her aunt from out of town came to visit once a year and would take her out for a weekend. Most of what I learned about life came from the older kids, and not the Nuns.

In June of 1951, Tim turned twenty-one and he expected his dreaded draft number to come up. He didn't want to quit the department, but needed to decide on what to do before he was drafted into the army. "I have to join the Navy or the Marines," he said, as he sadly presented me with his options.

"I love you and I don't want to lose you. If I go in, will you wait for me and not date anyone else?" he asked. "Of course," I said, "I love you Tim, so why would I date anyone else?" I wasn't interested in anyone except him. At that moment I felt he was my soul mate. I wasn't too nervous about him joining the service early, until Mrs. Wilkie talked about losing her son after I mentioned that Tim was thinking of joining before his number came up. That is when it hit me that I could lose him.

In late August of 1951 he turned in his uniform and badge, said goodbye to all on the police force and prepared to leave for the Marines. We spent our last date with his family. Later that evening after his parents and sister retired for the night we sat on the sofa together with our arms around each other. I began to cry. I reached my hand up to his face to caress his cheek. I couldn't help myself; I touched his face and his lips with my fingers. He had a square masculine jaw and I traced the slight dimple in his chin with my fingertip. I loved him so much that I almost collapsed from the exhaustion of crying. He held me tight and had tears in his eyes as he promised he would come back to me. We had only been dating eight months, but long enough to know how we felt about each other.

"Kathleen, I love you, I'll be back. Nothing is going to happen to me," he said, trying to reassure me, as well as him.

I didn't know how to express how I felt at that moment. It was like losing part of me to him. I had never bonded to another human being during all the years at the orphanage. I felt completely alone in spite of all the other children and the many nuns that surrounded me. I knew I never belonged to any of them. I was very fond of Mrs. Wilkie, but what I felt for Tim was so powerful that it wasn't like anything I experienced before. He was my first boyfriend, my first love, my soul mate, and my family. I looked up to him for protection. He was my, — well, everything, and now he would be leaving. I was frightened of being alone again and not feeling an attachment to anyone in spite of living with Mrs Wilkie. He held my face between his hands and looked at me for a long time. He kissed me many times. He was so gentle and affectionate that I thought I would collapse with grief at the thought of him leaving me. "I better take you home," he said.

The ride back to Mrs. Wilkie's was sad with both of us in tears. As we were driving past a large shipping trailer parked in a parking lot next to the airport, he looked at me and said, "Boy, would I love to take you into that trailer and make mad love to you."

I looked over at him and said "Oh no, you wouldn't," He leaned over while we were parked at a red light and bit the top of my ear. It hurt, but I realized the frustrations he felt. Later, when he walked me up to Mrs. Wilkie's porch and we sat on the swing for a few minutes, he apologized. "I'm sorry," he said, "I just couldn't help myself. I want you so badly, but that will have to wait, I know."

We both knew. Both raised Catholic and having it drummed into us to wait for marriage—for us there was no other option in 1951. We cried in each other's arms and then he was gone.

The next day at the station I could hardly keep my mind on my work. Everyone looked sad because of Tim's absence. They made it worse by trying to comfort me every time they passed my desk. I would start crying again. Sergeant Martino offered to drive me home at the end of the day. "Kathleen, let me drive you home tonight. You don't wanna ride the bus feeling the way you do," he said, after seeing how upset I appeared. I accepted his offer.

He tried to help me by talking nonstop as he drove. He told me he knew how I felt because he too worried about his twin boys, soon to turn sixteen, and if the war lasted too long they would be eligible for the draft as well. "I'm sure it will be over soon and Tim's a smart guy. He knows how to protect himself," he said.

When we reached Mrs. Wilkie's I asked him if he would like to come in and meet her. "Yes, yes I would like to meet her," he said.

When I opened the door and called to her, she came out of the kitchen quickly and was surprised to see a policeman with me. "Are you okay?" she asked, noticing that I had been crying. "I want you to meet Sergeant Martino," I said.

She smiled and said "Oh, I'm so happy to meet you," as they shook hands. "Kathleen has told me so much about you. Please come in and sit down. Can I get you anything?" she asked.

"No, thank you. I can't stay long, but I wanted to see Kathleen home since she's been upset over Tim's leaving." He said.

"Yes, I know how she feels. I lost my Gary."

She then went into all the details of losing her son and it made me feel worse. I was grateful when Sergeant Martino explained he had to leave. She thanked him for bringing me home before I could. When I tried to speak in spite of starting to cry again, he waved his hand and put his arm around me.

"Maybe this weekend you would like to come out and see Angie.

She talked about getting together with you. Would you like that?" he asked. He was trying to console me and I felt better after his offer. I thanked him and then he shook hands with Mrs. Wilkie and left.

The very next evening Angie called to ask if we could get together. I was happy to hear from her and I knew Sergeant Martino told her about the hard time I was having after Tim left. On Friday night she borrowed the family car and picked me up. We went to a movie but I couldn't concentrate on the movie, but didn't say anything and ruin her enjoyment of it. She took me to an ice cream parlor and we sat in a booth together. She knew the emotional state I was in, so she did all the talking.

"Kathleen, I'm sure Tim will come out of it just fine. Before you know it the war will be over and he'll be home."I wanted to believe her but found it difficult to believe anything anyone said to me because I kept thinking about Mrs. Wilkie's son.

"I hope you're right," I said. "I never knew what it felt like to have someone that loved me as much as Tim does." Angie looked at me with compassion. "You know you're welcome to spend as much time as you want with my family," she said. "Think of us as your family."

Throughout the next few weeks I spent the weekends visiting the Martinos. It helped to be with them as often as I could, because Mrs. Wilkie's constant chatter about losing her son was depressing. It seemed that since Tim left that's all she wanted to talk about. I understood her concerns, but it wasn't helpful to me. At first she seemed upset that I was spending almost every weekend away. I felt guilty about it, until Angie pointed out to me that I was simply her tenant and didn't owe her any explanation of where I went every time I went out.

I lived for Tim's letters and I wrote to him every day. He finished his basic training in California and wrote he was coming home on leave before being shipped out. The day he returned couldn't have come fast enough. He called as soon as he arrived home, and soon he drove over to pick me up. I waited on the porch for him and when his car pulled up I ran down the long walk into his arms as he met me just outside his car. He looked handsome in his Marine uniform. We hugged and kissed right on the sidewalk and I didn't care if anyone was watching our reunion. It seemed a few of the neighbors expressed their joy in seeing us reunited. Mrs. Wilkie came down to us and hugged Tim. We followed her into the house and she had set the table, to celebrate with cake and coffee. "How long are you in for?" she asked. Tim kept his arm around me and said, "Just two weeks and then I leave for Korea."

We sat at her table and finished the cake she served and then Tim mentioned that his family had planned a dinner for us that evening. "Oh, that's nice," Mrs. Wilkie said.

We left for his parents' home and I expected an evening with them would give me the feeling that I would have a real family once Tim and I were married, but I sensed coolness from his mother. On the drive home I expressed that I felt his mother might not like me. "Does she know I haven't any family?" I asked, afraid of what his answer would be.

"I explained your situation and I think my mother worries about background and family. It's because of Barbara. They don't know anything about her background and she has all the problems they mentioned. She'll come around about her fears eventually. In time she will come to love you," he said. I wasn't as sure as he was on the matter, but I kept my feelings to myself. I figured he had enough to worry about.

Tim and I would be together the whole two weeks before he left, mostly spent alone in Mrs. Wilkie's living room after she retired for the night. It was the only place we could be alone. There weren't many places one could go to be alone except lover's lane, a patch of grass on a hill outside the fence at the airport where cars would park and couples could kiss and do whatever else they were able to do. We went there a few times, but after the police shined their flashlights into the cars, we decided to stay in Mrs. Wilkie's living room. It wasn't easy to keep our hands off each other. The feelings we had were so strong that to part once more was harder than I expected. The first night after he left, I cried myself to sleep. If it wasn't for Angie and her boyfriend John, who included me in their lives, and also the whole Martino family, I would have been a real mess because being with Mrs. Wilkie was becoming a problem. She was so negative about the war and what could happen to Tim and she wouldn't quit talking about her son. Tim going to fight in Korea brought back all the memories of Gary and although I felt sorry for her, I felt she was dragging me down with her, into a state of despair and I was feeling depressed most of the time. I avoided her as much as possible. On the nights I wasn't with Angie or her family, I would go to bed early telling Mrs. Wilkie I was tired.

Meeting Angie one day after work, I talked it over with her. She thought it was a good idea for me to look for another place to live. "Kathleen, you don't owe Mrs. Wilkie anything, you're only her tenant."

"Why do I feel so obligated to her?"

"Because you don't have any family and she was the first person you met after leaving the home. It's only natural to feel the way you do." she said, looking at me, sadly. She tried to help me make up my mind on what I should do.

"Kathleen, for your own good and your own mental health, you have to leave her place. If you don't want to stay with her I'm sure my family would be happy to take you in."

I thought about what she was saying and I knew as much as I loved to visit her family, I wouldn't want to live with them. I wasn't used to such a loud and large family and it would be more than I could handle if I were there with them every night. Also in the back of my mind was the fact that the Sheriff was close to the family and visited them often. I wanted to avoid him as much as possible. He had a strong personality that reminded me of Sister Renada. I realized I was more comfortable around people who were less imposing.

One morning as I was getting ready for work and brushing my hair in the bathroom mirror I noticed the deep red tooth marks on the top tip of my left ear. I started to cry; it was all I had left of Tim. I began to regret not becoming intimate with him before he left, but it just wasn't done in our world at that time between two people raised Catholic who took the Religious indoctrination literal. I missed Tim more each day he was gone and was able to function solely on our letters that were filled with words of love and devotion to each other.

CHAPTER 5

Without Angie's help, I don't think I would ever have been able to move out of Mrs. Wilkie's home. I realized how timid I was when I needed Angie with me the night I had to inform her that I would be moving out. She appeared shocked at first until Angie explained that Tim and I would be getting married as soon as he came back and I would have to leave anyway. I tried to assure her that I would come back to visit her and would always be grateful for the kindness she showed me.

It was the first week of December 1951 when I arrived at my new home. Lorraine Perky was a friend of the Martino's, a divorced woman who rented out rooms in her large home in Clearidge. The woman welcomed me with open arms. She was in her late forties and she worked as a social worker. Her children were grown so she told me she looked forward to having young people living with her again. One of the rooms was taken by a young man in his twenties who worked for a company that made alarm systems. Lorraine told me he was a quiet fellow who kept to himself and didn't bother anyone. She said he was exempt from the draft due to a medical problem. Angie and I carried in my clothing and the personal items I had accumulated in the months I lived with Mrs. Wilkie.

My life took on a routine that was predictable—work, writing letters daily to Tim, hanging out with Angie, visiting her family and enjoying the company of the woman I boarded with. The young man who lived in the bedroom on the first floor hardly came out of his room, but was cordial when we passed each other in the kitchen each morning on our way to work. Two weeks after Christmas, in January of 1952, a Sunday morning, Lorraine picked up the *Chicago Tribune* newspaper from her porch and brought it in. When she opened it the front page had headlines that screamed out in big bold Letter's, 'Woman found dead in the Clearidge area of Chicago.' A picture of the girl was on the front page with her name and age under it. Lorraine read aloud to me as we sat at her table—'Jeannie Hunter, age 23, was last seen shopping on 63rd Street.' Her body was found in an open field near the railroad tracks that ran east to west across Central and Austin Avenue. She was dumped just west of Austin in a swampy area now turned to ice, in a field covered with snow. The article explained how two boys walking near the tracks discovered the body.

"I wonder who the person is that did this when nothing like this has happened in well over a year, she said. Jack, the other boarder was pouring a cup of coffee to go when he said, "I hope they catch the bastard before another innocent girl loses her life." Those were the first words I ever heard him express in all the mornings I ran into him as he passed through the house on his way out to work. His voice, strong and heavy, didn't seem to fit his demeanor. He was a tall lanky guy who looked somewhat emaciated, like he hadn't eaten a decent meal in some time. I found him to be strange and it left me with an unsettled feeling.

Later that afternoon I met Angie. Whenever there was a problem or a decision I had to make, I found myself depending on her for advice.

I was invited to the Martinos that night for supper and I looked forward to going. Everyone knew Tim and I were a couple and the many times I had supper with the family, I never ran into Sheriff Dan. If he visited the family, which I knew was often, it was never when I was there. I arrived early and Lottie prepared a great Italian meal. I always enjoyed the family and the laughs on the occasions I was invited for a meal.

"Have you heard from Tim?" Lottie asked. "Yes, very often, well, as often as he can write," I said. "It must be hard on you, waiting for his letters, but this police action can't last too much longer, can it?" Lottie asked, with a little sarcasm, directing her question to her husband. Sergeant Martino laughed and said, "Since Truman calls it a police action, maybe all the police departments should have been sent over instead of the military."

They all laughed, but I didn't feel like laughing. I worried about Tim every day. I wanted to call his mother, but the way she treated me after being told I was an orphan made me hesitate. I thought she didn't like me, so after Tim left I never contacted her. At times I felt I should have—after all, her son and I loved each other.

Lottie turned to her husband "Will the Sheriff's department be involved with the case of that murdered girl in Clearidge?"

"No, not unless the Chicago police ask for their help. Remember, Clearidge is in the city. It's a lot harder for police to investigate a crime that is in another jurisdiction than one in their own. If she's from Arden, of course they will be involved along with the detectives from the city," Sergeant Martino said, shaking his head in sadness over another crime so close to Arden.

"Isn't it odd that all the murder victims have been from either the Clearidge area or Chicago itself, but none were ever found from towns that border the city or from Arden," Lottie said.

"Let's not discuss the subject, the kids don't need to hear it," he said, giving Lottie a stern look across the table.

As the weeks went by I filled my days with my work at the police department and in the evenings I split the time between Lorraine Perky's home and the Martino's. Angie and I had become best friends and through her I met a few other girls our age. I visited Mrs. Wilkie a couple of times and never stayed long because her conversations were always the same. I knew in time my visits would be less often until I might never go back to visit her unless Tim returned. If he was along I reasoned she wouldn't be so negative— seeing he was safely back from the war.

It was going on many months since Tim had deployed to Korea from the states and I noticed I still had the bite marks. I would run my fingers over it and feel the indentation of his teeth. It was a silly thing to do, but it gave me comfort. I lived for the mail each day and when there wasn't a letter I was very disappointed. When March of 1953 came it had been a year and a half since he left. I went to the mailbox one Saturday morning to find a letter from him. It was only a few lines written in haste, as he explained he would be in a place where he might not be able to write for a while, and for me not to worry if I didn't hear from him. After that letter I hadn't received another in two months, so in July, when the fighting stopped in Korea I took the chance on stopping by his home to inquire if his mother had heard from him.

When she opened the door and saw me, she had a very sad expression on her face, and then she started to cry.

"On my God, Kathleen, I'm so happy you're here. I heard you moved and I wanted to get in touch with you," she said, in a very shaky voice. "Oh honey, Tim has been reported missing in action." She broke down in front of me and to my surprise she hugged me. I was stunned for a moment as I tried to take in what she had said.

"You haven't heard from him either?" I asked, in a trembling voice, and then I started to cry as I realized what the words 'missing in action' meant. "No, dear," she answered, as we hugged each other.

Barbara ran out of the room crying, and Mr. O'Malley appeared very sad and later we sat at the table together unable to enjoy the simple meal Mrs. O'Malley prepared.

I spent the rest of evening with them, staying well past my normal bedtime. Tim's father was a great source of comfort to us, because he appeared very optimistic.

"You know missing in action doesn't mean he's gone," he said, trying to convince us, as well as himself that Tim was alive.

He looked at both his wife and me crying inconsolably and put his arms around us. "Noreen, he's alive, I know it. When I was a medic in the Navy, we had to storm onto the island of Iwo Jima searching for the wounded, sometimes we had pronounced a Marine dead or wounded by mistake. If he lost his dog tag during battle and it was found near another poor guy that didn't make it, well you can see how it was, and not until much later could they identify the right owner of the tag. Until we know for sure, try to have hope."

I felt numb after receiving the news and I left their home promising to keep in touch leaving them with my new address and phone number, I walked to the bus stop and waited. How I was able to compose myself until I arrived at Lorraine's, I don't know, but once I entered my room I broke down and cried until there were no tears left. The feelings I had were indescribable. In spite of all the people who entered my life since I left the orphanage, I felt alone and quite abandoned. Without Tim, I was lost and frightened. The next day, at work, the men were all supportive having heard about Tim, and they did their best to keep my hopes up, but I was grieving as though the loss of the one and only person I loved was permanent. The Martino family was supportive and Lorraine did her best to lift my spirits and for that I was grateful, but the one person I stayed away from was Anna Wilkie. I couldn't bring myself to notify her about Tim.

My days at the police station kept me from falling apart completely, so my job was a blessing. It kept my mind off of thinking of Tim every minute; like I did after work and most nights when I couldn't sleep.

After three months I started to accept that Tim might never be found dead or alive, and I tried my best to go on with my life. One morning in September of 1953 as I was getting my usual cup of coffee before I left for work, the young man who lived in the bedroom on the first floor entered the kitchen. He seldom spoke except for a nod of the head or a whispered hello. This particular morning he remained quiet, not even acknowledging my presence when I said good morning. He quickly poured his coffee to go in a plastic cup and I noticed his right hand was bandaged. I looked more closely at him and he had a few red marks on his chin, more like scratches. "What happened?" I asked, but he just looked startled and said, "Oh nothing." and left quickly. Later that evening Lorraine opened the newspaper to another headline of a young girl's murder, and as we sat together eating the take-out dinner she brought for us, I mentioned the condition of Jack's hand and face.

"He works for that Alarm Company and sometimes they have to break into places when the alarms malfunction, especially if it's in a place like a warehouse," she said, seeming unconcerned. I wasn't comfortable around Jack before my last encounter with him in the kitchen and now I would be very uncomfortable when he was near.

Every day when the paper was thrown on the porch in the morning, I started to retrieve it myself to scan the pages looking for anything on the latest murder, hoping it was solved, so that my suspicions about Jack were expelled. After a few days, news of the murder was regulated to the second or third page of the paper and eventually disappeared. It left me with an unsettled feeling. Although I liked living with Lorraine I began to think of finding another place. I hesitated because Lorraine was a friend of the Martino family and I was afraid of hurting their feelings by leaving. I decided to mention my fear and suspicions about the other boarder to Angie. When I did, she laughed at me and said, "Kathleen, I'm afraid you're becoming paranoid. Jack is harmless, just look at him—a strong wind would topple him over."

I was embarrassed mentioning anything about my fears after that and the matter was dropped, but I made sure I locked myself in my room whenever Lorraine wasn't home and Jack was. I would sit up at night after Lorraine had gone to bed, and watch at my window that faced the front of the house, watching for Jack to return after a night out. It seemed he stayed out late most nights and I began to wonder where he could be spending his time. He didn't seem to be the sort who had anything like a real date with a girl. The best I could come up with as far as what I thought of him was that he appeared strange, in looks and manner.

CHAPTER 6

It was November of 1954, and there was another murder. The Korean War had ended in July of 1953 or at least the fighting did. Sheriff Dan came into the station one morning. The Sheriff usually stayed in the front office where Sergeant Martino's desk was when he came in and never came in the back where I worked. This time he did, supposedly to talk with one of the cops who worked near me. I knew he was within five feet of my desk but I didn't look away from my work, pretending not to notice him. He came over to me and stood in front of my desk where I had to look up at him.

"Hello, Kathleen, how've you been?" he asked, "I'm sorry to hear about Tim." I didn't know what to say, so I just smiled and nodded my head to acknowledge his presence. I thought he would walk away but he remained standing there looking down at me.

"Can I help you with something?" I asked, hoping he would just move on. I kept my eyes on my typewriter.

"I wonder if you would join me for a bite to eat, it's almost quitting time," he said.

"I don't think so, I need to get home," I answered, thinking I put an end to him standing in front of my desk, but he remained.

"I've had a hard day today, and I would really enjoy some company after work, just for a short time, no strings attached. You can leave whenever you want. It's just across the street—a sandwich and a cup of coffee? Like two friends, how about it?"

I looked up at him and saw such a sad expression on his face that I felt sorry for him. "Okay, for just a short time, I need to get home," I said, and then I was sorry I gave in, but at that moment I felt cornered by him.

We walked across to a coffee shop near the station. I was relieved, because I didn't want to get into his car and have him drive too far, and then have to bring me home. We sat in a booth and the waitress asked for our order. I could see her staring at us in a way that suggested she wondered what this older man was doing with a young girl. I always looked younger than I actually was and I hated to look

36

like a child. I was sure it was the presence of the few freckles on my nose that remained after childhood, and although I attempted to cover it with makeup they still shown through at times.

As stern as he often appeared, he looked at me with such tenderness and said, again, "I *am* sorry to hear about Tim."

"Thank you for mentioning him," I said, "I love him."

I thought I would put that out to him to discourage any thoughts he might have on thinking I would welcome more than these few minutes having coffee with him. He looked down at the coffee he was holding and said, "I've been under tremendous stress lately with all these murders unsolved and we can't seem to do anything about them."

"Why not?" I asked, pretending not to know anything about the fact that it was Chicago's case again not Arden's, and he had to wait to be invited to help.

"She was found in Clearidge, but so close to our town this time. I do what I can, but it isn't enough," he said, looking up at me and shaking his head appearing frustrated over the situation.

I began to think of Jack, the boarder and the suspicions I had about him. I thought even if I mentioned it to Dan, would he be able to look into it? What if I were wrong, I could do real damage to the guy. I thought of what the cops said at the first Christmas party, about how the Sheriff went after innocent people.

"I guess you're under a lot of stress with the job you have," I said, trying to make conversation with him. He looked at me with a very melancholy expression. "You have no idea Kathleen, what it's like to feel so frustrated — the kind of people I have to deal with."

At that moment I did feel sorry for him, and made the mistake of putting my hand on his, maybe to comfort him, but he took that gesture as a sign that I felt something for him. At that time I wasn't aware of what that small acknowledgement of what I thought was a sign of sympathy on my part, was taken as a license for him to continue to pursue me. I withdrew my hand but not before he put his other hand on top of mine.

"I really have to get home," I said, as I pulled my hand away and rose up from my seat. "Thanks for the coffee." He smiled at me and couldn't follow me out but had to wait for the waitress to bring the bill. I took that opportunity to rush out of the shop as quickly as I could and to my luck, a bus was just pulling up to the curb at its usual stop. I climbed in and sat by the window facing the coffee shop and watched as Sheriff Dan emerged out the door. The bus pulled away before he noticed it and I was happy about that. Somehow I was afraid if he saw me he might follow by jumping on, but then realized he had his car in the station parking lot. I thought about the coffee encounter with the Sheriff and a very unsettled feeling came over me. I regretted accepting his offer to spend any time with him. I decided it wouldn't happen again. I was relived after two weeks, and he hadn't come into the station. For the next three months there wasn't a sign of him anywhere and I didn't give him another thought. The rest of the year I felt free. I dated a few times, friends of Angie's boyfriend John, but wasn't interested in dating much and turned down dates. Angie and John gave up trying to encourage me and I stuck to my job and after work, the company of Lorraine Perky. On weekends I preferred to be alone, reading in my room or watching television. I ignored Jack who I seldom came in contact with except in passing him in the mornings in the kitchen as we each got our coffee to go.

I was invited to attend Thanksgiving dinner in November of 1954 at the Martino's with Lorraine, but she declined, planning to spend the holiday with her son and his family. I was apprehensive about asking Angie if I were the only guest, afraid she might say the Sheriff would be there, so I didn't ask. The night before Thanksgiving there was another murder of a young girl. Lorraine left early that morning to help her daughter-in-law prepare the meal, and I locked myself in my room until I had to leave for the Martino's. Jack, the boarder was still home and I avoided him like the plague. It was time to leave and as I came down the stairs I noticed his shoes were in the hall next to the stairs. I thought he was either in his room or the kitchen so I quickly headed for the front door, but not before I noticed the mud on his shoes. He must have come in late the night before and discarded them before he entered his room that was close to the front entrance. I didn't remember ever seeing his shoes in the front hall before and wondered if Lorraine had seen them. The mud surprised me because it snowed very little that November and it was the warmest November in years, it rained a cold rain instead. But the last time it rained was the first week of November.

When I arrived at the Martino's, Lottie greeted me with her customary smile. I loved being with the family and looked forward to another day of feeling like I belonged with them. I was relieved that I was the only guest. I listened to the family chatter and remained quiet, thinking about Jack's muddy shoes. I didn't dare bring up the matter in front of the whole family and decided to wait and mention it to Sgt. Martino when I found a moment alone with him. After everyone left the table, and he was about to get up from his chair, I asked him if I could have a word with him, alone.

"Of course you can," he said, looking puzzled. "What is it? Is it about Dan? I know you aren't interested in any attention from him. He told me how you fled quickly out of the coffee shop. Don't worry, he got the message and won't be bothering you again."

"It's not that at all," I said, "It's about another matter." He sat back down leaning on his elbows, and waited for me to tell him, so I did. I told him all about Jack, and how fearful I was, living at Lorraine's. I explained that the cuts on his hand and face came the day after a murder in Clearidge and now after the latest murder, of finding his shoes all muddy at the bottom of the stairs.

He looked at me with a sad expression. "Kathleen, do you think Mrs. Perky would rent a room to someone who could commit a murder? Heavens, she's a social worker. She of all people would know if Jack was a risk. I'm sure you're afraid because you feel alone most of the time. You shouldn't feel that way; you have friends, Angie, my entire family, Mrs. Perky and even Mrs. Wilkie. When was the last time you visited her?"

"I don't visit her too often, because she's so negative about the war after losing her son, and now with Tim missing, what could I tell her?" I asked, hunching my shoulders. He looked sadly at me, and shook his head.

"You could tell her to pray for Tim, I'm sure she's good at praying and also seeing you again might lift her spirits some, don't you think?"

"I guess you're right," I said, as we both stood up and left the table. I thought about what Sgt. Martino said through the next week and then one Saturday morning I did get up the courage to visit her. She was happy to see me, and greeted me with open arms. She seemed upbeat so I kept our conversation light, mostly about my job, the latest movie I had seen, and then I knew I had to tell her about Tim, except I put it off by first mentioning Jack the boarder at Mrs. Perky's. I felt I had to tell someone who might have a different take on my fears. Everyone I mentioned it to didn't take it serious and laughed off my suspicions. She listened with a serious expression on her face, then took my hand in hers and said, "Kathleen, if you're not comfortable living there, you can always come back here. Of course, I know, as soon as Tim comes home you would leave again."

I started to cry, and she touched my hand, thinking it was my fears about Jack. "You can come home," she said, as if her place was really my home.

"It's Tim," I blurted out crying, "He was declared missing in action!" She got up from her chair and came over to wrap her arms around me, and to my surprise, she said, "Don't worry dear, they'll find him."

I was surprised at how comfortable I felt telling her of my concerns and fears because she didn't judge me or make light of what I was worried about. She didn't go on a negative streak about the war, or the fact that Tim was missing. She tried her best to lift my spirits. I left her that afternoon feeling much better and was glad I went to see her. I knew I would return again for another visit. After Lorraine blew off my concerns, as did Angie when I confided in her, and when Sgt. Martino did also, I felt I had nowhere to turn so I took a chance on Anna Wilkie. She didn't disappoint me. It seemed my apprehension over living at Mrs. Perky's disappeared with that announcement, until we heard the suspect was released because of insufficient evidence and the guy had a foolproof alibi on where he had been the week of the murder, so I was back to my previous state of mind. I tried not to dwell on Jack so much and kept busy with my work and hanging out with Angie and her friends who I hoped were my friends also, but I never initiated contact with them on my own because I always felt I would be disloyal to Angie, after all they were *her* friends first. I began to have trouble sleeping at night and thought about Mrs. Wilkie's offer, and it was in March when I got up the courage to tell Lorraine that I might start looking for another place, closer to my work. After I mentioned it, I realized what I had done, lied, and knew she would find out where I was going; after all she was a friend of the Martino's. I finally got up the courage to tell her I would be moving back to Mrs. Wilkie, but the reason I gave was that she was ill and needed some help. I couldn't tell her the real reason of course. When I called Mrs. Wilkie, I made sure she understood it was a temporary move, until Tim came home. Somehow in my mind I knew Tim might never come home, but I would cross that bridge when I had to. My belongings were packed and I was waiting for Mrs. Wilkie to pick me up with her Ford. Lorraine wasn't too pleased to see me go, but when she watched the old woman pull up and get out of her car to open the trunk, she said, "I can see why that woman might need some help." She noticed the cane Mrs. Wilkie used which surprised me. I thanked Lorraine for the time I lived with her and she walked me out to the car carrying some of my bags. I introduced the two women and then we left. On the ride back to Vicker Street, I asked her why she was using a cane. " I've been having problems with my knees, it's the damp weather." She said, smiling at me. I sat back and took a deep breath, feeling safe again.

CHAPTER 7

After being with Mrs. Wilkie a week, I noticed how frail she appeared one morning. I was getting ready for work, when I heard her call to me from her room. "Kathleen," she called, "Do you mind if I don't get up with you this morning?"

"Of course not," I answered, peeking in on her. She was sitting up in bed. I went over to her and felt her forehead; it was cool to the touch. "Anna, don't you feel well?" I asked. She looked up at me and smiled. "I'm just a little weak this morning. I didn't sleep well last night."

"Well, you just stay in bed. I can make my own breakfast and I'll make yours too. What would you like to have?"

"Anything that's easy," she answered, closing her eyes, as she lay back down on her pillow.

I began to feel like she was family. All the reservations I had about her, or living with her, evaporated the first week I returned to her home. She had changed and I realized she wasn't as spry as she used to be, or as negative. I began to feel sorry for her. She had her sister Eva, but that wasn't the same as having her son. I tried to treat her as a daughter would and she mothered me in the way that I needed. I left for work that morning looking forward to starting over with a new optimistic attitude. With Anna Wilkie as my family and her home as my home, I looked forward to the future.

I loved my job, and was happy to be at work each day. As so much time had passed since Tim was listed missing, I came to terms with the reality that, that chapter of my life was over. I began to gain confidence and was less afraid of making decisions for myself. I knew there had been news of a prisoner exchange from North Korea back in 1953. Tim wasn't among them and I visited Tim's family for the last time after I moved back to Mrs. Wilkie and decided that it was futile to continue because I reminded them of Tim and they reminded me of him, and it was too sad. I had to move on.

Angie had introduced me to a friend of her boyfriend John's, and we double dated on our first date. Steve was a nice enough guy, and I really liked him, but just as a friend. He was someone to fill up time. In the back of my mind, I was thinking, maybe I could learn to fall in love with him, but it wasn't happening. I continued to date him hoping I would feel something that was more than just liking him, and on one of our dates, sitting in an all night diner after we had emerged from the movie theater, I looked at him across from me in the booth and felt guilty. He was kind, and I didn't want to hurt his feelings but I had to say something, to end it, to free him. He was getting too serious. He looked at me and sensed that something was bothering me.

"What's wrong Kathleen?" he asked, "Have I said anything to upset you?"

"No, of course not. You're always asking me that. Steve, you're a nice guy and I enjoy your company but in all fairness to you, I'm not in love with you. I like you, really, I do, but is it fair to you for us to keep seeing each other when I know you expect more than just my friendship?"

He looked at me and smiled, "You let me worry about that, will you? Maybe in time—and if not then, so be it, but right now you're not dating anyone else and neither am I, so let's just enjoy the friendship for now, okay?"

I couldn't argue with what he said, after all he was an adult and I let the moment when I should have ended our dating go by. As long as he knew the score, I didn't feel I needed to end it yet. He was the perfect buffer to any attention from Sheriff Dan, who was always lurking in the background it seemed, waiting for the right moment to get my attention again. He came into the room I worked in occasionally, appearing to speak to the other cops working around me, but out of the corner of my eye I would catch him staring at me and he always passed my desk on the way out to say 'Hi, Kathleen' without stopping to say anything more.

A month after I moved and in April just before Easter where I usually spent the holiday with the Martinos, and Mrs. Wilkie went to her sister's, another woman was found murdered but although she was found again in Clearidge, she lived in Arden. Everyone at the station was talking about the fact that it was so close to where an earlier crime was and she was the first homicide that came from Arden. That meant that the Arden police department and the Sheriff's department would be fully involved in this case. The woman lived in the Sheriff's county. Although she was found without any identification, like all the rest of the women, a picture of their face usually identified them, post mortem. Some of the cops I worked with were standing around the water cooler all talking about the latest murder. Jerry White, one of the older cops was mentioning the case. I overheard him say, "I think the killer slipped up this time."

I went over to get myself some water, because I wanted to know why he made that comment. I remembered Lottie wondering why all the murders were women who lived in the Clearidge area of Chicago but none were ever from Arden.

Another cop said that everyone thought the killer wasn't from Chicago but from Arden or another town nearby and he didn't want the town he lived in involved in the investigation. "It's just a theory Jerry said, but a good one, I think."

I thought if that were true, then Jack, the boarder at Mrs. Perky's couldn't be a suspect. In my mind I still hadn't ruled him out, because he made me so uncomfortable. I never mentioned him to Sheriff Dan after Sergeant Martino and Lorraine practically laughed at any suggestion that Jack could be a suspect.

Dan came into the station more often and I tried to ignore him, but it wasn't easy to pretend he wasn't bothering me because he was. He knew I dated Steve, but that didn't seem to stop him from seeking me out every chance he got. I wondered if the Martinos would invite Steve to Easter dinner since they knew we were dating. I asked Angie and she didn't seem to know who they would be inviting except me.

I was glad I had learned to drive Mrs. Wilkie's car. Thanks to Angie and John, who had the patience to teach me and when I passed the driver's test, it was my greatest achievement because it gave me independence. With Mrs. Wilkie's health problems, she encouraged me to get my license and use her car for shopping and running errands for her. I was able to drive to work if it was raining and I wouldn't have to walk to the bus stop, and wait for a bus.

After church, the morning of Easter Sunday, I drove Mrs. Wilkie to her sister's and then went back home to do a few last minute chores. I was bringing a cake I baked the night before to the Martinos. I looked forward to the dinner, knowing that Steve would be spending the holiday with his family. I held my breath as I pressed the doorbell at the Martino's that afternoon. I was so fearful that Sheriff Dan would be there because Sgt. Martino had spent a great amount of time with him at the station the past few days. The recent murder brought them together more often as they investigated. Angie opened the door. "Oh hi, come on in," she said smiling. Then she took me aside and whispered, "Now, don't get upset. Dan's here on business, but I think he's staying for dinner too. I'm sure he knows you're still dating Steve, so don't let anything about him being here bother you."

I felt my face flush, partly from anger and partly the fear of having to endure another encounter with a man who always made me feel so uncomfortable. As we entered the living room where Dan was seated, he quickly stood up to greet me. Of course I had to shake his hand when he offered it and then Sgt. Martino said, "Have a seat Kathleen." I looked over at Angie and she quickly announced that I would be helping her set the table. I followed her into the dining room where Lottie was already arranging the plates and silverware. They knew how I felt and were happy for the help. I stayed with them until dinner was served. Over the course of my friendship with Angie, she realized I didn't like Sheriff Dan and did all she could to make me comfortable that day. She whispered to me that she would take a seat on one side of the table and I should take one across from her. She put her sweater over the back of her chair and I would use my jacket on mine. If Dan happened to sit on her side we could switch seats. Her brothers were called to the table first so one took up the chair next to her and one next to me as a buffer between Dan and me if I were on the same side of the table with him. I thought Lottie thought, *all this maneuvering at the table, just to make her more at ease.*

When the men came in, Angie and I were the only ones standing, pretending to line up the napkins. I was relieved to see Dan sit on my side so I took my seat next to Sal Junior who sat between us. Angie, sitting across from me gave me a wink. At first everyone was busy filling his plate and then Lottie said, "We should say grace." One of her sons did, and we started passing the food. Sgt. Martino started the conversation by asking Dan about any new leads in the latest crime. Lottie tried to interrupt his question. She looked over at her husband and gave him a look he didn't seem to catch and he continued on with his intent on bringing up police business at the table.

"Sal, please," she said, "not on a holiday. You have all week at work to talk about that." Dan looked at her and smiled, nervously. "Of course, Mrs. Martino, you're so right."

I looked over at Angie and she looked annoyed. After that exchange, the talk was mostly about mundane things—the weather, what her boys were doing in school, and comments about the tasteful meal. I kept quiet because I had nothing to offer in the way of interesting conversation. After the meal the men went into the front room to smoke. I helped clear the table and then mentioned to Lottie that I promised Mrs. Wilkie I would pick her up from her sister's early because she wasn't feeling well. "Oh, you go ahead," she said.

I thanked her for the nice dinner and Angie handed me my coat. I had to pass the front room on the way out so I just peaked my head in the doorway and said goodbye to whoever might be in the room. I knew Sgt. Martino's sons were excitingly talking away, and I didn't stop to find out if anyone heard me as I headed for the front door. Once outside, I breathed a deep breath of air and felt relief. On the drive over to get Mrs. Wilkie, I thought about how oppressive the air felt when Dan was around, and if it wasn't for living with Mrs. Wilkie, again, I might have suffered the continued fear I had at Lorraine's. I felt so alone and afraid most of the time. I didn't have far to drive to get Mrs. Wilkie, because her sister Eva lived in Arden. As I waited for a red light to change to green, I thought about Dan at the dinner and remembered what Angie said about his mother choosing to spend a holiday with a date. I thought as mother and son they would be together on a holiday. It didn't make sense to me since everyone knew how he catered to her. I thought his mother was odd, but nothing about Dan made sense to me and as I parked the car in front of Eva's house, I was determined to put him out of my mind. On the ride home, Mrs. Wilkie, appeared tired.

"Anna, are you okay?" I asked, "You don't look too well."

"Don't worry about me dear," she said, smiling and patting my arm

46

as I drove. "I'll rest when we get home. I want to talk to you about my will, Kathleen. The old will was made out for Gary to receive my assets, but I have to change it. I'll leave the house to my sister, but I do want you to have something."

I looked over at her as I helped her out of the car. "Please don't talk like that," I said, nothing's going to happen to you." She laughed and said, "Dear, at my age anything can happen." The thought of her not being around for me never occurred to me at all because she wasn't *that* old. I began to worry about her and the old anxious feelings I had, returned. I found myself getting up during the night to check on her. I knew she was seeing her doctor, but I worried.

The month of July came and before the 4th, I refused the invitation to spend the holiday with the Martinos and accepted the invitation to spend the holiday with Mrs. Wilkie, and her sister. I didn't want to run into Sheriff Dan anymore than I had to at the station. He came in often as his team worked on the latest murder of the girl whose family lived in Arden. One day in the month of August, it was cloudy and raining, so I was using Mrs. Wilkie's car to get to work. On a Friday, she asked me to drop her at her sister's on my way to work. After work, I went to pick her up to take her home, but found her having difficulty breathing. Eva asked her if she would feel better if she stayed the weekend with her and not go home with me. I thought it was a good idea and was about to leave when she suddenly collapsed. We caught her and carried her over to the sofa. Eva ran for water, but I quickly called for help by phoning both the fire station and Sgt. Martino. It wasn't long before the fire department arrived and a medic was working on her and the police arrived as well. Two cops that I worked with entered and I felt relieved until Sheriff Dan appeared behind them. I thought it was strange for him to show up since it was a health problem, not a crime.

I felt faint as I watched them carry her out to the ambulance. Eva was going to ride with her and I thought I would follow in her car, but as I reached for my coat I couldn't stop shaking. I was worried and the implications were that if anything happened to her I wouldn't have a home. The thought made me cry and I didn't want to lose composure in front of Dan. He walked over to me and appeared concerned.

"Kathleen, let me take you to the hospital, you're in no condition to drive," he said, and I didn't know how to refuse at that moment because I was visibly in distress and he could see that. He was so gentle and kind in his approach toward me, and so I let him help me on with my coat and numbly followed him to his car. On the way to the hospital he tried to console me. "I'm sure she'll be alright," he said. "They have a great trauma center at St. Alexis."

I didn't answer him; I was deep in thought about Mrs. Wilkie. The drive to the hospital was silent as nether of us said a word after he tried to make me feel better by mentioning the hospital's credentials. He parked the car and we hurried into the emergency entrance. Dan asked about the status of Mrs. Wilkie. The nurse at he desk told us to wait as she phoned someone, but before she could tell us anything, Eva came out with a doctor and he had his arm around her. She was crying and ran up to put her arms around me. The doctor was talking to Dan, and I heard, "She didn't make it." Eva said nothing as she sobbed on my shoulder. I felt numb and asked the doctor to repeat what I thought he said.

"I'm sorry, we tried, but her heart just gave out. She expired on the way, but we still worked on trying to bring her back. I'm so sorry." It was then that I started to cry. Dan came over to us as the doctor left and hugged us both. "Come on, let me drive you both home," he said. I thought, *what home, whose home am I supposed to go to?* I was confused. We both followed Dan to his car. The drive back to Eva's place was wrought with tension. I let Eva sit in the front seat with him and I sat in the back crying softly into the sleeve of my jacket. When we reached her home, I could see Mrs. Wilkie's car parked at the curb where I left it. As Dan pulled in front of her house, he turned and looked back at me. "Can you drive yourself home?" he asked.

"Yes, yes, of course," I said, trying to compose myself. It was at that moment that it hit me; the car didn't belong to me. Eva must have been thinking the same thing. She put her arm around me as we got out of the car and she told Dan to go on, that we would be fine. When he left, she said, "Don't worry Kathleen, if you don't want to be alone tonight you can stay the night with me." I thought it was a genuine gesture of sympathy for me when she was mourning her sister's passing. I accepted her offer. I didn't want to be alone that night and I wouldn't think about what would happen next, until the morning. I lay awake most of the night thinking of what I would do, or where I could go, if I couldn't afford to rent Anna Wilkie's home. The desperate feelings I had when I walked out of that orphanage returned, and I longed for Tim.

CHAPTER 8

Eva was up early the next morning and I could hear her as she moved about the kitchen. She was nice enough to lend me a pair of pajamas the night before, but I knew I needed to get home, but not before discussing what my plans should be with her. At breakfast she talked about the plans for her sister's funeral and I wondered if I should mention what Mrs. Wilkie told me about her will.

I was nervous and hesitated for a moment and as she went on about what funeral parlor to use, I interrupted her. "Eva, recently your sister mentioned that she still had Gary on her will and she needed to change it. She said she would leave her house to you,"—and then I froze when it came to telling her that she also intended on leaving me something as well.

She looked at me with a disappointed expression. "Well, that complicates things!" she said, with anger. "You know we have two nieces from our eldest sister who passed years ago. I can just imagine what they will do, claim some of her money and without the will updated they will tie up everything in probate court."

I didn't know what to say to her after that outburst and knew I couldn't mention what her sister's intentions were pertaining to me at that moment, if at all. I brought up what she intended to do with the house in the meantime and that I didn't know if my paycheck would cover more than the board I was paying. I was sure renting the house from her would cost a great deal more than I could afford. "Oh, don't worry about that," she said. "If you can't afford to pay the utilities, I can cover you for a couple months until you find another place."

I knew then that I wouldn't have a home to go to after a couple of months. My mind was in frenzy as I tried to think of a way to find a new place. I knew I couldn't go back to Lorraine Perky, not with Jack living there. I wouldn't be comfortable. I was frightened of the thought of finding a place on my own from the ads people placed in the newspaper. I knew anyplace would bring me into contact with strangers. I was about to ask Eva if I could use her sister's car until I found a place, when she blurted out—"I'll drive you home today, because I need the car. Mine has been acting up and I don't want to take the chance it will quit on my way to work." I felt abandoned after she said that and knew from that moment — I was on my own.

It wasn't easy walking into Mrs. Wilkie's empty home that day. Everything reminded me of her and it was then I realized how much she had meant to me. She was the first person outside the orphan home that loved me like a mother would. I cried myself to sleep that night. The next morning I looked awful having had little sleep and my face looked it. Cold water didn't seem to diminish the dark circles under my eyes. When I arrived at work that morning I looked a mess. It started to rain and while trying to get my umbrella opened I got wet while waiting for the bus to arrive. Sgt. Martino looked up at me as I walked in.

"Kathleen, I'm so sorry to hear about Mrs. Wilkie," he said, with compassion. I started to cry and he came from behind his desk to comfort me. Putting his arm around me, he said, "I know how alone you must feel, but you're not alone, Kathleen. You have my family and all the boys here at the station."

I thanked him, and tried to give him a smile. When I entered the room where my desk was, the other cops came up to me to offer their condolences. Jerry, one of the patrolmen at Eva's the night before when the rescue squad from the fire department came, tried to comfort me. "If there is anything I can do for you, let me know," he said. I thanked him and sat down at my desk. It was then I thought of Steve. I would call him after work and let him know what happened. Although I wasn't in love with him, I liked Steve and he was dear to me as a good friend and I needed all the friends I could get at that time.

That evening after I returned home, the first thing I did was look at the ads for rooms to rent. It didn't look promising. I tried to make myself a sandwich but I took one bite and couldn't finish it. I reached for the phone to call Steve. When he answered, he could tell by my voice that something was wrong. "What's the matter? You sound upset," he said. "Mrs. Wilkie died yesterday," I answered, and then I started to cry. I hated that I cried so easily. I felt like a failure and a child instead of a twenty-three-year-old woman. "Are you alone?" he asked. "Yes," I said, then wondered if I should have let him know since he insisted on coming over and wouldn't take no for an answer. I thought since Mrs. Wilkie's neighbors knew she had died, thanks to Eva telling her next-door neighbor when she drove me home. I wondered what they would think if they saw Steve coming into her home knowing I was alone. I worried about everything.

He arrived about thirty minutes after we hung up. He must have flown out the door not to mention how fast he had to drive to make it in such a short time. He lived on the western side of Arden and the traffic on Archer was heavy that time of night. When the doorbell rang, I had mixed feelings of relief that I wouldn't be alone for a while and fear that he would use the opportunity to somehow take advantage of my vulnerability at that time. He entered the room and didn't do what I expected—wrap his arms around me, instead he took my hand and held it and expressed his sorrow over the death of Mrs. Wilkie. He knew how much she meant to me. He looked at me with sadness.

"I'm so sorry Kathleen," he said, "Can I give you a hug?" "Yes, yes, of course," and then I cried in his arms.

We sat at the kitchen table and talked about what my plans would be. I told him about Eva wanting me out of the home and that I needed to find another place. "My family has an extra bedroom since my sister got married last year," he said, "Maybe you could stay with us until you find a more permanent place."

I knew a trap when I saw it, so I let him know that wasn't a possibility and that I would find my own place soon. He left shortly after being satisfied that I would be all right. He promised to help me in anyway I needed and I was grateful for his friendship.

Later in the week Steve and I went out to dinner. He picked me up after work. I felt more comfortable with him since I expressed my desire to remain only friends. He honored my request by not trying to be affectionate in any way, but a good friend and listener. Somehow our conversation turned to the latest murder of the girl from Arden. It wasn't solved yet and I knew the police, the detectives and Sheriff Dan were working day and night to find the killer. Steve asked me many questions about how the investigation was going and if I knew anything about it and if the police had any idea of who could have committed such a crime. I shook my head, no, and said, "I feel so sorry for that girl and all the women that have been murdered. Just think of what their families are going through." He looked at me with a surprised expression.

"Why would you feel sorry for them?" he said, and I detected an irritation in his voice. "Well, no one deserves to be killed like that!" I said, "They were such young women." "Oh, yeah? They were tramps!" He said it with such hate in a voice that it took me by surprise. I had never seen that side of him before. "Why would you say such I thing about women you don't know?" I asked. "Women out late at night alone? What kind of women roam around at night alone? Only tramps, loose women, prostitutes, they deserve what they got, don't you think?"

After that exchange I tried to change the subject. I found some excuse to cut our dinner short. "I promised Angie, I would stop over tonight," I said. "Oh, good, I'll drive you over."

I thanked him when he pulled up to the Martinos, I couldn't get out of the car fast enough. Angie had no idea I would be coming to their home and I didn't want to go without calling first. As soon as Steve's car was out of sight, I looked over at the house and didn't notice anyone at the window so I quickly hurried down the walk toward Archer Avenue and the bus stop. On the ride home, my stomach felt queasy, like it did when I was near Jack, Lorraine's boarder.

I tried to find a reason why Steve would react the way he did, but couldn't come up with a reasonable explanation. I was left with only the thought that maybe Steve knew more than he should about the women, and maybe he had something to do with the latest murder. He was from Arden, and he kept asking me so many questions on how the investigation was going, didn't he? I reasoned. By the time I arrived home I was full of fear, fear that he could have done it. During dinner I mentioned how the police thought the killer was from Arden. I remembered how flushed his face became and then all his questions. I worried that I said too much about the case to him. I was sorry I was with him that night. I didn't know what to think. He was a friend of Angie's boyfriend, John. He couldn't have had anything to do with it. John knew him well. I must be getting paranoid, I thought. I knew I wouldn't mention what I feared to anyone, especially Angie. By the time I got myself in bed, I was so upset I cried out "Tim, Tim." It came out unconsciously since I never mentioned his name, even to myself. I thought about him and cried over him that night for the first time in years.

CHAPTER 9

Summer of 1955 had been a hot one. The humidity coming off Lake Michigan spread its cloud of moisture across Chicago and a good deal of the surrounding suburbs. I found a place to live in late September just before my time ran out at Mrs. Wilkie's home. The apartment I was living in belonged to the wife of one of the cops at our station. He lost his life during the takedown of a robbery around the time I was looking for a place, just after the death of Mrs. Wilkie. Rita Coombs was a hairdresser and with two small children to support, she moved her line of work from the shop where she was an employee to her own home, and a business of her own. Above her garage was a small three-room apartment that policeman, Ronnie Coombs, had built for his mother, but after his death, she chose to live with another son. Rita rented the rooms to me at a reasonable rate and I had a real little home of my own for the first time. I was careful not to divulge to too many people that I lived alone. In 1955 not many single women lived on their own, not decent women. A side door to the garage led to the stairs for the apartment, so for all intent and purposes it looked like I lived with Rita. The apartment was stuffy and hot even in September and the only relief I received from the open windows at night, was the one fan I managed to buy that helped move the air around.

I felt safe after my relationship with Steve ended shortly after that last encounter with him. I didn't mention how he reacted to the latest murder to anyone. I refused any attempt on his part to keep our so-called friendship intact by edging him out of my life. Angie knew we were only friends and thought nothing of our breakup. Sheriff Dan made himself available on my terms whenever I felt frightened or threatened. He led me to believe his interest was only to look in on Rita and me to make sure we were safe. Sgt Martino agreed with him and, after much soul searching on my part, with both Angie and Lottie convincing me that with the killer still on the loose, I agreed it was smart to have Dan around.

"He only has your best interest at heart, Kathleen," Lottie said, "He's a kind man and he knows you're alone. He wants to make sure you feel safe." I was happy that he never made a pass at me whenever he stopped by to check on Rita and me. Before he left, his last advice was always words of caution. "Make sure you lock your doors at night," he said to both of us. I would lock it after he said goodnight. I began to depend on him and I had to admit I judged him too harshly the last few years. He started to grow on me as a dependable friend. When he stopped by several times the third week of October, he only stayed a few minutes and I never asked him to sit down or encouraged him in any way, I began to relax with him coming around. I kept it simple. The last days of October there was a cool breeze, and the tiny apartment wasn't as oppressive, and I spent my evening hours sitting on the small balcony off the living space overlooking the back yard, reading books I brought home from the library. I loved to read and all I had was time on my hands after work or weekends unless Angie wanted to get together, or her parents invited me over.

I tried to be content with the life I lived and to be honest with myself, I often thought of how sparse it was. The boys at the station, the Martino family, Angie's friends, that was my world. Mrs. Wilkie's sister and I parted ways after I moved. Her anger that some one other than her would get any of her sister's money, made me afraid to mention what Mrs. Wilkie promised. Eva would never have believed me. When it was getting close for the time to move from what she perceived as her property, she became cold and pushy. She lost no time telling me how many weeks I had left. I became frightened because I hadn't found a place and when the boys at the station mentioned Rita Coombs and the recent death of her husband, and that she had an empty apartment, they arranged for us to meet. After I moved I never wanted to hear from Eva again and I didn't.

One Saturday morning as I was shopping for groceries, I noticed a new dry cleaning business opened next to the parking lot for the grocery store. It had a help wanted poster in the window. I decided to inquire about the job, hoping I could work Saturdays to increase my standard of living. A few extra bucks in my purse meant a new dress or shoes. I was living on a very tight budget. When I entered the store a pleasant young woman greeted me. "Can I help you?" she asked.

"Yes, I wondered if the job opening is for full, or part time?" Her smile put me at ease. "What are you interested in? We can use some help so whatever hours you can work would be a plus."

"I was thinking weekends," I said nervously. "Well, we are only open during the week and on Saturdays if that's what you're looking for." "Yes, that would do. You see I work for the police department here in Arden and I don't live too far from here, so if I can have the job for Saturdays it would be great," and I can start as soon as you want," I said.

She looked at her calendar and said, "Can you come in this coming Saturday? "Yes, I can, thank you." She took down all the important information she needed from me, and when I left I felt like walking on air. At that moment I felt the happiest I had felt since I was with Tim. Everything seemed to be coming together for me. I had a great job that I loved, a nice place to live, and privacy for the first time in my life, and now also a little extra money in my pocket. The only thing lacking in my life were friends I had made on my own. I considered Angie my closest friend, but I met her through her father, and I always felt a little wary of expressing too much of my feelings to her, never sure how much she shared with her parents, or her friends. I decided that day, that any friend I made on my own I would keep separate from the rest of the people I knew. I needed someone I could confide in and not worry about it becoming open news for everyone else. My landlady Rita was the sweetest woman, not too much older than I was, but again she was someone I met through the police department. Had I met her on my own, I might have felt more comfortable talking to her, but I didn't. I was yearning for someone to feel close to, like I began to feel when I returned to Anna Wilkie. At times the loneliness I felt almost drove me back to St. Cecelia's for a visit with Sister Mary Louise, but I didn't want the nuns to know how I felt. They would think I wasn't making it in the outside world and that I failed. I never went back to see any of them after I left and I would leave it that way.

My first Saturday at the dry cleaning shop went well. Betty showed me the procedure both at the register at the front desk, and how to line up the clothing on racks with the proper tags in the back room. Her parents owned the shop and they told me that occasionally her mother came in to help. Her father was in the shop with her most of the time. I liked both of her parents and they were very kind to me.

As we were having lunch in the back room while her father was manning the register, Betty and I confided in each other about our past. She looked at me with a whimsical expression.

"At least you were never mistreated in the orphanage," she said.

"No, but it was a lonely existence to be without family," I said.

"Well, you don't know how bad my marriage was. I fled with my son when Tom got crazy."

"Was he cruel to you?"

"Worse than that. They play with your head, you know. So sweet one minute and the next—Well, someone you hardly recognize appears. Right after we were married I became pregnant and he forced me to get an illegal abortion. He didn't want children he said, but soon as the Korean War started, then he wanted a child in hopes it would keep him out of the war. That's the only reason we had Ricky. I was lucky I had my parents to confide in, and they told me to get out of it, and come home."

I thought of what she said; having someone to go to, and I envied her. I told her all about the Martinos, the guys I worked with, Sheriff Dan, Steve, Mrs. Wilkie, all of them. It wasn't until later that night as I lay in my bed that I realized I never mentioned Tim. I found it too painful to talk about him.

I learned more about Betty—how she lived with a deranged man she hardly knew in the first years of the marriage. Her son, Ricky, was only a year old when she made her move after her husband left for work one morning, two years before.

"He threatened me if I ever left him," she said, "I had to leave when he wasn't there. I knew the first place he would look was at my parents. I was afraid of him, so my father thought it better that I go to my Aunt's in Indiana until things cooled off. He drove us there that same morning I left. Ricky was crying for his favorite Teddy Bear that I accidentally left at the apartment. I didn't dare go back because I never knew when he would walk in. It didn't matter if it was in the middle of the day, he would leave work to check up on me. He could be very charming and con anyone at anytime and they believed him. My father got a restraining order against him and I was lucky that after he met another woman, he moved to California and never bothered with us again."

After hearing her story, I grew more careful about any strangers I met. I was content with the knowledge that in Betty I had found a true friend I could trust. She didn't know anyone I knew and I aimed to keep it that way.

It was that winter of 1955 that I stayed indoors on the weekends when the weather turned bad. I used public transportation because I didn't own a car and wasn't sure if I could ever save enough money to buy one. Everything I needed was in walking distance or a short bus ride away. The move from Clearidge to Arden was the best move I could have made. I split my time between Rita, Betty's parents home, where she lived, and visiting the Martinos when I was invited. One night in the middle of November my doorbell rang. I was leery of opening the door to see who it might be because Dan had a key to garage door as well as Rita. They never rang the bell but just came upstairs to my door and knocked on it, announcing their presence before I opened the door. To answer the bell I would have had to go down into the garage to see who was outside the outer door. I hesitated long enough to call Rita from my phone, but she didn't answer. I thought she might have gone out. I ran to the only windows in my apartment that were on the opposite side of the garage or the back, but I couldn't see who was on the outside of the downstairs side door. After several more rings whoever was there left. I didn't hear a car motor or anything until about an hour later. I thought I heard tires on gravel and went to the back balcony to peek over the side. I could see part of the driveway closer to the street. All I caught a glimpse of was the back of a black Ford as it turned out of the drive. I couldn't see the front of the car or the driver and it wasn't Rita's car.

Around eleven pm I was awakened by a great deal of noise coming from the back of the garage. When I parted the drapes from the sliding doors to the balcony the yard was lit up with floodlights. I noticed a policeman in the yard and I quickly threw on my robe and a winter jacket, stumbled for my boots that I pulled on over bare feet and headed for the stairs down to the garage. Rita met me at the bottom of the stairs.

"I was just coming up to get you," she said. She was very upset and with extreme excitement and anger in her voice she cried out loudly, as I hurried down the stairs. "We've been robbed! Anything of value is gone, my few pieces of good jewelry and the place is ransacked, and everything is a mess!"

I put my arm around her to comfort her and followed her into her place. The four cops that responded were from our station. Jerry and Bob came up to me."Did you hear anything last night?" Jerry asked.

"Yes, it was about 6:00 pm. Someone rang my bell, but I called Rita first. When she didn't answer my call, I was afraid to go down to see who it was. Whoever it was rang the bell a couple times and then I presumed they left. I didn't hear anything until about an hour later when I heard a car in the driveway. I was only able to get a peek at it for a second as it turned out of the drive. I think it was black and it looked like the back end of a 1949 Ford."

"Thanks, Kathleen," Jerry said, "That's helpful." I think whoever it was that rang your bell wanted to make sure no one was home." Bob came over to us, leaving the two other cops who were searching the house for any other clues, dusting for fingerprints and doing what cops do during a robbery. He spoke to us with compassion in his voice.

"Whoever it was knew you weren't home, Rita, and he would have had to have known there was an apartment over the garage when he rang her bell."

He looked at us with great concern, "How many people know someone lives above the garage?"

"Well, of course my neighbors know. Ronnie had to get the neighborhood's permission to have a rental on the property. It was allowed because family would be living in it, my mother-in-law, but she chose to live with Ronnie's brother," Rita said. "Kathleen's not family so I didn't mention it to anyone else. For all they know she is living with me. What difference does it make if she's living in my house as a boarder and renting a room, or renting the rooms above the garage?" she asked, annoyed.

"Doesn't make any difference to us, but I think it's someone you know, Rita," Jerry said.

When the door opened, I wasn't surprised to see Dan; after all, he was a Sheriff.

He came over to me and put his hand on my back, "Are you okay," he asked, then as an after thought, he realized he singled me out when there were two of us who felt violated with this break-in. He took his hand away and touched Rita's arm gently for a moment. "Tell me what happened," he said, directing his questions to both of us. I felt better after he included Rita in his concern. He listened intently to both of us as we recalled the events of that evening to him.

"I'm worried about you living alone up there," he said, directing his concern to me, but then Rita said, "She's as safe as I am, Sheriff, I'm alone here with two children and my neighbors are good people, they look out for us."

He genuinely looked concerned and put his arm around both of us, "I know, neighbors can be helpful, but two women living here without a male on the property is an invitation to anyone who is up to no good," he said.

"I have my business here," Rita said.

"That's another thing I want to talk to you about," he said. "People come and go to get their hair done at your home and you leave yourself wide open for what happened tonight. It could have been anyone you knew from a customer to someone who knew one of them."

"I have two children under five, Ronnie is gone, my parents live out of state, and I haven't found anyone I want to leave my kids with in order to go out to work. I have to work out of my home," she said.

"I understand," Dan said, "but maybe it would be safer if you had a man living in the apartment and Kathleen living here in your place." He turned to Jerry, "Isn't that new rookie that's been hired looking for a place?" Jerry laughed and said, 'Yeah, I'll ask him if he's interested."

I could see Rita's expression; she didn't look too happy. She was probably thinking about the fact that her home had three bedrooms, but her children occupied two of them.

"She doesn't have room for a boarder," I said, "as you can see her home is small." Along with the bedrooms it consisted of a living room, dining room, and kitchen. The dining room was where she had a sink installed and it was used for the hair salon.

"Well, I guess we can think of something to keep you gals safe," Dan said. "How about it?" he asked Bob and Jerry, "Maybe one of the guys can park their cruiser temporarily in her driveway."

Later, after all the cops had left, with one of the police cars parked in the driveway, Dan stayed for awhile, and waited until I was ready to go back to my apartment. With my help and Dan's, Rita got her home back to some order, after she put her kids to bed. I thought he would leave as I walked to the garage, but he insisted on seeing me up the stairs and into the apartment.

"I know it's late, but could I bother you for some coffee to put in my thermos. It's cold out and I have another matter to check on before I head home tonight."

I looked at the clock above my kitchen table and it was 2:00 am.

"Yes, I'll put the pot on," I said, as he thanked me and headed to his car to retrieve the thermos.

When he returned, he sat at the table and I took a cup out and placed it in front of him. I sat across from him and noticed how tired he looked.

"You might as well have a cup before you go, to stay awake," I said.

"That's kind of you, Kathleen, will you join me?"

"If I do, I'll be awake all night, but I'll keep you company while you have yours," I said. He smiled at me and I didn't feel threatened, or uncomfortable with him. In fact I felt safe, and I was enjoying his company for the first time.

CHAPTER 10

After many weeks of investigating the robbery at Rita's, the police hadn't found any suspects, and under Dan's suggestion they kept a vigil around her home until they were satisfied that it was safe with just an occasion drive by the property. My Saturday job turned out to be more than just the extra pay because it brought me Betty, a friendship that I cherished. We became very close and spent a good deal of time together and I adored her son. Ricky was an adorable child and I began to think of one day having a child of my own. The only thing missing in my life was a husband and a family. I was twenty-three years of age and that was old in the social circles I lived in. Young women usually married right out of high school.

Angie and John were planning their wedding for June of 1956 to her parents delight, because she was twenty-four. She asked me to be a brides maid and I accepted, happy to be in her wedding party. Sgt. Martino was excited to plan and pay for his only daughter's wedding and he would spare no expense. I looked forward to it, but not without some reservation when I heard that Steve would be John's best man. Of course it came as no surprise since Steve was his best friend. I didn't want to feel uncomfortable around Steve, so I made up my mind to bite the bullet and be friendly and kind, but not too friendly to him. The way I ended our dating rather abruptly, left him angry, I'm sure.

I spent my time working as many hours as I could on Saturdays and I stayed after the shop closed working with Betty and the one employee that did the actual cleaning. By April of 1956 I knew how everything worked and could help in all situations. Spring brought us the customers winter clothing to be cleaned and put away for the next season. We were real busy, and I managed to work a few hours after I left the police station, about twice a week. I was half way to saving for a car of my own, albeit, a used car.

I spent Easter with Betty's family and then stopped over to visit the Martinos after Easter dinner, later that evening. Of course Dan was there as usual. I often wondered how he was able to be with the family for holidays when he had a mother who was alone, but Angie filled me in on the strange relationship between Dan and his mother. It seemed that she was a very big influence in his life, but when the opportunity arose for her to spend a holiday with a male friend, she chose the boyfriend over her own son. It didn't make sense to me, but nothing about Dan did. I only knew that the more I got to know him, I actually began to like him. He seemed to be a kind man who couldn't say 'no' to anyone in need. If his mother had a great influence over him, so did everyone else. Lottie once described him to me as a man with an invisible ring in his nose. I found the comment rather disturbing and blew it off as her way of saying he was at everyone's beckon call. I found that quality in his personality a tribute to his kindness.

Two months later, in June, I found myself dancing with both Dan and Steve at the wedding. I had to accept Steve's offer for a dance when Angie paired me with him to walk down the church aisle. She had no way of knowing why I stopped seeing him, but just thought we parted on amicable terms. Steve acted like a gentleman and I was relieved. Dan and I danced a few times and he seemed to follow me around the reception room in between the dancing. During one dance, he looked down at me and smiled without saying anything and I tried not to look up at him, but focused my eyes over his shoulder or at anything else in the room.

"Kathleen," he said, "Do I make you uncomfortable? You seem nervous. It's just a dance. If you'd rather sit down—"

"Oh, no, I'm alright," I said, not wanting to hurt his feelings. I did feel a little uncomfortable in his arms, because although I grew to like him, I was afraid he would expect more from me in the way of maybe dating in the future and I wasn't too keen on that prospect. I tried to cast aside the feeling I had as we danced. With his arms around me, and him holding me so close, I felt confused, and it was a feeling that frightened me. I also felt protected in some way and not so alone. It was somewhat like the feelings I had when I was with Tim except I loved Tim, but with this man I knew it wasn't love, more like what a daughter might feel for a father, I thought, since I had no clue what having a father figure in my life would feel like. Betty's father was kind and included me in his family, but he was Betty's father, not mine. With Dan the focus was all on me. It made me feel special and I

64

felt like a little girl around him. I enjoyed the feeling, but was cautious about getting too involved. I decided to confide in Betty about my feelings.

After the wedding, I didn't see Dan for a few weeks since he appeared busy with work and he wasn't stopping by to check on Rita and me as often. During a lull at the dry cleaning shop, I mentioned my feelings about Dan to Betty.

"That's normal to feel that way," she said, "after all, you don't know what it would feel like to have a parent figure since you never experienced having parents."

"Oh, I did, with Mrs. Wilkie, but it was more like I was looking after her, when I moved back with her than she was taking care of me," I said.

"Well, if he's a kind man, what are you afraid of?"

"He is so much older than I am, and— well, I really don't know."

"Age has nothing to do with anything, Kathleen, look at me, my husband was my age and it didn't work," she said, "He was so immature and cruel. Maybe if he were older he wouldn't have been that way. Have you ever known Dan to be anything but kind to you? More important, has anyone who knows him said anything unkind about him?"

I thought about what she said, and remembered hearing he was intense about the crime cases he worked on. "Only that he appears stern and intense when he's at work," I said.

Betty looked at me and stared to chuckle, "My gosh, he's a Sheriff isn't he? That has to be a stressful job."

"I'm sure you're right," I said, feeling better about Dan at that moment.

In July the police were planning a 4th of July Picnic. Everyone would be bringing their families and so I joined Rita and her children since I didn't have a family to bring. I thought of Betty and Ricky, who might have enjoyed coming with me, but I wanted to keep them separate from everyone else in my life, so I never mentioned the picnic to her. When she asked if I would like to spend it with her and her family, I simply said Sgt. Martino had invited me to spend it with his family.

Chasing the Unicorn

At the picnic, Angie and John were there and also John invited Steve who brought a date with him. I was happy about that since that meant he wouldn't come around me. I still harbored doubts about Steve, that maybe he was hiding a violent side to him. Dan came over to me and said hello, he then asked if he could get me anything in the way of a drink, or food. I nodded yes and he went over to where they had the food set up. I was sitting at one of the picnic tables with Rita and the kids. "You didn't tell him what you wanted, " she said.

"It doesn't matter," I said, "anything he brings I'll eat."

Dan came over to us and sat down next to me. He brought a hamburger and an orange crush. I thanked Dan, and then I noticed the expression on Rita's face, it was quizzical.

"I thought you didn't like orange crush," she said.

Dan turned to me and apologized. "I'm sorry, I thought you said anything I brought was ok." Then he noticed that Rita and her kids hadn't gone for their food yet. "Rita, let me get you and the kids whatever you want," he said.

Rita smiled and asked her children what they wanted, but Dan stood up and said, "Let me take them, and you stay. I'll get whatever you want."

Rita laughed, "Whatever," she said, "Just bring me a hotdog with everything on it and a coke, and thanks."

After he left with her son on his shoulders, and her daughter holding his hand, Rita said, "Kathleen, he's a gem and I know he really likes you, well it's more than like, I think he's in love with you."

"How can you know that?"

"Everyone at the station knows, Kathleen, except you."

I was about to say something to her when Dan came back with his hands full with their food, and her kids happily running behind him. He sat himself down at the table with us while we ate. I began to see Dan in a different light watching him engage her children in conversation and play. He loved teasing her little boy who was only three years old. Her daughter at age six held a sweet conversation with him. He turned his attention to Rita, asking her how she was doing and then to both of us. He wanted to make sure we felt safe after that break-in at her home.

"I don't think whoever did it would be foolish enough to repeat it after all the surveillance we had on your place," he said. Rita agreed and thanked him and then he asked if I wanted to join him in some of the games that were starting. Like all large picnics the police planned a lot of entertainment. It was a nice sunny day and I enjoyed the company and the attention and when the sun went down, Rita's little boy became cranky and she decided to take them home. She realized that I had come with her and asked if I minded if we left early.

"I'm sorry, it's past their bedtime and if you want to stay, maybe you could get a ride home. I don't want to ruin what's left of the day for you," she said.

Dan heard her and looked at me. "Kathleen, I'll take you home. There's going to be more games and you want to stay for the fireworks don't you?" I agreed and after Rita left it was just Dan and me at the table. We talked easily together and I enjoyed his company, really enjoyed him for the first time. He drove me home that night and I had no doubts about his feelings for me, but I wasn't sure of what I was feeling. He kissed me for the first time after he pulled into Rita's driveway and I felt happy and safe with him. It was a nice feeling and for the first time I didn't feel alone in my world. I was never lonely, not with all the friendships I had with the police, the Martinos, Rita and Betty and her family but having friends filled my life but not the empty feeling I carried inside of me ever since I lost Tim. Dan filled some of that but in a different way. I was content with that. We began to see each other often and on one of our dates I noticed a slight change in his personality and was puzzled. He seemed irritable and preoccupied with something on his mind. When I asked him what was wrong, he quickly changed his demeanor and smiled at me. "Nothing's wrong Kathleen," he said rather sharply, like I was annoying him by just asking a simple question.

I began to question my dating him and after another date where he appeared moody and sullen, I began to have doubts. After confiding in Betty I decided to rethink seeing him again and to end it the next time he called. When he called again for a date, his voice was all cheerful and happy sounding. He asked if I wanted to take in an early dinner and movie on Saturday, the next day. I took a deep breath and said, "I don't think so Dan."

"What do you mean?" he asked.

"I don't think we should see each other again," I said.

There was a moment of silence on his side until he sweetly said, "But why Kathleen?"

"I think I'm still too young for you, I would like to date others closer to my age."

He shouted back at me, "Wait until you're my age and everyone you know is married!" I thought he had some nerve getting angry and then he changed his tone and with pleading in his voice sweetly said, "Well, can I call you again in the future?"

I answered, "Well, maybe." The minute I hung up the phone I knew I shouldn't have encouraged him in anyway but I just couldn't continue to hurt his feelings. I figured in due time I would be dating some other person and I wouldn't hear from him again. I did date only once, a young man whom I met through Betty but it didn't turn into anything tangible as far as us becoming a couple and soon I was free again. The next couple of months I didn't hear from Dan and I felt free. I kept busy with work and was able to purchase a used 1949 Ford. I hadn't met anyone special and I devoted my time to enjoying both Rita and Betty's friendship and their children. When fall arrived again so did my birthday. In October of 1956 I would be twenty-four years old. I began to worry that I might never get married and I wanted to badly, to have a family and children of my own.

On my birthday, I had dinner at the Martino's and they had a cake for me. I thought it was kind to invite me over and help me celebrate. I left early and arrived home around 8:00 pm. It was a Tuesday night and I had to get up early for work the next morning. I had just settled down in my pajamas and bathrobe to enjoy a glass of milk and a couple of cookies before bed, when the doorbell rang. I looked at the clock and it was close to 10:00 pm. I knew Rita never rang the bell but came up to my door. I looked out of the side balcony, where I could see if there was a car in the driveway besides mine, and spotted a police car. I went back inside and quickly closed the sliding glass doors as a cool October wind picked up. I wondered what was wrong that the police arrived and went down the stairs to open the outside door. To my complete surprise Dan was standing there with a package in his hands, and also a large bouquet flowers. I was stunned and speechless and the only thing I could do was to invite him upstairs.

He proceeded to apologize for dropping by so late and unannounced and he had a sweet and sad expression on his face as he sat on my sofa still holding what he had brought, "I didn't have the key for the door downstairs on me, or I would have come up and knocked on your door," he said. "I miss you Kathleen," he said, nervously. "I can't eat, I can't sleep, all I think of is you, I need you," he pleaded. He then handed me the small package and the flowers. I was shaken up and sat across from him and like a robot I opened the package that held a small box. Inside was a beautiful American girl watch with two diamonds on the band and it was engraved, 'Kathleen, all my love, Dan, 10-10-1956.' I couldn't speak, I sat there like a dummy as he got up and gently put the watch around my wrist. He took the flowers out of my hand and went over to the kitchen and set them in the sink. He returned to where I was sitting, feeling numb and he took both of my hands in his. "I love you," he said, "please give me another chance."

He kissed me on the forehead like I was a child, and then on both cheeks. When I came out of the shock I was feeling, two thoughts came to my mind. What nerve he had, but also what courage it must have taken to come to me in this way and that he must really love me. After that night, Dan and I were together again, this time for good.

CHAPTER 11

I thought the year of 1957 would be the best year I had in quite a few years because Dan and I were steadily dating. I couldn't believe how attentive he was. I had gotten to know his mother and she seemed delighted with me, which was a surprise, after all I heard about her. She was a lonely person twice widowed and Dan was her only child. I realized she was just a very caring person, not only of her son, but she also transferred some of that maternal attention to me. I never took her constant attention to detail and involvement in our courtship as meddling in our relationship. I was like an empty shell when it came to knowing how a family functioned emotionally between themselves. She not only showered me with attention, but also was generous with taking me out shopping. She insisted on paying for everything and as a result of my tight budget, I let her.

I would confide in Betty and although she was happy for me, she did warn me a few times that she thought Dan's mother might be a problem in the future. I didn't see it that way because I was so needy of parental attention. By March Dan presented me with an engagement ring and I happily accepted. His mother insisted on throwing us an engagement party with the entire police department and whomever else I wanted, to help us celebrate. She booked a room in a fancy restaurant and everyone was happy for us, especially Rita. During the celebration, Nancy, wife of one of the cops, followed me into the lady's room.

Nancy was an older woman more Mrs. Martino's age and I got to know her the year before, at the picnic in July. I liked her and she seemed to take me under her wing when the police department had the Memorial Day picnic that year. We now found ourselves at my engagement party standing in front of a mirror refreshing our makeup when she gently took my hand in hers.

"Kathleen "watch out for his mother!"

"Why do you say that?" I asked.

She looked at me with an expression that I took for pity and said, "I know you don't have a family of your own, but Dan's mother is a very controlling woman. I can't believe she is so attentive to you when she drove away every woman he dated in the past."

I didn't know what to say after she expressed her doubts about Dan's mother and I just nodded to let her know I understood her concern, but I really didn't.

As I became more acquainted with Dan and his mother they appeared to be devout Catholics and she often remarked how sacred the marriage vows were to her. She would confide in me about her marriage to Dan's father and how he wasn't a very hands-on father to Dan, but that her second husband was.

"I don't think Larry ever wanted children, he wasn't kind to Danny, but my husband Tom was and when Larry died Dan was only ten years old so he needed a father. Marrying Tom was the best thing I ever did for Danny's sake. He loved him as if he were his own son," she said. After she told me that, I felt sorry for Dan, hearing how he was treated the early years of his life. I started giving Dan more attention in the way of being more interested in everything he talked about and what his interests were like baseball and most sports, even though I could have done without going to all the games with him, I did go. I was spending less time with Betty or Rita and although Dan knew many people he never wanted anyone else with us when he took me out. I took that as a compliment that I filled his needs in a way that no one else could. He was a true gentleman, never pressed me for more than a kiss after each date. I thought he was treating me with respect. Because I knew I didn't have the same feelings of passion for him that I felt for Tim, it was ok with me. I thought what I felt with Tim was a once in a lifetime thing and I had to forget it and move on to what was a more grownup realistic view of life, a feeling of comfort or contentment, and of just belonging to someone.

After the engagement party Dan suggested an April wedding and although both Rita and Betty thought is was too soon, I agreed. Working with Betty one Saturday, she cautioned me.

"You have only been dating a total of six months and engaged one and he wants to get married in a month?" she asked.

"Well maybe it's because of his age," I said, trying to defend Dan's rushing us toward marriage. He would be 35 soon and it made sense to me at that time. We planned the wedding for the first Saturday in May. His mother, who I now began to address as Mom, talked us into a May wedding. She couldn't arrange a wedding in the three weeks left in April to make an April date. When I mentioned to Rita that Dan's mother was planning the wedding for us, she replied, "Well, if you had parents they would be doing it, so just let her and enjoy whatever she can do for you."

"I think Dan and I should have a say about it," I said.

Rita looked at me and agreed, but then said "You know Kathleen, Dan is so busy with work and he's under a lot of stress, so just let his mother know how you feel and maybe she will accommodate some of your ideas."

I thought about what she said, but Dan's mother was kind to me and so excited to be involved in the wedding, that I didn't want her to think I was ungrateful for all she had done for us. So I said nothing, and let her do whatever she wanted. She took me for my wedding dress and insisted on paying for it. I knew both Dan and his mother were sharing the cost of the whole affair. Deep down I felt just a little resentment from time to time but it was pushed away by my feelings of not having a family that would have contributed to some of the costs if not all. I learned many things from her and at times I felt unsure and inferior to her when she bragged about her upbringing. She talked endlessly about her millionaire father who lost his fortune during World War I. She was left with some money from her second husband, and she lived not much different than most of the middle class wives of the men in the Sheriff's department or on the police force, but her demeanor and attitude was that of having the ambiance of a wealthy woman without the wealth. It caused many of the wives of the men her son worked with to dislike her.

I wanted to invite Betty and her family to my wedding after knowing her for some time. Everything would remain the same as far as not involving them with the Martinos or anyone else. As far as anyone knew, they were just the people I worked for. The first inkling that everything wouldn't run smoothly was when Dan's mother saw the list I handed her of the people I wanted at my wedding.

"Who are the Cheneys?" she asked. She knew everyone else I knew except for them and I hadn't invited Betty to my engagement party since it was only the wives of the police department. Rita was invited as the widow of one of their own. Dan's mother made it clear to me that it would be a small dinner party to celebrate our engagement with all of Dan's co-workers. I was nervous when I spoke and my voice quavered a bit as I tried to explain, "The Cheneys are the people I work for part time," I said. She looked at me and with an attitude of indignation said, "Kathleen, they are not close friends, you only work for them and besides you won't have to work for them after you and Danny are married, and you might have to quit your job at the department as soon as you're expecting a child." I was stunned and said nothing. I wanted to say that maybe I wouldn't have a child for a year or two but didn't and before I could open my mouth to say anything she went on speaking.

"My son is going on 35 in June and he doesn't want to wait too long to have a son," she said.

I felt cowed by her at that moment and all I could say was, "I know, but,"— she cut me off by telling me what her son wanted. She seemed to know exactly what his wishes were and it bothered me because he never spoke to me about such personal things, or what was on his mind and I was about to become his wife.

When I arrived at my part-time job on the following Saturday, I had to get up the courage to tell Betty that the invitations to my wedding wasn't going to include her and her family. "I have no say in the plans for my wedding," I said, "his mother is arranging it all." Betty looked at me with a shocked expression.

"How can you not be included in your own wedding plans? You're the bride for heavens sake! Don't let her browbeat you into submission. Kathleen, tell Dan how you feel. I'm sure he'll stick up for who you want to invite or anything you would like to do differently."

"I was planning to do that, but I feel like I'm obligated to her since she is paying for half of the costs."

Betty ran her hand through her hair with her eyes closed and looking toward the ceiling she said, "My God Kathleen! You're bought and paid for."

73

I didn't know what to say after that because deep down in my soul I knew it was the truth. I was selling myself for security with a man who was racing through life without a wife or children at the ripe old age of 35, as his mother put it to me, and she was focused on being a grandmother. That's all she talked about when she first knew we were a couple. I wondered if I were the perfect vehicle to give her that child. I was younger than all the other women he dated in the past, Angie said. I began to question if he really loved me. I knew it wasn't to the degree Tim expressed his love for me. I was confused and unable to think clearly so I put any doubts I had in the back of my mind and did nothing. I let the coming events carry me away. After all the invitations were sent out just a few weeks before the wedding I had second thoughts about not saying anything to Dan on how disappointed I was that I couldn't invite one family. We were alone in my apartment and I waited until we had finished the dinner I cooked for the two of us. He was in a pleasant mood so I gingerly approached the subject of how all the invitations were mailed and that I should have invited one more family.

"Who would that be?" he asked.

"The family I work for on the weekends, "I said, "They've been very good to me and when I was having a hard time making ends meet, they hired me for extra hours. I became close to their daughter so I consider her more of a friend now than just someone I work for." I hated that my voice shook toward the end of that statement. I waited for his answer but he took his time drinking his coffee first and then he looked at me and took my hands in his and in a sweet and understanding voice said, "Well of course you can invite them."

"But your mother didn't agree, she wants to keep it just the department and the friends we have together."

"Don't worry, I'll talk to her," he said.

I couldn't believe he would take my side and was so happy about it that I went to get the address of the Cheney family to give to him. He waved his hand away as I tried to hand it to him and said, "Let me talk to her first." I was stunned and said nothing except, "Ok." At that moment I felt like I was helpless. All the invitations were mailed, everything was planned, and everyone was excited for us. It was a speeding train I couldn't stop. The next day Dan called and said, "It's too late now and we have a pretty big crowd attending. You should have mentioned this to me weeks ago." Some how I knew if I had mentioned it to him earlier his answer would have been the same. I convinced myself that everything would turn out ok, and I dreaded telling Betty. I wondered if it would put a strain on our friendship but when I told her I was almost in tears and she could see the fragile state I was in.

"Don't worry about it," she said kindly, "It's alright, I understand the situation but I worry about, "—and then she stopped and changed the subject. I knew what she was about to say. That night alone in my apartment I couldn't sleep. I thought of what both Nancy and Betty warned me about, and it kept me awake. I knew if I had parents it would have been so easy to stop everything and go home, but I was alone and the only home I had to call my own was a small rented loft apartment above a young widows garage.

CHAPTER 12

The day of the wedding on Saturday May 4th had come and I was nervous. I had asked Angie to be my maid of honor and she was delighted. The two bridesmaids were Angie's friends whom I got to know well. They were happy to complete my wedding party. I told myself that after we were married things would get better. Dan was busy at work and left most of the planning to his mother and me, but I knew it was her decisions that counted, not mine. Because she was an older woman who had been married twice I convinced myself that she knew best when it came to weddings. After all, what did I know about anything pertaining to a wedding. I had never been to one until Angie's.

Dan's Mother whom I now called Mom because I accidently called her Mrs. Robson once and she corrected me sharply, preferring her 2nd husband's name. I kept forgetting that name so, I thought of her as just Mom. Mom expected me to dress at her home but since Dan lived with her I thought I would be with Angie at her parents home. That is where the bridesmaids would be at the invitation of the Martinos. Dan and his best man and the two groomsmen would be at Mom's home. Mom thought Dan should dress elsewhere and it wasn't settled until Lottie, and Sergeant Martino, spoke with her. If that misunderstanding was any indication of what our marriage would be like, we were off to a good start. I ended up at the Martinos to my relief.

Standing in front of the long mirror in the Martinos hall in my wedding gown, everyone crowded around expressing how pretty I looked.

"The dress is beautiful," Lottie said, "but why isn't it white?"

"Dan's mother thought an ivory color would be better because she said with my red hair and very pale complexion, white would make me look like a ghost."

"Well, that's crazy," Angie, said, and the other girls agreed.

"You're too easy going, Kathleen, you need to stand up for yourself and you should have demanded what *you* wanted, not his mother."

That surprised me because Angie and her family had defended Dan and his mother whenever I confided in them of my ambivalent feelings about them, when I first met Dan, and then his mother. When we started dating again, they thought it was the best decision I could have made. I could see the expression on both Angie and her mother when I told them it was his mother who insisted on the ivory wedding dress. They didn't approve and Lottie said, "I wish you would have told us before you went along with her. She's a bit—well, it wasn't supposed to be her choice."

"She paid for the dress, so I guess it was," I said.

After that, no one said anything more, but I could see the looks Angie and her mother exchanged. They were viewing Dan's mother differently. I needed them on my side, but little did I know how much in the coming days.

The wedding in the church was beautiful without anything more happening to cause any stress for me, but I couldn't help noticing how serious Dan looked. He never smiled throughout the service. When we had to face each other he almost looked stern and uncomfortable. It bothered me, because everyone else in the wedding party was smiling. I attributed it to his personality, and that he worried about all the cases he worked on. I almost felt sorry for him. I remember thinking, *I can't wait until we're together in our own home and I can help relieve some of his stress, by being affectionate and understanding.* We said our vows to each other, and when it was over he did smile a little as we walked down the aisle and out of the church. The whole police and sheriff's departments with their wives and children were ready and waiting with what seemed like buckets of rice. We ran to the limo Dan hired to take us for our studio pictures first and then to the reception. Once inside the car, Dan brushed the rice out of his hair and off his tux jacket like it was an unnecessary bit of a problem. I was covered in rice, but it didn't bother me. He was silent in the back of the limo for a few minutes and then I said, "Aren't you glad it's over," meaning the stress leading up to the wedding. He snapped at me in an angry voice.

"What do you mean it's over? It's just started!"

I said, "Wow! Where did that come from?" meaning his anger. He had never showed that side of himself to me when we were dating. His answer stunned me.

"Well, you're married to me now, and there's nothing you can do about it," was his comment.

I was shocked and couldn't respond. The thought that ran through my mind at that moment was that I was trapped. I had just taken a vow with the words, 'Til death do us part.' My religion sealed my fate and I filed that moment into my subconscious and pretended it hadn't happened.

The wedding reception was something I wanted to forget. He wasn't as attentive as I expected and almost ignored me most of the time. Except for cutting the cake together and a first dance, he was mostly with his work buddies at the bar. The honeymoon was by car, racing through the Southern States to view Civil War monuments. At one greasy spoon back country restaurant, we stopped for a southern fried chicken dinner, and a man quite drunk, leaned into the booth where we were sitting and tried to help us with the map Dan had spread over the table trying to decide where we should go to next. The man's incoherent rambling of words caused me to giggle, and Dan got upset with me. He spoke with the guy as if he was perfectly sober and his best buddy. Later in the car, I was scolded for my display of a lack of respect for the drunken stranger. I noticed he ordered a drink, which he never did when we were dating. At the reception he drank along with the guests and his personality seemed to change. As naive as I was, I thought the drastic change from sullen to appearing so silly and talkative was due to his happiness. The rest of the week-long trip was a combination of extreme tension between us, and his racing out of dry counties where selling liquor of any kind was prohibited, so he could have a drink with our dinner. I noticed for the first time how his hands shook when he wasn't moving them. I attributed it to nervousness on his part. His personality on that trip fluctuated between being real sweet once we stopped for the night, to constant anger and irritation when we were traveling. It left me confused. At night he would make the most endearing comments—" I don't believe you're mine," or "When I first saw you, with your red hair, it was like a flame that set my heart on fire." I was so needy and naïve, I took what he said as wonderful compliments, not as corny statements and manipulation. When we were driving through the state of Arkansas he informed me that he wanted to look up a World War II buddy. He pulled up to a pay phone and after reaching the guy, he announced we were meeting him that night in some bar. He appeared excited over meeting up with the co-pilot of the B-17 they were trained in during World War II, Dan being the navigator. When we arrived at the agreed destination, we found Charles Duncan and his wife sitting at the bar. They greeted us warmly and then we moved to a booth. Drinks were ordered and before long both Dan and the couple were on their way to an incoherent wonderland. I didn't drink except for a soda or two. The subject of how they chose different paths came up. It seemed that Charles chose OCS school and became an officer, but Dan took the discharge. Dan let me know during our courtship that he took the discharge because his mother had just become a widow and he didn't want to leave her all alone. In my naïve immaturity, I thought it was very noble of Dan. So I added to the conversation by mentioning that, and announcing how proud I was of Dan for making that decision.

"Oh, Dan wasn't chosen for OCS, because he never completed the applications, he didn't make the grade," a very inebriated Charles announced.

Dan was unaware of what his buddy had just divulged, he talked over everyone and his mind was on the next round of drinks. I was stunned; I was lied to. I wondered how many other lies he told to make himself look bigger than he actually was. When we were going through Missouri he hadn't had a drink for most of the day because the last eatery didn't serve liquor. He pulled into a gas station for gas and spotted a store attached to it, so he ran in with me following, preceeded to scan all the coolers looking for beer, the owner came over and said, 'Can I help you?' and Dan said, "I'm dry, I'm dry!" and the owner misunderstood and laughed, saying, "I know, I know, we are a dry county." After Dan caught on that there wasn't any beer sold in the county we were driving through, he became irritated, and until we found one that did, I knew not to inflame the situation by saying anything. Our drive out of that county was over the speed limit and in total silence on my part.

On our last day of traveling and when we were about an hour away from the apartment we had rented as our first home, Dan announced we were stopping to pick up his mother. He looked at me and said, "I want to surprise her and drive her to see our place and then I'll take her home." It bothered me because I thought we would arrive at our apartment together and alone for our first day in our new home. Dan had moved out of his mother's home a month before the wedding and rented a beautiful apartment overlooking a park. It was spacious and I loved it. We had furnished it together before the marriage and he let me pick out what I liked. It would be the first place that I could call a home of my own. I said nothing to him and was silent the rest of the drive to pick up his mother. She came out of her home after she spotted our car pulling into her driveway and ran out to us with a wide smile. After she settled herself in the back seat, she appeared excited and began to talk about something to do with some woman she didn't like that she had to work with at church. The rest of the way to our apartment the conversation was between her and Dan. I remained quiet silently seething inside and giving her a fake smile occasionally. When she realized we were pulling up to our apartment building, she excitedly said, "Oh, I was wondering when I would get to see it," then addressing me, she said, "Kathleen, he was so secretive about where you would be living and wouldn't tell me where it was."

"Well, maybe he wanted to surprise you," I said.

"If you both had let me in on it I could have helped in some way," she said, with annoyance in her voice.

Dan laughed, "Well, we wanted to surprise you, and we did."

Once we were inside and entered the living room, she noticed the furnishings and said, "Dan, I didn't know you liked Early American."

"Well it's not what I would have picked, but it's what Kathleen wanted." He said it like he would have picked something else, but resigned himself to my choice. It surprised me because he didn't give that indication when we chose it. His mother walked around through the rooms expressing her approval or disapproval, depending on what Dan said about each piece of furniture. When he left to take her home I was beyond relief, and told myself that once we were together, alone, I would try to make him a good wife and do all the things I imagined a wife should do. I convinced myself I could make him happy. Making myself happy wasn't in my consciousness back then.

As the days went by, it seemed I couldn't do anything right in his eyes. He complained about my cooking. I noticed in our conversations that were more like squabbles, he would always mention his mother. I never knew when he would blow up over something I said, or did, so I was determined to confide in Lottie and Angie to get their take on the situation since they knew him for quite some time in a way Rita didn't and Betty of course didn't know him at all. I cried a lot those first few weeks being newly married. I was still working in spite of Mrs. Clarke's suggestion that I quit. I began to think of Dan's mother by her married name, but still addressed her as Mom in her presence. I regretted calling her that. Mrs. Clarke constantly mentioned her late husband to me before and after the wedding. She talked about him like he was some kind of God. Dan never mentioned him at all. I was confused, angry, and disappointed the first four weeks of our marriage. I realized that Dan was not the person he led me to believe he was in all the months he courted me.

One evening I cooked my first beef roast and he looked at it with a frown.

"Do you always cook meat this rare? I can't eat this, put it back in the oven."

I was crushed, and put it in for an extra few minutes. I was so nervous I waited a few minutes too long and when it came out it was over cooked. He cut into it and slammed his knife down on the table and left the room without saying a word. I sat there in shock and after I calmed down I cleared off the table. Later he peeked his head into the dining room and announced he was going out and would be back later. When I heard the door close, I breathed again. I was glad he was gone. I went to bed early and was awakened when he returned sometime after eleven. I could hear him in the kitchen banging things around so I got out of bed to see what he was doing. As I entered the room he was leaning over the sink where I had left a bowl from some ice cream I had before I went to bed. He turned and stared at me with an angry look.

"Can't you clean up after yourself!" he shouted, and then threw the dishcloth at me. I could tell he must have had a few drinks, but he didn't appear real drunk, just angry. When he was drinking he never appeared drunk, like slurring his words or not walking straight, it was simply a drastic change in personality.

"I was going to do it with the breakfast dishes in the morning," I said, "Its only one small bowl."

With that said, he slapped me across the face and said, "Clean it up now!" I felt like I had entered a dark hole and would never see daylight again. That night I slept on the sofa.

Angie called me for a get together supper one night. She and John were now living in a small ranch house they had bought in Clearidge. I hadn't seen Angie since the wedding and looked forward to it. Dan was open to my friendship with Angie and Rita, but not with Betty. He considered her just my employer at the dry cleaning shop. I was still working on Saturdays and he kept pestering me to quit until I did, to stop his harassment of me. He felt it wasn't necessary any longer and he made enough money. We arrived at Angie and John's and while the men were in the living room after supper and I was in the kitchen helping Angie with the dishes, I confided in her all that was happening with both Dan and his mother.

"He's not the same guy I was dating," I said.

Angie looked at me, raising her eyebrows. "I knew you were going to say something like that because you don't look very happy. You were so quiet at supper."

"His mother is always in our business and she keeps at me to quit my job at the police department and so does he. I'm afraid to, what would I do all day and I'm also worried about getting pregnant. I want children, but not so soon."

"I agree with you. John and I wanted some time alone and we both had to work to buy this place first."

"Well, Dan is real religious and won't do anything to prevent it. It's a sin you know."

"Kathleen, it isn't. It's a man-made rule of the church. I ignore it. When John and I are ready, we will have a child."

"I'm afraid I won't have a choice," I said.

"I don't know what you should do. Talk to him, explain your feelings to him."

"I can't explain anything to him. He treats me like a child, and so does his mother. I'm not happy," I said, and started to cry.

Angie put her arms around me. "I'm sorry Kathleen, I guess he isn't the person my father thinks he is. My mother began to see a little of his real personality and how indifferent he was toward you at the wedding. She always thought he was too old for you, but my father didn't see it that way."

She looked at me with pity and it didn't help me feel any better. She couldn't help me, no one could and I resigned myself to the bed I had made by marrying Dan. I was somewhat comforted in the fact that both she and her mother knew the truth; they now knew the real Dan.

CHAPTER 13

It was at the end of June when I realized I might be expecting a child. I knew I was late and had possibly gotten pregnant on my honeymoon. I would know for sure by the end of July. I hadn't mentioned it to Dan, and I needed to see a doctor. He spent more and more time away from home, working day and night on that last murder of the girl from Arden. It had never been solved, and there hadn't been another murder since. Almost two years since the last murder and law enforcement from the City and surrounding towns held their breath.

Dan's mother would call almost every night and I would have to tell her he wasn't home yet. On the days he came home early, he would call her the minute he came in. It irritated me to no end, but I said nothing after he got angry with me the first time I asked him why he had to call her so often. At times I felt like he was married to her instead of me. He confided in her about all his work problems, and would say very little to me. I had to call Betty on the nights he wasn't home with my complaints and she sympathized. It was almost impossible to get together with her because I never knew what nights he would be home or when he would come home. On Saturdays he could pop in at anytime when he was working or he was at home the entire day. I felt isolated and alone most of the time.

I was so desperate for company I even thought about a visit to sister Mary Louise at the Orphan Home, but I decided against it. Angie worked during the day and her mother was busy with her family, as was Rita. I didn't want to bother them. When I had the first occasion to visit Rita to get my hair trimmed, I broke down and told her everything. She was shocked. I made her promise not to tell anyone, and hoped she wouldn't.

"My God, Kathleen, he's tied to his mother's apron strings. I don't know what you can do about it."

"There isn't anything I can do, I'm trapped between them and to make matter's worse, I'm pregnant."

She stopped cutting my hair and said, "Does he know?"

"Not yet, but I'll have to see a doctor soon, so I'll have to tell him."

"How long have you known."

"A little over two months, and I'm nauseous."

She looked surprised, "A little over two months, and you say you have morning sickness, and you haven't seen a doctor? Hasn't Dan noticed? You sleep together don't you?"

"Dan isn't tactile in that way. He isn't very affectionate and always so preoccupied with his work," I said. "He doesn't notice much when it comes to me, only when I'm not at home if he comes in early or if I do something he doesn't like."

She put the scissors down and said, "Like what Kathleen? That's no marriage. When my husband was alive—well, I know what a real marriage is. I miss him terribly. You don't have a real marriage from what you've told me, and you're only married less than three months; you should still be in the honeymoon stage."

I told her how his mother ran our lives, how I was treated like a child, how he would become angry over little things; I put the dishes on the wrong side of the sink to dry, I didn't make the bed with neat enough corners, I didn't cook a beef roast the way his mother did, on and on I went until the tears came and Rita hugged me until I couldn't cry anymore.

"Leave him!" She said.

"I can't, where would I go? And besides I'm Catholic. We are bound together for life. Please Rita, don't mention this to anyone, it might get back to the department and the other cops."

"Don't worry Kathleen, I'll never say a word, but you can't live like this forever, and you have to tell him about the baby, maybe that will mellow him, a little."

The following week I waited for one of the few times we made love and he was in his best mood.

"Dan, I'm late, I think I'm expecting," I said it bluntly, just like that.

"What? Already?" He looked surprised when he said it.

"Well, we haven't done anything to prevent it," I said, apprehensively. He looked at me and smiled which surprised me.

"That's wonderful Kathleen. I wasn't upset about it when I said, Already? Just surprised, that's all."

He took me in his arms and held me and I could feel all the tension in my body leave. I felt like a limp rag doll in his arms and the first thought that ran through my mind was, *Everything is going to be alright from now on. The baby has brought us together and he will change.* For the next few days Dan's mood was up and he was more attentive to me in a way he hadn't been. It gave me hope. He also took it upon himself to tell Sergeant Martino that I wouldn't be returning to my job in the department.

A week later I made that appointment to confirm my condition and just as I thought, the doctor gave me the last week of January as my due date. When we told Dan's mother she was ecstatic and began planning to be a grandmother. She offered to design our extra bedroom into a nursery after the baby was born, and that upset me. When she came over one evening, by bus, she walked around the empty room and told me where everything should go.

"But not until after it's born, it's bad luck to buy things beforehand. What if something should go wrong?" she said.

"That's an old wives tale," I answered.

"Kathleen, I know what I'm talking about. Before Danny, I lost my first son at seven months and I had a room full of baby things. Do you know what it was like to come home from the hospital empty-handed and have to look at all the baby stuff?" She looked like she was going to cry, so I changed the subject. After she left and later when Dan came home after working late, I brought up what his mother had said.

"The best time when having a baby is the planning and setting up the nursery." I said, as I put my arms around his neck. He pulled my hands away.

"I think what my mother said has some truth to it. After all, she's had the experience of losing a child, you haven't."

I watched his weeklong pleasant mood, change back to the real Dan. It seemed his mother was good at controlling his moods. She had a hold on him that I couldn't figure out. I tried to excuse it at times when I thought of Anna Wilkie's obsession with her only son. It had to be because it was the only child they had. It made me think of making sure there would be a 2nd child in this marriage. I didn't want to be like either of them, when it came to my child.

As the months went by I had to admit that Dan was slightly worse than he had been before the pregnancy. He was irritable most of the time and I tried to stay out of his way as much as possible. Any desire for intimacy on his part was gone and many nights when he came home late, I could smell the liquor on him even if he didn't appear drunk. He usually went straight to bed without eating if it was real late. I began sleeping alone on the sofa more often as my belly got larger. I was more comfortable away from him. He didn't show much interest in knowing what was going on with the pregnancy. At Rita's, in the middle of August, I was having my hair cut real short, mainly because the summer heat and my long hair was too much for me to take care of. Putting my straight hair up in curlers every night in the heat of the apartment drained my strength. We had several fans in the windows but it wasn't enough to keep the rooms cool.

"You're wanting me to cut this beautiful long hair off?" Rita asked, as she stood behind the chair I was sitting in, looking at me in the mirror. "What will Dan say?"

"I don't care what he'll say. It's my hair, and it's a job taking care of it in this heat."

"I agree Kathleen, and red hair is much thicker than blond or brunet."

I watched as she clipped away until I had my first pixie cut, and I loved it. So did Rita.

"You look beautiful, it brings out your features more, the eyes and cheekbones too. I think Dan will like it. It's sexy," she said.

"I don't think he'll notice. Since I've been pregnant, he's been drinking more and I stay away from him as much as I can. He's seldom home and I like it that way."

"It's gotten that bad, hasn't it?"

"Can't get any worse. But I don't think about it, only about my baby."

In December, a month away from giving birth Angie and Lottie approached me about a baby shower. They wanted to have one for me. I filled them in on the taboo a baby shower was to Dan and his mother. They looked at me like they couldn't believe it. While I was at it, I let them know how the marriage wasn't working through this pregnancy.

Chasing the Unicorn

It was a Saturday and both Dan and Sgt Martino were working, and the women invited me to lunch at Lottie's.

"That's the craziest thing I ever heard, " said Lottie. Angie agreed with her mother.

"Ma, let's you and me have the baby shower here at your place. Dan will have no say in it and besides Dad will embarrass Dan if he objects. You can leave all the baby gifts here until the birth, Kathleen."

"I can't thank you both enough," I said, and I meant it. Angie and her mother had become my closest confidant many times when I was feeling low. They were my salvation. At one point in the last few months, Dan was so verbally abusive to me, that if it weren't for the Martinos I would have been reduced to a shell of my former self. Lottie's advice during one bad episode was to speak to the parish priest at St. Joe's in Arden. I took her advice and then left after the meeting feeling worse. Advice like, 'Go home and be a good wife and your husband won't drink as much,' was totally useless. When I informed Lottie what he said, she shook her head and laughed.

"What the hell does an unmarried priest know about marriage? Absolutely nothing," she said, and then she apologized for recommending him to me. Between Dan's moods and his mother's constant calling day and night, asking how I was feeling, telling me what I should be eating or doing would have driven me insane if it weren't for my friends. Mrs. Clarke was in the dark as far as what the marriage to her son was like. I told her nothing. Dislike would be too kind a word to describe what my feelings were for her. In one conversation about her to Lottie, I looked at her across the table we were sitting at and started to cry. All through the summer and fall, all I did was cry over everything. I felt I was near the breaking point. Angie reached over to comfort me when Lottie's eyes grew larger and a look of surprise came over her face.

"I got it!" she yelled, addressing her daughter, "Angie, remember how we tried to figure out why Mrs. Clarke welcomed Kathleen, but drove away all the other women away that Dan showed an interest in, in the past?"

"What are you getting at, Ma?"

"She's a devil, that woman, like the black widow spider. Kathleen

88

is young and an orphan, she's quite aware of that. Someone like Kathleen with no family of her own can be controlled; can give her a grandchild she can take over; won't take her son away."

Angie gave me a hug and said, "That's it! The church expects you to stay married, but that doesn't mean you have to live with the person, does it?" She looked to her mother for the answer. Lottie looked at me and said, "No one should have to live like that!"

I felt trapped in the marriage and my religion with all its rules kept me in the prison I was living in at the time. With all the friends I had made, I didn't have family and family made one feel secure and I didn't feel that way. Knowing Betty and her family gave me a glimpse of what a family could do for one in crisis. I didn't have the support Betty had when she removed herself from a bad marriage. I still clung to the hope that after the baby came things would change.

CHAPTER 14

On January 16th 1958, two weeks early, Thomas Daniel Robson was born, a five-pound bundle of joy. The doctor figured he was early due to some of the stress I was under after I confided in him about my problems. The baby was small and had to gain the few ounces he lost so he was kept in an incubator and I thought I got pregnant on my wedding night— it was a possibility. Dan was ecstatic the minute he saw him. I stayed in the hospital eight days until they would release my child. The minute we entered our apartment with the baby, my mother-in-law met us at the door and took him out of my arms. For the rest of the day she held him when he was awake and only gave him to me at feeding time. She relinquished him to his crib when he was sleeping. With her and Dan looking at the baby, I heard her say, "He looks just like the baby I lost." It upset me. I got the feeling she was going to take over my child. I couldn't wait until Dan took her home, but when evening came she tried to insist that I needed help, and she would sleep on the sofa that night. Before I could protest, Dan took charge and gingerly told her that the sofa was uncomfortable and that he would pick her up after work the next day and bring her over.

"Oh, I'll miss seeing my little Tommy," she said, as he escorted her out the door. I pretended to be busy in the nursery and didn't follow her to the door to say goodbye. I was proud of Dan at that moment for getting rid of her, and it gave me hope, but I should have kept my mouth shut when he returned, instead I said, "I'm so glad you took her home." His happy mood changed.

"What? How can you say that? She's his grandmother. She has a right to see him whenever she can."

"I only meant—I was tired, and I looked forward to our first night with the baby alone, just the two of us."

"Kathleen, I know you don't like her, but she's *my* mother! You don't have any idea what a mother is. If you did, you wouldn't treat her that way."

I had no idea what he was talking about. I never treated her with anything but respect. I seemed to have no say in anything when it came to my own life; they decided everything, even the baby's name. I didn't have any particular name in mind since there wasn't any family member on my side to name him after, but I would have named him Daniel, after Dan. Mrs. Clarke insisted he be named after her second husband who wasn't a blood relative of Dan's, and give Daniel as his middle name. Dan didn't object and never consulted me. While I was in the hospital, he came into the room laughing and said, "I'll name the boys and you can name the girls." I said nothing, but felt the anger rise in me. The first week home I was upset and angry most of the time but hid it well. Little did I know the birth of Tommy would be the beginning of a living hell.

Lottie and Angie came over the next day with most of the baby clothing I received at the shower. Dan had a crib and dresser delivered while I was in the hospital. It was one he allowed me to pick out some months before. They went to peek at the sleeping baby, and Angie thought he looked like me.

"He's so cute! He does look more like you," Lottie said, "but his hair looks light brown. It could change."

"I'm glad he doesn't have my color. Being a boy he would get teased growing up," I said.

"How are things going lately?" Lottie asked, appearing concerned.

That was my opening to unload all my feelings. I filled them in on everything that was so upsetting to me and I cried.

"You couldn't even name your own baby?" Angie's voice was filled with anger, "You suffered the labor pains, not him. It's a mother's choice, not a grandmother's."

Lottie looked sad and voiced her opinion. "What was Dan's real father's name? I can understand if they wanted to use his name, not his step-father's."

"His father's name was Lawrence, I think. Mrs. Clarke refers to him as Larry. He died when Dan was around ten, that's what I was told."

"She probably drove him to his grave," Angie said, laughing.

"Her second husband died when Dan was in his early twenties. Sal said Dan never cared much for him," Lottie added.

That bit of news surprised me. "To hear it from his mother, you would have thought otherwise," I said. "If he was as great to Dan as she said, why didn't he adopt her son?"

Lottie shrugged her shoulders; "I wonder why Dan went along with naming his son after him, if he didn't care that much for him?"

"Nothing makes sense to me when it comes to Dan and his mother," I said.

We spent the rest of the visit talking about the baby and more pleasant things. I was in a better mood by the time they went home. I was still optimistic regardless of what had taken place since we were married. A month later, planning the Christening would again shoot down my naive optimism.

I wanted Angie and John as Godparents. Being young and both Catholic, I thought there would be no objections, but Dan and his mother had other ideas. They wanted some old Aunt in her seventies living in California, who wasn't able to travel to Illinois. For the Godfather Dan asked Sgt. Martino. That was my saving grace, because with Lottie explaining my feelings he managed to talk up his daughter and son-in-law as a more fitting couple. One Sunday during supper at the Martino's, Sgt Martino said, "I'm too old Dan, and if your Aunt can't be here, it doesn't make sense. Who would fill in for your Aunt?"

"I thought my mother could hold the baby in her place," Dan said rather sheepishly.

"Having Angie as Godmother would make Kathleen happy, after all she hasn't any family and my daughter was her first friend after she left the orphanage."

After that comment by Sgt. Martino, Dan never brought it up again. Not in their presence that is, but once we returned to our apartment, he tried, but I carefully said, "You will have to think about what Sgt. Martino said. He'll refuse to be Godfather and you don't want to him to mention it to the whole department, do you?"

I thought, *try explaining that to your mother, and good luck.* I was so pleased that Angie's family stuck up for me. I had no idea what he told his mother, but the Christening went off without a hitch much to Mrs. Clarke's chagrin, and Angie and John were the Godparents. I ignored Dan's mother's unhappy expression and enjoyed the day.

In April Dan was working around the clock and seldom home because another murder had taken place after two years of hoping the killer or killers had left the area. We weren't getting along too well and having him at home with his sullen attitude depressed me. One night in August there was another murder and he came home late with blood on his shirt and on one sleeve, but there weren't any cuts on him. I was afraid to ask him about it, but it began to prey on my mind. I was folding the clean laundry I had washed and I took the shirt to put aside to iron but noticed a rip in the sleeve.

"Dan, I found the sleeve torn, isn't this a new shirt," I asked.

He was sitting reading the paper and looked up. His stare frightened me. It was an angry look, as he threw the paper down and stood up; taking a few steps toward me he reached out and pulled the shirt out of my hands.

"What did you expect? I'm a Sheriff, we apprehend criminals!" he shouted, "We don't sit around the office all day!"

"I only wondered how it got torn, and there was blood on it," I explained.

"Questions, questions, that's all you're good at, asking questions. You're stupid, you know that!"

With that outburst, I said nothing, just picked up the shirt off the floor where he had thrown it and walked out of the room. His moods were getting darker and he frightened me most of the time. I didn't understand what was happening to him. Everyone knew a killer or killers been on the loose, but after so many years I began to panic and suspect any man I came in contact with, including my own husband. I stayed home with the baby most of the time, and if the doorbell rang, I was afraid to press the button to open the downstairs door in the outer hall. I would ask who it was over the speaker. If it weren't a person I knew, I wouldn't open the door.

Summer came and it was a hot and humid one. In August, only five months from the last murder, another one, this time again the body was found in a field near a creek. I didn't feel safe when I took the baby out in the buggy, but I managed to take him for a walk in the park across from the apartment. The heat in the apartment could become too much in the late afternoon so I found the park with all its trees a bit cooler. I stayed close to the edge of the park, where I could still view our building and not venture too deep inside.

One day I was talking to Betty on the phone. The new wall phones came out and mine was in the kitchen, so as we talked I could be doing the dishes at the same time. I hadn't seen her in some time but we kept in touch by phone. She was the only person I could confide my worst fears to because the Martinos and Rita were all connected to the police and Betty wasn't. I told her about my fear of Dan and how he was becoming a stranger to me; one I thought was coming unglued.

"I'm afraid of him, afraid of who he really is," I said.

"Why don't you mention his behavior to Sgt, Martino," she said, trying to comfort me, but she didn't understand that when it came to police matters the Sgt. and Dan were attached at the hip as far as I was concerned. I was telling her about the bloody torn shirt and I didn't hear the door to our apartment open. I don't know what he heard me say—describing the shirt, or that I suspected him of something, but the conversation ended when I turned around and saw him standing in the doorway to the kitchen.

"I have to go!" I managed to say as I hung up on Betty.

"Who were you talking to!" he asked, with anger, "Telling tall tales to your friends? telling lies about me?" He grabbed me by the arm and with his face an inch away from mine, he yelled—"I could kill you right now!"

I pulled out of his grasp and ran to the baby's room and locked myself inside. I could hear his rage, taking it out on the dishes I had just washed and left to dry on the rack. I sat in the rocking chair next to the crib that held my sleeping eight-month-old son, and held my hands over my ears to shut out the sound of breaking glass. When it became quiet, I listened for his next move and then he was pounding on the door.

"Open this door!" He shouted.

I was shaking, but managed to yell back, "No, go away, you'll wake up the baby!" I was afraid he would break the door down and my heart was beating so fast, I was grasping for air in the stuffy room. After a few minutes he stopped and I held my breath until there wasn't any sound on the other side of the door. I waited for what seemed like forever. The baby was awake after all that noise, and started to cry. I picked him up and tried holding him until he fell back to sleep. I don't know how long I sat motionless with my son in my arms. I was afraid to move, to make any sound. I knew then that whatever Dan's problems were, I had to get away from him. I tried thinking of what my next step would be. I thought of how Betty escaped a bad situation by going home to her parents. I didn't have that option. I felt trapped like a wounded animal, afraid to leave the apartment and afraid to stay. When I heard the outer door slam shut, I knew he had left. The baby's room faced the street so I stood near the window until I could see if he emerged from the building. Sure enough, I watched as he walked to his car in the lot in front of the entrance. When he drove away, I thought of what to do next.

I calmed down enough to call Angie. I told her what had happened, my breathing coming in gasps between words.

"My God, Kathleen, do you want me to come and get you? You and the baby can stay the night with me until he cools down," she said.

"Yes, please come and get me. I'm too nervous and upset to drive myself tonight."

I lost no time in packing the diaper bag for Tommy and threw a few things in a small bag to get me through the night. I had no idea what I would do the next day. My heart was beating fast; I was sweating profusely and I felt dizzy. I was terrified he would return before Angie could get to me. I waited in the downstairs hall watching for her car to pull up. I thought if he returned he would never try anything where the other tenants would come upon us. As soon as she appeared, I ran to her car with two bags and the baby in my arms. Once in her car, I started to cry.

"Hurry," I said, afraid he would appear before she drove away.

"Calm down," she said, trying to console me. "You'll make yourself sick. He's a Sheriff, he works with the police, he knows the law, —he isn't going to harm you."

"I wish I could believe that. If you could have seen his face, his eyes, when he gets angry."

"Did he ever hit you?"

"Yes, once. He slapped me when he came home late one night after finding a bowl in the sink that hadn't been washed."

She looked at me like either he was crazy, or I was.

"I can't believe it. I know he's wound up pretty tight—my Dad's words not mine, but I never thought he was capable of physical abuse."

"The verbal abuse he throws at me is worse. He calls me dumb, stupid, whatever he can think of to degrade me."

Angie took a deep sigh and said, "I want you to tell my Dad what you have just told me. He can talk with him and see if he can get to the bottom of Dan's behavior."

When we arrived at her apartment it was dark. She helped with my bags and as we entered her living room, John came to help us. "You're welcome here," he said, and that made me feel comfortable. After we were settled and she made a bed for Tommy by pushing her guest room bed against the wall, with John's help, she then added a plastic cover on the mattress on the side Tommy would sleep on. I couldn't thank them enough. She lost no time calling her father and explaining what had happened, and then came into the room to let me know Sgt. Martino was on his way over. I felt relief, but still not sure what he could do about Dan.

He arrived with Lottie and they both listened to my tale of woe. Lottie had her arm around me as we sat together on the sofa, but Sgt. Martino kept repeating; "I don't believe it, I just don't believe it. I haven't seen a sign of it in his personality when he's comes to the station or when I have conversations with him. I'll talk to him; get it straightened out for you before you go home. I'm sure things will cool down. He might be home already. Let me call him."

He went to use Angie's phone and came back to say no one answered. He came over to where I was and put his hand on my shoulder and said, "Don't worry, I think I know where he might be. I'll drop Lottie off at home, and try to find him. By tomorrow you'll be able to go home."

I thanked him and Lottie gave me a hug.

"Don't worry, Sal will straighten it all out for you," she said, as they left.

CHAPTER 15

On her way to work the next morning, Angie drove me home, after her father called and explained that after he spent several hours looking in their usual hangouts, and not finding Dan, he found him at home. He sat up late with him trying to calm him down and now it was safe for me to go home. I had worked myself into a complete wreck the night before. I couldn't sleep thinking of what would await me when I returned to my apartment, and wondered if telling the Sergeant about our troubles would incite Dan to more violence. When I arrived home, I didn't see Dan's car in the parking lot so I was sure he left for work. Once inside, I was surprised to see everything neatly in place. He had cleaned up the mess of broken dishes in the kitchen. I opened the refrigerator door and was surprised to see he put the pot roast that was in the freezer in there to thaw, presumably for the meal he expected me to cook that night. I didn't know what to think, because he had never done that before.

I kept busy with the baby all morning and when I put him down for a nap, I thought I'd watch some television to keep my mind off what Dan would say or do when he returned. I worried and wondered if I should call Lottie to inquire about her husband's encounter with Dan the night before. When I thought about it, it was late afternoon. I was afraid to know what happened; maybe it was nothing to worry about. I was preoccupied thinking about all that and didn't hear the key turn the lock in the door. I looked up as it opened to Dan, coming in early and I panicked. I started to tremble and tried to stand up but before I could move, he fell to his knees and put his head on my lap crying, "I'm so very sorry, so sorry, forgive me Please. Please forgive me."

Having never seen him cry before, it left me feeling a little shocked because here was this big tough guy in a sheriff's uniform who I'd come to first think of as my protector and then later, my tormenter, crying like a baby, and for the first time seeing him as he really was. I struggled with mixed feelings of disgust at such a display of weakness and at the same time maternal instinct allowed me to stroke his head in a gesture of sympathy like one would do with a child.

"Don't worry about it," I said, "I forgive you."

At that moment I really did forgive him, and believed we had turned a new page in our lives. At least I was hopeful. He made dinner that night and was attentive to the baby and me. When I tried setting the table for supper he said, "Sit down Kathleen, I'll do that." I sat and watched him as he took the roast out of the oven, and then went into the dining room. I could hear him in the kitchen getting the meal together. He insisted we eat in the dining room that night, which I thought was a little over the top. It was a Tuesday night and we always ate in the kitchen during the week. I didn't know what to make of it. It was so unlike him. I wondered what Sgt. Martino said to him. For the next few days he acted like we were on a honeymoon. Although I relaxed, I wasn't feeling very amorous and just went through the motions to keep the peace.

By the end of the week, I was surprised the truce lasted and he made no effort to bring his mother over after work as he usually did on Wednesdays and Fridays. She called less often than she did when we were first married but his calls to her continued almost every night when he was home. She had no clue about what was going on in our marriage and his conversations to her were about mundane things or they talked about Tommy's first milestones; his first tooth, and at almost nine months how he began trying to pull himself up in the playpen. I had very little contact with her when she wasn't visiting. Some nights when she called, I wouldn't talk long if he wasn't home, but have some lame excuse to cut the call short.

I talked to Betty often and tried to visit, but she was always at work and when she was free it was when I wasn't. Rita and I would see each other more often because she worked out of her home. She would have me over during the day, and her younger son wasn't in school yet so he would keep Tommy amused while we could visit between her customers. In September I helped her by giving a hair washing to a few of the women who came to get their hair done.

One elderly woman, who was born in Germany, was Rita's customer. I came to like her, and she would tell us all about her miserable marriage. She moved from Wisconsin to live with her daughter after her husband died. She began to tell us about her life on the farm.

"You know, mine life vas hard. I did most of the vork," she said, "Fritz did nothing. I should have left him years ago, but he die anyvay."

Rita looked at me and smiled, as the woman continued, "He vas a drunk, mine Fritz, you know, and he vas a cruel man. All that I put up vith and then one day, Poof, I vas free."

Rita looked over at me. "What happened?" she asked, trying to keep from giggling.

"He come in from the barn at supper time and vee vas eating, then he put his hand on his chest and his eyes get so big. Next ting I know he fall out of his chair to the floor."

"Oh my God!" We both said in unison," and then what happened?"

She sat up, straightening herself in the chair while Rita started cutting her hair, as we waited for her to continue her story.

"I finish mine supper until he vas goot and dead. Den I call for help."

Rita and I were left speechless and we said nothing. After the woman left, Rita said, "Boy, am I glad my husband wasn't around to hear something like that. He would have walked her out in handcuffs. I guess in her day the only way a woman could escape abuse was do what she did,"

"Well, she didn't kill him," I said, as I wondered if I wouldn't have done the same thing. I thought about Dan's abuse of me, but things had changed for the better.

After a few weeks had passed, I began to relax and enjoy the baby more. Angie was right, he did favor me and he had my blue eyes, but light brownish blond hair. Dan's hair, what was left of it, as he started to go bald on top, was dark brown and his eyes were so dark that when he became angry they seemed to turn black. His eyes looked frightening at times when he looked that way. I began to feel happy for the first time since our wedding. I wondered what Sgt. Martino had said to evoke such a positive change in Dan. Angie called and asked me to supper one night when Dan had to work late, I accepted. I hadn't spoken with her since she drove me home that morning. She was busy with her job and being without children yet, she and John were busy with other friends and they were free to go out often, unlike Dan and I.

I tried to limit the number of times I allowed Dan's mother to sit for us. I didn't quite trust her with Tommy. I arrived at Angie's home and placed Tommy in his jumper seat, giving him his teething ring to chew on. John wasn't home yet so I helped her set the table while we talked.

"How are things going?" she asked, "I hope everything is okay now."

"It couldn't be better. I don't know what your father said to him, but he's changed. He's not the same Dan."

She smiled at me and said, "Kathleen, how have you been feeling lately?"

I thought it was a strange question to ask when I just told her how happy I was.

"Why do you ask? Why would you think I'm not okay?"

"Well, my father said that Dan—Please don't let Dan know I'm telling you this—he said you were having some issues and you were not rational at times. He said you had a bad temper and would have a melt-down over trifle things."

"What? None of that is true!" I shouted, "How could he say such things about me? You know me Angie, don't believe it."

She looked at me with compassion and said, "I never believed any of it, but he's got my parents convinced you're not well. I even told them it's not the Kathleen I know, but they think because you haven't any family and was left in an orphanage, you might have mental problems you keep hidden."

"If anyone's crazy, it's Dan and his mother, not me!"

My thoughts went to Tim's mother when she first met me, thinking I was damaged goods because I didn't have a family.

"Don't trust him then, just be on your guard around him, and call me if you need me," Angie said.

"Angie, I was just beginning to relax, he's been so nice. Why is he so nice to me? I don't get it. Dan's like two different people, like Jekyll and Hyde I never know which one is going to appear when he comes home."

After that conversation, my trust in Dan was completely gone. I went home that night confused and beside myself with fear. I kept thinking—*how do I get out of this, how can I pretend any longer?* I knew I had to talk to Betty. She once lived with what she called a 'nut case' for a husband. When I returned home from Angie's that night, Dan wasn't home yet. It gave me time to compose myself and do some acting, which I wasn't good at, to convince him everything was okay. I could have saved myself the trouble because he came home the old Dan. Dr. Jekyll disappeared and Mr. Hyde walked in. I was in bed and I heard his loud entrance. He sounded drunk, which wasn't unusual. I jumped out of bed and threw on my robe and ran into the living room. He was completely disheveled and his face was red. Again his shirt was torn. His eyes looked deranged. He was looking at me but not seeing me.

"What's happened?" I asked.

"What's happened? What's happened? You ask me *that*! With the miserable job I have. Everyone wants a piece of me—my wife, my mother, and the lousy lawyers that protect those guilty sons of bitches. I could kill them all!"

He was yelling and threatening, acting like I wasn't there, referring to me in the third person. He was blocking the bedroom door, so I ran into the bathroom and before I could close the door, he came in and grabbed me by the throat.

"I could choke the life out of you and no one would know, I could claim I found you that way. One of those low-life defense lawyers would defend me and prove me innocent. If they saw me kill you they could prove me innocent!"

He let go of me, but I could see he was coming unhinged. I slipped out of the bathroom and left him in there. I heard him lock the door. I took that opportunity to get dressed as quickly as I could. I picked Tommy up out of his crib and wrapped a blanket around him. I grabbed my purse and car keys and ran out of the apartment. Once in the car I tried to stop shaking and started driving aimlessly down one street and another in the middle of the night. I didn't know where to go. Tommy was crying, and I was crying. I left behind his diaper bag where I kept extra diapers and one of his bottles. I had nothing for him. I was thankful it wasn't too cool in late September. I stopped at a drug store that was still open at 10:00 pm. I had the money Dan had given me for the weekly groceries. I carried Tommy into the store with just his sleeper on and the blanket. The clerk looked at me strangely, probably wondering what I was doing out so late with a baby. I ignored her and searched for a baby bottle, formula and hopefully some diapers that were found in the isle where the baby products are kept.

Back in the car, I sat for a few minutes thinking, *where can I go? Not Angie, not Rita, not Betty, none of them could protect me. He knew where they lived, what if he came after me?* The police came to my mind, but not just any policeman. I found myself driving to Sgt. Martino's home. I would feel safe there and I would convince them it wasn't me, but Dan who was sick. I convinced myself that Sgt. Martino could handle Dan, he could reason with him. He thought he knew Dan, and they were best friends.

When I pulled up to their home, all the windows were dark. It looked like everyone had gone to bed. I carried my sleeping child, my purse and bag from the drugstore and climbed the stairs to their door. I rang the bell and waited, shaking from head to toe. I wasn't sure how they would receive me. After what seemed like more than a few minutes, Sgt. Martino came to the door in his bathrobe. He shouted back to his wife who was coming down the stairs, "It's alright, it's only Kathleen."

CHAPTER 16

Having told the Martinos all that had happened, they kept Tommy and me overnight. The next morning, Sgt. Martino assured me that he would leave early and stop by our apartment to check on Dan before he had a chance to leave for work. He would talk with him and when all was well, he would call to let me know it was safe to go home. I knew I had to return because there wasn't any place else to go. It was then I thought of Mrs. Wilkie. She would have taken us in, no questions asked. I missed her.

When I entered our apartment later that morning, of course Dan wasn't there. I fed Tommy and put him in his playpen and paced the floor, wondering what to do if he came home in the same condition as the night before. I hoped Sgt. Martino realized how sick he was and it would quell any suspicions he might have of me being mentally ill. With all my anxieties and fear I could be the one mistaken for losing touch with reality. I tried to appear calm but inside I was a total mess. What to do next was constantly on my mind. I knew then I did not love Dan, if I ever did; it was mistaken on my part with a need to be taken care of. I also knew I had to leave, but how and when? What would I do for money? We had a joint bank account, but if I took half the money could he arrest me for theft. He knew the law, I didn't.

The afternoon dragged on with me being unable to do anything except walk around in circles waiting for the hour he would return. At 6:00 pm Dr. Jekyll walked in. He was as nice as he had been several weeks before and he bought me a birthday present a week early, I would be 26 years old the 10th of October. He was very kind, but this time I didn't buy it. I played along and bided my time. I acted like nothing happened and so did he. This time there were no apologies or begging for forgiveness. Did he even remember what happened? I wondered.

"I'm sorry, I haven't started supper yet, I haven't felt well," I said.

"Oh, that's okay, I'll go for take out—some hotdogs from Hippo's."

"Yes, that would be nice."

As soon as he left, I quickly packed a bag of all the necessities Tommy would need if and when I needed to leave again on short notice. I put the bag on the floor of Tommy's closet. Dan never went in there and I would wait until he left for work the next morning to pack a suitcase for myself. I didn't know what would happen, but wanted to be ready at any time. If I had to flee again, I didn't want to think ahead about where I would go. I had no clue and knew the next time it couldn't be around anyone we knew, because I wouldn't be talked into returning to him again.

He returned and put the hotdogs on the table and went to phone his mother. He knew she would have called the night before. What he didn't know was that I seldom answered the phone when it rang around the time she usually called, if he wasn't home. I pretended to be busy placing the meal on paper plates, but I caught some of what he was saying.

"I was busy Ma, I didn't get home until late! Well, I don't know where she went, no, I know, Okay, I'll pick you up when I pick you up, Okay! Friday, Okay!"

I left the room and he hung up and came into the living room where I had placed our hotdogs and fries on TV trays. I poured lemonade and sat down. He took his jacket off, loosened his tie and sat down abruptly, his face showing a strain he didn't possess before the phone call. We ate our meal in silence. He finished first and on his way to dispose of the remnants of his meal, he stopped and turned to me.

"Would you like more lemonade?"

"Yes, thanks."

He paused for a moment and I thought he was about to say something, but he went back to the kitchen. We spent the evening watching TV and he tried several times to comment about the program, but I remained silent with just an occasional— ah huh. I stayed up late and waited for him to go to bed. When I was sure he was asleep, I got undressed and made up my bed on the sofa. I made sure I was up before him to clear off any evidence that I wasn't in our bed. He usually slept soundly and never woke up during the night. I was waiting for the next shoe to drop: so to speak, before I made my move, but I didn't know exactly when that would be. I had no plan other then to just leave. The more I thought about it, the more frightened I became. I was in a constant state of anxiety and felt extremely tired. The next morning after he left for work, the phone rang. I answered it thinking it might be Betty, who usually called in the morning, but it was Dan's mother. It shocked me to hear her voice at that time of day. She knew he wouldn't be home in the morning. I tried to sound normal, although my heart was racing. I waited for her to speak after I asked her how she was.

"Kathleen, my friend Clara, you know, my neighbor next door, she offered to drive me over this morning to visit Tommy, and you too of course. I should be there in about thirty minutes."

I managed to get out "Alright," and then panicked after I hung up the phone. I was still in my nightgown, Tommy was sleeping and he needed his bath and to be fed. The house wasn't too tidy with all the turmoil I had gone through, so cleaning up wasn't high on my list of things to do. I managed to get dressed quickly, and picked up Tommy to waken him and I rushed to change his diaper and put a clean sleeper on him, plopped him in into his highchair and opened a jar of baby farina, when the doorbell rang. I let her in, and with barely a hello to me, she asked where the baby was.

"In his high chair, I was about to feed him," I said.

She rushed into the kitchen and pulled him out of the chair. She hugged him, walking around the room talking to him like he understood every word.

"Oh, my sweet little boy, you've grown so big—I hardly know you. Your Mommy and Daddy should allow me to spend more time with you, but they always say they're busy. Busy, busy, busy, too busy for your Nanny."

I could have thrown up my breakfast had I eaten one that morning. I picked up the baby food and stood with the jar and the spoon in my hand waiting for her to put him down. He started to cry.

"He's hungry, he hasn't had his breakfast yet," I managed to say.

"Oh, of course."

I watched her put him back in the highchair.

"Let me feed him," she said, as she took the food and spoon out of my hands. Tommy continued to cry, but that didn't stop her from shoving the food into his mouth. I thought he was going to choke between crying and trying to swallow.

"He's upset," I said, "He needs to stop crying before he chokes on the cereal."

"Oh, nonsense, I always fed my Danny this way."

I watched helplessly and was relieved when the last spoonful was gone. I was shaking with rage, but tried not to say anything more. I watched as she again picked him up and carried him to the rocker in the living room. After a few moments of her rocking him, he stopped crying and I took that opportunity to ask her how long she was staying. She took that as an insult, that I didn't want her there.

"When my friend finishes her errands, she'll come for me!"

She said it in a huffy way, with anger. I tried to defuse the situation, by engaging her in small talk. It was difficult to do because I loathed the woman.

"I think he'll be an early walker, he's already pulling himself up to stand," I said.

"Of course he will; my Danny walked at eleven months."

She always had a comeback for what I said. I left her alone and went into the kitchen pretending to be busy and hoped her friend would come early. When noontime approached I thought I should offer her lunch. She put my sleeping baby in his crib and came to the dining room where I had set the table. Lunch was simple, sandwiches, chips and lemonade. She sat and looked at her plate and its contents and said nothing—she didn't have to, her distasteful expression said it all. She brought up Dan in her conversation.

"You should know Kathleen, a man in Dan's line of work needs rest and a peaceful place to come home to."

I didn't know what to say to that— should I tell her the condition he came home in? I wondered if it was a smart thing to do, and then she blurted out what I feared.

"I have the name of a good doctor I think you should see. He can help you with your problems, and don't worry dear, I'll look after Tommy until you're well."

What she said didn't shock me, not after hearing what he told Sgt. Martino and his wife about me. Lottie didn't believe him, but I wasn't sure about the Sergeant. I didn't answer her. *Let her think what she wants,* I thought. Nothing I could say about her son would convince her I was telling the truth, if she thought I was the one who was crazy.

When the doorbell rang, I let her friend in. She introduced me to a woman, who appeared nervous and gave me a look that convinced me she had been filled in on my mental state. After saying hello, she announced she would be waiting in the car. Mrs. Clarke paid a last visit to Tommy who was sound asleep and then she thanked me for the lunch, and left.

Later that afternoon, I went into the bathroom to take out the laundry bag of dirty clothing. I would do the wash in the basement where laundry machines were to service the tenants. I usually waited until Tommy woke up from his nap, I would feed him and take him downstairs with me along with his bouncy chair, hoping the girl who lived below me was doing her wash and I could count on her to watch him while I went up for the load of clothing to be washed. If she weren't there, I'd leave the chair and go back up for the wash with Tommy in one arm and the wash in the other. As I was sorting through, to put the whites in one pile, a small black wallet fell out of either Dan's shirt pocket or one of his trousers. It was very flat, there was nothing in it, until I turned it over and noticed just a driver's license. At first I thought it was Dan's until on closer inspection the face of a young woman stared back at me. Where had I seen that face before? I studied it until goose pumps rose up on my skin. A flash of recognition filled me with indescribable fear. I couldn't stop shaking. This was the clothing I put in the wash bag the day after Dan came home red faced and disheveled, with his shirt torn again. This was same face in a picture in the paper of the last victim found murdered in August.

I don't know how long I was on my knees, trembling with fear. I looked at my watch. Two or three hours before Dan would be home—*I have to get out of here before he comes home, I have to get out of here,* I was thinking, my mind in a frenzy, racing, thinking quicker than my body was able to move. I knelt there in the bathroom; my body frozen in fear, but my mind was already fleeing out the door, with Tommy, the pre-packed diaper bag and my small suitcase.

I don't know how long I knelt in shock, until I gathered my senses and stood up, quickly putting all the laundry back in the bag. What to do with the evidence that Dan had committed a crime, or had he? Maybe he confiscated the woman's license during the department's investigation, but on second thought, he couldn't have. The latest victim was in Chicago's jurisdiction. The Arden police and Sheriff's department would not be investigating this case, unless invited. *What if, what if, what if Dan was guilty, but what if he was innocent,* kept going through my mind. What to do with the evidence; I would throw it in the apartment's incinerator. Every floor had a place to dump the garbage. I ran into the hall and with the license wrapped in a piece of clothing I pulled the door open to the shaft that led to the constant fire below and dropped it in.

I gathered up Tommy and our belongings and raced out of the building. I ran to my car and once on the road, had no idea where I was going. I kept driving thinking of going as far away as possible. I needed money so I took the chance of stopping at the bank and I withdrew five hundred dollars. Back in the car I wondered; would the clerk remember me when Dan put out the word I was missing? All the more reason to get out of Illinois, I thought. I made plans, to drive east through Indiana, but I passed a Greyhound bus station on the way, and that gave me another idea. I didn't want to leave my car parked anywhere near the station, so I drove a good half mile past, parked the car along the street, but reasoned that the car shouldn't be anywhere near the bus station. I started up the motor again and drove to Betty's shop and parked the car in the shopping centers parking lot next door. With Tommy in my arms I rushed into her shop hoping she would be there alone and thankfully she was. She was surprised to see me and knew instantly something was wrong.

"What's happened?" She asked, as she took Tommy out of my arms because I appeared so distressed. Between sobbing and trying to tell her what happened, I managed to tell her all that happened the past few weeks.

"I can't go back, I have to leave now!" I said, "Can you take me to the Greyhound bus station? I can't leave my car anywhere near it."

"Where can we leave it Kathleen? Not anywhere near here, he

knows my shop is here," she said.

We spent the next twenty minutes making plans. We decided that I would follow her in my car, north to the canal. It rained often the last week of September and the water level in the canal was high. After reaching it I put my belongings in her car and making sure no one was around I took the car out of gear and we both pushed it down an embankment and watched it disappear into the deep water. We were both shaking over the ordeal and I was grateful we were in a deserted area. We were sure no one was around to see what we had done. Betty assured me no one would know anything, not even her parents. I trusted her completely and when she dropped me off at the bus terminal, we hugged and said our tearful goodbyes and I promised to call her in the future to let her know I was okay.

I checked the bus schedule and the first bus to leave was going to New York. I couldn't go any further east than that. I bought my ticket and sat on the bench inside the station with my heart pounding, waiting for thirty minutes, before we were permitted to board. Finally, I climbed into the bus. My suitcase was stacked on the sidewalk with the other passengers' cases until the driver loaded them in the compartment beneath the bus floor. It started to rain as I watched him load up from the window seat I had chosen. I put the diaper bag on the floor behind the seat in front of me and with Tommy on my lap, watched the raindrops hit the window. I felt such fear that I wanted to scream— Help me! But I held on and as the bus pulled away from the station, the silent voice that was deep inside me cried out, hurry, hurry!

CHAPTER 17

The bus had made many stops along the way, and each time we were allowed a rest stop I would check the newspapers in the bus terminal. Our first stop was in Southern Michigan where there wasn't any mention of a missing woman and child from Illinois. The further away we would travel, the less likely there would be. I began to relax. I would spend my twenty-sixth birthday on that bus. The rest of the trip was uneventful, up until we stopped in the large town of Addison, Pennsylvania.

I followed the other passengers into a little restaurant where we were to have lunch. Tommy was fussy and I needed to change his diaper. I spread the only blanket I had on the very end of the rest room sink counter and laid him down, hoping no one came in while I changed him quickly, tossing his dirty diaper in the trash. Being a cloth diaper I couldn't wash, I was now down to seven clean diapers from the package of a dozen.

I noticed a newspaper someone had discarded in the trash when I threw the diaper in. My eye caught the word missing and I pulled it out far enough to see my picture on the front page. The wrinkled page of an early morning Chicago paper was enough to cause me to grab Tommy and bolt out of the restaurant. I wasn't about to board the bus again when I realized most of the large cities sold their papers across state lines. I was in a panic, trying to figure out where to go. All I had was my purse, the diaper bag and Tommy. My suitcase was in the storage compartment of the bus. I wouldn't draw any attention to myself by asking for it, but then realized my name was on it. I needed to ask for it, so I waited until everyone was ready to board the bus and I told the driver I would be getting off at this stop. After he retrieved my suitcase I kept walking, not knowing where I was going. When the bus passed me and was well out of the town, I stopped to gather my thoughts. The driver would remember I stopped in this town if ever he knew about me missing and was questioned. I found myself walking until I noticed a local bus that served that town was about to pull away from its corner stop. I quickly pounded on its door and the driver

110

opened it and watched me trying to struggle with my bags and the baby, so he stepped down and helped.

"Where are you going Miss?" he asked, "to Wilding?"

"Yes," I answered, not knowing where Wilding was.

The bus pulled out of the main street of that town onto a country road. The bus was empty except for one elderly woman in the back who seemed to be dozing. The driver was elderly also and hardly seemed to pay much attention to me struggling with a baby and the luggage. It was near dusk and it looked like rain clouds were gathering. I prayed it wouldn't rain. When we were nearing the town of Wilding but still on the country road, I noticed there wasn't any traffic except for the bus. I asked him to stop before we entered the town, to let me off. The weather had turned cool. Tommy would be ten months old soon and too heavy to carry for too long. Worse, I didn't know where to go or where to hide. I didn't want to appear in that town on the chance someone might remember seeing me there. I walked away from it toward some farms in the distance. I was in shock and had no idea where I was going.

Noticing farms on each side of the road the further away from the town I got, I also realized there weren't any lights coming from those farms as the sky began to darken. I knew I had to find shelter soon. My state of mind was completely in disarray, and I was crying. Exhausted after walking what could have been a mile with my suitcase, and the diaper bag and purse hanging, my arm became numb and now Tommy seamed to gain weight with every step I took. It became dark and the emerging moon shed some light. The empty road and the stillness of the night allowed me to hear faint horse's hoofs in the distance hitting the blacktop country road behind me long before it came into view. I turned in time to see a horse and buggy approaching. The gray bearded man driving the buggy stopped along side me. I was cold and shivering, with Tommy over my shoulder, covered with the blanket and carrying my suitcase with a purse and diaper bag dangling from my arm, I must have looked totally out of place on that road, and it started to rain.

"Hello there!" he yelled out. He looked startled at seeing a young woman carrying a child on the dark road in the middle of nowhere. I sensed he didn't expect to see a total stranger.

"Woman! What are you doing out here with that baby on a night like this?"

I couldn't answer; he steadied the horse and climbed down from the buggy. He looked closely at us and spoke a few words in what sounded like German, but when I didn't respond, he again spoke in English.

"Are you from around here?" he asked.

I shook my head, no. He looked closer at me and a spark of recognition seemed to appear in his face. "Are you from Indiana?"

"Yes, yes, I am," I lied.

"Oh, I thought so, you look just like her—like my cousin Frieda, she left us years ago."

I didn't know what to say to that, and just nodded, yes.

"You must be her daughter Elizabeth then, were you going to Emma's? Emma is your Aunt—Frieda's sister. Come, I'll take you to her."

I didn't answer him, but just numbly nodded yes again. He helped us into the buggy. Tommy's blanket was damp from the rain and the warmer clothing he should have been wearing was in my suitcase, I hadn't had time to open the case.

"Cover that baby with the blanket back there," he said, pointing to one on the back seat where we were sitting. I was thankful the buggy had a roof over us as the rain came in a downpour just as I climbed in.

"Well then," he said turning to look back at us, as he led the horse into a faster gallop, "I'll take you right out to Emma's place."

I was trembling inside. The damp night air coming from the open sides of the buggy sent a chill throughout my body. I was filled with fear as I felt myself getting deeper into a lie. I wasn't good at lying, but I could only think about the moment and not what lay ahead. He looked over his shoulder and yelled above the horse's hoofs hitting the road and the thunder above us, "Emma hasn't seen you, her niece—you were five years old. Frieda ran away from the Amish ways."

That gave me hope, if she thought I was her long lost niece, we would have a warm bed for the night. I would worry about tomorrow, tomorrow. I cradled Tommy in my arms; covered with the warm dry blanket. The bouncing of the buggy wheels on the gravel road we had turned onto finally lulled him to sleep. I sat back and closed my eyes and tried to relax. The uncertainty of what lay ahead paled compared to what I had just escaped from. The Amish man led the horse up to a little white frame house set next to a larger house. The horse came to a stop and he climbed out of the buggy to help me by taking Tommy from me. I looked around at what I could see in the moonlit night. Everything was in total darkness. Faint light came from a window in the smaller home.

"Miss, excuse me, but I'd like to introduce myself. I'm Otto Voss, a cousin of Emma's and your mother," he said, as he stuck out his hand in a friendly shake.

I had to think fast, and then I heard myself say, "I'm Elizabeth Brown, glad to meet you."

He knocked on the door with Tommy still in his arms as I stood next to him with all my belongings. The door opened to an elderly lady with wisps of gray hair peeking out from the little white Amish cap she was wearing. She looked surprised and said something in German to Otto.

"Emma, look what I bring you," he said.

She looked puzzled, and then with a wave of her hand beckoned us in. I walked into a dimly lit room. The only light in the room was coming from an old fashioned lantern. She walked over to it and raised the wick to shed more light, then she turned to look at us and her hand went up to her mouth in surprise, as she looked closer at me.

"Oh my, Lizzy, are you Lizzy?" She cried as she threw her arms around me. "You look just like your Mama, I'd know you anywhere with your red hair, and eyes like my brother Joe."

I didn't know what to say to that, and I knew then that she thought I was her long lost niece. I had worried about what to do with the color of my hair. Red hair was rare and I thought I might have to dye it brown, but now it came in handy. Luck was with me so far, but having to keep a lie going wouldn't be easy on my conscience. She released me and held me at arms length and then hugged me again. When she took Tommy out of Otto's arms is when she started to cry.

"What a beautiful baby!" she said, and then took us into her kitchen. "You're all grown up Lizzy, and married with a child of your own?" and then she handed Tommy to me as we sat at her table. She insisted Otto join us in a cup of Nescafe.

She studied my face across the table like she couldn't believe I was there.

"How is your mother?" she asked, "You know she ran away when you were five years old and took you to live among the English. We never heard from her again."

"My mother died," I said, knowing it was just the beginning of the many lies I would need to tell to remain safe. She looked sad and shed quite a few tears on hearing her sister passed away. I felt guilty about bringing her bad news that might not be true, but I didn't have a choice at that moment. I only worried about keeping myself and my child safe from what I thought was a man out of control and capable of murder. Tommy was hungry and needed to be changed and he started to cry. She took him from me as I tried to get into the bag for a clean diaper and the one jar of baby food I had left. Otto stood up to leave so we said our goodbyes, and I thanked him for the ride, and the concern shown for us. Emma asked him to go next door to her son's home and notify them of my presence. Soon after, a young couple rushed over. Emma introduced them as Jacob and Elsa Fisher. I was greeted with apprehension as Elsa stared at us.

The couple appeared confused that an English woman was in their Mother's home so late in the night. Elsa looked at Tommy and me and questioned Emma.

"Who are these people, Mother?" she asked, looking concerned.

"Didn't Otto tell you?" Emma said, shaking her head.

"No, all he said was to get over here quickly."

The older woman's excited explanation assured them not to worry, that I was the lost niece who was taken away when I was a child.

"She's Aunt Frieda's child, she informed her son, Jacob— your cousin Elizabeth, we called her Lizzy, remember?"

Elsa's frown turned to a smile quickly and I was greeted with hugs and smiles that put me at ease as she reached her arms out to take Tommy from me.

"He's a beautiful boy, what's his name?" Jacob asked.

"Timothy, Timmy," I replied, without thinking. There it was; Tim was never far from my thoughts, especially when I was under stress. I knew when I left I would have to change our names and what better name could I call my son under the conditions we found ourselves in. I never liked the name he was given, so it wouldn't be hard to think of him as Timmy.

After my son's needs were taken care of, and Emma laid him down in one of her spare bedrooms where she kept a cradle for her grandchildren, we returned to the kitchen, and talked about where I had been and my supposed mother's death. I tried to appear calm, but I was as nervous as could be, having to tell one lie after another to these fine people. Jacob took leave of us the first hour explaining he had to rise early to do his farm chores. As I sat listening to the two women fill me in on the Amish way of life and who was related to whom, I paid half attention to what they were conveying and the other half to my surroundings. The kitchen was spotless, of what I could view in the dim light. Emma brought in another lantern and set it on a cupboard across the room. It shed light on a large black immaculately polished wood-burning stove. The room was rather austere with a table and four chairs. The walls were bare except for a paper calendar.

"Where is your husband?" Emma asked.

I had to think fast, I was afraid to say he died also, that would sound too contrived, I thought, so I quickly let her know that I was divorced. The minute I said it, I wondered if it was the right thing to say.

"Oh, that's too bad, do you plan on staying with us or are you here just for a visit," Elsa asked.

"I wanted to come back to my mother's family to stay, if it's okay with you," I said.

"We would love to have you, wouldn't we Mother?" Elsa said, looking to her mother-in-law to affirm that I was welcome back to the Amish way of life. They explained that they belonged to the Old Order Amish and their Ordnung (Church rules) were very strict. I knew nothing about the Amish except for once hearing the name Amish mentioned when I was in school. I was unaware there were many branches of the religion that differed from one another. When Elsa suggested I stop by her place in the morning and she would give me some proper clothes to wear, all I could do was thank her as she said goodnight to us.

That night I didn't sleep. The room was plain, almost barren, just like the nun's rooms at the Orphanage, except for the missing crucifix. My mind was in overdrive wondering what I had gotten myself into, and if I did the right thing. I thought back to my rash decision to toss the damning evidence of my husband's crime, or maybe proof of his innocence away. I wasn't sure of making the right decision about anything. In a moment of panic it seemed I might be complicating my circumstances. I had to stay hidden until at some time in the near future I would try to contact Betty.

I awoke to a hand on my shoulder gently telling me it was time for breakfast. Emma held the kerosene lamp high and I noticed it was still dark out.

"What time is it?" I asked, trying to shake myself out of a deep sleep.

"It's 5:30, time to go next door and help Elsa with the breakfast," Emma said.

I was confused and tried to sit up as she put the lantern on a dresser and left the room. The baby started to cry and I hurried over to him and picked him up out of the cradle. He needed to be changed so I took care of him first and then dressed myself and carried him into Emma's kitchen. The room was warmed by her woodstove that had already produced the tray of biscuits sitting on top of it. I wasn't used to getting up that early and Emma could see my confusion, so she took Timmy out of my arms and told me to wash up at the sink where she put some warm water in a large tin wash bowl. A towel and bar of soup was next to the bowl. After I washed my face and combed my hair she handed me my son and took the tray of freshly baked biscuits' covered with a towel. I wrapped Timmy in a blanket and followed her next door to Elsa's. It was quite chilly in the morning and Elsa's kitchen was warm and inviting with its smells of pancakes and sausages cooking away. I couldn't believe they were so awake and busy that early. I was to learn much about the strictest order of the Amish in the days to come. Elsa greeted me with a wide smile and soon her children and Jacob came down to breakfast. The two eldest were boys around ten and twelve years of age and three girls. Elsa introduced them to me and I noticed the eldest girl looked no older than eight and already taking charge of the baby not much older than my son. She handled the youngest child like a pro and the six-year-old seemed just as proficient in handling adult business. I was impressed. We all sat at the table after it was covered with various breakfast foods, cereal, sausage, pancakes, and jam. I was startled when they all bowed their heads in silent prayer. I was used to saying grace before a meal aloud at the Orphanage. They explained to me that the cows needed milking as soon as Jacob and his two sons finished eating. I thought such young boys forced up so early to do chores was unusual. I was ignorant in the ways of these strange people so I asked if the boys went to school, knowing it was a weekday.

"Yes, school starts at 8:30 so they have plenty of time to complete their chores," Elsa said.

I sat with Timmy on my lap. The only high chair held Grace, their youngest child. Emma mentioned the extra high chair at her home and that it was inconvenient to carry it next door.

"Oh, is she staying with us?" Elsa asked.

"Well, we have to inform the elders about the situation and they will decide," Emma said.

"I don't want to be a burden to you if I can't stay, I'll go," I said.

Emma put her hand on mine, "Where will you go? I'm sure you'll be able to stay with me, after all, you're my sister's child."

I noticed Elsa's expression of doubt as she looked at her mother-in-law. Later after eight-year-old Lydia and six-year-old Lucy did the dishes, they along with their brothers left for school. They walked to school, to a one-room schoolhouse they informed me. I noticed how everything was cleaned up in an orderly fashion. I offered to help, but they said as a guest I didn't have to this first day. Emma didn't seem to be in a hurry to return to her place so I wasn't sure if I was to stay with her daughter-in-law or go back with her. Both women began to bake bread and seemed to be planning for the lunch that they informed me was the largest meal of the day. I realized Timmy needed a diaper change and informed them that my extra diapers were next door.

"Oh, don't worry, Elsa has plenty of diapers," Emma said.

Elsa smiled and took me upstairs to her baby's room where she laid out several diapers for me.

"Take the extras with you when Mother Fisher goes home," she said.

She left me alone and returned to her food preparation in the kitchen. The sparsely furnished rooms left an echo and as I changed Timmy, I could hear their voices downstairs clearly even though they weren't speaking loudly at all. I felt unsettled when I heard Elsa's reservations on the Elders unlikely accepting someone who lived among the English and knew nothing about their way of life.

"You know what they will say, she will bring news of the outside world to corrupt our beliefs," I heard her say.

CHAPTER 18

The next morning the same ritual applied as the day before. Rising at 5:30 and attending chores, but we didn't go next door and instead waited after breakfast for the Minister and several elders to appear to question me. I was nervous and could hardly eat any breakfast after Emma informed me of the impending visit. At exactly 10:00, three men came. Emma ushered them into the kitchen where I was sitting at the table holding Timmy. They each occupied the remaining three chairs looking rather expressionless. They didn't smile as Emma and Elsa had, but looked rather stern. Their clothing of plain cotton shirts and pants held up by suspenders mirrored their bland expressions. They wore beards but not mustaches and I felt intimidated by them. They stared at me and the one who appeared to be the Minister spoke first.

"I'm told you're related to Mrs. Fisher? Explain in what way, please."

I knew Emma had no way of getting in touch with them since I arrived so I reasoned that Otto, the man who brought me to her filled them in on who I was.

"I'm Elizabeth Brown, her niece," I said, with my voice shaking and barely above a whisper.

"Brown! We don't have anyone here with the name of Brown," he said, his dour face never changing expression. It was hard to guess what they were thinking. Emma could see I was frightened and she interrupted to explain my presence but the second man to speak in a stern voice said, "The young lady can explain herself to us."

I told them my mother left the order when I was only five and I didn't have any memories of that time. It was so nerve-racking talking to these men who sat in judgment over me. Each time Emma tried to intervene they shut her up. She quit trying and remained standing in the background. I had to explain that Brown was my married name and that I was divorced. That information didn't go over too well with them so I made up a story about how I wanted to return to my mother's family and the Amish way of life and he didn't, so I divorced

119

him. I knew in an instant that was the wrong thing to say so I applied another lie on top of that one.

"After we were divorced, he died in a car accident," I heard myself say.

The older man who I thought of as the Minister or leader looked at me skeptically and then introduced himself as the Bishop of thirty-five families and told me they attended church every other week in members homes. He explained that his was of the Old Order and he viewed all other Amish and Mennonites as brethren who strayed from the true church. He explained that because I came from the outside English world, I could stay only on a temporary basis until I took instruction in the Old Order beliefs and only then would I be considered permanent, if I choose to accept their way. I wondered what I had gotten myself into, and noticing how cowed Emma appeared in their presence gave me reason to wonder if I shouldn't bolt from this web of lies I found myself in, in the same way I left my modern world, but where would I go? Where could I hide? I had no choice but to stay and let fate take me where it will. Emma poured Nescafe for the men and after they left I breathed a sigh of relief. I knew I was trapped and didn't want to think of what tomorrow would bring.

Over the next few weeks I would learn much about the Old Order Amish, enough to leave me feeling self-conscious. I didn't belong. I was glad I mentioned my husband died. They viewed divorce a disgrace and one was considered married for life unless one's spouse died. Their clothing was bland, with women appearing sexless in their boring dresses in muted colors of dark green, gray, brown and black. The men reminded me of peacocks with their more colorful shirts of solid pale blues, greens, and whites. It was a man's world and women were there to serve the men and bear the children. They all dressed like they were from the eighteenth century. The black chunky shoes the women wore reminded me of the nuns' attire at the orphanage. So much of their dress reminded me of the nuns and some of their beliefs did also. They were strict and everything they did was like a ritual, even daily chores. They all resembled each other dressing alike, plain and austere. Although I knew I didn't belong in that setting, the calmness of their lives was an environment I badly needed to be in at that time, since leaving the chaotic life I had led with Dan.

I became used to the German dialect they spoke among themselves, and they could switch back and forth between German and English with ease. After the first few days with Emma I was dressed in the same clothing they wore and I found it simple and somewhat freeing. It was the religious instruction I endured that I found quite stifling. Believing that only the Amish could get into heaven reminded me of my Catholic upbringing where we were told only Roman Catholics could get to heaven. I attended the classes and pretended to believe in their teachings.

In November they celebrated the harvest and that is when all thirty-five families gathered at the largest farm for the celebration. It was there that I met Levi Yoder. Levi was a widower with three small children. His wife had died in childbirth leaving him with sons age two and four, and a newborn baby girl. He wore a beard and his hair was long to the shoulders like most of the married men. Unmarried men shaved. His status was different and I guess he was considered a single man but he kept his beard. He was tall and blond and rather good-looking, but his beard hid most of his face. Elsa told me, that his chin wasn't as square as Jacob's and the reason he kept his beard so full. I was never sure of all their rigid rules and how they changed depending on the whim of the Bishop. November and December, after the harvest, were also the months that weddings occurred. The Bishop announced the wedding of a young couple at the Thanksgiving meal. I was busy serving all the men who sat at long tables when I accidently spilled some of the lemonade I was serving. Levi got up to help me and struck up a conversation with me after that encounter. He knew all about me, as did almost everyone in the community. I was the lost Amish child who returned after living with the English and more importantly, I was a young widow. At Christmas the celebration was very austere. No decorations, no colored lights, nothing except prayer and church services.

For the rest of the winter I would run into Levi at the church services twice a month and we would exchange a few words and that was it, until spring came and planting time along with it. I noticed he would come up to Jacob and Elsa's farm to help with the planting, along with others. The Amish helped each other in everything that needed to be done. Building a barn, the whole community helped. Plowing, planting, everyone did his or her part. Spring brought sunshine and warmer weather and I noticed all the children ran barefoot and carefree, including my son who had turned a year old in January of 1959. It was now April, 1959, a full decade had passed since I left the orphanage and Timmy at thirteen months was walking all over the place usually under the watchful eye of one of Elsa's daughters. Lucy and Lydia took turns tending to both Timmy and their baby sister Grace, who was a few months younger than my son. Both babies tottering around and playing together and I was at times confused about the quiet calmness of their lives when I watched the happiness of my son. I was brought back to reality whenever Jacob was hard on his two boys. They were expected to do a man's work and they did, all during the spring planting. I was permanently living with Emma and doing what all the women were expected to do. I did more than my share, wanting to be accepted in their world so they would have no doubts about my intentions living among them. I completed the religion lessons and was accepted into their order. I was sure they all believed I was the long lost Elizabeth, daughter of Frieda Voss. During the day I was Lizzie, at night when I lay awake thinking, I was Kathleen Kelly Robson, just biding my time until I could one day return to my life. I wondered at times if I ever had a life. I felt guilty for deceiving these people who didn't know who I was, but coming from an orphan home, I myself would never know who I was.

During the serving of lunch one afternoon when about five men came in for the meal, Levi was one of them. He made a comment on how big my son was getting and I asked him out of politeness how his children were doing. I knew his sister helped in raising them. Having seen them at the services, I knew the now three and five-year-old were boys. His baby daughter was just a few months younger than Timmy, and turned a year old in April.

"The boys miss their mother," he said, wistfully, "I do the best I can."

I knew his best was probably next to nothing since the women were the only ones I saw tending the children. Occasionally I would notice a father holding a young child but mostly it wasn't the father's job to raise them. Children were made to work hard as soon as they were able. I thought Levi was interested in me, but I also knew by then that my son's childhood would last a lot longer than the Amish children because I intended to leave at some point in time. I felt sorry for his children and hoped he would find some single Amish girl he fancied, but I was afraid it was me he was interested in.

Later that evening after the men came in from a full day's work in the fields, Levi's sister and her husband's buggy arrived with the family. Her husband was one of the farmers helping with the planting. Levi introduced me to his sister and her teenage son who drove the buggy and her other two younger children along with Levi's three small children. I felt sorry for his children and in my kindness toward them during the evening meal, Levi came up to me to thank me for giving his children extra attention. I noticed he was affectionate with them in front of me and that was a rare sight among the Amish men. I thought the gesture was to impress me.

"You're a kind woman," he said.

"So are you," I inanely replied.

I was thankful the men took up all the room at the table and the women and children ate after the men had finished. I could see Elsa and Levi's sister whispering to each other and looking back at me. I knew they were plotting something that had to do with Levi and me.

In the following month of May, 1959, there was a barn raising on the Sherman farm. Except for attending the strict church services twice a month, it would be the first time I would meet all thirty-five families in a different setting. The day was warm and sunny and Emma and I arrived early along with her son's family, all packed into their black buggy with the horse I came to know and like, pulling us up to the Sherman farm. Emma, Elsa and I rode with each of us holding a child on our lap and the older children sat on the floor at our feet. It was a bumpy ride and I longed for the smooth ride of a modern car. After our hellos we women went into the house to help prepare for the very large crowd that would soon arrive. I looked out to check on Timmy and observed how all the children ran wild all over the grass in bare feet, happy, squealing with delight, enjoying each other without the aid of toys or anything else except seeing each other, chasing each other and playing tag.

It was during a gathering like building a barn that I learned how the Old Order Amish really lived. So much of their teachings reminded me of life with the nuns in the orphanage. Once I was out on my own I realized how confined I felt with the teachings of the nuns and what I was experiencing with the Amish wasn't much different. It was while living with Emma and such people who opened my eyes to how one's life could be controlled by outside forces. I wasn't honestly accepting this way of life and I began to question my own faith that I had left behind. I stayed close to the farm and never ventured into town the whole eight months I was still missing. I wondered if anyone ran across a paper in the small town with my picture on it. I reasoned if they had, I would have been reported to the authorities.

Out on the lawn behind the farmhouse was a very long farm table constructed especially for this gathering. Dozens of women of all ages were busy preparing the food, both indoors and out. They all looked alike, resembling penguins all dressed in their shapeless dresses and aprons, with the women wearing the little white caps on their heads at home and some wore black when they went out. I wore a white cap. No one questioned it and since they weren't sure what I should wear since no one had ever been divorced in their order although some widows wore black caps. I knew I was an enigma to these people as was their way of life to me.

In the kitchen I helped prepare the large vat of potatoes boiling away on the black wood-burning stove. Soon more women arrived and took on other dishes assigned to them. They moved in unison never getting in each other's way and I marveled at how they seemed to enjoy every movement when it came to the steps in preparing each special dish. They lived their pious religion in everything they did. Levi's sister came up to me on her way out with a large tray of food, and paused to say—"Lizzie, have you thought of settling down with someone?"

"Not recently," I said.

"Oh, you must still be in mourning then," she said, giving me a smile as she went out the door. I wondered how much she knew about me because I was beginning to realize she thought of me as a widow, divorce not being recognized in her world. Elsa came up to me and whispered in my ear.

"Levi is a good catch, he's more gentle than Jacob and most of the men," she said.

I hardly doubted what she said; he did appear less stern than her husband and what I viewed among most of the men.

"I'm not ready to settle on any man just yet," I said.

Their quiet manner was unsettling. They seemed to blend in with their drab surroundings. Their long dresses of deep dark colors lent to my memories of watching nuns quietly going about their daily rituals that included daily prayer. Their long sleeves never showed naked arms. I was dressed in the same way and at times I felt like I was both free of deciding what to wear, but also imprisoned in their cotton and polyester sameness. When the potatoes were done, I took the potato masher and proceeded to mash the giant pot by hand until it felt like my arm was about to fall off. What I wouldn't have given for my electric mixer at that moment. Levi came in and carried the pot out to the long table where most to the men were seated. I followed him with a large ladle and as he held the pot for me I began to serve ample portions onto each plate. Most of the men stared at Levi and several said something in German to him. Levi answered back in German. I didn't understand what they were saying but could tell by their demeanor and the sound of their voice that they didn't agree with him carrying the pot for me. He carried it by the handle and set it down at the end of the table once we finished one side of the table.

"You should be able to carry it now," he said, "It's not as heavy anymore."

I could see by his expression, he wanted to continue to help me and I was sure the men were teasing him, causing him to stop.

"Thanks Levi," I said, "It's ok, I can finish the rest."

As he passed me to take a seat at the table, he whispered so quietly I could barely make out what he was saying, but I caught the word "Sorry." After that day, I began to see him as different from the other men.

Later after all the men went back to constructing the barn, the women began to tend to the children and the rest of us. Sitting next to Levi's sister Miriam, I asked her why men frowned upon a man helping a woman. I mentioned how her brother was helping me and what transpired with the other men. She looked at me like I was asking a foolish question.

"That's women's work," she said, "Men have their work and we have our work."

I thought about Elsa helping her husband planting, pitching hay, and helping to clean out the pigsty, the chicken coop and other chores. I was confused.

"Elsa helps her husband," I said.

"That's farm work, not house work," she said, in a matter of fact way, like I understood the difference. I didn't. It was a long day and I was tired so I changed the subject and we talked about the children. I noticed one of the younger women who I knew belonged to one of the families was absent.

"Where is Ruth Kruger?" I asked. Ruth was a seventeen-year-old girl, who appeared feisty and overly friendly whenever I ran into her at gatherings or at church services.

"She is being shunned," Miriam said. I knew what shunning was and wondered what that spirited girl could have done to receive such punishment. In all the months I lived among the Amish, I knew the Old Order was the strictest. I was afraid to ask what she had done. Before I could ask, Miriam shook her head in resignation at what the girl was being punished for.

"She was caught with a boy from the Mennonites, in *his car!*"

I knew the Mennonites were a sect of the Amish that allowed cars and telephones and were the most liberal of all the Amish.

"How long will she be shunned?" I asked.

"Until the Bishop decides, of course!" she said, like I should have known the answer.

I thought the punishment didn't fit the crime, but I was still ignorant of just how strict some of the Old Order's rules really were. I found shunning quite cruel because no one was allowed to speak or eat with the girl. She was confined to her home and virtually a prisoner in her own room, not allowed to have contact with her family except for necessities. After that conversation, I knew for certain I would eventually make a mistake and not just be shunned, but tossed out of the order completely. When such a calamity might happen was anyone's guess. I knew I was beginning to chafe under their way of life. It was time to make other plans, but I didn't have a clue as to what they should be. All I knew was I had to get out, and soon.

CHAPTER 19

Summer arrived and with it the hot weather that was stifling in homes without electric fans. Open windows did little to help, and the air was oppressive. Sitting idle under a tree in the shade and hoping for a breeze was wishful thinking for anyone over the age of six. No one sat unless it was mealtime because the men worked from dawn to dusk in the fields or with the farm stock and there were always things to repair around the farm and the women were preparing meals all day long. They were cooking, canning, mending clothes, working on quilts, and helping the men in the fields. After hanging up the wash on the clothesline outdoors, my dress was drenched in sweat. I needed a bath badly but baths were once a week on Saturday nights. A large tin tub kept in a separate room was filled with about six inches of water, heated in a large pot on the stove. I bathed at Emma's and thankfully there was more privacy there, but the primitive way of existing with the Old Amish was wearing me down.

One afternoon I went to the chicken coop on the farm when to my surprise Levi appeared. He came in from the fields and stopped to watch me until I became aware he was there. I turned and said hello and mentioned how hot it was. I was inside the coop searching for eggs and he leaned against the doorway, smiling.

"You must find our ways hard to get used to," he said.

I brushed my damp hair out of eyes and off my forehead and said, "No, not hard, but different, well, sometimes it's hard."

"I guess living with the English most of your life was different, huh?"

"It was a lot easier and more free, and I miss the electric appliances. Work wasn't as grueling."

"You know, when my wife Becky was alive, I tried helping her especially in her last few months of carrying the baby, but the men laughed at me, so I stopped, it's not our way."

"Well, I find some of your ways too strict," I said. I wanted to say they were ridiculous, but I didn't want to insult him. I was beginning to feel uncomfortable because we were alone in the small coop with its low ceiling and Levi was too close to me helping to take out the remaining eggs from the last nest. I worried that Emma would appear at any moment. I hurried out as quickly as I could with my basket of fresh eggs and started back to the house, with Levi following. I felt sorry for him and I didn't want to encourage him, so I said nothing more and hurried into Elsa's kitchen. I must have rushed in because Elsa looked surprised, but it was mostly because Levi was right behind me.

"What do you need?" she asked him, thinking he was after something, coming in from the fields early. "It's too early for supper," she said.

He stuttered a bit trying to think of a reason to be there alone with two women who were not a sister or wife.

"We could use some drinking water, it's hot in the field without any shade."

Elsa filled a large jug of water from the outdoor pump. I stayed indoors and watched from the window as she handed the water to Levi. I thought she could have just given him the empty jug and let him get the water, but nothing the Amish did made any sense to me. At least he was outdoors and returning to the field where the other men were and not following me. I didn't want to feel anything when it came to him because I would feel guilty knowing I couldn't live his life even if I did care about him. What I felt was pity and wished he wasn't so kind around me. It made me uncomfortable.

The men labored hard during planting time and later harvesting the crops. I learned all about farm life living with the Amish. I found watching them harvesting hay without modern machinery ridiculous when they could have used modern equipment. It was against their beliefs, so they had to bale the hay with old-fashioned equipment. The Fishers hitched their workhorses to a mower made in the early 1920s. The combination of heavy hay and the horses moving quickly made it difficult for the mower to cut. Hay is cut on a breezy hot day when the hay is dry. From May through November they worked planting and cutting several times. It was agonizing watching them struggle when I compared their way of farming to the farms the nuns took the children from the orphanage to visit and learn about farming with modern machinery.

Emma, Elsa and I prepared Supper for the six men who came to help Jacob that day and with Levi almost becoming my shadow, it was quite noticeable to the other men and they teased him in German. I felt sorry for men coming in looking totally exhausted and drenched in there own body sweat and I was grateful they were served on Elsa's outdoor picnic table. Levi, upon seeing me come out of the house carrying the large caldron of stew, quickly got up and relieved me of the hot pot that I carried with its handle wrapped in a thick pot holder. This time the men didn't chastise Levi, but whispered to each other and laughed. They were getting used to the idea of maybe Levi and me becoming a couple I guess. Later when the men returned to the fields and I was helping both the women clean up in the kitchen, Emma asked me about my feelings when it came to Levi.

"He really likes you," she said. "He's different from the other men and I'm sure you've noticed."

"Yes, why do you think he's that way?" I asked.

Emma dried her hands on a towel and took my hands in hers. "Be kind to him, he lost his mother at a very young age and was raised by his very strict and not so nice father, he passed away when Levi was seventeen, and then he lived with his sister.

"Not just strict," Elsa said, "He was cruel to Levi as a child, I remember, because we played together as children. Although I was younger than him, I liked him a lot as a boy, because he didn't seem as rough as the other boys."

"Losing his mother and then his young wife made him more sensitive I think," Emma said.

"He's a lot nicer looking since he grew his beard because he has a small chin and it covers it. He looks more manly with the beard," Elsa said, laughing. "I was attracted more to Jacob when I was of courting age."

I couldn't see how she found Jacob attractive because he had a round face and very square chin that made him look like a pumpkin. I began to take an interest in Levi after learning more about his life. I had been on the farm since Otto picked me up in his buggy and women surrounded me often so I was never alone, but I was lonely. I began to fantasize about being in a man's arms again, and what it would feel like, especially the arms of one so kind. I began dreaming at night about Tim and sometimes I couldn't make out whose arms I was in, Tim's or Levi's when they blended together in the dream. That fall I celebrated my 27th birthday in October. Elsa and Emma made it a special day for me. During the harvest that November after all the men came in for the evening meal at the Fisher's, I knew it would be the last time I would see the men together in one place except for church services unless there was another barn going up that fall, but there wasn't. According to Emma, remarriages happened by writing letters and meeting at the singings on Sundays. From her I learned that the bishop was remarried having lost his first wife to cancer. I didn't know how Levi and I would even get together because there wasn't anything called dating for widows or widowers. I was so lonely for love and affection that I was lost in a fantasy and began to forget I was still married to Dan. I didn't know what I was thinking half the time.

That same month during the Thanksgiving meal, Levi wouldn't necessarily be attending Elsa and Emma's meal. Amish families were large and the only time all thirty-five families came together was at church services or if a barn was going up. Thirty-five families meant entire families that were related that could include several generations, cousins, uncles, aunts, grandparents on each side was considered one family. Thirty-five families could swell to over a thousand people or more. I didn't know when I would be close to Levi again. I knew from the first Christmas spent with the Amish that they celebrated privately each family baking cookies and exchanging gifts but there wasn't any Christmas decorations, no stockings hung, no Christmas tree, no Angels, they didn't believe in graven images. They might put a candle on the table surrounded by greenery. Christmas was strictly about the birth of Jesus. They celebrated Zwedde Grischldaag, which meant second Christmas. It's usually the day after Christmas. Both days are holidays for the Amish.

After Thanksgiving was over, I felt restless and one night after putting Timmy to bed and Emma had retired for the night, I put on my winter coat, wrapped a woolen scarf over my head and headed for a brisk walk down the road. The night was cold and the air felt freeing after being indoors. I wanted to clear my head and think. Lately I hadn't been doing much of that, just living for the moment. I began to realize my infatuation with being with Levi was ludicrous. My head was swimming with thoughts of what my next step would be; I knew I couldn't remain with the Amish forever. I had to think of my son as well as myself, but where could I go? It was over a year hiding out and I wondered what was going on back home. I never left the farm to go into town, being afraid someone might recognize me, but now I felt it was time. I turned to go back after having walked up to the next farm where the Krogers lived. It was very dark and the moon wasn't out, maybe hidden behind clouds. I thought I heard a rustle in the roadside bushes so I stopped.' "Who's there?" I asked, wondering if it was a person or animal. A small figure of a girl emerged from where she was hiding and I knew it was Ruth Kroger, the girl who was shunned.

"What on earth are you doing out here in the dark?" I asked the shivering girl, who wore only a sweater on such a cold night.

"Please, please, don't tell anyone you saw me," she said, almost in tears.

"You're Ruth, aren't you? Are you still being shunned?"

"Yes, but I climbed out of my bedroom window, I couldn't take it anymore."

"Where were planning on going on a night like this and without proper clothing?" The girl was cold and crying. I felt sorry for her, so I put my scarf around her shoulders and as she walked with me she told me her sad story. She was in love with a twenty- year- old Mennonite boy and she was trying to walk to his farm. She was running away. It was at that moment that I knew I had to help her. I decided for good or not, I would bring her back to Emma's with me and get her some winter coat to wear. I couldn't take a chance Emma would awaken if I brought her to the house so we made plans to have her hide in the barn in the hay where it was warm and I would bring her warm clothing. I knew I was doing something that could get us both in big trouble, but I didn't care. I thought back to when I was desperate and the help I received from Angie, Betty and Lottie. I had no way of getting in touch with her boyfriend and I talked to her about what we could do to get her to him. After she told me she was actually seventeen and would turn eighteen in a few weeks and that they both planned on leaving the Amish way of life and go into the English world together, it was what I needed to hear to brave what I was about to do for them. She needed to stay hidden in Jacob's barn without him knowing until I could get word to the young man.

How I managed to enter the house and gather up some warm clothing and go back to the barn without waking Emma was a miracle. She was a light sleeper. In the barn there was a hayloft. It was full of hay and I managed to climb up and fix a place hidden from Jacob if he entered the barn. I knew he wouldn't be climbing up to the loft anytime soon. Ruth settled in and I cautioned her not to make any noise if she should hear anyone enter the barn the next morning. It would be Jacob and his boys milking the cows. I prayed his boys wouldn't decide to play in the barn and climb up to roll around in the hay, but I knew they had to leave for school early the next morning. Emma drove her buggy to town but always with Elsa or Jacob doing the driving. I needed to have a reason to go to town the next day. Ruth had given me the name of her boyfriend, Noah Wagner, and I managed to write down the telephone number she'd given me.

The next day after Jacob and his sons milked the cows and his boys left for school, I entered the barn to check on Ruth. I went to Elsa and asked to be taken into town but both Emma and Elsa said it would have to wait until the next day. Jacob had promised some farmer he would come over to his farm to help him with something and he needed the buggy. His mother's buggy was parked in one of the sheds needing a wheel repaired. I was at my wits end because I needed to get the girl out of the barn by that night. I didn't know what to do. Ruth was frightened and didn't sleep during the night. She was cold and the hay and one of my winter jackets didn't keep her as warm as I had hoped. She was chilled to the bone. I was determined to get her out, but I didn't know how. Unable to get to a phone I felt helpless in trying to help her. After checking on her again later in the morning, and promising to think of something, I started back to Elsa's kitchen with a few eggs from the chicken coop in my basket. As I approached the house I noticed a buggy parked in front of the porch.

The voice of Levi filled the room as I entered. He was sent by

133

Jacob to see if he could take a look at Emma's buggy and maybe fix the wheel in question. Jacob knew I wanted to go to town and I thought it was kind to send Levi but wondered why he didn't just ask Levi to take me in *his* buggy. Then I remembered the strict rules about courting. Levi couldn't be seen alone with me I reasoned, but if one of the women were with us, wouldn't that be enough, I thought. Everywhere I turned I felt restricted. It seemed the Amish did everything the hard way.

"Hello!" Levi said, as soon as I walked through the door. "I hear you need to get to town so let me have a look at that buggy wheel."

"It's in the shed," Emma said, and then turning to me she said, "Show him where it is, Lizzy."

I was shocked, but didn't waste any time wondering why she allowed me to be alone with him. I left quickly with Levi right beside me. I prayed neither of the women would follow us. I had to get him alone for what I was about to do. I looked back to make sure we were alone and led him to the shed. Once inside, I turned to him before he had a chance to inspect the buggy and poured out what had happened the night before. I was near tears and wasn't sure how he would react, but to my surprise he took my hands in his and gently assured me that no one would know what I had just confided to him. I started to tremble and he took that opportunity to embrace me. I shouldn't have let him, but it felt so good to be hugged by anyone. The Amish were not demonstrative in that way. I never saw any affection between husbands and wives. They were quite stingy with showing affection to their children also. Maybe they were different in private, but I never observed any such displays in public.

"Don't worry, Lizzy," he said, as he held me close. "Where is she?"

"She's hiding in the barn, up in the hay loft since last night. Her parents went to visit the grandparents for two days but are due back late tonight. I need to get her out of there tonight." I was shaking with fear and he held me tighter, then after kissing my forehead he let me go.

"Will she be okay up there until tonight?" he asked. "I'll wait until dark, later, around eight and come back with my buggy so have her on the road far enough away from any buildings and I'll pick her up. I

134

need you to come with me, in case we are stopped where no one knows us; it won't look too suspicious with two women along because she's so young."

"Yes, I think she can spend a few more hours up there. I'll make sure Emma and Timmy are sleeping before I leave. Emma usually goes to bed early."

"I'll be waiting in the buggy, so try to get there as soon as you can," he said.

"I don't know exactly what time I can get to Ruth, and there isn't any way of letting you know," I said.

He looked at me tenderly, and I felt guilty using him in this way but I was desperate. My getting caught was one thing, but for him it would be catastrophic.

"We better get back before they wonder about us out here, alone," I said.

"I'll tell them I checked the buggy and it might need a new part," he said.

"Why wouldn't they let you take me to town?" I asked. It seemed the logical solution, but nothing the Amish did had anything to do with logic as far as I was concerned.

"We are both single," he said.

"Well, we aren't exactly teenagers, we don't need chaperones, do we?"

"It's the rules, but I agree with you Lizzy, what can I say?"

At that moment, I really liked Levi.

At noontime I purposely took my time bathing Timmy, so Emma went next door to Elsa's before me. On the way with Timmy in tow, I went into the barn and gave Ruth some food. My son was a toddler and at almost two years old, running all over. He was busy chasing the cats that lived in the barn to notice what I was doing. When we entered Elsa's kitchen, she eyed me suspiciously.

"What were you doing in the barn?" she asked. I was sure she was watching for me because I usually came in with Emma.

"Timmy wanted to see the cats," I said, holding my breath. The day was one of the coldest so far and Ruth had a full day of freezing in the hayloft before nightfall. I was afraid when Jacob milked the cows again in the evening, he might discover her. I had to get her out sometime that evening and hold my breath that she wouldn't be discovered before I could come for her.

We had just returned from Elsa's after we cleaned up the lunch dishes. I wished that Emma would stay home and we could eat a meal together at her place, but we spent most of the time at her son's during the day doing chores and ate all our meals with Jacob and family. I marveled at the patience Elsa showed in having her mother-in-law with her everyday. I compared Emma with Dan's mother and it was like comparing apples to lemons as far as I was concerned. Emma was a sweet woman and always deferred to her daughter-in-law over family matters. Dan's mother could have used a few lessons from her on how to be a mother-in-law.

At exactly 8:00 pm Emma retired for the night. It was dark early during the winter months and there wasn't much to do by candle or kerosene lamplight. I too would go to bed early most nights but I had to stay awake this night. Timmy was fussy and I couldn't take the chance he would cry and wake Emma. I had to make sure he was sleeping soundly before I made any attempt to leave. I rocked him in the big rocking chair in our room, singing softly all the little songs I remembered in hopes it would lull him to sleep quickly. It was nine before he really was sound asleep. I waited another half hour to make sure he wouldn't awaken and then I put on my coat and scarf and quietly opened the back door. It was the door that squeaked. Darn, I thought, *I should have oiled the hinges*, but I had forgotten about that door. I held it and opened it ever so slowly until there was just enough space for me to squeeze out. I had to close it in the same manner. I ran to the barn in total darkness. No moon to light up anything and I was grateful for that.

Once inside the barn, I could see nothing. I heard the movements of the cows in their stalls and they heard me. One of them mooed and it startled me, but when Ruth heard it she crawled over to the ladder to look down and waited until I called up to her. Slowly, she came down the ladder.

"Hurry," I whispered, as if the cows could make out what I was saying. I was shaking and so was she. Together we left the barn and made our way to the road hoping everyone was asleep and not looking out of a window spotting two figures in the dark rushing down the driveway. I was thankful for the trees and tall grasses that lined the road but most of the foliage was gone in November. In another two days it would be December and only a matter of time before the first snowfall.

Ruth began to cry, "Oh if we get caught they are going to kill me," she said, between sobs.

"No, no they won't, the Amish don't commit murder," I said.

"No, they don't, but living this way you die slowly." she said, "Noah finds his order too strict and wants to leave, but compared to our Old Order, it's heaven. They can have cars, and telephones."

I knew that as far as Christian doctrine was concerned the two faiths were the same. It was in the practice that they differed. Some Mennonites believed in some modern technology. The branch Noah belonged to also believed in higher education. I learned all about the different beliefs from Emma, now a widow, who seemed to know a great deal. She was once a member of the Mennonites as a young girl, but she found herself falling for an Old Order boy and left to join him. Emma of all people should understand this young girl wanting out, but I couldn't take the chance of confiding in her. She had been in the Old Order too long and was now completely indoctrinated in their beliefs.

We hurried in the dark along the side of the road and prayed no buggy was out this late except for Levi's. Half way between the Fisher and Kroger farms I could make out a horse standing off the road in the grass, so we started to run and soon we could see the buggy with Levi sitting with his hands firmly on the reins, holding the horse still. We climbed into the buggy and we were on our way. Levi seemed to know where Noah's farm was. The Mennonites lived among the other Amish groups and I noticed how they were used by other Amish orders. They thought nothing of riding in cars, or using the telephones of the more liberal Mennonites. They used the English in town in the same way. I found it all so hypocritical.

"I didn't see any lamp-light at the Kroger place as I passed it so I don't think anyone's home yet," he said, noticing how nervous Ruth was.

"How would Noah know you're coming to him?" I asked Ruth.

"I left word months before the shunning that he was to always watch for me and if I could get out, I would."

After traveling a few miles in about forty minutes in a span of time that would have been a few minutes in a car, we arrived at the farm. It was after ten at night and to see real lights on in the farmhouse and on the porch, was a feast for the eyes as far as what I felt at that time. Levi helped us down from the buggy.

"Do you want us to go to the door with you?" I asked.

"No, its ok, they'll accept me. They know all about us."

She assured us she would be fine and to go on before we got into trouble. We watched her walk up to the door of the house and Levi said, "Lets wait until she's inside." We both watched as the door opened to a young man who embraced her. We quickly left.

CHAPTER 20

We expected to get back to the Fisher farm without any problems. The night was clear and cold. Levi's horse seemed to know the way in total darkness. I was still sitting behind him in the buggy and we talked a little. I had to shout above the clopping of the horse's hoofs and Levi would turn his head when he spoke, so I could hear him. We were less than a half-mile or so from the Fisher's when we noticed what looked like lights on the road in the distance. As we approached a little closer and about the distance of two blocks from the farm, we could make out men on the road and in the fields on each side of the road holding lanterns. Levi pulled the horse to a stop.

"Oh, oh, you better get out, *here*, looks like they're searching for Ruth," he said, "You can't be seen with me, and alone at this time of night."

I began to panic, "How can I get back into the house? What if Emma is awake? It looks like they are around her place too," I said, my voice breaking. I was terrified.

"Get out *now* and go through the field until you get to the back of the barn, if she saw you coming in the back door you can say you went to check on a noise you heard in the barn," he said, trying to help me.

"What excuse will you have for being out this late?" I asked, worried about what they would accuse him of.

"Don't worry about me, I'll think of something. *Now go!*" he ordered.

I jumped out of the buggy and into the brush at the side of the road and watched as Levi continued on and then I ran as fast as I could quite a distance from the side of Elsa's place around to the back field and slowly made my way up to the large cow barn. I entered the barn though the double doors used by the cows, and ran to the other side to enter the milk house. I could view the back of Emma's kitchen from a window in the room the milk pails were stored, and noticed a dim light coming from her window. I knew she was up and by now noticed I was missing. I was sweating profusely even in the cold, and my heart was pounding fearfully. I thought of what to say when I had to face her. I would do as Levi said; I heard a noise coming from the barn and went to investigate. Somehow I knew it wouldn't wash, but I couldn't think of a better excuse.

I entered the room where the washtub was kept and stopped before entering the kitchen because I heard voices. I recognized them as Emma and Jacob's. What were they talking about? I couldn't make it out, but had to walk in and face them with a story they wouldn't believe, I was sure. Emma turned when she heard me come into the room, she had an angry look on her face and she had Timmy in her arms.

"Where have you been?" she shouted. Timmy started crying and Jacob lost no time in scolding me. I tried to explain about a noise in the barn but they both jumped on me, both yelling at the same time.

"Don't lie to us!" Jacob shouted, "It's been over an hour since your son was awakened by the men searching for the Kroger girl, so don't give me that tale because I was in the barn with a couple of the men searching for you. You know something about her disappearance, don't you?"

I had no answer; I just shook from nerves and knowing there was no way I could lie my way out of this. I couldn't say anything because I needed to protect Levi. I knew they wouldn't think it was a coincidence that both of us were out late at night and at the same time.

"I'm sorry," was all I could say. After that I remained silent to all their questions. For some unexplained reason, I couldn't cry, but remained stoic. That was unusual because I cried so easily over minor things. I didn't know what story Levi came up with so I made sure I said nothing at all. Emma handed me Timmy and told me to go to my room.

"The Bishop will want to question you tomorrow," she said, not too kindly.

Jacob stared at me, "We know you helped that girl, didn't you? Don't lie to us."

Then he held up the white cap single women wore, and the horse blanket. Knowing where he found them, I froze and said nothing.

"We found it in the hay loft so we know she was up there. You'll have to answer to her family and the Bishop tomorrow."

140

I didn't answer, but went into my room and closed the door. They didn't know anything about Levi, not yet, but I knew by the next day everyone would know if Levi told the truth. Somehow I couldn't picture him telling lies, but I was sure he wouldn't mention I was with him. I got Timmy back to sleep and lay awake anticipating my punishment. *Would they shun me, or throw me out of the order all together, thinking I couldn't be trusted anymore having spent my life among the English. I was sure they would think I was a threat to their way of life.* I wondered if they would begin to doubt I was Emma's niece. All those thoughts kept me up all night.

The next morning I was prepared to face my fate. When I came into the kitchen with my son, Emma wasn't around. I realized I dozed toward morning and she went next door to Elsa's. This would be the first time I would not go with her but stay where I was, and wait. I couldn't face Emma or Jacob again, not to mention Elsa. For the first time since I entered their world I found myself cut off and desperate much like I felt the day I discovered that woman's driver's license in Dan's clothing. The same fear that almost paralyzed me then, had me in its grip again. This time I couldn't run. The primitive world I had entered, void of communication and transportation, rendered me frozen to the spot, unable to escape.

It was after noontime when two buggies appeared. I heard the horses coming up the drive and braced myself for what was to come. I watched by the window as Jacob walked up to them. I was sure he was waiting for them. He escorted them to his mother's front door. I quickly ran back to the kitchen and sat at the table and waited, relieved that Timmy had gone for his nap. The same three men that questioned me when I first arrived over a year ago entered the room. They were intimidating as they took their seats. Jacob stayed, leaning against the kitchen cupboard. The Bishop, who I had come to know as Moses Kerchen, spoke first.

"We know you helped that girl, so no use lying to us. Where is she?"

I knew I couldn't talk my way out of this, so I braced myself to tell the truth, but take the blame without mentioning Levi.

"I did help her because she came to me by accident, you see, I was taking a walk and I found her walking on the road without her coat and it was cold and so I couldn't bring her into Emma's, because of the shunning, so I took her to the barn and gave her a warm jacket." I knew I was in big trouble and waited for his reply.

"Where is she?" he asked.

"I don't know, I last saw her when I gave her the jacket. I thought she went back home."

"What you tell us makes no sense. If she was cold you could have just given her the jacket, not hide her in the barn. She couldn't escape by herself could she?"

"I don't know how she got out or where she went," I said. "Maybe she walked to town."

"That's unlikely," one of the men said. "We know how she got away."

"Well, if you know, then why are you asking me?" I said, as I began to shake a little. I began to think of leaving with my son as soon as the interrogation was over, not thinking how it would be possible in the middle of winter, alone without transportation. I wasn't thinking rationally at all.

Moses stared at me in a menacing way and that helped fuel my anger toward this man who held everyone's life decisions in his hands alone. I thought of the priest who told me to go home and be a good wife and I could see the comparisons between them. I got angrier.

"I helped her, so what? She's a young girl in love with a Mennonite boy. She's almost eighteen."

"So, is that where she is? How did she get there by herself?" Moses asked, "We know you couldn't have taken her there yourself."

I didn't answer. I sat there in silence.

"What if we told you that Levi took her and you were with him, weren't you?"

I wondered how they would know that, unless Levi confessed I was with him. I couldn't believe he would do that so I stuck to my story thinking they were hoping I would fall into the trap of admitting Levi and I were together. I was confident Levi didn't mention me.

"You were both seen together in his buggy by a farmer near that boy's farm, when you dropped her off," one of the men said.

How could they know anything without communication with the Mennonites, I thought, so I stuck to my story because I wasn't sure if Levi confessed to helping Ruth.

"I don't know how she traveled, the boy must have picked her up in his car," I said. I knew they didn't believe me, but by then I didn't care. I knew my days were numbered, maybe hours, with this group. I was ready to move on. The men quit questioning me and abruptly got up and walked out, leaving Jacob behind to let me know they would decide my fate, but I was prepared to leave even if I wasn't told to leave.

Jacob looked at me with pity. "If it's up to me and my mother, you being her niece and all, but its not up to us." Shaking his head sadly, he went out the door.

Emma stayed away the rest of the day and I spent it alone with Timmy, while contemplating my next move. There wasn't any way to get in touch with Levi, or anyone for that matter in this Godforsaken Order. At least the Mennonites could communicate with each other by telephone. I thought of what to do, because regardless of my punishment, I knew I wasn't going to stay with these people a day longer than I had to. I felt so bad for Levi, what would happen to him? I wondered. The qualities I admired about Levi were his kindness and his life in its simplicity showed me how good and honest he was. I felt guilty having gotten him mixed up in my mess. Even in his innocence about the wider world, I found myself attracted to him in spite of the fact we had nothing in common. He needed a plain and loving Amish woman, innocent of my world. Levi had an innate goodness about him and having only an eighth-grade education made him an innocent man in my eyes. If only one like Levi would exist in my world I thought, and I knew they did, because of Tim, my first and only love. In some ways, Levi and Tim were both sides of the same coin. When I thought of them I thought of how life was like a coin toss, you never knew what side you would come up with. I felt sorry for Levi and needed to see him before I departed for God knows where.

That night Emma wouldn't speak to me, so after I fixed something for my son to eat, we returned to our room. It became one of the longest nights I would spend at Emma's. I didn't think it would ever end because I was awake the whole night. Early the next morning, again the horse's hooves' striking the gravel driveway drove my anxiety to a fever pitch and again I started to shake and sweat and with my heart racing I awaited my fate by the Old Order Amish. Not that it mattered as I intended to leave anyway.

Emma came in from next door just as I walked into the room, and was about to open the door for the Bishop who I was sure was arriving in one of the buggies. I didn't say anything to her, but she nodded to me that she would get the door.

The same three men entered the kitchen and removed their black hats and sat around the table. I remained standing holding Timmy as an excuse not to have to sit with them. Old Moses spoke first relaying to Emma that they knew I was her niece, and they felt bad about having to tell us that they didn't think I should remain but because I *was* her niece they would resort to shunning as a punishment until I repented. That wasn't what I was expecting because I had no desire to repent anything.

"I don't think I should stay in my aunt's Order," I said, " I would like to leave because I find your ways too hard to get used to."

Emma tried to explain for me, "She isn't used to our way and I'm afraid it's been too difficult for her."

The Bishop looked at me, "Is that what you want to do, leave?"

I knew they couldn't hold me there against my will. "Yes, tomorrow, if I can get a ride to town to look for a job, it would be fine with me."

"What would you do with your son? Who would care for him if you work?" Emma asked. She appeared honestly worried. She knew in the year I was with her I had never asked to be taken to town. She knew I didn't know anyone in town.

"I'm sure I can find a babysitter for him," I said, but I wasn't sure of anything.

Moses could see I was determined to leave and he probably welcomed my decision, afraid I could be a continuing problem for his flock. I took that moment to accept all the blame for Ruth's escape.

"None of this is Levi's fault," I said. I wasn't sure what they were told when they questioned him but I was sure they did. "He tried to help and I'm sorry, it's all my doing so please don't take it out on him. He was going by and saw us both on the road and offered us a ride. Where was the harm in that? He had no idea Ruth was running away." It felt better telling some truth.

"So, it's true, you knew she wanted to go to that boy and you helped her by hiding her in Jacob's barn," one of the men said, with a smirk on his face. The other man who was silent until that moment said, "You lied when you were questioned by Jacob yesterday, how do we know you're telling the truth now?"

"Because I'm leaving tomorrow, and what difference would it make for me to lie now."

The men nodded and agreed and then left leaving it up to Jacob to take me to town the next day. That couldn't come soon enough for me. Another sleepless night reduced me to a zombie the next morning because I worried all night on how I was going to survive. I thought, *What if I couldn't find work in town?* I knew it was a small town and I wasn't sure how many opportunities there would be for me to find work. I counted my remaining cash, only two hundred dollars left of the five I started out with, enough to stay in a motel if there was one. Motels were starting to pop up across the country in the late 1950s but not too many. I might have to rent a room in someone's home. The more I thought about it the worse I felt. I was beginning to panic and think the shunning might have been a better alternative to living on the street, if I couldn't find anything.

The next morning I went in to take a bath before Jacob would come for me. It was a Saturday morning and I didn't know when I would have an opportunity to bathe again or where. Emma took care of Timmy, feeding him his breakfast and I prepared my bath. I had to carry the hot water in the large teakettle to add to the water from the well that I had already poured into the tin tub. I gingerly stuck my toe in and although the water wasn't warm it wasn't as cold with the added hot water. I eased myself into the tub and thought about hot water coming out of a facet or from a showerhead. What I wouldn't give for that sensation again. I heard the door to the tub room open and it was Emma, holding Timmy, wanting to ask me something. Whenever I took a bath she never invaded my privacy but today was different, I would be leaving and she wanted to ask me a question.

"What is it?" I asked, with my back to her. I turned my head to wait for what she wanted to ask me. She was silent for a moment.

"Lizzy! What happened to that large birth mark you had on your back?"

I was stunned; she had never seen me undress, not in this Amish world. There was never a time it would be possible. I tried to come up with an answer.

"Oh, that? My mother had it removed when I was around ten," I said, hoping she would believe me. I could feel my face flush hot and was glad she couldn't view my shocked expression. She didn't say anymore about it and asked me if I wanted to take the extra stroller for Timmy that she kept at her home.

"Yes, that would be helpful to me," I said.

Later as we waited for Jacob to come for me, I thought she eyed me with suspicion. I wondered if she was beginning to question if I was really her niece. It mattered to me that she wouldn't have any doubts because I still had to be near the Amish community as her niece in order to hide; I had to remain Elizabeth Brown.

I felt bad having to say goodbye to Emma and I promised her that since I was leaving I was sure shunning didn't apply to our situation and whenever she came into town we could still see each other. I thanked her for everything and I could see she was near tears, still believing I was her niece, I hoped. I tried to appear as upset, but of course I didn't have the same feelings. She was just a kind woman to me, not my aunt. Jacob readied the buggy and pulled it in front of the house. He helped me with my bags and I noticed that Elsa hadn't come outdoors to say goodbye. I wondered if I should go to her, but then I realized if she didn't care enough to come out, I would just leave. I knew from what Emma said, about how angry she was about what I had done. Elsa was a devout Old Order Amish to the core, but her mother-in-law having lived at one time, as a Mennonite, seemed a little less stringent and more understanding when it came to their religious rules.

I climbed into Jacob's buggy and reached for Timmy as Emma planted a kiss on his cheek before handing him to me. It was a sad parting for all of us, even for Jacob. He put aside his anger and wished me well. As the horse turned and started to trot away, on the fresh snow that had fallen the night before, I waved Timmy's hand and watched as Emma waved back. She didn't smile. I turned away to look ahead, again facing the unknown.

CHAPTER 21

The town I avoided when I first arrived was larger than I had expected with a long block of stores and businesses lining both sides of the street. There was a section for horse and buggies where Jacob parked. The town of Wilding, mostly inhabited by the so-called 'English' was all decorated for the Christmas Holidays.

I didn't have a clue on what to do next, or where to go. He advised me to leave my bags in the buggy until he brought me to one of the stores, a mom and pop kind of little quaint restaurant that also sold Amish trinkets for the tourists. Once inside, Jacob introduced me to Clara Holsteder, a short and stocky, cheerful Mennonite Woman.

"Lizzy needs a place to stay, until she can find work," he said, "Do you know of anyplace?"

Clara looked me over, noticing my Old Order dress, "You're leaving the Order?" she asked.

Before I could answer, Jacob explained how I was a relative of Emma Fisher's and I was leaving because I could no longer live according to their rules. He didn't mention I had been shunned.

The woman smiled and said, "Yes, I know how stressful that can be, Mr. Fisher. Leave her with me and I'll see what we can come up with." She smiled at Timmy. "She has a child; she can't be roaming the streets." Addressing me, she said, "As soon as Mr. Holsteder comes in, we'll figure out something."

"Thanks, her Aunt Emma will be relieved to hear she's in good hands," he said.

He turned to me and took my son's hand, "My Gracie will miss this little guy," he said, and then mentioned he would bring my belongings from the buggy. I realized the woman and Jacob knew of each other, as did some of the different Orders. After Jacob delivered my bags and Emma's stroller to me, he bid me goodbye and assured me the family would see me again. I hoped they would come into town for supplies from time to time. I watched him walk back to his horse and buggy and a feeling of loss engulfed me again.

"Please, come into the back room and make yourself comfortable,"

Clara said, directing me to a large kitchen in back of the shop.

"I can't thank you enough," I said, as tears began to gather in my eyes. I hated when I couldn't control my emotions. It seemed when I felt in most danger, I didn't cry, and if I became angry I felt stronger. It was when the danger was over or someone showed kindness toward me is when the tears would come. Clara sensed my fragile state and took my child from me.

"Here, sit yourself down and rest awhile," she said, directing me to a chair. "Everything will work out, you'll see, as soon as Mr. Holsteder gets here." She placed my son in my lap.

"I have to attend to my customers, so you make yourself at home."

She left me and I sat trying to hold a squirming child who wanted to get down and run around. I was surrounded by a large stove and other modern appliances including boxes of supplies, too much for Timmy to get into, so I walked around holding him pointing out various objects to distract him. I had to keep in mind that Tommy was to be called Timmy around the Amish. It wasn't long before her husband arrived. She must have filled him in on my presence because he rushed into the back room and greeted me like a long lost relative. I felt relieved.

"Clara and I decided we could use some help in the store. It gets quite busy during the holidays" he said.

They were kind to me and I was so grateful for their help that the dam burst and I did cry in front of Mr. Holsteder. I was embarrassed and apologized.

"Mrs. Holsteder suggested I bring you to our farm. Our youngest daughter Rachel is home, she's fifteen, she'll keep you company until we close up for the day."

The Holsteder's were an older couple more Emma's age, and I sensed a more relaxed attitude and certain cheerfulness about his personality, unlike the staid Old Order Amish.

It was a pleasure to ride in a real automobile again. I had forgotten what a smooth ride felt like after so many months riding in bumpy buggies whenever the fisher's had to attend church services or we visited other farms. The Holsteder farm reminded me of the farms I remembered back home in Illinois. I found their daughter Rachel a warm and sweet girl who took to Timmy immediately as I entered their home. I was sure her mother had called her to let her know we were coming. What a convenient appliance, the telephone. It felt like I was half-way back to the real world. Rachel held out her arms and I gave her Timmy. She cooed over him and took him into another room before I could get my coat off.

"Make yourself at home, we close up shop at five o'clock," Mr. Holsteder said.

I thanked him several times, and before he left he said, "Just call me Jim, my wife's name is Clara. You can call us by our first names." I was thankful for that because Holsteder was a mouthful to say and I mispronounced it several times.

The afternoon went by quickly as Rachel talked on and on about her family and my 'Timmy', how cute he was, and how the family was waiting for their first grandchild to be born. She kept my son entertained with a set of building blocks and a toy truck.

"How many siblings do you have?" I asked.

"Oh, they are five of us. Two are married and I have two younger brothers, they are at grandfather's farm today. They help out on Saturdays."

Rachel was a pretty girl and although she wore her hair in the customary bun at the back of her head, with the white cap, as did the Old Order women, her dress was a colorful pink print. I watched her play with my son and it calmed me. I knew then that the Mennonites were people I could be comfortable with. As I sat waiting for her parents to arrive, my thoughts were of Levi. I had to see him, to let him know how sorry I was for getting him in trouble. I knew he had to be punished in some way, but I didn't know what his punishment would be. Of all the adult people I met in the Old Order, Levi was the one spot of sunshine in a cloudy gray world. That is how I viewed that Amish group.

Shortly after five, Jim and Clara came home, laden with packages from their store. Leftover food from the restaurant was brought home. Nothing was wasted. They smiled their broad smiles and it made me feel accepted. They invited me to stay the night and after supper we talked about what they were able to do to help me.

"We could use some help in the store, serving the customers," Jim said, "Clara has her hands full trying to cook in the back room and watch up front at the same time. As you can see I have the farm to take care of. Rachel helps her mother some on most weekends, but she goes to school."

I was surprised when he said Rachel went to school. At fifteen most Amish children were finished with school. Elsa's children's education was finished after eighth grade. "Is Rachel in eightth grade?" I asked. Rachel started to laugh; in fact both parents thought the question was amusing.

"Oh, my, no, I'm in high School," she said.

During that evening I was to learn much about the Mennonites, in fact about the Amish themselves, more than I ever did living with Emma. It seemed this family's sect were the most liberal of the Mennonites as there were many different groups of Mennonites as there were different Amish groups going from very conservative, like Emma's sect to very liberal, but still more conservative than the most conservative Mennonites. My head was swimming with all the information of these unique people and I thought it wasn't much different than the entire regular Christian religions I was used to, that all differed from each other. After supper Clara showed me to a room with two double beds where their sons slept.

"You can sleep here tonight, I'll bring two chairs to put against that bed near the wall, so your son can safely sleep there," she said.

I thanked her and as she showed me around her home Jim brought my belongings upstairs. I knew she offered us to stay that night but wasn't sure where we would go after that and before I could ask her, she and Jim assured me that they would work something out and that I wasn't to worry.

"We can't pay you enough, to rent any place in town, where you could walk to the store and then there's the problem of being able to pay for a sitter for Timmy. So Jim and I decided if you didn't mind staying in the two rooms above the shop, we could fix it up so you both can sleep there. You could use the restaurant kitchen when you needed to and there is a full bath upstairs. We use the rooms for storing supplies, but we can clear out one for you and your son. We won't charge you rent and you'll be able to pay for a babysitter. The building has central heating so you will find it nice and warm up there," she said.

"I can't thank you enough," I said. I couldn't believe my luck with such fine people, so the tears came.

"Please don't cry," Clara said, as she put her arm around me. "I know it's hard, what you've been through; taken away so young and then coming back and trying to fit in to—"

"Oh, you know about me?" I asked, surprised.

"Of course, news travels fast in these parts. From farm to farm, everyone knows everyone's business, I'm afraid."

"Then you might know Levi Yoder. I need to get word to him about how sorry I am for getting him mixed up in the mess I made of things."

"You mean, about helping the Kroger girl?"

"You know about that?" I was surprised she knew.

"Yes, of course, we all know. Noah's family belongs to our church."

I thought of Noah, and what Ruth said about them leaving the Amish and going into the outside world, or the English, as they called it. Having spent just a few hours with these fine people made me wonder why Noah would want to leave.

"Ruth told me he wants to leave the order," I said.

"Noah is sowing his oats, he'll come back, they usually do," she said, seeming unconcerned.

I was to learn much about the Amish world and the more liberal Mennonites and how many young men go live among the English before they take their final vows to remain Amish.

"I need to get word to Levi somehow, but I don't know what kind of punishment they gave him for helping me," I said.

Jim was sitting quietly listening to our conversation. "I'll see what I can find out about him," he said.

"Thanks, it would mean a great deal to me," I said, hoping he would bring me news of Levi.

I noticed the look exchanged between husband and wife, they smiled the kind of smile that told me they thought Levi and I might have feelings for each other. I was always sure of Levi's feelings, but certainly not my own. My need to see him had to do more with guilt than any amorous feelings I might have for him. At least that's what I told myself. I was desperate for a connection to anyone I could relate to and so far among the Amish, Levi seemed to be the only one. Levi was regarded as different, even by the Amish, which were a patriarchal society. I was drawn to him because he put women on an equal footing with men, much to his sister's chagrin. She considered her husband as manly and her brother as lacking in that department. I saw Levi as the kind man he was, nothing less and nothing more. I just plain liked him—a liking that I withheld for any of the other men.

CHAPTER 22

The room above the store was cleared out and Jim brought in a double iron bed for me. Clara found a used crib somewhere for Timmy and we settled down in our little warm nest. It was a shock to the system, but a pleasant shock, to have hot water at the tip of one's fingers and the bath upstairs was heaven. What I took for granted all my life felt like something new and wonderful. I helped in the restaurant and it wasn't hard work. The meals we served were mostly Amish meals consisting of fried chicken, mashed potatoes, vegetable dishes, various casseroles and sandwiches of all kinds. The front of the store wasn't large, just large enough for three small round tables in the center and six booths, three against each the wall. The very front held racks of various souvenirs of Amish life.

I found a woman who kept my son for me during the day and Rachel kept him on the weekends, our busiest days, were when the tourist season, would begin, I was told. Clara would open the shop on Sunday afternoon as soon as tourist season started, from spring through fall. She was closed on Sunday during the winter. On Sunday if I wanted, Jim would come and pick me up to spend the day at their home, and I did occasionally, but after being with someone everyday most of my life except for the time I rented Rita's apartment, I preferred to be alone with my son for a day. I played with him. I pulled him on a sled in the snow and he enjoyed it. I enjoyed him fully. It was a pleasure to spend so much time with him. At Emma's, I was always working and Timmy was left to the older children to watch, or Elsa or Emma shared him with me when the girls were at school.

It was nearing Christmas and it had been almost three weeks since I came to the Holsteder's. I would spend Christmas with the family. As liberal as they were in dress and appliances, they worshipped Christmas in the same way, no tree, or other decorations. The holiday was celebrated for two days. I went to church with them and everyone stared at me. It was the only time I attended their church services and to my surprise, Ruth and Noah came up to me to thank me for helping them. I learned they were now married and were still living with the

Mennonites. I was happy for them, but the one thing I hadn't heard anything about was Levi. Jim promised he would ask around and no one seemed to know. I was sure he was being shunned, or confined in some way. I knew he never came into town and when I lived with Emma, the Old Amish only went to town for supplies. I kept busy in the restaurant and never knew if any of them were in town since none of them came into Clara's shop. After Christmas, we had a larger snowstorm and I stayed home. A few days Clara didn't make it in, but I kept the shop open for the few customers that wandered in and I managed to serve them. I learned to make all the recipes Clara had, and was becoming a good cook.

In January 1960, it would be a whole decade since 1950 and the start of the Korean War. I couldn't believe I had been gone almost a year and a half and not a word of my missing in the news, or any papers I came across. It bothered me and I began to think about what could possibly be going on back home. There was television that many homes had and although the Amish didn't have any, you would have thought someone somewhere heard something about a missing woman and child. I felt bad about never letting Betty know how I made out, but I was afraid to make any contact with anyone back home. I thought, *what if they were tracing phone calls to all my friends*, and Dan knew I thought of Betty as a friend.

On the sixteenth of January, Timmy would be two years old and he was talking up a storm of quite a few words, but mostly gibberish. I thought it was cute. I worried over how mixed up he might be over me having to call him Timmy. The only word he never used was 'Daddy.' It bothered me that he didn't know what a father was. I was sure he heard the other children at Elsa's call Jacob, 'Daddy,' but I never heard him use it. The Amish celebrated birthday parties for their children in a big way. When I first came to Emma's in October of 1958, Timmy was almost nine months old. When his first birthday came the following January, my mind was in such a turmoil that I didn't remember his birthday until the very day. I had been with the Old Order just a few months when I realized it was his birthday, Elsa made a cake and her children helped us celebrate by sharing ice cream and cake and singing to him, but he didn't know what was going on.

Turning two years old with the Holsteder's was going to be a big celebration for him. The two young Holsteder boys, Rachel, and her two married sister's, one with a newborn baby of her own, would be attending his birthday party. Clara insisted on having it at her home with her entire family present. The Holsteders thought of me as family in the short time I had been in their lives and I was grateful for that.

In early April the weather began to slowly warm up, melting what remained of the winter snow. It was a Tuesday morning, when Clara and I were preparing the menu of the day, when Jim burst in the door of the shop calling for us. We were in the kitchen and customers hadn't started to arrive yet since it wasn't lunchtime. I ran out to see Jim, and to my surprise, there was Levi. Without thinking my first impulse was to run to him and he moved at the same time and before I realized it we were in each other's arms. He hugged me tight until both of us became aware of Jim and feeling embarrassed we quickly parted.

"Where have you been?" I asked, not thinking of what else to say.

Jim smiled and said, "I ran into him just down the street working at the lumber yard behind the hardware shop."

"I have a job here, and I live nearby with the kids," Levi said, proudly.

"What about your sister Miriam? Does she still take care of the kids?" I wasn't sure of what he was doing. "What are you doing working in town? Didn't they punish you in some way for that night?" I asked. I was confused.

Jim suggested we sit down so Levi could explain. We sat in a booth and Jim went in the back, I guess to explain what was going on to Clara. I looked at Levi and he looked a little different or maybe it was my imagination. He still had his beard, but his eyes seemed brighter. I had my hands on the table, fingers intertwined waiting to hear his story. He reached over and took them in his and although it felt nice to have a man hold my hands, it was the way he looked at me—I felt a little uneasy.

"That night on the road, they stopped me and gave me hell because they knew you were missing, as well as Ruth. They had been to the Fishers before we even reached Noah's. Her parents came home just minutes after we left. That was close," he said, as he rolled his eyes in the realization we could have been caught before we were able to get Ruth out.

"What was your punishment?" I asked, "I'm sure you had to face it the next day. What did you tell them about me? Did you tell them anything at all that night?"

"Lizzy, I didn't have to tell them anything, they knew it was me, and I knew what was coming the next day, shunning or worse. I didn't wait to find out."

"What do you mean, you left? — You never met with the Bishop?"

"No, I went home, late as it was, and took the kids out of their beds telling Miriam I was leaving. She looked shocked, she didn't know what was going on, and I didn't stop to tell her. I piled them into the buggy and took off, for where I didn't know, until I could think straight. I remembered this farmer I worked for once, he's Amish but not Old Order, and he lives alone, kind of cut off from the others. He has a small place about five miles from here. I felt sorry for my kids having to be in the buggy and the cold for that long ride, but I couldn't think of anywhere else to go. Henry is sort of a recluse among the Amish. He doesn't attend any church service but still considers himself one of them. He keeps to himself and the Amish leave him alone. I knew I could count on him, so he put us up for the night."

I admired Levi for the guts he had, but I felt responsible for him having to leave at all. The feeling I had at that moment was a feeling of responsibility and I didn't know how I could help him without feeling trapped by his situation.

"Levi, I'm so sorry, its all my fault getting you mixed up in this mess. I never intended for this to happen, please forgive me," I said.

"It's not your fault at all, if it wasn't this, it would have been some other thing that gave me the push to leave. Lizzy, after my wife died, I thought often of maybe going over to another more easy church group or maybe the Mennonites, so you see, it wasn't you."

I always felt Levi was different and what he was telling me just confirmed what I had suspected, that he didn't belong in the Old Order, not the kind of man *he* was. He told me how he stayed with the old man until he could find a job.

"Who takes care of your children?" I asked.

"I found an English woman here in town. She's a lady I did some carpentry work for last year."

"Where do you live?"

"I rent one of her apartments and I work for anyone who hires me. I have plenty of jobs to help pay the rent and to pay her for the kids."

I had heard that Levi was a master carpenter as were most Amish men when they weren't farming. He was still holding on to my hands and I quickly drew them back when Jim came in. A few customers came into the store and I had to begin to serve them, so I stood up to say goodbye and wished him luck. Jim and Levi left together.

I thought of Levi's children. I felt sorry for them, wondering how being taken away from the only home they had known was affecting them. I mentioned it to Clara.

"Jim is building a new chicken coop, the old one has seen its day, do you think Levi would like to come over on Sunday and help. Jim can use an extra hand and he can bring his children. We can have a picnic supper outdoors. Rachel loves small children," she said, laughingly, "Look at how she is with Jenny's baby and your Timmy."

Against my better judgment, I heard myself say, "Oh, that would be nice." There wasn't anything else I could have said. I knew it would make things worse as far as trying not to encourage Levi. I was sorry I mentioned his children to Clara. It was the guilt I felt and also I had a soft spot for children, especially children without a mother.

I guess Jim invited Levi because on Sunday afternoon he showed up with all three children. His baby was now running around and Rachel took to her like she did to my son. His two boys ran around with Jim and Clara's boys. All the commotion, the kids running around and the noise, reminded me of the time all the children ran around yelling during the barn raising I attended. The men in the Old Order kept most of the young boys between six and twelve busy pounding nails into the lower boards on the barn. At the Holsteder's, their two boys ten and thirteen weren't helping Jim and Levi, just chasing the little kids around. It was quite a contrast to Jacob's poor boys who where made to do the work of men.

I didn't talk with Levi much that afternoon because he was busy helping Jim with the new chicken coop and Clara and I remained inside getting supper cooked. When everything was ready, she sent Rachel to get the men and gather the children around the outdoor table. The weather was warm, the sun was out, and it was a nice day to spend outdoors. Levi and Jim came up and Jim sat down, but Levi came up to me where I was standing placing plates and napkins on the table.

"Here, let me do that for you," he said. Before I could protest, he took them out of my hands and finished setting the table. I looked at Jim and his reaction was to smile. What a contrast to the men of the Old Order, I thought. After the meal was over and the children ran off to play, Jim mentioned how far along they were with the new chicken coop. He got up from the table to carry some plates in with Clara when he looked back at Levi and said, "Why don't you show Lizzy what a good carpenter you are. He had some better ideas on the design than I had."

How I wished Jim hadn't said that, because I found myself alone with Levi, out of sight of anyone else, once he led me to the new building. It was bad enough that I allowed him to take me by the hand, but once standing behind the coop he never let go and before I knew it he grabbed me and kissed me full on the lips. I can't say it wasn't a pleasant feeling, it was, and I liked and admired him, but I was trapped in the moment and confused about what I was feeling. I felt I was hanging on for dear life between two worlds, and Levi belonged in only one of them. I knew I had to do something before this went any further, or there would be no turning back. I had to make another move, and uproot my son and myself again. I had to remind myself that I was still married to Dan. I was twenty-seven years old and more confused and constantly upset than I ever was. I dreaded Levi telling me he loved me, because I knew he did, or asking me to marry him, because I knew he eventually would, so I had to think straight, be reasonable, and act, soon.

I pulled out of his embrace, and it was hard to do. I wanted to be in his arms, I wanted to be kissed again, but I knew it was wrong. I was a married woman and my Catholic guilt wouldn't allow me to let it go on.

That night sleep wouldn't come; I had to have a plan. I couldn't just up and leave, not after what this fine family had done for me. I couldn't disappear on Levi without an explanation, and hurt him like that. I started thinking about what might be happening back home. I knew I would have to get the courage to make a call to Betty, but how, and when?

CHAPTER 23

In June, I found myself with the Holsteders, biding my time until I could get up the courage to make that call to Betty. I couldn't bring myself to do it and my relationship with Levi was getting to a point where I was getting in deeper as far as my feelings for him were at that time. In a way I thought I loved him, but with reservations, about my feelings, not his. I watched him struggle with the gulf between the Old Order he left, and English world and maybe the Mennonites he espoused to join. He asked me out to a horse show and unable to hurt his feelings, I went. We were leaning against the rail fence watching the horses going through their performances when he wistfully said, "Why am I checking out horses? I should be learning to drive a car."

I could see the painful expression on his face. He put his arm around me and feeling sorry for him, I let him. The last time he touched me was at the Holsteder's behind the chicken coop, when he kissed me. He stopped by the store twice back in May but except for that, we hadn't spent any other time together. What a dilemma I found myself in. I was lonely and missed him when he wasn't around and I was nervous when he was.

Jim and Clara encouraged our friendship, that's what I told them it was, but they didn't believe me, I'm sure. At night I would lie awake thinking, *If only I knew what Dan was doing, what was happening back home?* I had very little sleep, and I was caught up in a web of lies, but fear of returning home kept me from doing anything. I was afraid of Dan and the power he could have over me. I was sure if I returned, he would find a way, both he and his mother, to declare me a kidnapper of his child and I might lose Timmy, or worse Dan might have killed that girl, or he might have totally cracked up and would kill me if I returned. All those thoughts were going through my mind and I couldn't share my fears with anyone.

On the buggy ride back to the restaurant, Levi apologized for the horse and buggy ride knowing the Holsteders drove me in their car. I thought he was ashamed of the transportation he was stuck with. That's the impression he gave me.

"I don't mind the buggy at all," I said, "It's summer and it's fun to ride this way when it's nice and warm out."

He looked at me like he didn't believe me. "I'm going to take driving lessons," he said, "then first chance I get, I'll get myself a car."

Levi still kept his beard but I noticed quite a few Mennonite men had shaved their faces. It was a matter of choice in the most liberal of the Mennonites. I wondered what Levi would look like without his beard. I remembered Miriam said he looked better with the beard. He looked at me when he parked the buggy and complimented me on my dress. I began to wear more colorful print or bright solid colors, not as drab as the other Amish, but I still wore the little white cap and my hair was always pinned up in a bun like Clara and her daughter's. I enjoyed the horse show and thanked him. He made no move toward me except to take my hand for a moment.

"Thanks Levi," I said, "It was fun," before I climbed out of the buggy, and crossed the street to the restaurant. Clara was waiting for me, about to close up for the day. It was at her suggestion that I accepted Levi's invitation.

"Lizzy, he's a good catch and a very sweet man. You could do worse."

"Yes, yes I know, but I'm afraid of hurting him and I don't want that to happen."

"Why would you hurt him?" she asked, giving me a quizzical look.

I couldn't tell her the real reason so I had to think fast after saying that without thinking.

"I like him, but I don't think that's enough," I lied, knowing that he was growing on me and what I felt when he touched me was a great deal more than just liking a person.

Not having parents and growing up without a family left me feeling empty until I met Tim. For a short time Tim gave me a sense of belonging, if only just to him, but with Levi, he came with children. Against my better judgment, I thought, I began to feel sorry for them, and I knew they needed a mother. They filled an emptiness that even my own son alone couldn't fill completely. Watching Timmy run around with Levi's little Alice, who turned two in April and his two boys, Samuel and Paul, soon to be six and four years of age gave me a sense of family. In between spending more time with Levi's family and thinking about what was happening back home, I knew I needed to do something and soon. I was a married woman, keeping company with a single man and his family. It wasn't fair to him, not even thinking about the moral aspect of it. Although Levi and I never got beyond kissing and general attempts of showing affection to each other, my Catholic upbringing left me with the feeling I was being unfaithful.

On one trip we took by buggy, to a wooded area for a picnic with the children, there was a river nearby that was great for fishing. Levi planned on taking his boys and Timmy down to the river's edge to see if he could catch a fish for them. I set up the blanket and picnic basket of food while caring for Alice. After laying the blanket down and sitting, waiting for Levi to come back, Alice climbed into my lap and to keep her from wandering off I began to sing a little lullaby that I often sang to Timmy. Her little blond head resting against my chest while I held her caused me to be filled with emotion and then the tears came. I didn't know what I was feeling—wishing she were my daughter? Wishing I were her, being held by a mother? Wishing she was Tim's child? Wishing Tim would be here instead of Levi? Wishing I had never married Dan? But then wishing all that would have meant I wouldn't have had my son. By the time Levi came back with the boys, I looked a mess. He could tell I had been crying, but didn't say anything until after we finished our picnic lunch and Alice and Timmy had fallen asleep on the blanket. The two older boys were playing off to the side catching bugs in a jar that we had given them. Levi took my hand in his.

"What's wrong?" he asked, "Lizzy, tell me, please."

The tender expression on his face and the way he cupped my chin in his hand, the way he looked at me, I fell apart in his arms. I cried like I had never cried before and he held me tight, saying nothing until I finally I had to compose myself.

"I love you Lizzy, whatever it is, I'm here for you, so please tell me. If it's this way of life you find hard and you're missing living among the English, I could fix that."

I looked up at him and moved away, "What do you mean? You

would leave the Amish and live outside the religion forever?"

"Yes, if that's what you wanted, of course I would, I'm almost doing it now."

I pulled my hand out of his, not letting him touch me, thinking, *My God, what have I gotten myself into? What have I gotten him into? I'm married, I can't tell him that. I'm Kathleen Kelly Robson, not Elizabeth Brown and I can't tell him that either.*

What could I say to him that wouldn't devastate him? Absolutely nothing.

"It isn't anything, I get this way every once in a while," I said.

"Oh, I understand, it's that time, huh," he said.

I nodded my head, confirming what he thought and thinking of how sensitive he was that he would think of that. He moved closer to me and I couldn't hurt him so I let him hold me again. I let him kiss me, many times. I was mixed up in my feelings and while I lay in his arms watching his two boys running around, I was thinking, *why am I letting this go on like this? Why can't I do what I must before things get worse?* I was afraid of what would be coming if I didn't do something.

Later that night after Timmy and I were back in our little cocoon of a room, where I felt safe, I tried to put what happened out of my mind, but I couldn't. I was awake for many hours. In the morning when Clara came in, she could see I hadn't slept well. She didn't say anything. After I took Timmy to the sitter and returned, she sat me down in a booth for a talk. "Give me ten minutes before we set up for the day," she said. "Now tell me what's wrong, you don't look well and you look tired and upset, I want to know."

"I'm afraid Levi is going to ask me to marry him, and I'm not ready for that yet."

"Is it because he has three children? I know that it's quite a responsibility to take on," she said, looking at me like she understood what an undertaking that would be for any woman.

"It's not that at all," I said, trying to come up with a better excuse. "I'm not sure if I love him enough to marry him,"

"Love grows after you're married, at least it was that way for Jim and me," she said, like it was a natural evolution in marriage. Having lived with the Amish long enough to realize they didn't think of falling in love with someone was all that important at least not in the Old Order. Love came from living together. What I viewed didn't look like the love I expected in a marriage. I began to think *if only I were free of Dan*, I might cast aside everything I had known, and maybe it would work, then I thought of how would it work when I didn't want to live the rest of my life as Amish. When Levi mentioned he would leave, I thought of his lack of education, would he become frustrated, would he feel inferior, lose his confidence, bring stress into the marriage? Of course it couldn't happen at all, I was married to Dan. I had to keep reminding myself of that. Clara mentioned the large gathering that would take place at one of the Mennonite farms in August. Another barn raising and I was expected to attend with all her family. We would celebrate Samuel's sixth birthday that month.

"Don't worry about anything Lizzy, just look forward to the gathering this weekend, it'll be fun. Lets get back to the kitchen," she said.

I followed her and put all my negative thoughts aside for the day. I needed to keep busy.

The first Saturday in August came and we worked in the restaurant. When the last lunch customer left, we closed up. It would be almost three pm before we arrived at the gathering. Everyone was there, including Levi and his children, and the Holsteder family including Rachel who was minding Timmy and Levi's children. Timmy ran to me with Alice trying to keep up, as well as little Paul. His children were becoming attached to me, and I felt guilty about that. All the women were preparing the supper for when the men would finish for the day. I marveled at how quickly the Amish could put up a large barn in one day. The building was set quite a distance from the house, so from where I was viewing it, the men in their black pants or bib overalls reminded me of at least a few dozen ants crawling all over its sides and roof. In winter the Amish and Mennonite men wore black hats, in summer straw hats, and the women always wore the little white caps, but some wore black when going into town shopping or to church services.

We were at the Kirkman farm, a family I didn't know at all, but had come across a few times. One of Mrs. Kirkman's sisters had gone over to the Old Order I was told, but they still saw each other. It was mostly Mrs. Kirkman's sister who came to visit her. Olive, a woman I just met filled me in on all the gossip about the sisters.

"The sisters didn't speak to each other for a few years," Olive said, "but they got over it. The Old Order sister usually brings her all the gossip she hears about the various groups. It's a sin to gossip like that you know. Olive thinks it's lies she spreads."

I wondered what Clara would think if she knew the lie I was living and the real me. That thought almost paralyzed me and I pushed it to the back of my mind. Clara introduced me to a few other women I hadn't met and we worked in the kitchen together preparing the meal. I enjoyed the Mennonite women who were more jovial and open with their conversations. Laughter was one of their endearing traits; they seemed to take great joy in teasing each other and joking around. I listened to their conversations but didn't have anything to contribute to the merriment. One of the women was whispering to another and the laughter stopped.

"No, you must be joking," one said to the other. I couldn't hear what was being said, but Olive joined them and soon there were four women huddled together. I didn't feel comfortable going over to them so I kept busy with peeling the mountain of potatoes piled high on the table. The group broke up and went back to their individual dishes they were preparing. Olive came over to me.

"You won't believe what I just heard," she said.

"What did you hear?" I asked, wanting to hear what I was sure was a bit of gossip.

"The rumor is that someone in one of the Amish Orders, I don't know which one, it's not Mennonite, had a woman living with her that she thought was her sister or cousin or some other supposed family member for awhile and the woman thinks it was all a sham. She discovered that her family member had a large wine mark on her body that was missing on this person, but she also noticed some other flaws as time went on that didn't match. They say the so-called relative left the Order."

I froze, almost unable to speak. Clara knew nothing about the Fisher family, didn't know them, and all she knew about me was I was shunned for helping Noah and Ruth. She knew me as Elizabeth Brown and so did Levi, but a name wasn't mentioned when the woman repeated the tale. No one knew who it was. I pretended to be interested.

"Did they say what family that was?" I asked, trying to keep my voice from quivering.

"No, there are so many families and who knows what Order of Amish it's from. It could just be gossip."

The rest of the day I spent in a fog, knowing that I couldn't go on this way. Sooner or later I would be found out. So far I had been lucky, no one came into the shop from the Fisher family and I wondered about that since it was Jacob who brought me to Clara. He seemed to know her, or maybe he didn't know her that well, just knew of the shop. As far as I knew, Levi had no contact with them since he left, not even with his sister. But it could be only a matter of time. I was sure with Levi gone from the order, Emma's suspicions would eventually reach Levi's sister Miriam. I had been with the Holsteders almost nine months, and knowing Emma, who desperately wanted to believe I was her niece, I hoped it would take some time for her to add it all up. How I got through the day, I don't know. I went through the motion. When serving supper Levi sensed I wasn't myself. I noticed he had shaved his beard very short, just a stubble of a beard remained and I thought he looked quite handsome, and his chin wasn't like Elsa described at all.

"I'll take you home tonight," he said, "we need to talk."

I knew in my heart that I couldn't stay with these fine people much longer; I needed to make that call to Betty. I had to bite the bullet and go home and face whatever needed facing. I couldn't keep running and most importantly I had to divorce Dan, and free myself. I had friends back home that would stand by me, vouch for me, I had Betty, Rita, Angie and the entire Martino family, also the police department. I was sure by this time someone noticed how Dan was becoming unstable, ready to come apart if he hadn't already, with my disappearance.

Levi took us home and once we were in the buggy, he said he wanted to have some time alone with me, to talk. "We need to be alone, without the children," he said. I agreed. I owed him at least that much. Except for those few minutes behind the chicken coop we always had our children with us whenever we were together. He said he would get the English woman to look after his children for a few hours. He planned on coming back to the store, so I put Timmy to bed and waited downstairs. When I heard him at the door I quickly opened it, hoping no one noticed him. It was dark and I purposely had the outdoor light turned off. As soon as he entered and closed the door behind him, he pulled me into his arms. I was too weak both physically and emotionally to refuse his embrace. We went into a booth to sit beside each other.

"Are you okay? I hope you're ready to tell me how you feel, because I need to tell you," he said. "I love you Lizzy and I want to marry you, if you'll have me."

"You're the finest man I know, Levi, truly, but I have to go back home to straighten out a few things before I can give you any answers."

He was holding me close. "Where is home? With the English?"

"Yes, it is, and I need to go back for awhile before I can make any decisions."

"Do what you have to," he said, "I'll wait. Remember, I love you."

He kissed me and we sat there holding each other for quite a while. He didn't ask me any more questions and I didn't commit my feelings to him because I wasn't sure of my feelings. I wasn't sure of anything.

CHAPTER 24

It had been raining all night in August 1960 and he threw his muddy shoes and socks in a dumpster so he wouldn't bring mud into his car. After breathing heavily, exhausted and sweating from the August humidity, and from all the tension that built up, he was relieved, and ready to switch off the demon and return to himself. The woman was a little heavier than the others and he had to drag her body far enough away from the road and deeper into the woods. Many times he promised himself it wouldn't happen again, but the tension would build and the demon he tried so desperately to control always appeared to release itself in him. He told himself it wasn't him, it was *it*, the thing that invaded him and it was *it* that forced him into the monster he wasn't.

Driving straight into the garage, he turned off the motor and closed the door behind him. Remaining seated behind the wheel, he lit the cigarette so badly needed. The garage was his oasis, where he kept extra clothing, shoes, and socks, everything that would be needed. After purchasing two of everything to match what he would be wearing when he went out with *it,* he kept them well hidden, locked in a large metal toolbox. Inhaling deeply as he smoked, and still trying to catch his breath, he dug into his shirt pocket for the only item he ever kept of his victims, a driver's license or some other ID or a piece of their jewelry. Keeping them in the locked box with all the newspaper clippings of the crimes was the proof he needed of what the monster made him do.

Always priding himself on being smart and clever, he was devastated over that one mistake, and would never be that careless again. Acting carefully, not wanting the police from his town snooping around, he chose his victims carefully by making sure they were from the city of Chicago. Investigating a crime committed in the big city was out of his town's jurisdiction. How was he to know that one time the woman was from *the town he lived in.* He wouldn't make that mistake again and he didn't, going deeper into the city for the last two. He convinced himself he could keep everything in check, but just that one mistake with the woman from Arden was his Achilles heel. He searched for his service pin after he got home. It was missing and he was afraid he lost it in the weeds where the body was, but there was no mention of it when her body was found. The sheriff wouldn't let go of the crime. He was the first on the scene, being it was in his county and he kept investigating the murder, snooping around, wouldn't give it up. He was getting too close. He tried to deflect the direction of the investigation by trying to implicate the Sheriff, but it didn't work. Hating to do what needed to be done, he kept the Sheriff close, as his best friend, what better way to keep a step ahead of the law, and to know every step the Sheriff's department took. Sheriff Dan took his work too serious, asking too many questions and he was the best Sheriff in the department, so when he got the chance, he planted that driver's license of the victim, in the laundry the day he went to smooth over the sheriff's marital problems. He couldn't understand why Dan's wife hadn't found it. She would have turned it in to the police, he was sure, because she suspected her husband was having problems and she was afraid of him. Maybe after she disappeared his mother found it and thinking it implicated her son she disposed of it.

The Sheriff's dogged determination in solving the murder made him fear the worst, maybe it was the sheriff who found it. He knew the man had a volatile temper but he didn't believe what his own daughter suggested, that Dan might have done something to Kathleen. He brushed that ridiculous assumption aside knowing Dan loved his son and the baby was missing too. Dan was emotionally destroyed when her car was found in the canal and the search for their bodies was in vain. Two weeks after they dragged the canal he thought Dan was on to him, playing a cat and mouse game with him—maybe Dan found the license and knowing he was the only person in their apartment that morning that could have planted the license there.

At his wits end, he had to do something. He didn't know what happened to the license or to the Sheriff's wife. He called over to the Sheriff's department asking Dan to meet him at the bar they frequented after his shift was over, and before going home. As he entered the bar he mentioned he thought someone was trying to break into the back of the store across the road. The Sheriff was going to call it in, but he suggested they walk over first to make sure. He didn't want anyone else there. As they approached the building, he knew it had to be now. It was easy, he was a cop himself, he knew the ropes, and he could make it look like he was killed in the line of duty. Everyone knew the Sheriff was under stress, and coming apart even before his wife went missing and with her disappearance it put him over the edge, he became careless, not quick enough, police work was dangerous, the robber got off the first shot. He also knew the Sheriff wore a bulletproof vest that night having come straight from another case and would approach with a gun in hand. The Sheriff led the way walking a few feet in front of him to the back of the store.

The next day the headlines read; 'Arden's Sheriff, Dan Robson, was killed in the line of duty during a robbery at the Winston store. Sergeant Sal Martino, his back up man, pursued the shooter over back yard fences but the criminal got away. Sergeant Martino said the sheriff was a friend of many years. The Sergeant called for backup and the police are searching diligently for the robber. Martino was devastated and blamed himself for not having the Sheriff's back, quick enough.'

Everyone bought the story, and he breathed a sigh of relief and told himself he should lay low and not let the demon control him, but here he was, once again having to clean up after another victim for what *it* forced him to do. Smoking another cigarette, he got out of the car and began to change his clothing. From the large steel box he took out the exact matching shirt, pants, shoes and socks he was wearing when he left home. Always afraid there might be the woman's hair on his shirt or pants and not wanting his wife to handle his dirty clothing, he put them in a plastic bag and locked it in the trunk of his car, feeling relieved knowing he would burn it the next day. He walked over to the sink he had installed in the garage against his wife's wishes, telling her he needed it to wash up after working in the yard. It came in handy on nights like this. Dressed in clean clothing he left the garage, walking up to the back door of his home looking the same as when he had left—like the proud family man and brave cop his friends and family knew.

CHAPTER 25

Levi understood my wanting to return home, and when I confided to Clara at the end of August of what I had to do, she understood too. They thought I was Elizabeth Brown wanting to return to my deceased husbands' place and maybe see his family. They all thought my Amish mother who ran away and took me with her years before had died. I told the same story to them that I told the Fishers. All the lies were becoming hard to bear. I spent the weekend saying goodbye to the Holsteders at their home. On Monday I didn't want to call from the restaurant afraid the call might be traced to that number, so I waited a few days and made the call from a phone booth in town. Betty would be ready to close up on Saturday just before five, Chicago time, so I called her place of business.

When she heard my voice, all she could say over and over was, "Oh my God! Kathleen, where are you? Are you okay?" I assured her I was, but didn't tell her where I was. Before I could ask her anything, she very excitedly yelled into the phone, "Kathleen! Dan is dead! He was killed during a robbery!"

I was stunned, unable to speak for a moment, "Hello, are you there?" I heard her say, "Yes, Yes, I am," I answered, and then she filled me in on all the details. I started to ask questions, but all she said was, "Come home Kathleen, come home." I promised I would as soon as I settled things where I was, and that I would call her again, when I was ready to leave. "I'll come back by bus and call you when we arrive," I said. She told me she would fill me in on everything she knew and that she now had her own apartment and we could stay with her as long as I needed. I thanked her and left that booth feeling free for the first time.

Later that evening I called Levi and asked him to come over after we closed up for the day and Clara went home. I needed to see him again before I left. I put Timmy to bed and went downstairs to wait for him. When he arrived, we sat together in a booth where it was comfortable, in the dark, so it didn't look like the shop was open. After he kissed me, he held me and for the first time I didn't feel like I was doing anything wrong. Dan had been dead the whole time I was missing. My relationship with Levi took on a new meaning and I sat in his arms free to let him hold me without feeling uncomfortable. I said nothing for a few minutes, not knowing what to say, but at the same time the freedom I felt hearing I was a widow, left me for the first time with the dilemma of telling the truth to him and risk losing his respect. I knew I couldn't leave this life and these fine people without being honest with them. I made up my mind to tell Levi first and then the Holsteders. Whatever their reaction, I would accept it and go home. I might never see them again, but I needed to be honest. It was the hardest decision I ever had to make. I told myself, he would get over me and find a nice woman to love. I sat in his arms thinking all that.

"What's wrong, you're quiet tonight. Have you changed your mind about making that trip home?" he asked, probably hoping I had.

"Everything's wrong," I said.

I was surprised that I didn't feel any sorrow over Dan's death and yet I had to tell myself, he was my son's father, so I should have felt something, but I wasn't able to feel anything. I thought maybe it would hit me later, after I returned home. Levi took his arm away and moved to face me.

"What do you mean, everything's wrong?" He looked worried.

"I'm not who you think I am," I said, my voice failing me and then I started to cry. All he could do was hold me again and wait until I was ready to speak. I told him about my life in the orphanage in Illinois, my love for Tim who perished in Korea, my marriage, running away, Otto picking me up that night in his buggy mistaking me for a relative. I told him everything. I waited for him to say something, to be shocked, angry, or at least disappointed. But he never let go of holding me and I knew then how much he cared. It made me feel worse.

"That's all behind you now," he said, "Don't beat yourself up over it, it's done."

"But all this time, I thought I was a married woman and I let you kiss me, led you on, it wasn't right."

"But you weren't married, so don't let it bother you. Go home, make that visit, and call me when you're ready to come back."

When he said that, I felt like the lowest of the low. I had deep feelings for him and knew I wouldn't be coming back, because I couldn't live in his world, but could never tell him that, not after just unloading what I considered a land mine on the man. I would worry about that later. I told myself once I was gone for a time, it would make it easier to say goodbye in a letter or phone call. I was a coward.

"How am I going to tell all this to the Holsteders?" I asked.

"Don't tell them anything, you've been through enough, leave it to me to explain, once you're gone. It will be easier on you. I'll explain why you couldn't tell anyone and how you've lived in fear all this time."

I looked at him and felt terrible. In a way I loved Levi, but what I felt was only here in his world, in mine it might disappear. It was not the same as the intense feelings I had for Tim. I wasn't sure what love was. I never felt loved as a child and what I had with Dan wasn't love, but my needing someone who I thought loved *me*. We sat together for a long time. I had used Levi and with my single status I was feeling real guilty. I remembered how I regretted not being able to make love to Tim. We were kids, and it wasn't done back then, but now I was soon to be a twenty-eight-year-old woman and Levi was a thirty-one-year-old man. How unfair I had been to him. How could I ever make it up to him? And what would his beliefs allow. After the emotional few hours, we had both been through, I wanted to make things better, but wondered if it would make it worse for him in the end. He kissed me again and it was getting late. I moved to get out of the booth and he got up holding on to my hand. He didn't make a move to go to the door, so I turned and still holding my hand, he followed me up the stairs.

CHAPTER 26

The bus pulled into the same station I had left from, and on the 12th of September I returned with Timmy and my one suitcase. Before I left Pennsylvania, I had to buy us new clothes. When I left home I found myself traveling back in time, now I was traveling into the future. My son was over two and a half years old, when we returned home that September of 1960. I wondered what Dan's mother would say when she found out we were alive. Maybe after having lost her only child she might have mellowed, I hoped. How would I explain my disappearance? What could I say to her about her son? Certainly not much—what would it serve to tell her how badly he behaved, or what I found in his clothing. I figured she suffered enough with his untimely death. I would tell her I left because he wasn't kind to me and his drinking was becoming more than I was willing to put up with, and I left in the way I did because I was afraid of him. I would leave the gritty details out. She wouldn't believe me and I was sure she might not believe what little I was willing to tell her.

I made a call to Betty to let her know we arrived. Timmy and I waited in the bus terminal for her. When she came, we embraced and I was so happy to see her. She likewise was happy to see me again and said how much Tommy had grown. I told her to address him as Timmy and not Tommy because I changed our names when we left. She knew I didn't choose his name and how upset I was about it when he was born, so it didn't come as a surprise to her. She also knew about my love for Tim. When I worked for her family and we became close, we confided in each other, so she knew about everyone in my life, but no one knew her.

On the ride to her apartment, she told me we would stop at her parents to pick up her son. Her parents were gracious and happy to see me. Her father offered me my job back at their store, but I knew I would need to find full time work also, and soon. On the way to her apartment, her son Rickey who was now eight years old, kept Timmy amused in the back seat of the car.

"Where have you been all this time?" Betty asked.

"It's a long story, I'll tell you everything," I said, and I did, once we got the boys to bed. Betty and I sat up most of the night and she listened while I explained the entire time with the Amish. I told her about Levi, and my relationship with him and his children. When I finished all she could say at first was "Wow!"

"Kathleen, Levi sounds like such a nice man, what a shame he's Amish."

"He's as nice as I explained, maybe in my description of him I didn't do him enough justice."

She told me everything she knew about Dan's death, most of what she read in the papers and on television. I sensed that Betty was looking at me strangely, like she wanted to comment about something else but held back. She was quiet and didn't ask any questions, but suggested we retire for the night. She had a pull out sofa bed that I would sleep on and I helped her with getting it ready. We put Timmy in the bottom of the bunk beds she had in Ricky's room. She mentioned how Rickey wanted bunk beds and always slept on the top bunk. At first she didn't think it was necessary but he loved climbing up the ladder in the store, so she bought it. Now she was glad she did and so was I.

The next morning Betty announced we should take the boys out shopping for Rickey's school clothes. School had started after Labor Day and it was more than a week later when I arrived. She wasn't going into the shop this day and asked if I didn't mind tagging along.

"Of course not, I need to pick up an outfit for Timmy. All he has is what I bought him to make the trip home and a few pants and shirts the Amish kids wear," I said.

All I had left was a hundred dollars after I bought my bus ticket and the clothing we would need to come home in. I knew I needed to work and make some money soon, and later that week I found myself back in the dry cleaning shop part time and then I found a full time job next door at a grocery store as a cashier. It didn't pay as much as I had hoped but it was better than nothing. I had been with Betty for two weeks and she found a woman she knew to take care of Timmy when I was at work. When I worked in the dry cleaning shop on Saturdays, I was able to take my son with me. There was a back room where

Rickey would play when he was small and that's where we kept Timmy in between tending our customers and arranging the clothing in the back. The little room held her father's desk, and enough of Rickey's toys to keep him busy.

In the days we were together I made no effort to contact anyone and each time a costumer came into either store I worked in, I held my breath that it wasn't anyone I knew. I wasn't ready to see anyone and I was afraid of what the reaction would be. I thought of all I put the police department through searching for me, and dragging the Canal. I was able to acquire my new job using my maiden name, Kelly, to remain anonymous, because the name Robson was well known having been in all the papers due to my disappearance, and Dan's death. I was sure Betty wanted to tell me something, but was holding back. One night two weeks after I had returned, and after the children had gone to bed, I asked her if anything was wrong.

"Kathleen, I'm not sure of this because I forgot about your first boyfriend until you called your son by that name, then I remembered he went to Korea and you said he went missing. About a year and a half ago there was a newspaper article about a South Korean Soldier and an American Marine who escaped from some North Korean Gulag and made it to Japan. Some Japanese freighter picked them up from a small boat in the Sea of Japan. I wondered if it could be him, but it was a far-fetched idea, after all, many Americans went missing."

"Why didn't you tell me?" I asked, excitedly.

"I didn't want to get your hopes up when the chances it would be him were so slim. The article didn't give too much information, but I remembered he was from the Chicago area."

"Do you have it?"

"No, I don't."

I wasn't going to get in touch with Angie yet and thought I would wait another week, until I was settled. Now I knew I had to call her. I couldn't wait any longer. That night, I got out the little book of phone numbers I kept hidden in my locked suitcase when I lived in hiding. I was as nervous as I was the night Otto brought me to Emma, maybe even more so. I hoped she had the same number. I heard it ring twice and then the soft voice I remembered, answered.

"Hello, Angie?" I heard my shaky voice say. "It's me, Kathleen, I'm back."

There was silence and then she screamed, "Oh my God! Kathleen, where have you been? Do you know about Dan?"

"Yes, yes, I know he was killed, while working," I said.

"When can I see you? I have so much to tell you. Where are you now?" she asked.

"I'm staying with a friend but I don't have a car yet. Are you still working?"

"No, I can meet you any time."

"There's a restaurant on the corner of where I work so meet me when I get off work," I said.

I gave her the directions and told her not to tell anyone I was back yet. She promised she wouldn't. I told Betty when I left for work the next morning, I was meeting Angie and she said she would pick Timmy up from the sitter.

I was a complete wreck waiting for her as I sat in a booth in the back corner of the little sandwich shop where we were to meet. She arrived rushing in the door and I stood up and waved to her. She came quickly to me and hugged me.

"Oh Kathleen, so much has happened."

"Is everyone angry at me for leaving like I did," I asked.

"Well, at first it was terrible, everyone thought you had drowned in the canal."

"Yes, I can imagine, but I had to get away from Dan, he was so crazy, Angie, and I didn't think anyone believed me. He tried to choke me and I was afraid he might kill me."

She listened to me and agreed. It made me feel better; I knew she always believed me. I reminded her that her father thought it was me who had problems.

"Oh, he changed his mind about that," she said, "He could see how unraveled Dan was becoming after you disappeared, and he tried to get him off for a while convincing the Sheriff's department to give Dan a leave of absence, but Dan was stubborn and refused to leave and take time off. About two weeks later Dan was killed. My Dad feels real bad because he was with him, but couldn't save him."

I felt bad for Sergeant Martino; I knew how close he and Dan were. Angie looked at me funny and said, "I need to tell you something, it's about Tim—"

"Oh, I think I know what you're going to say, was it Tim who was found?"

She looked surprised, "How did you know?"

"Betty, the woman I work for read some article in the paper and wondered if it was him."

"Well, it was," she said, anxious to tell me. "He's been back about a year now and he's at his old job in the police department. My Dad helped get him back on, about six months ago. I heard he went through quite an ordeal, but he doesn't like to talk about it, according to my Dad."

I was excited, anxious, happy and so on cloud nine. I wanted to know how he was, and if was he okay.

"He's not the same guy you remembered," she said, and then shook her head sadly.

"Kathleen, he's aged. His hair is almost gray and he's only thirty. He's been through a lot."

"Did he ask about me?" I asked, with apprehension.

"I'm sure he was told by his parents what happened to you because when you disappeared it was in all the papers. They had your name as Kathleen Kelly Robson. I'm sure his parents knew you were married and went missing."

"Do you know if he ever mentioned me to anyone at the station?"

She looked at me with a kind of pity, or maybe she felt bad for me. She smiled a little and said, "You'll have to ask my Dad about that. He sees Tim at work, I've only seen him a few times around town, but I never spoke to him."

I didn't know what to say after that exchange because I didn't know what to do to get in touch with him. I would have to ask Sergeant Martino when I saw him, which I hoped would be soon. We parted with Angie taking my phone number at Betty's.

"I'll call you," she said, and then we went our separate ways. There wasn't an immediate invitation to visit her, or her parents, and I had an unsettled feeling, almost like the warm friendship we once had cooled a bit, or maybe time and distance caused me to feel that way. Two years is a long time and people change, even staying in the same place. I went home that night and lay awake thinking every negative thought.

A week later Angie called. I had her phone number and thought of calling her, but was afraid after meeting with her. I wanted to leave our friendship up to her to rekindle. I wasn't feeling well that entire time; the stress was getting to me. I was in a state of anxiety most of the time. When Angie invited me to her home and asked me to bring Tommy, I didn't tell her I had been calling him Timmy and now realized it would be a problem. What would Tim think? Or worse, what would his parents think if I ever saw them again. What would Dan's mother think? I was worried. I was so upset thinking about so many 'what ifs' that Betty noticed how I was near tears most of the time.

"What's wrong?" She asked, "Tell me."

"I have to go back to calling my son by his real name, but how do I do that? He'll be three in January and for almost the last two years he's heard everyone say Timmy."

She looked at me like I was worrying about something trivial.

"Kathleen, just start saying it, the two names almost sound the same. He's still a baby, he won't notice after a while, he'll forget."

She was right; he didn't pay any attention to the difference in sounds because I managed to blend in both names softly almost to a whisper in the beginning.

I arrived at Angie's by bus. I didn't want to impose on Betty any more than I had, so I didn't ask her to drive us or lend me her car. Angie greeted me like she was happy to see me and when I entered her front room I was startled to see Lottie and Sergeant Martino sitting there. Lottie lost no time in getting up to greet me with a smile and a hug. Her husband stood up and shook my hand lightly and when he said just simply hello, nothing more, I realized he didn't seem too enthusiastic over my return. I felt badly about his reaction to me, because I knew he was upset over all the problems I caused with the police having to search for me. I thought he might even blame me for Dan's death. I always thought he believed Dan more than me when it came to our marriage problems. I was embarrassed over disappearing and I didn't know what to say to them. Lottie said, "We worried so over you and the baby." And then she picked my son up and gushed over how big he had gotten. Tommy didn't know them and was shy. Angie showed him a lot of attention and I noticed for the first time that she looked like she was pregnant. I hadn't noticed it when she met me in the restaurant. The visit was strained and I wished her parents had met me at another time. Lottie turned to her husband who remained silent and pointed to Tommy.

"Isn't he cute Sal? We can't wait to be grandparents," she said, trying to make conversation in a very strained atmosphere. Her husband smiled at Tommy and then said to me, "Are you working?"

"Yes, I am, but I will look for a better job later," I said, all the while thinking about my old job at the police station, wondering who had it, and thinking that I was sure they wouldn't want me back. I was afraid to ask Sgt. Martino anything about Tim. I didn't have to mention him because Lottie mentioned him first.

"Oh, Kathleen, did Angie tell you Tim is back and back on the police force?"

"Yes, she did," was all I said.

Lottie turned to her husband, "Sal, have you mentioned to Tim that Kathleen's back, he might want to see her."

"Yeah, I told him."

"Well, what did he say?"

"Not much, I'm sure he wants to see her, but he doesn't know where you're staying," he said, looking at me.

Lottie said, "Give him your phone number so he can give it to Tim."

I wrote it down and gave it to him. He didn't sit back down, but said it was time for them to leave. They said goodbye and then I asked Angie if she thought her father was angry with me.

"No, I think he has a lot on his mind with his job and all," she said.

I was sure he didn't think of me in the same way as he had in the past, and it bothered me. He was the first person I met after Mrs.

Wilkie and he made me feel so welcomed in his family, there was so much warmth coming from him. I always thought of him as a big Teddy Bear of a man. Something changed in his attitude toward me and I didn't blame him after what I had done, and I began second guessing myself on maybe I made a mistake and should have turned the license in to hIm first, if not to the police department.

CHAPTER 27

I lay in bed one night thinking of how my life had become one trauma after another. I don't remember ever feeling at peace at any time except when Tim and I were together. As much as I had feelings for Levi, I was living a lie during that time and it brought me constant stress. I often thought of Mrs. Wilkie and how much I missed her. She was the first person who made me feel wanted until I met Tim. I worried about how much he had changed, and if we would connect in the same way. I worried mostly because it had been a week since I gave my number to Sergeant Martino, and Tim hadn't called yet. Maybe he didn't pass it to him, *but why wouldn't he?* I thought. I made no effort to contact Dan's mother, I was afraid. I couldn't imagine the Martinos or someone in the police department not informing her I was back or giving her my phone number. I had her grandchild, so it didn't make sense to me that she hadn't called. Out of fear, I hoped she would call me. I don't know why I thought it would be better if she contacted me first.

I confided all this to Betty and she said I should call, because of Tommy. I was a mess emotionally. I wasn't able to think straight. At times I wanted to crawl in bed, under the covers, and never come out. The call from Tim finally came one night and Betty answered the phone. I heard her say, "Yes, she is, one moment please." She handed me the phone.

"Hello," I said, not knowing if it was Tim or Dan's mother.

"Hello, Kathleen?" His voice sounded the same. I was so nervous that all I could say was, "Yes."

"I know you heard I'm back," he said, "Can we meet tomorrow night, somewhere? Or can I pick you up?"

"I'll meet you," I said, and I gave him the time and address to the same place I met Angie. I could hardly speak, and he didn't say anything more, except, "See you then." I was left with the same feeling I had meeting Angie and her parents, a feeling of loss that I couldn't put my finger on. I told myself it was to be expected after so many years. Right after I hung up the phone I felt terrible. Why wasn't

I excited over hearing his voice, shouldn't the normal reaction have been, "On my God, Tim, I'm so happy to hear from you?" *But he should have said that too*, I thought. He sounded so cold and formal. I was racked with doubt about us and faced another sleepless night. Of course our relationship would be strained, I told myself, look what has happened to him, but worse I thought, *look what you have done, you married the very man he knew you detested. What must he be thinking about that?* I borrowed Betty's car and somehow got up the courage to meet him and while I waited in the same booth I had waited for Angie, this time there would be no standing up and waving, I sat waiting for him to find me. I purposely sat with my back to the door, frightened to death of what our first meeting would feel like. I didn't have to wait long. As I had my eyes fixed on the cup of coffee in front of me, he appeared, sliding in across from me, he didn't smile, just looked at me and said, "Hello, Kathleen." I sat frozen with fear. Here was a man I would hardly recognize if I ran into him on the street. His hair was streaked with gray and his face appeared drawn, thinner, with small hollows beneath his cheekbones. He had aged beyond his thirty years. We both stared at each other as if we were total strangers. I remained uneasy about our relationship, if there would be one, and I could not grasp the significance of the change in him. He spoke first.

"I hear you were married," he said.

"Yes," was all I was able to get out, my voice trembled.

He looked at me with a frown on his face, "And to Sheriff Dan Robson? I thought you didn't like him at all."

"Tim," I said, trying to explain, " I thought you would never come back, I was afraid and lonely and Dan appeared to care. I didn't rush into anything; it took me quite a while. He was kind at first. When you didn't return after the armistice, and the prisoner exchange I gave up hope you would ever return."

"I got separated from my Company and I was hidden by a North Korean family up North near the Yalu River. They were relatives of a South Korean soldier who was with me," he said.

I couldn't believe this was the same Tim that made my heart beat so. I felt sorry for him, maybe pity, and I wanted to embrace him in a bad way, but he seemed so aloof. I asked him how he managed to escape.

"There was no question of us going south, we were encircled on three sides by the Chinese and it was completely dark, he said. "The Hwachon Reservoir provided water and electricity for the City of Seoul and eventually it was bombed. Oh, the terrible odor that permeated the air of North Korea. I will never forget and I can't get the smell out of my mind. It was from a lack of modern facilities. What I remember most was the cold. It not only numbed your bones but your brain as well. We made our way North to my companion's relatives who lived in Unsan. They hid us for a year until we were all caught. We were separated and they threw us in a prison camp. I don't know what happened to his relatives, I can only guess—tortured or killed I'm sure. We were used as slave labor. I can't talk about the time in there."

I felt like crying and I did, as he tried to console me.

"Kathleen, please don't, I didn't mean to make you cry. I won't say another word."

"No, I want to know," I said. "How long were you in that prison camp and how did you escape?"

"Four years in that hell hole and then on a lucky chance one night— in total darkness, we slipped by the guard who had passed out from drinking and we headed North East. It wasn't easy; North Korea was always dark after the sun went down. They had little electricity. We hid out among the most downtrodden people we could find, people who were starving. They hated the communists and shared what little they had with us. By the time we reached Chongjin, as far north as we could go— it's on the Sea of Japan— we were able to steal a small motorboat one night, and that was a year after we escaped the prison. We traveled at low speed not wanting to make waves that might be noticed by any Korean ships, hoping to reach Japanese waters. In the morning we found ourselves in the middle of the sea with no ship in sight. I prayed we wouldn't be spotted by a North Korean ship, but we were lucky, a Japanese freighter came upon us late in the day."

I wanted to hug Tim, but all I could do was reach for his hand across the table. I thought he might pull his away but he didn't. He held my hand and continued to talk. I was thinking, *he needed to get this all out to someone and I was grateful he chose me.*

"We were in a Japanese hospital for a time until we were well enough to be released. By then the state department and my family had been notified."

"What happened to the South Korean soldier you were with?"

"Minh Chong kyu was reunited with his family in Seoul."

He quit speaking and remained silent while holding my hand across the table. He reached for my other hand and lowered his head, looking down at our hands, and said, "I've thought of you on all those terrible nights in prison, and it got me through. I didn't expect after all these years to find you single, but Sheriff Robson? I never liked him even when I first joined the force, years ago. He would stop in at the station occasionally. He was arrogant son of a bitch and had a bad temper. Were you so desperate Kathleen, that you had to marry *him?* "

I didn't know what to say to that, and withdrew my hands. How could I explain how lonely I felt, even when I was with Angie, Rita or Betty. I was getting older and so far the few single men I met, like Steve or creepy Jack didn't leave much to choose from. Everyone else I knew was married. I wasn't brave enough to go searching on my own and relied on the few friends I had to meet anyone new.

"I know you've been through a terrible time," I said, "and I don't mean to equate your experience in anyway to mine, but I've been in a hell of my own."

He looked at me skeptically and said, "Like what?"

I was taken by surprise at that comment and simply said, "Dan wasn't what he made himself out to be. He was cruel at times and nice at other times."

"Well, anyone in the department could have told you that!" he said, like he couldn't believe I hadn't known.

"I never witnessed that side of him, and the Martinos were close with him. They of all people would know of his dark side," I said.

"I hear you have a son," he said, shaking his head like he couldn't believe it. It upset me. "Yes, I have, he's almost three. His name is Thomas." I said it almost defiantly. I knew what he was thinking, like father, like son, what his mother would have thought. I thought of his sister, and to change the subject I asked about her.

"How is your sister, Barbara? She should be all grown up by now."

"Yeah, she's grown alright, left home at the grand old age of seventeen, came back pregnant and it all went downhill after that."

"She wasn't married?" I asked.

"Of course not, what did you think? She's always been a problem for my parents and they told me she left to go live with this guy after they had a big blow up with her. They find out he wasn't the father, and the real father was in jail. They washed their hands of her after that."

"What happened to her baby?"

"Who knows? I guess she had it. It wasn't my parents' problem any longer. The baby would have been a second generation of problems."

After that, I began to see where his thinking was going. It was upsetting to me. I was sure he was thinking of Dan and my son. We seemed to run out of things to say and I was ready to accept that he might not want to get together again, but I was wrong. I was about to say I needed to get back home, when he said, "Kathleen, when can I see you again?"

I decided to give it another try. I had feelings for Tim; I just wasn't sure what kind they were. I knew the excitement of being near him when we were younger wasn't there in this meeting, but I wanted to see him again. I had hopes we could rekindle what we once had. I also thought once he met my son, he would see there was nothing to fear.

"Yes, I would like to see you again," I said. "Just let me know when."

"How about this coming Sunday, maybe out for a bite to eat—somewhere where we can talk."

"Well, I need to check with Betty to see if she can watch Tommy," I said, hoping he might say, bring him along, but he didn't.

"I'll call you Friday then," he said.

He got up and took my hand, just for a moment, and then he walked out. Not a hug, nothing that would have been a gesture of what we once were. It left me feeling empty. I went home wondering if Tim and I could ever be the couple we once were. Too much had happened to both of us, but I was willing to give it a try.

The day I got up the courage to call Dan's mother would be a milestone for me. I had been back exactly four weeks and couldn't believe she hadn't heard I was back. I was to find out she didn't know. The Martinos never called her and I heard she moved out of Arden. She bought herself a home quite a distance from where she lived before. After my first meeting with Tim, I got in touch with Rita. She filled me in on all Mrs. Clarke had done after the murder of her son.

"She emptied out your apartment of all Dan and your things and left the area," she said. "I think she moved to a town pretty far south of here. I can get her number from one of the sheriffs' wives for you."

Rita was happy to see me and invited Tommy and me to her home. It was nice to see him play with her children, it reminded me of the noise and laughter of children running all over when I was with Levi. I didn't fail to notice the difference between the Amish children and the children in my world. There were both good and bad differences. I missed the gentle innocence of Alice, Samuel and Paul, but at the same time I noticed how Betty's Ricky, and Rita's children appeared so much more astute, but a little more aggressive, less politeness. It left me with ambivalent feelings.

I finely got up the courage to call Mrs. Clarke. My hands were shaking as I dialed the number Rita had given me. I could hear that authoritative voice of hers, when she answered, "The Clarke residence."

"Hello, Mrs. Clarke?" I said. I wasn't about to say Mom. I was no longer married to her son.

"Yes?" came her reply.

"It's Kathleen, I want you to know I'm back." There was silence on the other end of the line. Then she screamed loudly,

"What! Oh, oh, oh my God! Where have you been? How could you do this to me? Do you know what happened to my son?"

"Yes, I do, and I'm so sorry. I'm calling because I thought you might want to see your grandson."

Her voice seemed to change quickly, like she just realized I had her grandchild. It became softer, almost pleading, as he said," Oh, please, I do want to see him, is he alright?"

"Yes, he's fine, and walking and talking too. It would be nice for him to see you again."

I felt sorry for her in that moment, and we set a date for me to bring Tommy to her after she first insisted on coming up to us. I let her know I didn't have a place of my own yet and it would be more convenient to visit her.

"Oh, all right then, I can't wait to see *my* Tommy," she said, leaving me with the feeling that doing the right thing might only be right for her.

I had to take public transportation and found a way down to the town of New Lonex. It was quite a distance from Arden. At one point the bus route ended and I had to call a cab. I wondered how I would get back once I was in her home. I could just envision her trying to keep me there longer than I planned on staying. Just a quick visit, I thought. I would have to think again.

"Oh my God!" She exclaimed, as she opened the door to us. Without any attention to me she scooped Tommy up in her arms and turned her back to me as she settled on her sofa cradling him in her arms. She started crying and my son tried to wiggle off her lap. He succeeded, and then she finally seemed to notice me standing just inside the open doorway. She stood up and came toward me glaring at me for a moment, and then she closed the door behind me and offered me a seat in her living room. There wasn't any kind words of happy to see you, or are you ok, nothing like any concern for where I had been or why I was gone for so long, just anger in her expression. I had to speak first.

"I'm sorry I never contacted you after I left," I said, waiting for her to ask me any question. She took her time wiping her eyes of any tears she shed while holding her grandson.

"My son went crazy after you disappeared, did you know that? Have you no idea what you put us through?" she cried, in an accusing tone.

"I'm sorry about that," I said, not knowing what else I should say without destroying her son for her.

She was so hostile, which I didn't expect with Tommy being there with us that it triggered anger in me and I let loose.

"I left because he was cruel to me, that's why I left. He was drinking more and I became afraid of him. He tried to choke me one night, that's why I left. What did you expect me to do?"

She looked at me like I was crazy, "My son would never treat you or anyone that way," she said, her face flushing red.

"Oh, no? Ask anyone in the police department, ask Sergeant Martino. He tried to talk him into a leave from work until he calmed down."

"That's because you disappeared without a word and when they found your car in the canal, how did you expect my son to react?"

I could see we were getting nowhere and she wouldn't listen to what I was saying so I went to take Tommy by the hand, ready to leave, when she started crying again.

"Mrs. Clarke," I said, "I'm truly sorry for leaving and I realize you lost your son and haven't seen your grandson in some time and I want to make it up to you if you'll let me."

"I just can't believe my son could be cruel to you," she cried, "but I know he had a bad temper. It was the stressful job he had."

Her voice became softer and a little kinder and I decided I would appeal to the pain she was feeling on losing her son, and mentioning Tommy might calm her down enough to hear me out. She sniffled and held her handkerchief up to her nose as I again told her that I wanted her to be able to see her grandson. I needed to get her on my side, to find out more about Dan. Finding the slain woman's identification in his clothing hung over me like a dark cloud. For my son's sake, I needed to believe Dan was innocent of any crime. She calmed down and went through the motions of making tea. She held Tommy on her lap for as long as he let her in between our conversation. I asked her questions about Dan.

"I know Dan had a bad temper," I said, "But did he ever get into any fights when he lived with you?"

"Oh, yes, many times he would go out with the boys for a drink after work and I would have to mend his shirt or wash off the blood from someone's bloody mouth. Sometimes his, or some other guy he punched," she said, shaking her head, in remembering what she would rather forget.

"Do you know what the fights were about?" I asked.

"Dan had a strict code of honor, right was right, and wrong was wrong. There was never a gray area in his thinking," she said.

When she said that, it eased my doubts about him. I couldn't tell her anything about what I knew; I wanted to develop a good relationship with her. I think she realized I held all the cards when it came to her grandson because I was the sole parent now. We spent the rest of the visit on a more pleasant topic, talking about my work, how I was getting along, and mostly about Tommy, how he had grown, his first milestones of when he began walking and talking. I promised her we would visit her again soon and I meant it. As we began to leave, and after she kissed Tommy, she held my hand for a moment, and thanked me for bringing him to her. She had a little weak smile and I was sure hidden behind it she was seething with anger over what she thought I had done to her son. I knew she believed if I had stayed he wouldn't have lost his life the way he did.

"Next time you come," she said, "you can have a look at all that I stored in my basement from your apartment. Of course I had to sell the furniture, but I kept my son's personal stuff, and some of your personal stuff and jewelry."

I was surprised, and thanked her, promising I would return soon.

On the way home I thought of how sad she appeared and tried to put myself in her place. She lost her only child and I looked at my son sitting beside me on the bus and couldn't imagine ever losing him.

CHAPTER 28

My visit to Dan's mother confirmed what I had hoped, that the blood I found on Dan's shirts twice, was over his fighting with someone and not what I feared it might be. When she mentioned he came home with a bloody mouth, it was one more confirmation of his bad temper. I didn't want to believe that a man with such a rigid conception of right and wrong could be guilty of any crime. I still didn't know how he had come by that woman's driver's license.

Tim called me for another date and I agreed to meet him. This time he picked me up in his car and we went out to dinner and later we sat in the car, in the parking lot of his apartment building, and talked for hours. He asked me in, but I refused. Somehow it didn't seem right. He was now living in his own place. My feelings for Tim were a mixture of still caring for him but needing to get to know him again. He wasn't the same guy I knew before, but nether was I the same person. He was cautious in his approach to me also. He seemed more abrupt, more hardened, and I couldn't help comparing him to the gentle and kind Levi, devoid of any cynical view of life.

"Kathleen, I thought of you often, and I know we're both older and changed by our circumstances, but I know in time we can find a place where we feel comfortable with each other again," he said.

"I thought of you too," I said, "Even when I was with Dan, it was you I wished for. I thought you were dead, and at some point I knew I had to put you out of my mind or I couldn't go on."

"I can't believe you didn't know the real Dan," he said, "Everyone at work knew the temper he had. He hated two defense lawyers involved in a couple cases he testified in. Once you were on his shit list, you stayed on it."

"I know, I realize now he was a rigid person, but I wasn't aware of it when he dated me," I said. "We didn't see each other all that much, his hours took him away most of the week." I was trying to ease any thoughts Tim might have on the severity or degree of any passion during our time together. "I liked him at that time, but to be honest with you Tim, I didn't love him, not the way I loved you."

"So, you would marry a man you didn't love? Just to feel taken care of?"

He posed a question I found hard to answer. "We weren't married long enough for me to feel any real love for him. I knew on the honeymoon something wasn't right," I said. He looked at me with what I guessed were dozens of questions on his mind, so I began to tell him everything—about our marriage, beginning with our less than desired honeymoon trip, down to his threatening rampage the night he tried to choke me. I left out anything about my child, or what I found that night in his clothing.

He looked at me with such compassion and said, "My God! Kathleen, why didn't you leave him sooner?"

"Where was I to go? Besides I was pregnant the first month. It was the Catholic thing, you know?" and he did know, he was Catholic himself, an Irish Catholic. I knew he would understand my predicament, and he did, to an extent. He changed the subject and talked about my seeing his parents soon. I didn't say anything to that proposal and he was quiet for a few minutes and then he took me in his arms and kissed me. It surprised me; I didn't expect it and it happened so quickly that it didn't feel anything like what I remembered when he last kissed me. I thought it was different then, we were young and the excitement of youth was more intense. That's what I told myself. We made plans to see his parents but I was uneasy about it, not sure how they would receive me. I wanted him to meet my son and so far he hadn't mentioned him, didn't ask about him and I was afraid to ask him to include Tommy on any future meeting we had. Betty and I were taking our boys to a carnival the coming weekend, so I invited him.

"This Saturday? I'm off duty this Saturday, sure, I have a stop to make in the morning so why don't I meet you girls there around two," he said.

I was happy he accepted. He would be the first person Betty would meet from my friends associated with the police department.

It was half past two and I began to wonder if Tim was going to show up. Betty had just gotten the boys cotton candy when he spotted me bending beside Tommy, trying to adjust his little hand around the cone that held the sticky candy.

"Hi," he said, looking down at us. I introduced him to Betty and then the boys.

"This is Rickey, he's eight," I said, nervously, and then I picked Tommy up in my arms so he was eye level to Tim, I guess. I didn't know why on impulse, I picked him up. He would be three in a few months; he was perfectly capable of greeting Tim standing up. Tim looked at him seriously at first and then smiled. He patted Tommy on the head.

"He resembles you," he said.

"That's what I said, first time I saw them together," Betty added.

We spent the afternoon together, the five of us and whenever the boys wanted to ride a kiddy ride, I noticed it was Betty and I that lifted Tommy in and out of whatever we put them in. He was too young for some of the rides but he loved the merry-go-round. He sat on the horse with me holding him on throughout the ride. I noticed Tim made no effort to help us; he stood outside watching the ride go around. I found excuses for him. He wasn't used to small children, I told myself. Except for when he first met us, his attention was on me, and Betty too, whenever we talked together, while waiting for the boys to finish a ride. I don't know what I expected, but his lack of attention to my son in particular, annoyed me. I thought of Angie's reaction to seeing Tommy and later her husband's, and I thought of Levi with Tommy. I realized I was being unfair to Tim. He wasn't used to children. Levi had children of his own and Angie and John were expecting a child, so they were excited over seeing Tommy. Around five, we parted at the carnival and Betty and I left together. She was driving us home when she asked me if anything was wrong. I must have appeared worried.

"You're so quiet," she said, "Is it because Tim seemed so disinterested in the children?"

"Oh, you noticed that? I thought he would at least help me lift Tommy each time he wanted to ride the horse," I said.

"Well, he really didn't say much to Ricky either, although Ricky was old enough to engage him in some conversation about the kiddy cars on the track, remember? He asked Ricky how he liked the ride, if it went fast enough?"

I thought my son was old enough to render some attention from Tim. It left me feeling that his dislike of Dan would always come between them.

Later in the week Tim picked me up for a visit to his parents. He didn't mention Tommy, so it was just the two of us. On the ride over, I looked over at him; his profile was the same as the man I once was crazy about, the square chin, the dimple, the eyes, and the smile. The gray in his hair didn't bother me; I kind of thought it made him look more distinguished looking. He parked the car and turned to me. He reached for me in the darkened car in his parent's driveway and kissed me. This time I felt something. I ran my finger along his square chin and felt the dimple

"You always did that," he said laughing, "What's so interesting about my chin?

"I don't know, it's your trademark I guess. It's what I remember most of you, well I take that back," I said, "You branded me before you left, so I always had this—I brushed my hair away from the ear he bit—to remember you by."

He looked closely at my ear and laughed, "I did that?"

"Yes, you did, remember? You said I was driving you crazy."

"I remember how frustrated I felt, only being allowed to hug and kiss you, but I don't remember biting your ear."

"Well, you did, and when I missed you all that first year you were gone, it was a comfort to feel your tooth mark on my ear, like you left a part of you with me."

"Come here," he said, as he pulled me toward him again and this time kissed me for a long time, several times. I was happy to come up for air. Did I still love Tim? I asked myself that in that split second, and told myself I did, at that moment.

His father greeted us in the front hall and announced our arrival to his mother, who came in to greet me. Something about the way she smiled reminded me of Mrs. Clarke's smile, strained, not real, but badly needed in an awkward moment.

"Hello, Kathleen, so nice to see you again—after all this time," she said, "Please, come in, make yourself at home—Tim, take her coat."

I told her it was nice seeing them again, and we sat together in their living room and it was so painfully strained as we talked about Tim's escape, his recuperation, how he needed to gain some weight, and how happy they all were that he was able to get his old job back. No one brought up the elephant in the room—my marriage and my child—I wasn't going to say anything unless they asked me questions, but they didn't. Tim's mother did bring up their daughter's problems, explaining how they were glad when she turned eighteen, because they were no longer responsible for her. After Mrs. O'Malley served us coffee and cake, there wasn't much more anyone was willing to discuss, so Tim said it was getting late and after thanking them for the evening, we left. On the ride home, I felt numb. I thought, *how are we supposed to get back to where we were—pick up the pieces of our lives again, without acknowledging my son?* I was quiet on the way home, and Tim asked me if anything was wrong. I said, no, and thought, *My God, if you don't know what just happened, I'm not going to clue you in, not going to remind you that I have a child.* He stopped the car in front of Betty's and when he went to kiss me goodnight, I gave him my cheek and slipped out of the car. "You don't have to get out," I said, as I ran to the door of the apartment. Once inside, I told myself he has to know I'm upset. Let him figure it out. I went to bed that night angry instead of upset, so I didn't lose any sleep over it. Anger I could always handle, it made me stronger, more determined to hold my ground.

Near the end of October we were looking forward to dressing the boys for Halloween. It would be Tommy's first Halloween. The Amish ignored the holiday; they considered it a heathen day related to the devil. I also made plans to visit Mrs. Clarke again. Tim and I got together at least once a week on Friday or Saturday night. I wanted so desperately to feel about him the way I used to. He was very loving to me, but I kept our relationship just plain dating with a few kisses. One night after we had returned from seeing a movie, Tim asked if I would please come up to his apartment so we could spend more time together other than sitting in his car. The weather was getting a little nippy. I had no place to invite him to, where we could be alone, so I agreed.

Once settled inside, he put on a pot of coffee and we talked. He didn't try to force himself on me like I imagined he might. He was still the gentleman I remembered, or maybe it was his Catholic upbringing. I had long ago discarded any notion of being intimate with someone you loved or had deep feelings for as a sin. He poured my coffee and I decided to confide in him about more than I already had.

"Tim, I need to tell you something I have been holding in about Dan," I said.

He looked at me, put the coffee pot down and grabbed my hands across the table.

"What is it, you can tell me," he said, sensing I was afraid to tell him.

"I don't want you to say anything to anyone because it might not be what I think, but I need to tell someone. One day when I was getting our laundry ready to wash, I found a thin wallet holding only a driver's license in Dan's clothing. I think it fell out of his shirt or pants pocket." I paused as his expression took on a real interested expression.

"Go on," he said, "I'm listening, if it wasn't his, I'll reserve judgment, I'll try to keep an open mind."

"Tim, it belonged to a woman who was killed in Chicago. I recognized her face; she was in all the newspapers. It happened before I left. What would Dan be doing with it? He wouldn't be on that case because it wasn't in his jurisdiction.

"Where is it, do you still have it?" he asked.

"No, I was afraid, I wasn't thinking straight, and I threw it in the apartments incinerator."

"You threw it away? Do you think he was involved in some way? God, Kathleen, how would he come by that? He was the Sheriff of our county but I don't think he had anything to do with investigating crimes in the city, unless he was invited."

"I'm sorry, I panicked and I should have turned it in to the police or at least to Sergeant Martino."

"Who else knows about this? No one I hope—you didn't mention it to Angie, did you?" he said, rubbing my hands between his. "I didn't like Dan, but I would never believe for a minute he would be capable of murder," he said, trying to reassure me.

"Neither do I, not after his mother told me about how solid his thinking was, about right and wrong," I said.

"How could he come by such a thing unless someone else gave it to him, but who? Don't worry about it now, but I'm glad you told me. I know a guy on our force that is friends with a Chicago cop; maybe he can find out something—if the case is still open of the murder around that time. I would like to know something about that investigation," he said.

We agreed to keep it just between us. I felt so much better hearing Tim defending Dan, and sharing what I had carried alone for so long. It was what I needed—to go on without guilt about hiding the whole mess. We parted that night with me feeling like I wasn't alone.

The next time we got together, Tim began to have second doubts about Dan. I asked him why he felt that way.

"You know Kathleen, there was a priest in our parish once, when I was in grade school. It was at Saint Joe's. I heard my parents talk about it. This priest was the most devout priest in his order and he was the assistant pastor. No one wanted to go to confession to him, he was so strict, he gave out impossible penance and no one liked him; to him everything was a sin, until he shocked the congregation one day by running off with a woman from our parish who went to him to complain about her marriage. So you see Kathleen, sometimes people can fool you. The ones you would never guess, can leave you in shock. They are usually charming to your face. Every cop knows some killers could be psychopaths."

He left me stunned, feeling as bad as I had when I first came upon the damning evidence.

"Oh my God, Tim, I don't know what to think," I said. What I was thinking was, *if it were true, my poor baby.* I wanted him to like my child, but with that kind of belief on his part, it would never happen.

We parted that night with me just going through the motions. I let him kiss me goodnight, but felt nothing except fear, fear of what Tim might uncover, fear for my son, and fear for our future.

CHAPTER 29

I borrowed Betty's car to visit Dan's mother so I could go through the personal things she said she saved from our apartment. On the ride down, with Tommy busy playing on the back seat with the few toys I took along, I thought of all Tim said the week before. My mind was in turmoil; I lay awake most nights praying that Tim was wrong. When I arrived she welcomed me with a more pleasant attitude than she displayed on my previous visit. She again picked Tommy up and gave him her immediate attention.

"I made lunch for us," she said, while kissing her grandson until he wanted down. She took him by the hand and talked baby talk, "Tommy, my wittle munchkin," she said as she led him to her kitchen table. I noticed she had set the table and had roasted a small chicken. Mashed potatoes, and a bowl of vegetables, a mixture of corn and peas, were included. It looked more like supper to me than lunch. I thought she wanted to make up for her first confrontation with me, that wasn't too friendly.

"Sit down Kathleen, please, and have some lunch. You didn't have lunch yet, did you?"

I looked at my watch, it was almost one, "No, I haven't," I said. She poured lemonade and then milk for Tommy. I noticed she had a thick telephone book on the chair for him to sit on. I wondered if she sold his highchair, but I didn't ask. It was a strained few minutes; I didn't know what to say to her. I felt sorry for her. She talked to my son most of the time and I didn't interfere. I ate my lunch and waited for her to mention the articles she stored in the basement. Finally, she spoke to me.

"How is your work going?" she asked, "If you need any help, with money, please let me know."

"Oh, no, I'm fine, but thank you for offering," I said. I wouldn't take any help from her if I could help it because I didn't want to be indebted to her in any way. I wanted to remain free of the control she could have over me, and I was sure that's what would happen if I accepted her offer. She would expect an obligation on my part, like more time with Tommy, or expecting me to leave him with her on the pretense of helping me out. I remembered the control she had over Dan. After Tommy finished his lunch, she took him over to the sink and wiped his hands, and then she turned to me.

"Kathleen, feel free to go downstairs and see what is down there that's yours. I know you had some jewelry. I didn't save any clothing."

"Thanks," I said, expecting her to come down with me, but she motioned for me to go alone.

"I'll keep Tommy company," she said, "You go—holler if you need any help."

I lost no time in going down the basement stairs. It was a finished basement, the usual knotty pine paneling on the walls, and a few pieces of furniture. On a table I noticed several small boxes. On the floor were several large cardboard boxes. I opened them. Books, Dan's pipes, papers, some of his cuff links and tie pins along with notebooks, address books, his watch, the one I gave him for our wedding, our wedding album, Tommy's baby book and photo albums. I took the baby book and his photo album and set it aside. I left my wedding stuff in the box. The second box held my jewelry, what little I had. Dan bought me a few pieces and I left them as well. I didn't want anything except what I had bought for my son and myself. The two boxes on the table held more of our wedding trinkets, engagement party keepsakes. I lifted out a small steel box from the cardboard box. It was locked. I searched for a key, but couldn't find one. I shook it but couldn't tell what could be in it. I remembered Dan storing that on the top shelf of our bedroom closet. I once asked him what was in it and he said law enforcement stuff. I believed him and didn't ask again, but wondered why he kept it locked.

I was just about to put it back in the cardboard box when something white caught my eye. I reached in and pulled out my little white unicorn. I couldn't believe it. I hadn't thought of it in years. At times I had forgotten were it was. I emptied the one small cardboard box and put everything I wanted in it, including the little figurine of the horse. I held the metal box in my hand again wondering what could be in it, and why Dan kept it locked. I decided to bring it upstairs along with what I was taking.

"What have you got there?" Mrs. Clarke asked, as she took the metal box from me.

"I wondered what's in it," I said, apprehensively. "I know it's Dan's, but he always kept it locked. He said it was police business. I wasn't able to find the key to open it. I thought I would take it with me, and get someone to open it."

"No, dear, let me keep it. I'll find the key, it has to be somewhere in the basement," she said, holding the box tightly in her hands. I knew she wasn't going to give it up, so I let her have it. I thought it probably wasn't anything of interest to either of us.

The following week was Halloween and Betty and I bought costumes for both boys. I dressed Tommy in a little Davie Crocket costume, with a raccoon tail hat that was from a popular Davie Crockett television show. Rickey was dressed as the devil. I laughed at the thought of what the Amish would have thought of that. Lately I began thinking of the Holsteders and Levi. I wondered how they took the news about me after Levi told them. I thought I should write Levi one day soon, but kept putting it off, not knowing what I could say to him. I had no intention of going back, and I felt guilty about that.

When Tim called the afternoon we were taking the boys trick or treating, I invited him to come along, but he declined.

"I need to see you," he said.

"Can it wait until tomorrow?" I asked. "After we take the boys out, we promised them ice cream, at the ice cream parlor."

"I need to see you tonight!" he said. It sounded urgent, so after the ice cream we brought the boys home and Betty said she would handle the children.

I was wondering what was so important that he needed to see me on a weeknight. When his car pulled up, I was already outside the apartment waiting for him. I climbed into his car and as he drove, I asked where we were going.

"To my place, we need to talk," he said.

"What's happened? Have you found out anything?" I asked.

"Yeah, I'll tell you when we get there. I need to ask you questions about Dan. Are you okay with that?"

"Yes, of course," I said, but I wasn't okay with it. I was a wreck

201

inside, hoping against hope it wasn't about Dan's lack of innocence.

We arrived at his apartment and he lost no time in telling me that he met with his Chicago friend and the cop his friend knew.

"Kathleen, was that the only driver's license you found in your apartment?"

"Yes, why?" I asked, and then I became nervous.

He sat me down on his sofa and put his arm around me, trying to calm me. He could see how upset I was.

"This guy who is on a police force in Chicago was involved in the investigation of that murder involving the woman who lived in Arden. He told me the case is still open, but they have run out of leads. I found out none of the victims going back at least nine years had any identification on them. Their purses and its contents were found, but nothing that could tell the police who they were. Identifying them wasn't easy. They had to rely on missing persons reports and photos of their facial features taken in the morgue. They would run fingerprints but none of the women had any encounters with the law, so that was a dead end." He looked at me and realized how frightened I was. He hugged me and then tried to console me. "This might not have anything to do with Dan," he said, "but I need to know if that was the only one you found."

"Yes, it was, and I'm sorry I got rid of it."

"Well, I think the killer, or killers—They seem to think it's one guy, and that he keeps all the driver's license or identification of those women as some kind of a sick token of his crimes. Some of the women didn't drive, so he must have taken something else that belonged to them."

He was quiet for a few minutes, neither of us talking, and then he asked me if I was sure there wasn't anything else I came across that would leave me with questions about Dan. I froze, as my mind went to the locked box at Dan's mothers. The box that sat on our closet shelf all those months we were married. I didn't want to think of my son's father as a suspect, or the kind of person who could kill anyone, but I knew deep down, it was a possibility. He had a bad temper; he frightened me when he was drinking and in a bad mood. I had to face that there was something wrong with him, but a cold-blooded killer of strange women? That was the one thing I couldn't get my mind around. I broke down crying.

"Kathleen, are you alright?" he asked, "What is it?"

"Oh Tim, I need to tell you, but I—"

"Tell me, don't be afraid," he said, trying to comfort me and at the same time pressing me for anything I could give him that would condemn my son's father.

"I took Tommy to visit Dan's mother, and I found the little metal box she had taken from our apartment after Dan died and—" He interrupted me, grabbing me by both shoulders, his face inches from mine, his voice softened.

"What can you tell me about it," he asked.

"After Dan's mother emptied our apartment, she took all our personal things home. When I was visiting her she mentioned she had all our stuff in the basement and I should go through it to take what belonged to me, jewelry, photo albums, things like that and I found the box that was always on the top shelf of our bedroom closet. I asked Dan why he kept it locked and what was in it, and he said it was papers that had to do with police cases. I still don't understand why it had to be locked. I wanted to bring it with me but she insisted it remain with her because the key was missing and we couldn't open it. She thought she would look for the key."

He looked at me with a seriousness that told me he thought Dan was the number one suspect.

"We need to get that box before she opens it!" he said with an urgency that left me trembling. "How can we do that?" I asked. If I go back to her, she wouldn't give it to me, I'm sure of that. What do you think is in it?"

He hesitated for a moment looking at me with what I thought was pity, sorrow, or maybe just feeling guilty that he was about to hurt me with his answer.

"All the killer's trophies," he said, hanging his head for a moment.

"But, I shook it, it didn't sound like a bunch of cards would be in it, it didn't rattle," I said.

He shook his head, "They could be in an envelope, inside the box. We need that box!" and then when he realized I was shaking he tried to tell me that maybe it wasn't what he thought.

"Wouldn't you want to know either way, for sure?" he said.

I had to agree with him. Not knowing was unbearable for me. We had to come up with a plan to get the box, so I decided I would go down to visit Dan's mother and talk her into going out with Tommy and me to the park, or anywhere, to get her out of her home. I thought it through; I would find a way to leave a door unlocked for Tim to enter while we were gone. He would drive his car and be in full uniform on his day off, so if a neighbor saw him, there would be no questions about seeing him enter her home. I didn't think about Dan's mother finding out about it later, and if her son were guilty, it wouldn't matter what she thought. That was my thinking at the time. I would borrow Betty's car and leave around the same time Tim would. I wouldn't know how long it would take me to get her to leave the house so he would have to cruise around until he noticed my car gone from her driveway. That was my plan, until Tim said it wouldn't work.

"You do realize I'd be breaking the law," he said. "To enter a person's home without a search warrant is against the law."

I felt foolish recommending such a plan, and it showed my lack of knowledge of the law.

"Tim, I'll just have to find a way to get that box out without you. I'll—"

"I've got a better idea, why not let me take you to her. She knows me from when I was working with her son years ago. I could say you needed a ride, and I wanted to tell her how sorry I am about her son."

"And then what?" I said, "sneak you the box and you put it in your car before we leave?"

"You got it!" he smiled—the first smile he showed me since he arrived.

We talked about the exact steps to take to locate the box and I hoped she put it back in the basement.

"What if she put it where it was hard to find? We're not going to have much time to find it," I said, and then Tim's face took on a look of something between a bright idea, or he had seen a ghost.

"What's wrong?" I asked, wondering what he might be thinking.

"The thought came to me, that if she opened it and what I fear was in there, there is no way we would ever see it. She would certainly protect her son's name, and the game would be up," he said.

"She would need the key," I said, "and I doubt if she found one, it's made of steel."

"We'll see, " he said, "We won't worry about it until we get there."

I called Dan's mother the next day and she was happy to hear I would be bringing her grandson for another visit.

"I'll be coming with a friend who worked with Dan at the department," I said.

"Oh, you won't be alone?" she asked, sounding disappointed.

"Tim O'Malley is driving me down. The bus ride is too long for Tommy, he gets restless and I don't have a car yet."

"Well, okay then, I'll be looking forward to seeing Tommy, and you too of course."

I had to laugh at that comment, knowing that if her grandson were old enough to make the trip alone, she would be delighted.

CHAPTER 30

Dan's mother welcomed us into her home with a gracious smile that never left her face the entire time we were there. I thought she would be capable of receiving an academy award had she been an actress. I introduced her to Tim, minus his uniform and of course she recognized him. She gave Tommy her full attention at first, and then she asked Tim about his escape from Korea. He filled her in on just enough, and then I brought up the box.

"Have you found the key to that little box?" I asked, hoping she hadn't.

"No, I know it's either downstairs somewhere or it's lost. When I emptied your apartment, I never found a key. It might have been on Dan, I presume his car keys and your apartment key was in his pocket when they rushed him to the hospital after he was shot, but somehow they went missing during that time," she explained. "Oh, I bet the key was with his other keys," she said.

Tim remained silent, and I asked her if Tim could take a look at the box and maybe he could figure a way to open it for her. He looked startled, not expecting me to ask for it, but I thought with him being here she would be more inclined to hand it over. She knew he was a cop and even without his uniform, he represented the law.

"Oh, well, yes, of course, if you think you can," she said, addressing him.

I couldn't believe our luck. Tim and I looked at each other; we were surprised it was that easy. He whispered to me as she left to go to her room to retrieve it.

"It's in her bedroom, you would have never been able to get it," he whispered.

She came back and handed it to him. "Thanks, I'll take it home and have a locksmith I know get it open for you," he said, letting her feel the box was still her possession. We didn't want to leave too soon, having her think we came just for the box, so we stayed long enough for her to spend some time with her grandson. Tim and I couldn't believe our good luck.

Once back in the car and on our way home, Tim laughed out loud, "Kathleen, all your planning and worrying was for nothing. She was a piece of cake. I think her son's death cut her down a peg or two. She doesn't seem like the witch she was when he was alive."

"Oh, I don't know about that," I said. "Remember she thinks of you as representing the law. I'm sure if I were alone she would have never turned it over to me."

"She mentioned her son kept a diary as a boy, maybe that's all that's in there," he laughed again. "All this for nothing, probably."

On the ride home Tommy fell asleep in the back seat. We didn't talk much the rest of the way home and I thought of how Tim really wasn't that interested in getting to know my son. He hardly bothered to say anything to him. I wondered if he was going to carry him out of the car for me since he was sleeping. In two months Tommy would be three years old. He was talking and capable of holding a child-like conversation with his grandmother and with Betty and her parents. It annoyed me when Tommy would say something to Tim, and he would get an, ah huh, or something short of a word out of him. My memories of Levi, taking my toddler son by the hand, down to the river, with his boys running ahead, excited, wanting their Dad to catch a fish for them, I couldn't help but make comparisons.

When Tim pulled up in front of the apartment, I was feeling anger after comparing him to Levi, when it came to my son, that I asked him to carry Tommy in for me. Of course he couldn't refuse, that would be a blatant confirmation of his attitude when it came to my child. He carried Tommy and Betty greeted us at the door. She pointed to her son's bedroom, that Tim should carry him in there. He did, of course, placed him on the bottom bunk and came back out smiling at Betty. She asked him to stay awhile, and he sat, long enough for a cup of coffee and then he left. As soon as he was gone, Betty said, "It was nice seeing Tim with Tommy that way. Did you guys have a good visit? Were you able to get that box?"

I filled Betty in on the box Dan's mother had, that belonged to Dan, that I wanted, but it was all I told her. She knew nothing about why the box was important to me, only that I wanted it because it was with our possessions.

"Don't get excited over Tim with Tommy," I said, "I asked him to carry him in."

"You don't think he would have thought of it on his own?"

"No, I really don't. He can't seem to get past the fact that I married Dan, and Tommy is Dan's son."

"He'll get over it one day," she said. Betty liked Tim, but Betty liked everyone. She saw only the good in people. I considered Angie and Rita my friends, but I knew Betty was my best friend. I trusted her completely, but I had to keep everything Tim and I were involved in concerning Dan and the suspicions we had, just between us. I wouldn't burden Betty with anything I was going through. She couldn't help me this time. It was different when I needed emotional support during my ordeal living with Dan, but this was different. I wasn't the scared young wife and mother that I used to be. I had changed—frightened or terrified was replaced with anger and determination. I was a stronger person. I felt like I had lived several lives, and I was racing through them searching for a happiness that seemed to elude me.

The call from Tim came a few days later. "I'm taking the box to a lock smith, and I think you should be here when we open it."

"I agree," I said, "Whatever it is I don't want you to tell me, I need to see it for myself."

"The box belongs to you, not me, I'm sure there's nothing in it to cause alarm," he said, trying to assure me.

I thought that was quite a switch from what he thought earlier, but he knew how upset I was at the thought my son's father would have anything like what I found in his clothing, hidden in that box. He had to be deaf not to notice how quiet I became on the ride from Dan's mothers home. He asked me several times if anything was wrong. I told him I was just tired. He drove over to pick me up and I had to rely on Betty to care for Tommy, again. The locksmith was able to turn the lock and it opened. I was amazed at how easy it was, when he was able to find just the right key, but as soon as I heard the click, I began to sweat. It was fear of what we would find. Tim chose not to open the lid until we got in his car. My heart was beating so fast I thought I would faint. Inside we found a notebook, and under it was a ten-year service pin.

"What's this? a simple note book he kept locked?" Tim said, staring at it. We sat close together as he picked up the book. The pin was in the form of a shield. Tim's first words were, "Holy hell! This can't be *Dan's* service pin. It's a patrolman's service pin. It's for ten years on the police force. Dan joined the Sheriff's department, not the police department. I would have been on the force eleven years if it were not for Korea. It Looks like he kept a list of dates here, and, oh no, looks like he's written about all the murders."

"What? What is it?" I asked, I wasn't able to make sense of what Dan had written, but Tim knew police jargon.

"This is about information he was gathering about all the murders and the time line he was keeping about the murder of the girl from Arden, Kathleen, it's not Dan, because he seems to be investigating our own department."

"What do you mean?" I said, unsure of what he meant.

"He suspects someone on the Arden police force is the killer. He writes here that the medal belongs to someone in our department."

"Oh, my God! Who?" I said,

"He was in the middle of investigating when he died. He mentions here—he pointed out the words to me—"several of the guys, and then eliminates Jerry.""

"Jerry? He thought Jerry might be the suspect?" My head was swimming with all Tim was reading to me. I became confused.

"No, see, he eliminated him, as well as Joe Keller, but he writes here that there are others who can't account for things that don't make sense to him."

I looked at Tim like he was crazy, or maybe it was Dan who was crazy, suspecting his own town's law enforcement, and some were his friends? *How crazy is that?* I thought. Tim was breathing heavy, going through a couple pages and then back to the beginning again. "He wrote about his suspicions and why," he said. I stopped looking at the pages; they became a blur to me.

"I can't go to anyone with this, not yet," Tim said. He looked visibly shaken. "I'll take this home and read it."

"What are you going to do," I asked, I began to breath easier knowing we didn't find anything that would implicate Dan.

"Didn't you say Dan was becoming unglued, that he might have had mental problems, that he would go into a rage?" Tim asked, becoming excited.

"Yes, but he didn't do anything or we would have found evidence of it, right?"

"I'm talking about him becoming paranoid, suspecting the police? That's a sign of a breakdown. The police? Kathleen, come on—except for two things. How did he come by that woman's license?"—He held up the service pin— "or this?"

"I wondered about that myself," I said.

Tim shook his head like he couldn't believe what he was reading in Dan's notebook. "It was like he was putting down all his suspicions and findings on paper so he wouldn't forget, or hoping he would see a pattern in someone that would lead him to the suspect," he said. Then looking at me, eyes widening, he asked, "Do you remember the date on that license you burned?"

"I never thought about looking at the date, and I was in such shock, all I remember is her face, why?"

"If it belonged to the woman from Arden, maybe he would have had access to the pin, if not, there wouldn't have been any way of it coming into his possession."

"If I'm not mistaken," I said, "that woman from Arden was years before, so I don't remember much about it, and I don't know what she looked like. The face I saw wasn't her, well, I don't think it was."

"Kathleen, lets keep this just between us. I'll start watching every guy I work with, his habits, and things like that. I'll keep a close eye on who Dan didn't eliminate in his writing, that seems to be everyone except Jerry White and Joe Keller."

"Tim, I'm so relieved because I don't think it's Dan."

"I'm not ruling anyone out yet," he said, "Remember, Dan had problems. Psychos live in an imaginary world of their own making."

With that remark, I was left stunned. "I need to get home," I said, "I have a child to look after. Drive me home, please." I let him keep the box and its contents. "Do what you have to," I said, as I got out of his car without the usual hug or kiss, not even the cheek. I was angry. Just when I wanted to accept Dan's innocence, Tim brought doubt back again. A doubt I couldn't shake, because I had to admit that Dan *wasn't* acting normal, and that's why I left him.

Three days later Tim called again, wanting to get together, this time he wanted to take me out to dinner. During dinner, he brought up Dan, asking me questions I couldn't answer.

"Why are you bringing Dan up? He's dead, and another murder occurred after his death," I said, "So explain that!"

He looked at me and realized the subject of Dan was off limits during this date, if I wanted to think of it as a date.

"I'm sorry Kathleen, it's just that I'm trying to figure out who Dan suspected. I *know* that last murder was after he died. I'm not accusing him of any crimes; I don't want to leave anything out. I hate speculating, I want the facts."

I sat across from him noticing the intense expression on his face. It seemed that look never left him. It was his persona since the first day I saw him again. I blamed his Korean ordeal for the change in him. He didn't seem like the old Tim I remembered, that Tim was gone. Nine years is a long time and people change. I sat across from him not hearing what he was saying, I was thinking about my son. He would be three years old in January and it would be the new year of 1960. So much had happened to all of us in the past decade.

"I'm sorry Tim, what did you ask me?" I said, feeling guilty that my mind had wandered and I wasn't paying attention to him.

"I said, we should get together with Jerry White and his wife one day. He's been asking me to come over, maybe play cards, something, anything, I think we should be with other people too, and not just alone all the time."

I smiled at him, thinking, he was right. "Yes I agree, and Angie and John also. You need to meet John; he loves sports, same as you. Did I tell you they are expecting their first child?"

He looked surprised, "No you haven't. I know how close you were to her parents, I see Sergeant Martino at work. He asks me about you often."

After that night out, I made an effort to get together with Angie. I called her knowing I hadn't heard from her and I attributed that to her and John being busy preparing for their baby that was due in

December. The month of November brought cold weather and Betty and I didn't take the boys to the park as often. I had been living with Betty since September and I felt bad about having to impose on her in the small two-bedroom apartment. Sleeping on her sofa bed was becoming a chore. I needed to find a place of my own. I wasn't sleeping too well. It was a combination of the uncomfortable sofa and all that was happening around me. I couldn't help thinking about Mrs. Wilkie, how she would have loved Tommy. It seemed that happiness escaped me. My entire life consisted of loneliness and loss. Tim leaving for Korea so long ago was a loss, Mrs. Wilkie's death was a loss, a bad marriage was a loss, and I began thinking that leaving Levi was a loss, but a necessary one. The greatest loss of all was when my birth mother left me on the steps of that orphan home.

Angie was happy to hear from me and invited Tim and me to her home. We got together on a Saturday night. John whispered to me that Angie's friends were giving a surprise baby shower for her and I would be receiving an invitation soon. I thought of how Lucky Angie was, and it made me think of the stressful time I had during the baby shower she and her mother tried to give for me. I was envious of her. She had two parents to help her and a loving husband who made her impending motherhood an enjoyable time, unlike what I experienced.

Angie laughed at her large stomach getting in the way of how she normally did things. I couldn't help comparing her relationship with John and all the attention she received from him with what I experienced with Dan. It made me angry that I put up with it as long as I did, but I knew no other way. If weren't for Angie and her mother pointing out to me things they didn't like that Dan and his mother were doing, I would have thought it was all normal. We finished dinner and the guys went to sit in the living room. John and Tim talked sports while Angie talked on and on about her coming baby, how she hoped it were a boy for John, but she said John didn't care as long as it was healthy.

"I think John would really like a little girl," she said.

"What makes you say that?" I asked, thinking most men want their first to be a boy.

"Oh, just the way he is with his sister's two girls. They wrap him around their little finger."

I couldn't help remembering Alice, Levi's little girl and how loving he was to her and her brothers, but especially to Alice. I found myself comparing Levi to Tim, Levi to Dan, and other men. He was different from the Amish men, but he was Amish and I had to remind myself of that. I could never live that kind of life. I told myself maybe what I felt for Levi was guilt. Almost three months and I made no effort to let him know how I was doing. What could I tell him, I wasn't coming back? I kept putting off writing to him. I had more than enough to think about with what Tim and I discovered.

Angie suggested we get together for Thanksgiving at her parents, but Tim mentioned his parents usually expected him home for the holiday. His brother was a career navy man who lived in Baltimore. He was married with his own family and if he didn't come in, Tim wouldn't leave his parents alone on thanksgiving. I was happy to see how well Tim and John got along since they had just met at this first visit.

"I'll let you know about thanksgiving later," I said.

Our evening ended with promises to get together again, soon. In the car on the way home, I let Tim know that if he wanted to spend the holiday with his family, I would understand, but I intended to be with Angie and her parents. At the Martinos Tommy would get the attention he didn't get from Dan.

"So you wouldn't want to spend it with me?" Tim asked, with a kidding tone. I think he knew I was determined to do what I wanted to do, and I wasn't the same clinging young girl he once knew.

CHAPTER 31

Betty understood my desire to spend thanksgiving with my oldest friends. Although I was happy to know her family invited us, she knew how close I was to the Martino family. John and Angie drove Tommy and me to her parents. The lack of transportation of my own was getting to me. I planned on talking to Sergeant Martino about my old job, if there was a chance of getting it back. I didn't want to take some other secretary's job away, but hoped they could find a spot for me in the department again.

The Martinos greeted me warmly and of course Tommy was the focus of their attention as soon as we walked in. Mr. Martino smiled and said, "He's a big boy," as he looked at my son.

"Yes, he'll be three in January," I said.

Lottie picked him up and carried him to the living room. I noticed they had a few toys on the floor for him, a couple of small cars, and a jack-in-the box. The kind you wind up and it plays music. Lottie put him down and he went to them as quick as he could. It kept him occupied until dinner was ready. Between Angie and her mother, I didn't have to watch after Tommy at all. They took him over. I knew Lottie was going to make a wonderful grandmother.

When seventeen-year-old Tony entered the room, I couldn't believe he was the same little boy who blurted out loudly, 'Is she the orphan?' the first time I met the family. He greeted me warmly. He was all grown up and in his last year of high school. He was very friendly and got down on the floor with my son. Later their son Sal arrived with his wife, they were newly married, Lottie said. We were about to be seated in the dining room when Frank came in wearing his navy uniform. The Martino boys all remembered me, and sitting around the table celebrating thanksgiving dinner with this fine family I couldn't help but notice how happy Mr. Martino looked. I thought he was a lucky man.

After dinner, Lottie told me Angie and her daughter-in-law would help her clean up and since I was a guest I should relax and visit with her family in the living room. I sat across from Frank, who lit a cigarette and then was telling me all about his childhood desire to join the navy and see the world. At twenty-five-years old, he said he had been many places and he was telling me about one of them when his father entered the room.

"She doesn't want to hear about all that navy stuff," Sergeant Martino said, "I tried to talk him out of joining the navy. He's getting old, he should have a wife and be looking forward to a family, like his brother."

Frank answered back, but not too nicely, I thought. There appeared to be tension between them.

"It's my life, you joined the police force, so you could show what a big tough guy you are, and I joined the navy!" Frank said.

With that statement he left the room. Sal left with him and Tony followed. It was just Mr. Martino, and I with Tommy playing on the floor. During dinner I felt he kept staring at me but he didn't direct too much conversation to me.

"How are you doing, with your jobs?" he asked.

"Fine, but I wondered, if there should be an opening for a secretary in the future, would it be possible for me to work at the station again," I said. There was something in his demeanor that made me uncomfortable. He would never forgive me for what I did and for Dan, I thought.

He looked at me and smiled, "Well, I'll see what I can do," and then his smile disappeared and he looked serious. "Kathleen, what did Dan's mother do with all your stuff from the apartment?"

"She sold all the furniture," I said, "but she saved our personal things."

"What about your clothes, what did she do with them?"

I thought it was a strange question, why would he care what happened to our clothes.

"She got rid of it all, probably to the Salvation Army clothing center or some other charity," I said.

He nodded and smiled and didn't ask any more questions. I couldn't help thinking of what he must think of me, running away like I did and then losing his best friend, he couldn't possibly have the same warm feelings he had for me before all that has happened. He was going through the motions of being nice for his family's sake, I thought. I wasn't as comfortable around him as I once had been, and it was entirely my fault. I relaxed when Angie, her mother, and Sal's wife Cheryl, entered the room and joined us. The rest of the afternoon I enjoyed the family. Lottie didn't leave me with the feeling that I in anyway contributed to Dan's breakdown or death, because both she and Angie understood what Dan had put me through.

The first week of December Tim and I got together again for a Saturday night dinner. He never included Tommy and by that time it didn't bother me, I didn't care. We were together to solve something bigger than both of us. I knew Tim still had feelings for me, but my feelings for him were in doubt. I felt sorry for him, with all that he had been through, but it caused the love I once felt for him to become murky. I wasn't sure if it was love or pity, and the obstacle in the way was my son. With Levi, I told myself it was guilt for allowing him to become too close and the obstacle was his Amish way of life.

When we were settled in the restaurant and had ordered, Tim appeared anxious to talk about Dan's notebook.

"I read it through over and over Kathleen," He said, "and the reason Dan suspected one of our own on that case of the Arden woman, is because he found the pin at that crime scene. It was a pin only a cop would have, a ten-year service pin. Quite a few of the men have been there over ten years. Except for the new rookies, and me, most have been there long enough to receive that pin. Dan was the first sheriff on the scene after the Arden police arrived, because she was from their town. Her parents reported her missing and they identified her as soon as they found her.

"Well, if the police were there first, couldn't one of them have accidentally lost it?" I asked.

"No, it was found under the body. Dan picked it up when the body was taken away. He writes that he grabbed it and shoved it into his pocket. He had it dusted for fingerprints and none were found. It seems he kept this bit of information to himself because what he noticed is it came from our own department. Kathleen, do you know what that means? Someone we work with committed that crime."

"Did the pin have a number on it that would trace it to the person," I asked.

"No, it's just a plain pin with years of service and the name of the town. Dan didn't want to tip anyone in our department off that he had it, I think."

I now realized the heavy burden Dan must have carried during that time. "He kept it to himself?" I asked, "Why would he do that?"

Tim looked at me with a disbelieving expression, "Didn't you say he was becoming paranoid, cracking up? He didn't trust anyone, that's why."

"I almost feel sorry for Dan, the hell he must have been going through, but he took it out on me," I said.

Tim looked at me with an exasperated expression and said, "He knew that pin wasn't the same as his deputies from the Sheriff's department and the two patrolmen, Jerry and Joe, they weren't on the force long enough, so that leaves at least the older guys. It's definitely a cop, so I'll have to check on how many years they've been there."

He lit a cigarette, blew the smoke off to the side and said, "Dan wrote he was about to check on that, and then his writing ends. Who he suspected, I can't guess. He didn't write it down."

Tim was smoking more than he had before Korea. The smoke bothered me lately, and I couldn't help comparing sitting in the smoke filled restaurant to being in a room with the Amish and Levi. The Holsteders didn't smoke and nether did Levi.

"So you think he was going around checking everyone's badges or medals?" I asked,

"I don't know what he did, I just know he was close friends with some of them, so only he would know."

"Well, he was a very close friend to Sergeant Martino," I said.

Tim laughed, "Martino? He's beyond reproach and they were attached at the hip. I'm sure he eliminated him first thing, Kathleen, it's the other guys, you know, some of the hot heads, the cocky ones with hair trigger fingers. A few have been suspended for a period of time due to their all too aggressive actions when confronting people over a stupid back tail light that was out, or driving over the speed limit by just five miles. Some of those old guys are bullies, and joining the police force suits their personalities and feeds their egos. They've been on the job long enough to have seen the terrible seedy side of life and they've become hardened."

I had to agree with Tim. He himself had changed. He displayed more aggression when it came to his job than he had when we first met, back then he was a young rookie, now I thought he was becoming hardened, somewhat like Dan.

In December I found another job to replace the one at the grocery store. It was as a secretary in a real estate office, and it paid better. Between the new job and Saturdays at Betty's shop I made enough to look for a place of my own. Rita's garage apartment was rented out to her cousin, so even though I would have loved to live there again, it was not available. Having access to rentals in the office I worked in helped, and I found a small apartment—one bedroom was all I could afford—Tim helped me move in. Tommy was young enough to sleep with me, later I would get him a bed of his own. The first day all I had to move was our clothing and personal stuff.

With Christmas a few weeks away, I had plenty to do. I found a woman who would keep Tommy for me during the day. My budget was tight, having to pay the rent and her too. Betty's father insisted I take their old second car that they were replacing and I could pay them the little they asked for as often as I could afford to pay. I made sure I would give them something each month. I was getting by. Tim and I were still considered a couple by everyone, so I kept my feelings about him to myself.

Lottie called me one morning, as I was getting ready for work.

"Kathleen, Angie's had her baby last night, it's a boy! Sal is on cloud nine, as we all are," she said.

"Congratulations," I said, "I'm happy for you. Tell Angie I'll call her when she gets home." We talked for a few minutes, and then I got Tommy ready to take to the sitter. She was a neighbor of Rita's, so when he was with her, with Rita just a few houses away, I felt he was in good hands. I was looking forward to Christmas and having a tree of my own. It would be Tommy's first real Christmas, because the Amish way of celebrating was sparse and he wouldn't remember. I was surprised when Tim's mother invited me to dinner. She called me herself and not through Tim as she usually did. She surprised me when she asked if I would bring my son. I wondered what Tim would think of that. I didn't have long to find out. We were seeing each other more often since I moved to my own place. He came over one night, a few days after we moved in. He brought me some kitchen utensils his mother contributed and between his mother, Betty's family and Rita, they helped by donating their extra stuff. My apartment took on the look of a resale shop, but I was grateful for anything I could get. All the guys in the Sheriff's department got together a fund for Tommy and me to buy a new bedroom set. They said it was in memory of Dan.

"So, your mother wants me to bring my son over for supper," I said.

"Yes, she wants a grandchild so badly, but my brother's wife can't have any," he said.

"I thought your brother had a family." I was confused because I heard her mention her daughter-in-law and the children.

"Oh, that's his wife's two girls from her first marriage, my mother wants a grandchild of her own."

When he mentioned the words, 'her own,' that bothered me. I noticed he paid a little more attention to Tommy lately and I thought a little was better than nothing. I made supper for us on the used table set from the resale shop. He helped me this time, bringing a booster seat he had bought for Tommy to sit on, and that surprised me. I watched him lift him up on it. I looked at Tim across the table and wished he were the old Tim, and I imagined us young again and Tommy was his child and his name wasn't Thomas. All those crazy thoughts went through my mind as we ate in silence for a few moments.

"Have you been able to track down the owner of the pin?" I asked.

"Not yet, and don't mention this to anyone in the Martino family," he said.

"I won't," I assured him, "but certainly you don't think it might be—"

He looked at me like I was crazy, "Kathleen, why would I think that? Of course not, I just want to keep it between us for now, ok?"

I agreed and the Martinos weren't mentioned again.

I drove over to Tim's parents and was grateful for my own car. Tim wanted to pick me up but I refused, saying I had to run an errand on the way and I would drive myself. The real reason was I didn't want Tim at my place that night. It was a Saturday and he was off on Sunday, that meant he would be staying late and on a few occasions when he came over and stayed late, I didn't know what he expected of me. He didn't know anything about my life before I returned, and might now expect me to sleep with him. He had changed so much and his world was different. He wasn't as religious as he once was. I was afraid to become intimate with him; afraid he would expect it. We were together, but except for one time when he told me he loved me, it wasn't mentioned again. I didn't reply back because I had just returned and hanging over me was the fact that I became intimate with Levi before him.

When Tommy and I entered the O'Malley's home, Tim's mother scooped my son up in her arms.

"What a beautiful boy!" she said, gushing over him. I felt it was a genuine gesture and I was happy over her response. Tim relieved me of the booster seat that I held and he carried it to the dining room.

"How old is he?" Noreen asked as she held him. Timmy wanted to get down and she put him down.

"He'll be three in January," I said, pleased at her reaction to meeting my son for the first time. I wished her son had the same reaction.

It was strange, years before it was Tim I loved and she was the one who I wasn't comfortable with, things were reversed now. She gave Timmy a lot of attention and I noticed Tim's reaction, he was smiling. Maybe seeing his mother accepting my son would change his attitude and his thinking, or whatever he thought that caused the emotional distance he put between himself and Timmy.

The evening went well and we talked mostly about my job, Tim's work, what Noreen was doing with her volunteer work at her church. Tim's father was quiet, but friendly. He made a few paper boats for Timmy and when it was time to leave, I thanked them and we hugged goodbye. This time Tim carried Timmy to the car for me, and I carried the booster seat. I wondered if it was just for show in front of his parents.

The next time Tim came over, his attention to my son was greatly improved. He came in one night without calling me as he usually did before he came. I had just come home from picking Tommy up from the sitter. I was tired, it was a Tuesday night and I didn't stop to visit Rita as I did on occasion when I was picking up my son. I was surprised to see him.

"Kathleen, I hope you don't mind, but I was on the way home and didn't have time to let you know I was coming," he said, apologetically.

"Oh, no, it's alright. Are you ok?" I asked, noticing he looked worried about something.

He removed his jacket and sat down. Tommy walked over to him and he put his hand on his head to tussle his hair. I thought it was an affectionate gesture and it pleased me.

"What's wrong?" I asked.

"Nothing, just tired," he said.

He did look tired and I asked him if I could get him anything, but he shook his head no, and closed his eyes with his head back against the sofa.

"Angie has been home with her baby for over a week now and I thought we could go over to see them, it you want, or I can go alone," I said.

"Yes, of course I'd like to see them," he said, opening his eyes. "I'm just so tired lately, so make a date and we'll go."

I invited him to stay for supper and when it was ready, I went into the living room and found him sound asleep on my sofa. He had taken one of the sofa pillows for his head and was lying down. I sat across from him and stared at his face. He had put weight on and the hollow look he had when I first returned was gone. He looked more like the Tim I remembered, albeit, older. I loved that face once, and at that moment I felt I still did. He resembled the same man, but time had changed him and I loved what he once was. Maybe, he could be that man again if I gave him time and was more understanding, I thought. He was rough around the edges and that came home to me in his approach when it came to affection. His hugs and kisses were different. I thought back to Levi, so gentle in his lovemaking, and so kind. I longed for that again. I was confused, and I felt a tear trickle down my cheek. I knew I would have to contact him again. It wasn't fair to him that I hadn't. He would be worried about me and so I decided after Christmas I would write him a letter. I didn't have the heart to wake Tim, and so I covered him with a blanket and went to the kitchen where Tommy and I ate our supper. I would heat up a plate for Tim when he was awake.

CHAPTER 32

Christmas was days away and Tim helped pick out a tree. It snowed the day before, and Tommy loved the snow, kicking it up with his boots and running between the trees in the Christmas tree lot. I could see how hard Tim tried to give Tommy attention, but wondered if he had problems relating to small children and not necessarily just my son. I knew some men could not connect with young children. At times I thought he did it just to please me, and not because he really wanted to. When we went to visit Angie and John, I noticed he didn't make a big thing out of their new baby either. I thought I was too judgmental, and I needed to cut him some slack. With the tree tied atop Tim's car, we stopped at a restaurant for lunch. I opened the back door to get Tommy out, and Tim picked him up.

"He's old enough to walk," I said, "He likes to walk in the snow."

Tim laughed, "No problem, but we can get out of the cold quicker if I carry him."

Once settled in a booth, Tommy and I on one side with Tim across from us, Tommy, like most young children wouldn't sit still and I noticed Tim's expression. Patience wasn't one of his attributes.

"Have you come up with anything new in the investigation?" I asked.

He ran his hand through his hair, a sign of frustration, and said, "No, I looked through the files on that murder and nothing sticks out, but I can't figure out how Dan got his hands on the driver's license you found in his clothing. It belonged to a woman from Chicago."

"I wish I hadn't thrown it away, it was done on impulse and I regret it," I said.

We talked about Christmas, and where I would be spending it. I was invited by almost everyone, the Martinos, Betty's family, and Tim's parents and I hadn't made up my mind yet. I knew I would have to take Tommy to see his grandmother and decided to take him Christmas Eve.

"I need to visit Dan's mother, so she can spend it with her grandson," I said.

He looked surprised, "You're awfully nice to her considering what she put you through, during your marriage."

"Well, I feel it's the right thing to do."

His expression changed to one trying to mask his true feelings. "You're too forgiving Kathleen, I wouldn't give her the time of day."

"She's his grandmother, the only one he has," I said, thinking I knew what it was like to not have one family member I belonged to by blood.

"Well, I hadn't thought of that," he said.

I was thinking at that moment that the Tim I once loved wasn't present at all, and the man sitting across from me was bitter and unable to forgive.

I decided I would spend Christmas Eve with my son's grandmother and Christmas Day with Betty's family. I didn't need the stress of being around Sergeant Martino and all the feelings of guilt that would arise in me, it would ruin my day, or at Tim's parents, watching Tim trying hard to please me, with forced attention to my son.

On Christmas Eve, I arrived at Mrs. Clarke's and she greeted me warmly. Picking up Tommy who was no longer a baby, she mentioned how heavy he was.

"Well, he's almost three," I said.

"Yes, I forget he's not a baby anymore, but I missed all those months when he was a baby," she said, giving me a certain look. I knew it was my fault. She said it in a way that made me feel guilty that I deprived her of her grandson while he was still an infant.

We settled down to the nice dinner she prepared and then she busied herself with having Tommy open his presents. She decorated her tree in unbreakable ornaments and allowed him to touch everything on it. I offered to clean up after the meal and she let me, so while she was in the living room with Tommy I spent a good deal of time leaving her alone with him and I stayed in the kitchen until everything was washed and put away. I found myself having to ask her where some things were stored and she yelled back at me, "Just put them where ever you find room, I'll find them." Nothing was going to take away a minute she could spend with her grandson.

I might as well have been invisible, as I sat in the room watching her on the floor playing with Tommy. She bought so many toys and she told him Santa told her to buy them. She needed to take credit for what should have been Santa's gifts. I hoped I could get them all in the trunk of my car, a tricycle, a wagon, and many smaller toys. I sat there thinking of how generous she was and she made up for the other grandmother he would never have, not to mention, aunts, uncles, cousins, and a Grandpa. He would never know any real extended family. Dan was an only child and his mother didn't have any family nearby. Her only sister lived in California. I never met her and she was too elderly to attend my wedding.

As I sat watching them, I told myself I did the right thing; Tommy needed a Grandmother as much as she needed him. I was leafing through a magazine when she looked up at me and said, "Kathleen, I'm thinking of selling my house in the spring and moving back to Arden."

I froze, taken by surprise; I said nothing as she continued to tell me of her plans. "I wish I had my old home back, it was perfect for Tommy, the back yard was large and I could have put a swing set there for him. I had plenty of room for him—Well, for both of you, whenever you could stay," she said.

I wasn't expecting that, and it brought back all the negative feelings I had about her. I envisioned her taking over my life if she moved back to the town where the only friends I had lived. I could feel my face flush, but I didn't say a word; certainly I wasn't going to comment at all and give any hint of encouragement.

"It's getting late," I said, "and I think I better pack up and head home, before the roads become dangerous."

I could see it started to snow again, so I had a good excuse to leave.

"Yes, it's dark and you need to get home before there's more snow on the roads," she said.

She dressed Tommy in his snowsuit and boots while I went out to the car and loaded up the Christmas gifts in the trunk. I piled the smaller gifts in the back seat next to Tommy and we said our goodbyes. All I could manage was to allow her to hug me with difficulty. Once on the road, I found myself shaking with anger, and feeling that things were spinning out of control in my life and I didn't know how to stop it.

Christmas day at Betty's parents was the reprieve I needed. The only place I didn't feel obligated, guilty, or angry, in the presence of someone. I didn't mention any of my problems to them, wanting the day to be free of all negativity.

New Year's Eve was another hurdle to overcome. Who would I spend it with? Tim and his stressed out demeanor or the Martinos and my uncomfortable feelings around Sgt. Martino. Rita was dating again and had her own group of friends. Betty was spending it with a guy she was dating and that would mean, I would be expected to join her with Tim. I was still reeling from Dan's mother's announcement of moving near us. I wasn't in the mood for a night with Tim, especially on New Year's Eve. There would be drinking and Tim taking me home, maybe expecting something other than a kiss? I decided to feign illness and stay home with my child to see the New Year in. Tim was disappointed when I told him and he wanted to come over and spend it with me, but that wouldn't solve anything, so I told him I was going to bed early as I wasn't feeling well. I could tell by his voice when I called, that he was disappointed, but I didn't care.

I put Tommy to bed and sat up on New Year's Eve, alone, crying and trying to decide what to do about my life. I wasn't happy. I still harbored a tiny doubt about Dan's innocence, about my feelings for Tim, and about the threat Dan's mother posed in my life. After I went through a box of tissues, I poured myself a glass of wine, a rare thing, and sat down to write a letter to Levi. He would be worried about me and it wasn't fair to leave him not ever hearing from me, I needed to tell him that I was okay, but I knew I wasn't. I sat at the table with paper and pen for a long time, not knowing what I could say to him. I had to write that I wasn't coming back, but what excuse would I give? Maybe I wouldn't need to tell him that, not yet, because I didn't want to break off contact with him. I wouldn't do anything impulsively again, so I decided to tell him very little, only that I needed time to settle things and that I would write again in a few months. My hand was shaking as I managed to write: "Dear Levi, I'm so sorry that I have not written before this—"

I finished the short letter letting him know I needed more time to settle things and would write again. I had no idea what I was doing—was I stringing Tim along? I didn't know which way to turn, what to do next. I sat in a stupor hardly knowing the New Year arrived and it was 1961. I wondered what the year would bring. So many people around me, at work, in my life, and yet, except for my son, I was alone.

New Year's day, Tim came over to check on me. I wasn't expecting him. He brought us a dinner his mother fixed and I felt guilty lying to him. I pretended to have a bad headache, which wasn't too far from the truth since the night before I sat drinking wine, crying and trying to write the letter. I looked like the mess I felt. He made me lie on the sofa and he got a cold washcloth to put across my forehead. I felt terrible pretending I was sick when it was the wine I had the night before.

"Thanks," I managed to say.

"No problem," came his reply, and then he kissed me. I hoped he didn't notice the empty wine bottle in my trash can, so after a few minutes of lying down with the cloth to cool my forehead, I got up and covered the bottle with paper towel, later the remnants of our dinner would be added to conceal any trace of my little white lie.

We spent the rest of the day with me lying on the sofa and Tim putting together a toy for Tommy. I watched him and felt confused, in that moment it seemed like the old Tim was back. He was affectionate, kind, and showed concern for me. He didn't mention anything crime related, and he played with Tommy for the first time. I looked over at them together and fantasized what could never be— Tommy being Tim's son. I regretted ever marrying Dan. I should have waited for Tim, but then I had to realize if and when he came back after so many years, it would never be the same Tim.

CHAPTER 33

On the 16th of January, Tommy would be three years old. I often thought of how Dan would have been when his son was able to talk and run around. Would that have helped Dan to relax more, maybe helped in relieving stress for him? There was no doubt that he loved his son. I often thought of so many *what ifs* and it was driving me crazy. I knew I needed to stop that way of thinking.

Angie called me and wanted to know what I had planned for his birthday.

"I haven't thought of it," I said.

"Well, my parents wanted to know if you would be okay with us having a big party at their home for Tommy," she said.

"Oh, I don't know—"

"Come on Kathleen, let them, because all the men who worked with Dan want to do something special for Tommy."

I was surprised, "You mean they would be at the party?"

"Yes, of course," she said, "everyone Dan worked with in the Sheriff's department and a few of the cops, and you can invite whoever you like."

I thought of Dan's mother, if we left her out she would find out about it, because she kept in contact with a couple of the older Sheriff's wives, I was sure.

"What about his grandmother?" I asked, "she'll find out about it and if she's not invited, I'll never hear the end of it," I said.

"Yes," she laughed, "My Ma said we can put up with her for one night."

After I hung up the phone, I wondered what I had gotten myself into. All the men and other deputies who worked with Dan would be there, including some of the police with Tim among them. The very men he was suspicious of, all together. I wondered what he would think about it when he found out. That night after work, I called him. I asked him to come over, that we needed to talk. He usually came on weekends unless it was for something special.

"Is anything wrong," he asked.

"No, it's about Tommy's birthday," I said.

"What about it?" he sounded a little distant.

"The Martinos want to throw a big party for his third birthday and invite the whole police and sheriff's departments," I said.

He was silent for a moment and then he said, "I'll be over soon as I can get there."

He must have flown over because before I knew it he was at my door. He came in with a big smile on his face and I was relieved, at first believing he might not be interested in a party for my son. I would have preferred a small affair with Betty's son and maybe Rita's kids for him but as usual things were spinning out of control when it came to my wishes.

"I don't know about this, Tim," I said, "Is it a good idea?" I was thinking it was an over the top party for a three year old.

"Best idea I can think of," Tim said.

I looked at him wondering what he meant. Was he happy for my son to have a big party with so many grown ups? It wasn't what I planned.

"All I wanted was a small kids party for him," I said.

Tim's eyes widened with excitement, "Kathleen, this is perfect—a chance to maybe flush out who lost that service pin, without anyone suspecting."

I looked at him and was disappointed that his interest had nothing to do with my son's birthday, but a chance for Tim to play detective.

"Please don't make any trouble," I said, "It's Tommy's birthday."

"Don't worry," he said, convincing me that he wouldn't do anything, tip off anyone about what we found. "I won't say a word, about anything," he assured me.

I didn't know what to expect, and preferred to keep both Betty and Rita out of attending. I gave them the option of a kid's party or attending this debacle at the Martino's. They knew how I felt and would attend a small party at my apartment for Tommy with their children. I was surprised that Rita would pass up being around all her former husband's coworkers, but she was now engaged to a nice man and had moved on with her life. She confided in me that being around the police brought back the pain of losing her husband. Betty and Rita now knew each other and would prefer to be alone with our children celebrating Tommy's birthday.

On the day of the big Sunday afternoon party, a few days before Tommy's actual birthday, Tim drove us over, arriving early and Lottie greeted us warmly at the door.

"Hi, come on in and make yourselves at home," she said.

I noticed Tim went right over to Sergeant Martino, who was in the living room talking with Dan's mother which surprised me, seeing her there so early, but then it shouldn't have since she would never miss a moment she could spend with her grandson. The minute I walked in with Tommy, she picked him up. Lottie looked at me and smiled, and I knew she was thinking the same, that Tommy wasn't a baby. Dan's mother carried him over to a chair and sat down expecting him to stay on her lap, but he managed to slide off and run to Angie who came into the room holding her baby son. I laughed at that, three years old and he had a mind of his own. He wanted to see the baby who interested him more. Angie knelt down so he could see little Johnny, now six weeks old.

I followed Lottie into the dining room hoping I could help her with something, anything to keep away from whatever was going on in her living room between Dan's mother, Tim and the Sergeant. Lottie and I began to ready the table where she would put on a large buffet of food when most of the guests arrived. It wasn't long before the other men and their wives filled both rooms, walking around talking and eating, drinking and having a great time with each other.

I was so afraid of what Tim might say to a couple of the older men, that he knew were on the force over ten years. What was supposed to be a child's birthday party appeared like a gathering in a courtroom, as I heard Tim and the other men talk about the one crime their department was still involved in, that hadn't been solved. At that time I knew the murders of all the women over the past ten years had never been solved. After the fifth murder everyone thought it might be the work of just one killer.

I noticed Sergeant Martino and Dan's mother speaking together in a corner. I wondered what he would have to talk to her about; he never cared much for her and I thought he was just trying to make an old lady feel comfortable. Knowing Dan's mother, she probably cornered him to talk about her son. I was uncomfortable all afternoon and couldn't wait until it was over. There must have been at least forty people, not counting the Martino family and Tim and me. We all gathered around the table when Lottie lit the candles on the large cake. Someone picked Tommy up to stand him on a chair, and I noticed it was John, Angie's husband. Tim was in the background deep in conversation with Jerry, one of the guys he was close to. He had to be reminded that it was Tommy's birthday when everyone started singing Happy Birthday. Then John helped my son blow out the candles. I felt disappointed that it wasn't Tim who took an interest. When one of the men, Dan's deputy sheriff, Jake Sebik, spoke up he got everyone's attention. He held an envelope in his hand, waved it and announced, "Kathleen, here is a savings bond for your son, for his education. Everyone in the department got together and we want to present you with it, in memory of his father," he said.

He went on speaking about Dan, what a great Sheriff he was and all the years of service he gave, and then I noticed Dan's mother crying in the background. Sergeant Martino went to her and put his arm around her.

"Thank you all, so much," I said, "I can't thank you enough for what you've done for Tommy."

It was getting late as most of the people left after saying their goodbyes and wishing my son the best for his future, I thanked everyone again as they left. Dan's mother came by bus since she never learned to drive, which wasn't uncommon for women her age. It was the one saving grace for me when I was married to her son. She couldn't show up at our home unless he went and got her or a friend drove her. I felt we needed to drive her home. I thanked the Martinos more than a few times; I was overwhelmed over what they had done for my son. I mentioned to Tim that we needed to drive Dan's mother home. He gave me a look that told me he really didn't want to, so I quickly said, "Tim, It's late, drive us home and I'll take her home."

"No, that's okay, I don't want you driving that far alone if you don't have to," he said.

He knew it got dark early and the weather was very cold. It hadn't snowed in a couple weeks but there was still plenty on the ground, much of which had turned to ice. Tim put the few toys Tommy received in the trunk and we climbed into the car. It was cold, and he started the motor to get the heater going. Dan's mother thanked him for offering to take her home. She settled in the back seat with Tommy and enjoyed the long ride. He fell asleep in her arms, and that, I'm sure made her day. On the way she talked and talked about what a nice thing they did for Dan's son and I could see the expression on Tim's face. I knew what he was feeling and thinking, he didn't want any reminder of Dan. I tried to say a few words to her, agreeing it was a nice gesture on the Sheriff's department giving a savings bond for him. She agreed and then she addressed me.

"Kathleen, I'm sorry I threw away all your clothes, I should have waited, it would have helped you in not having to buy new clothing again, it's quite an expense since you said you came back with very little."

"Oh, don't worry about that," I said, "you didn't know if I would ever come back, and besides what would you have done with them. You needed to get rid of it all."

"Well, I took all the clothes to the Salvation Army thrift store. First I washed all the dirty laundry and packed it in boxes. They were happy to get them."

"You didn't need to do all that, I'm sure they were happy to get them in any condition."

"Mr. Martino, asked me what I did with the clothes, maybe he wanted something of Dan's, like his ties. You know Dan loved bright ties when he wasn't working," she said.

Tim looked over at me with a dumbfounded expression. He turned his head looking back at her, "Did you save any ties," he said, "or anything belonging to Dan?"

"No, and I should have, shouldn't I? It was too painful for me, I guess."

The rest of the ride to her home we didn't say much. We let her talk about how happy she was that the Martinos invited her. When Tim pulled in her driveway, she thanked us for bringing her home. Tommy was asleep on the back seat, and Tim managed to find a blanket he kept behind his seat and he covered him. I thanked him. It was quite cold, even in the car with the heater going, so it surprised me that he thought of doing that.

Once we were on the road again, Tim said he thought it was weird that Sergeant Martino should care where all the clothing went. I agreed with him.

"He asked me the same thing," I said. "I didn't much of it at the time, but asking her the same question? That's weird."

Tim looked startled, "That makes no sense unless he really wanted—no it still doesn't make sense. Did you tell him what she did with the clothing?"

"Yes, I did, so why ask her the same question? She said she washed all the dirty Laundry, didn't she say that?" I was beginning to think of the license I found in the bag of laundry and Tim thought of it at the same time.

"Kathleen, if it were the license of the dead girl from Arden, Dan might have come across it when he found the service pin, but it couldn't be, if you were sure the face of the girl belonged to a later murder. Are you sure? Think, Kathleen, think, are you sure?" He sounded excited and desperate for an answer.

"I'm sure of it", I said, It's what made me think it had something to do with Dan, that maybe he was involved, but I only thought about it for a minute, and I panicked and threw it away, I'm sorry."

I thought about how happy Tim was that the entire company was together under any circumstances, even during a child's birthday party.

"So, did you ever find out if anyone lost his service pin?"

"I'm sure it wasn't any of the guys who have been on the job ten years or more, because I asked each one of them if they still had their service pin, and I took a chance doing it without tipping one off if it was one of them," he said, and then he stopping talking and I thought he was concentrating on the icy road, but he blurted out loudly, almost waking Tommy, "Martino! No, can't be. I didn't ask him, afraid he might think I was nuts, and in his home in front of everyone, no, I don't think so, but I've ruled the other guys out," he said.

I detected nervousness in his voice. I was upset too, and didn't know what else to say. I thought of what Lottie said during the party when I thanked her for what she and Angie had done for Tommy. 'Oh, it was Sal's idea, she said, 'and we thought it was a great thing to do.'

"It was Sergeant Martinos idea for the party," I said, "Lottie told me he thought of it."

Tim had to stop at a red light at a railroad crossing and while we waited for the train to pass, he turned to me, "When did you find that license? Do you remember exactly when?"

"Well, it was during the worst time in my marriage when he was coming home with blood on his clothes and after we had that terrible fight and I went to stay with the Martinos overnight. I was afraid to go home in the morning and Sergeant Martino said he would stop and talk to Dan. He left early and I remember he talked to him at our apartment. He called and told me it was safe to return home. When I got there, Dan had already left for work.

"It fits!" Tim said loudly, "it had to be him, there's no one else. I've ruled out the others and Jerry told me that Dan was working day and night with the detectives on that case of the Arden girls murder. Jerry mentioned that some of the Sheriffs and cops would go out for a few drinks together and everyone knew Dan and Sal were close, but after a few drinks they would get into arguments over the Arden case. Jerry didn't think it was anything serious, just two guys with different opinions. I wasn't here, so I can only go by what Jerry told me."

I started to get a sick feeling in my stomach. I was thinking, *it couldn't be what Tim's thinking, could it?* "Tim, are you thinking what I'm thinking?" I said, my voice shaking.

"Who else? But how can we prove it?' he said. "If I'm wrong—no, I can't be. Is there any way you can find out if he has his service pin? If I ask him, Oh, boy, I can't let him suspect I'm on to him, you have to find a way to find out about it without him knowing. You're close to his wife and daughter, try to find some way."

When we arrived home, I was so upset I was crying. Tim carried Tommy in and after I put him to bed we sat together in my living room. I was as nervous as I was the day I found that damn license. I was frightened and all I could do was cry.

Sobbing, I said, "It can't be— Tim, my God! Angie, Lottie, the family, what will happen if it's him, worse, what if we accuse him and he's innocent?"

He put his arm around me for a moment to comfort me, but I could tell his thoughts were not on how upset I was, but on what to do next in trying to find out about that missing pin.

"Did you notice the point at the bottom of the service pin was bent back?" he asked.

"No, but shouldn't you mention something to Jerry, you can trust him, can't you?" I asked, hoping we wouldn't be alone with this awful suspicion.

"No, I can't take a chance, not until I know for sure the pin could be Martino's. I want to know more about what went on during Dan's investigation of that Arden murder and that I could only get from Jerry. Dan was Sheriff for the whole county but he could only get involved in other cases outside our county if invited. All you need to do is find some way to find out about Martino's service pin."

"I wouldn't know where to start," I said, "Ask Lottie straight out? What do you want me to do?"

He stood up, ready to leave, "You'll find the right words at the right time," he said, and then with a quick kiss, he left. He left me frightened, and alone with the problem. I began to think of Levi's uncomplicated life, how lucky he was. I went to bed feeling like I was getting sucked up in a whirlwind.

CHAPTER 34

In February around Valentines Day, Angie invited Tim and I to join her and her husband to a Valentine party they were attending to be held in a restaurant, one they usually went to with the friends they hung out with. Tim thought it was a great opportunity to meet other couples our age. It would be a reprieve from the turmoil we found ourselves embroiled in.

We arrived at the party and were introduced to many of Angie and John's friends. We were chatting with one couple when I noticed Tim's expression change as his attention went to the entrance of the private room. He quickly left us and went to greet a young man whom he brought over to us, his girlfriend in tow, and introduced him as a new police rookie who recently joined the Arden force.

"Kathleen, this is Patrick Keegan, he's new in the department," and then he introduced him to the other couple and in turn Patrick introduced Tracy, his girlfriend.

Angie came over to us and said, "Oh, I see you met Pat, he's new on the police force. My Dad became friends with him, and Pat expressed how much he wanted to join the police department so Dad got him started." Turning to Pat, she said, "It's been almost a year since you and my Dad met hasn't it?" and then she excused herself and joined the other guests.

Pat smiled, "Yeah, it's been about eight months", he said, addressing Tim. "We met one night having a few beers but I didn't know he was a cop, so I was telling him how much I wanted to be involved in the law in some way and that's when he told me he was a Sergeant on the Arden force. He guided me in how to apply and I took it from there," he said. He laughed when he recalled how he at first didn't think Sal was a cop and thought he was putting him on. Tim looked at him and said, "What made you think that?"

"Well, it was pretty late that night and I wondered why a cop and a Sergeant at that, would be sitting alone in a bar so late at night. He wasn't wearing his uniform so I didn't take him for a cop. He told me he had been a cop for thirty years."

Turning to me, Tim said, "Pat's just joined about eight months ago." And then said, "Let's sit down." The others followed and took their places at a long table. We had a nice time that night, but Tim looked bothered about something and on the way home he told me how he was surprised to hear Martino helped him get the job, and how odd it was that Martino would be out drinking alone, and so late.

"Didn't you tell me the guys liked to stop for a couple beers some nights," I said.

"Alone, and that late? No, that isn't what I meant. I bet he was up to something. I should have asked Pat how late it was, but I thought it would sound like a stupid question and it's really none of my business—in a way it is."

"I can't imagine Lottie going along with him staying out so late, I wonder what excuse he gave her. Maybe it was the only time," I said.

"I highly doubt it, and I'm going to try to get close to the kid and see what information I can get out of him about that night, if anything," Tim said, excitement in his voice. "He said they met eight months ago, that would be about in July, early August. You weren't here Kathleen, but there was another murder around that time. I have to look up the exact date she was found and then try to find out the day the kid met him in the bar."

I glanced at him and he could see I was afraid of what he would find. "I almost don't want you to find out," I said, and then quickly changed my mind. "Oh, I do, but then what do we do? The same date too close proves nothing," I said.

"Let me handle it. It can't hurt to ask questions," he said, as he parked the car in front of my apartment.

"Tim, I'm tired tonight, and after I pay the sitter for Tommy, I'm going to bed."

He pulled out his wallet and handed me ten dollars. "What's this for?" I asked, knowing it was for the sitter. "I can't take this!"

"Yes you can, come on, take it, I insist. You had to hire that girl for tonight, so please let me pay for it," he said, in a pleading way.

I don't know why I felt that I shouldn't take it because I knew if it were the old Tim, I would have thought nothing of allowing him to pay for anything pertaining to me, but I didn't want to be obligated to him when it came to my son. I accepted it so I wouldn't hurt his feelings.

"Thanks," I said, and we kissed goodnight. He waited until I entered the building before he drove away.

Tim and I would see each other every weekend and his attention to my son improved, but my feelings about him was always changing depending on what was going on with his investigating Martino's nights out. We both knew the answer to who the killer might be depended on who owned the service pin bent on the bottom. The killer unknowingly placed the body of the woman over the dropped pin and only he could have lost it there.

Tim came over one week night and I made supper for us. He brought Dan's notebook and after he helped me clean up and I put Tommy to bed, we both sat at the table with the note book Dan had written on, about the complete time-line of every murder starting with the first one in 1949.

"See here," he said, pointing out the murder that took place in Clearidge in December of 1949. In March 1950, another one, and at that time they were two women found three months apart, one behind the school, and one near the railroad tracks.

"I remembered Mrs. Wilkie mentioning it to me when I came to live with her in October of that year because she warned me to be careful whenever I went out," I said.

"That's when it started, and those two were close together," Tim said. He pointed to the following year, 1951, "One more murder, and this time the killer put a whole year between the last victim and this one."

I looked at the dates. It seemed there was one almost every year until Tim pointed out how the killer tried to put more space between them. He pointed each one out.

"Look," he said pointing with his finger. "January 1952, another, then September of 1953, another. In November of 1954 another, and then he didn't strike again until April of 1955. That was the girl from Arden. It's when our department along with the Sheriff's department got involved, when Dan found the service pin. The killer seems out of control, if it's the same guy.

"How would they know it was the girl from Arden?" I asked.

"Her picture was in the paper as missing before they found her so they knew the minute they came upon the body." Shaking his head, Tim said, "I looked up the old news reports and she was wearing the same clothing her mother described. That's when our police and sheriff's department's were notified, before they removed the body."

I was sitting close to Tim watching his finger move from one date to another.

"Look at the date of the next two, three years later, April 1958?" I said, surprised, "One in April and then another in August. How did the Killer? —If it's one guy, control himself for three years and then strike twice in a few months?"

Tim shook his head in disbelief, "He's one sick bastard," he said, with disgust. "I think it's the one from August of 1958 whose face was on the license you found, not the Arden woman, and not the woman found in her kitchen."

"The one in August, was that the last one?" I asked, hoping it was.

"I'm afraid not, the last one was this past August, just before you returned. It seems like he's trying to put more time between them, but he can't control it. I'm afraid he's a born psychopath."

"What if it's more than one person? Gosh, how can it be the Sergeant, he seems so normal," I said.

Tim laughed out loud, "Kathleen, psychos appear normal most of the time. They're clever and deceptive, don't you know that?"

I was taken aback with the statement and tone of voice he used, like I was supposed to know about something I would know nothing about. It reminded me of some of Dan's expectations of me, which left me feeling less than adequate. I looked over at Tim's face as he kept his eyes on what Dan had written and then watched as he went over Dan's book of notes, again. He had the intense look of a hunted person. I moved away and quit looking over his shoulder. At that moment if I were able to disappear from this web I was caught in, I would have.

"Look here!" Tim ordered me to look at the notebook again. I wasn't sure what I was supposed to see. He looked up at me when I didn't comment.

"He writes here that he found the pin at the scene of the murder in

April of 1955 and kept it, realizing it was from the Arden Police department."

"He's had this for over four years or more?" I asked, wondering why it took him so long to figure out who it belonged to.

"He was probably in shock to think it could be any one of the Arden police. He wanted to bide his time, to make sure, to eliminate each one, one at a time," Tim said.

"Have you found out anything more from Pat about the night he met Martino?" I asked, apprehensively, not really wanting to know anything, but out of curiosity I had to ask.

"I was just about to tell you. He mentioned they left the bar together around closing time, two am, I think, and he wondered where Martino lived because he noticed when he pulled out of the parking lot ahead of him, he went toward the city. He said he thought he heard Martino say he lived in Arden. I asked him if he asked the sergeant about it later and he said he never thought of it after that, and didn't want to appear nosey."

"Well, wasn't he curious that *you* were interested with what Mr. Martino was doing?" I asked.

"No, I distracted him and he quickly forgot what we were talking about. He's young and easily pulled into another conversation. I asked him how long he had been dating Tracy, and then that's all he talked about. I got the information I was looking for—he didn't drive in the direction of home that night—I should say early dawn. Where the hell do you think he would be heading at that time of the morning? We both know, don't we?" he said, a slight smile on his face that reeked of 'Gotcha.'

"You missed your calling," I said, "You should have been a detective instead of just a plain cop."

Moving his chair back, he said quite angrily, "What do you mean a *plain* cop? We risk our lives everyday, more than any detective, you should know that!"

I didn't say anything after that outburst and waited until he calmed down. I couldn't wait until he went home. He insisted he knew it was Martino, and he was sure that was the night, or early morning and thought it was the woman killed in her home.

"But all the other women were found outdoors," I said, "So why would he enter a woman's home?"

"Who knows why, he's crazy, that's why! That's all we need to know."

Tim's voice softened and he moved closer to me, taking my hand in his, he whispered as though someone would hear him besides me.

"Kathleen, I don't know how to tell you this but—"

"But what?" I asked, feeling my heart beating faster, afraid of what he was about to tell me.

"I don't think Dan died by anyone committing a robbery, I think Martino knew he was on to him and—"

"Oh, no!" I interrupted him, not wanting to hear what might be true, but he put his arm around me and said, "It was Martino, I'm sure of it. That's why it's important that you find a way to find out about his service pin. How you're going to do that I don't know, but I can't point blank ask him myself, or I could be next with a bullet in the back of my head."

"Is that the way Dan died?" I asked, as I started to cry, and he tried to console me.

"Of course, if he faced him he would have to look him in the eyes, no, Martino is a coward and then when Dan turned his back to him, that's when he shot him, but he must have realized a shot to the back of the head during a robbery would look suspicious. Why would a criminal shoot a cop who had his back to him? I read the police report, he had a very believable story. He told the investigation team how Dan turned to make sure he was ok and the gunfire between Martino and the robber were exchanged and the robber somehow got a shot off just as Dan turned to make sure Martino wasn't hit. It was believable. If he suspected for any reason that I was questioning him, he would know I suspected something and he could sneak up on me under some other circumstance, and bang. I wouldn't necessarily need to be facing him."

At that moment, with my heart racing and tears streaming down my face, I imagined myself in that field back in Pennsylvania, with my son running barefoot in the tall grass, holding on to Levi's hand and little Alice snuggled in my arms. That's where I took myself when the fear engulfed me; except my body was sitting next to Tim and he was hugging me, but at that moment I found no comfort in his arms.

"What made you think of that?" I asked, still shaken by Tim's analogy.

"It all adds up, Dan's suspicions laid out in his notes, the service pin he found, the woman's driver's license in your laundry bag, and he was at your place during that time period, his late night out with Pat and driving in the wrong direction for home when they left the bar. You don't need to be a rocket scientist to figure it all out. The last link in this chain is that damn pin, it has to be his," Tim said, looking intense and upset, which only made me feel more afraid.

He looked at me sadly and his demeanor changed, he knew he put me in a dangerous position if I had to be the one to connect the last dot to this indomitable crusade we were on, to expose the killer of not only all the women, but my son's father as well. It now became personal to me and I wasn't about to be encumbered by fear. As frightened as I felt a few moments ago, the feeling evaporated as soon as anger consumed me. Anger over the death of a man probably fighting for his sanity, as well as his determination to help solve what most in law enforcement thought of as the crimes of the century. Whatever demons haunted Dan, I began to feel sorry for him, and tried to think of the few good times we had where he made me feel loved and safe, mostly during the courtship. It would give me the courage to do what I had to and forget all the rest. I had to tell myself I was doing it for our son, so I could tell him his father was a hero, and he was the one who charted the course for Tim and me to flush out the culprit. I would have the notebook as proof.

Tim got up to leave and I walked him to the door. He put his arms around me and spoke gently, "The next time you're invited to the Martino's, go, and don't say anything. All you have to do is be you. Bring up subjects like how proud they must be of their family, or how many years Mr. Martino's been a policeman—bring subjects up like that whenever you're alone with his wife and daughter. Someone will say something, eventually. You don't have to do anything, just observe the family and keep your eyes and ears open. The moment will present itself when you least expect it," he said.

CHAPTER 35

I reached into the mail slot on my return from work one night in April. Juggling the mail and Tommy while climbing the stairs to my second floor flat wasn't an easy task. He insisted he wanted to climb them and could only do it one step at a time. Usually I gave up and picked him up under my arm and went up as quickly as I could. This night was no exception because as I scanned the mail, my eye caught the stamped date with Pennsylvania on the envelope even before I noticed the return address, and name.

Once inside my apartment I put Tommy down leaving him to his own resources on removing his jacket, and lost no time in tearing open the letter. I sat down in the nearest chair and read Levi's letter.

'Dear Kathleen,

I remembered your real name because I have thought of nothing but you, and happy of how you confided in me before you left and allowed me to love you. Thanks for letting me know you're ok. I was beginning to worry when I didn't hear from you. You asked how I was doing and so I'm happy to tell you I've been extremely busy. My work as a carpenter at a lumberyard now keeps my children and me taken care of with a steady income. The children are doing well and we have now joined a little church nearby in the small town of Deering. I left Reding and the Amish life completely. At first it was hard to leave people I have known all my life, but I put my children first and want them to get a good education. I enrolled myself in night courses in the High School here and hope to graduate in the near future. How is little Timmy doing? Well, I hope.

I bought myself a used car, about five years old and took the driver's course. What a difference getting places in minutes instead of hours. It hasn't been easy leaving everything behind, but nothing good comes easy I guess. I don't see the Holsteders unless I'm in Reding near their shop, which is seldom. At first they were upset with all I had to tell them about you, and also about the changes I have made, but at least he said hello to me the last time I ran into Jim Holsteder. I'm living in a small apartment but saving and planning on looking for a house in town or another town nearby, in the near future, with a yard for the kids to run around in. They miss that, unable to play indoors unless the sitter takes them to the park.

Take care of yourself and Timmy. Let me know when you're ready to come back, I hope it's soon.

I love you, Levi'

I felt terrible after reading that letter, I forgot to tell him Tommy's real name. I hoped he wasn't making changes in his life because of me, and not because he wanted it for himself and his children. I knew in my heart that he was aware I would never live as Amish again in any form. I looked forward to his letter, but now it left me feeling guilty and torn about my feelings, and believing he loved me, I wondered if the sacrifice he was making to enter my world was to entice me to come back and would he regret it at some point? — I didn't know.

I put the letter back in the envelope and placed it in the top dresser drawer in my room and then noticed the little white unicorn that was supposed to bring me happiness, but so far it hadn't. I placed it on top of the dresser where I could view it, maybe then it could cast its spell. I realized I hadn't removed my coat. I sat on the bed deep in thought until Tommy came running in with a toy in his hand and still in his jacket. I removed it as well as my own, and went into the kitchen to prepare us supper, while wishing I had waited before I wrote Levi, but I waited long enough. I left him in September of 1959 and it was now April of 1960. As I stood by the stove fixing our supper my thoughts were on how mixed up and complicated my life had become. The stress I was feeling was getting me down. My unhappiness made me want to flee or bury myself under the covers in my bed and never come out, but of course I couldn't do either ridiculous thing. My child needed to be protected and cared for, the only one that I loved dearly. He came before anything else in my life. He was the one person related to me by blood and he looked like me. In all the years I spent in the orphanage, no one else resembled me. I would look into every face I came upon in the community, in church, on the street, and wondered if I was related to any of them. I knew from now on whatever I did would be for my child.

The invitation to spend Easter with the Martinos was a welcomed one. I knew with or without Tim I would be spending Easter with the family I was bound to in an awkward way. My determination to find out if Sergeant Martino killed Dan was uppermost in my mind. I wasn't as concerned about the other murders since I now knew it wasn't Dan who had anything to do with any of them. It wasn't his service pin found under that woman and the fact that Dan found it eliminated all doubts I previously had about him. I felt ashamed to have thought that about him, but during the marriage I was enmeshed in a bad union to a sick man. I told myself Dan couldn't help being the way he was and I was able to forgive him.

It was just Tommy and me that would spend Easter with the family. Tim thought it would be easier if I were there without him and besides he explained his parents would be alone if he wasn't with them. I dressed Tommy in a cute little suit with short pants. I bought him new Buster Brown shoes that he loved and off we went for our Easter dinner with Lottie and her family. As I drove over to their home I was thinking of who would be there. I knew Tony and Angie would, and maybe Sal and his wife, but wondered if Frank might. I hoped he would, because I wanted to see more of his interactions with his father. I knew being in the Navy it would be unlikely. I was sure he was sailing away somewhere to another place if he wasn't at Great Lakes. He was never home whenever I went there in the past except for that one time.

Angie opened the door to me with her son in her arms. Johnny was five months old and as cute as could be.

"Kathleen!" she said, in an excited voice, "I'm so happy you came."

"I wouldn't miss seeing all of you—the baby, he's gotten so big!" I said.

She looked down at Tommy, "Oh my goodness, he's not a toddler anymore is he?

He looks more like you than ever, except for his hair, it's almost blond."

"I know, it turned during the summers, the sun bleached it lighter."

Lottie scurried into the room giving me a hug and making over Tommy. I always felt welcomed and comfortable in their home, but not anymore. I thought I was betraying them. It was a terrible feeling and I found it hard to pretend everything was the same because it wasn't. I had to hide my true feelings.

Lottie took our coats and we went into the living room where Tony, Angie's husband John, and Sergeant Martino were having a conversation.

In the presence of Mr. Martino I began to feel ill. I knew I wasn't, but I was so nervous near him that I had to quickly leave the room, following Lottie to the kitchen. Cheryl, Sal's wife, was mashing potatoes.

"Oh, Hi," she said, "Nice to see you, Kathleen."

"You're looking good," I said, noticing she was expecting.

"Yes, I'm feeling great, Sal and I will be parents in June."

"Congratulations! I'm so happy for you."

I realized I hadn't seen Sal. "Where's your husband?" I asked.

She looked at me with an odd expression and leaned over to whisper, He went to pick up Frank. I hope there's not going to be another nasty blow-up with Frank and his father butting heads."

"Why? Don't they get along?" I asked.

"Hardly, that's why when he's in port he never lets us know, but his mother insisted he come home this Easter. He hasn't seen Angie's baby yet."

"Oh, I didn't know—Mr. Martino was always kind and pleasant to his other kids," I said.

"Not to Frank. Sal tells me it's been like that since they were small children."

"I wondered why, the first time I met Frank, at age 15, he appeared testy around his father." I said.

Cheryl looked over at the kitchen door making sure Lottie wasn't about to come back in, and began to fill me in on the family dynamics.

"I think they both have the same personalities. Frank can be a hot-head and my father-in-law—well, I've seen his bad side once, and you don't want to get between them when that happens."

After hearing her describe him that way, it confirmed what Tim and I suspected about him. I felt sorry for Frank, although good-looking, he resembled his father more than his other siblings. Cheryl went back to her potatoes and we quit speaking when Lottie and Angie came in to carry dishes to the dining room.

Once we were all seated at the table minus Sal and Frank, who hadn't arrived yet, Mr. Martino said annoyingly, "Where the hell are they? They should have been here by now!"

"It's the traffic," Lottie said, "You know everyone is on the road on a holiday."

"Well, we're not gonna wait all day!" he said, rather loudly, and then we heard the door open in the hall. I noticed how Lottie relaxed from her previous stiff demeanor and stood up to greet Frank, as they came into the room. Sal said he was sorry they were late, but it was the traffic. Frank went over to Angie and she stood up to give him a hug.

"Where is he?" Frank asked, referring to his new nephew and before Angie could say anything Mr. Martino shouted," You can see him after we eat, the foods getting cold!"

No one said anything after that and Frank took his place at the table. His father reminded everyone to say grace before we started and I looked at him not believing what I was witnessing. I thought, *how could this family man and a cop besides, act like this pious head of a family, at this table, encouraging his grown kids to say their prayers on an Easter Sunday and hide the monster he really is, if he is.* I felt sick. I must have looked sick because Lottie asked if I were all right and I assured her I was, while all the time noticing how her husband eyed me with suspicion, or so I thought. I almost choked on my food trying to appear normal, but was too nervous and the Sergeant looked at me with a quizzical expression. I could feel my face flush.

"Kathleen, you're blushing," Angie said, as she laughed. And then looked over at Frank who was sitting next to me. Frank had helped himself to the dish being passed around of buttered corn and after he put a spoonful on his plate he preceded to put some on mine too. He was trying to be helpful, but Angie thought either it was cute or her brother had an eye for me. He was three years younger than me, so that never entered my mind. I was glad he did it because it was the excuse I needed for blushing. My face turned red, but not because of him. I found it very uncomfortable being in the presence of his father knowing what I suspected about him.

I turned to Frank and thanked him for the help, and then was occupied with fixing Tommy's plate. He was sitting on the other side of me on two phone books set on the chair so he could reach the table. The conversation at the table turned to Angie and her baby, and Frank saying he couldn't wait to see him.

"Well, he was born five months ago, if you called you would have known about it and came to see him!" Mr. Martino said, not too nicely.

"I was at sea, I called soon as I could!" Frank answered back, loudly.

"He's your first nephew, I would have thought you'd be here sooner. When the hell did you get back?" his father asked, not too nicely.

Frank didn't answer, he looked angry and looked over at Angie. "I called as soon as I came in, didn't I?"

Angie said quietly, "Yes, you did," and then she got up from the table. "Come on," she said as she waved to Frank to follow her. He left the table and followed her out. I wished I were going with him. I was so uncomfortable that I knew after dinner was over I would have to find an excuse to cut this visit short. I didn't know what Tim expected me to do in the presence of Sergeant Martino because I became emotionally paralyzed with him in the room. I tried to refrain from making eye contact with him and directed my conversation to Sal's wife, asking her questions about the impending birth of their child. Frank and Angie came back and everyone finished their meal. Mr. Martino returned to his old charming self and talked about how proud he was of his first grandchild.

After most of the family left the table, with Lottie, her husband and Tony remaining, I got up and took Tommy to the bathroom. When we came out to the living room, Angie was holding her baby and about to give him a bottle while sitting in one of the chairs.

"Sit down, Kathleen," she said. I knew she wanted to talk, but I wasn't about to stay much longer, and I explained that I wasn't feeling well. It was believable because I wasn't, and looked it. Frank came into the room and apologized for the angry exchange between his father and him. It was Angie, Frank and I in the room until Tony came in. The rest of the family was left in the dining room or kitchen.

"You're not leaving so soon, are you?" Tony asked, "We have a surprise for Tommy, so please, stay a little longer."

I didn't want to disappoint him since he gave my son so much attention the last time we visited.

"Ok, I'll stay for awhile," I said.

He went and got an Easter basket for him and after I gave my son a few jellybeans, Tony handed him a gift-wrapped box of Lincoln logs, and sat on the floor showing him how to build with them. I thought Tony was the kindest teenager I knew. He was playful and enjoyed my three year-old. It was unusual, I thought, but he was just a loving kid. Angie and I sat and watched them as she fed her baby. Lottie came into the room and said, "Oh, look at Tony, he never outgrew playing with toys" and then she laughed. Angie agreed with her mother.

"Remember the time Tony got into the bottom of your china cabinet, Ma?" she said, "He stacked all her good cups together until one of them was found broken," she said, telling me about how her youngest brother loved playing with anything he could get his hands on.

"How old was he at that time?" I asked.

Lottie laughed, "About Tommy's age," she said.

I was forgetting how nervous I felt earlier and was enjoying the conversation until Sergeant Martino came in and sat down on the sofa next to me. He smiled his usual smile and silently watched his son and mine playing on the floor. Frank left the room as soon as his father entered. Soon everyone was in the living room except for Frank. I could feel Sergeant Martino staring at me.

"How's Tim?" he asked.

"He's fine," I answered, wondering why he asked about Tim since he saw him at work every day.

"I think Tim should take it easy, he's really been up tight lately. He should take a vacation. He's due one, I think," he said.

I could feel myself shaking inside and hoped it didn't show. I thought I would respond in Tim's defense.

"After what he's been through in Korea, I'm not surprised he's tense," I said, hoping that would put an end to the conversation about Tim.

"Korea has something to do with it, he wasn't acting so serious before he went away and, well, he isn't the same guy since he's come back," he said.

He was soft-spoken and so condescending as he spoke to me about Tim, like he was so concerned and gave the impression he expected me to find out why Tim was acting differently. I hated how in his patronizing way of speaking to me, he was trying to get me to agree with him—that Tim needed time off from work. I decided to curtail his questioning about Tim and rose up to announce it was time for me to take Tommy home.

"Oh, Kathleen, it's early, and he's having a great time, stay a little longer," Lottie pleaded.

"Well he's used to taking a nap and he didn't get one today. He gets very overtired by bedtime," I said, "It's almost three and I don't want to drive after dark."

"That's two hours away," Angie said, "So stay just another hour."

I couldn't disappoint Angie and Lottie after the great meal they put together with Cheryl's help. I agreed and sat down in a chair John had just vacated. I wasn't about to sit next to Mr. Martino again. I ignored him and directed my conversation to his wife and daughter, so he got up and went out of the room. It wasn't minutes later when we heard loud shouting in the other room. Lottie quickly left the room to intercede in an argument between Frank and his father. I was embarrassed for Angie and Tony, who along with me had to endure the angry voices that could be heard throughout the house. I could hear Lottie and Sal trying to cool down the precarious situation in the next room. I wanted to go home and suddenly the opportunity arose when Frank stormed into the hall to get his pea jacket out of the closet. Sal was pleading with him to wait, and he would drive him back to the train he came on from Great Lakes. Frank said, "No, I'll take myself."

I told Angie I had to leave, and she didn't try to talk me into staying again; she was embarrassed over the heated outburst between her brother and father and sensed I was uncomfortable. I went to the closet to get our coats, as Frank was putting his on and took the opportunity to offer Frank a ride.

"I'm leaving and I'd be happy to drop you off," I said.

"Are you sure you won't mind giving me a ride to the train station?" he asked.

"No, of course not, I'm going that way," I said, trying to reassure him that it wasn't a problem for me. Tony packed up Tommy's gifts and Lottie, Angie and Tony, along with Sal's wife came to say goodbye, but before Mr. Martino came back into the room, I went out the door quickly pulling Tommy to the car, with Frank close behind carrying his Easter basket and Lincoln logs.

On the way to the station, we didn't speak for a few minutes. I think we were both trying to get over the loud confrontation that had taken place. Frank looked over at me, and apologized. "I'm sorry about what happened back there," he said, "I didn't mean for you to leave when I did."

"I was going to go anyway, so don't blame yourself. You and your father don't get along, do you?" I asked.

He laughed a little, "I can't remember when we did," he said, sighing with a resigned acceptance like it was always that way between them, and it would always be so.

I looked over and felt sorry for him. He was a tall good-looking twenty-five-year- old guy, unlike his father who was a shorter version of him, and stocky, but with the good looking features of Frank's tall dark and handsome looks. Of all the Martino boys, Frank was the handsome one. I found him serious and pensive, unlike his brothers who displayed a more easy-going jovial side.

"Why do you think your Dad clashes with you?" I asked, knowing it was none of my business, if he didn't want to tell me.

"As long as I can remember he's picked on me if anything went wrong. I got out as soon as I was eighteen, joined the Navy and never looked back. If it wasn't for my siblings and my Mother I'd never come back, not even for a visit," he said.

"Your father always appeared to be a kind and charming man and he helped me when I first came out of the home, you know—"

"Yes, I do, it was Saint Cecelia's wasn't it? I remember the first day you came to our house, just before Christmas, I think."

He looked over at me and snickered like he thought something was funny, and said,

"You don't know the real Sergeant Martino. Yeah, he's charming all right. He could charm the birds right out of the trees, like he charmed my mother." He said it with an expression of anger.

"What do you mean?" I asked, even though I had a pretty good idea of what his father might be like behind closed doors.

"He's fake, the real person behind that good cop crap, is a liar, and my mother believes everything he tells her."

"Tell me—what is he really like Frank, I want to know, and I'll never say a word, it's just between us," I said, trying to reassure him that whatever he chose to tell me, I wouldn't tell a soul, but I knew it was information I wouldn't keep from Tim.

"I wouldn't know where to start," he said.

I looked over at him and placed my hand on his arm for a second, "It's ok, anything you say will help you, maybe get over the anger you feel. Why do you say he's a liar?"

"Well, when I was around seven, he took my brother and me to a carnival in the neighborhood. Sal wandered away to look at something and I was standing next to my father. He told me to go over by Sal, and I did, except I looked back and saw my father go up to a strange woman and they disappeared behind one of the concession stands, so I ran back to see where he had gone. He didn't see me at first, and I saw him kissing that woman. In my seven-year-old innocence, I made the mistake of calling out to him, and things were never the same between us from that day on because I saw him for what he was, and he came over to me and walked me to where my brother was all the time telling me I didn't see what I thought I saw. I never told my mother because at that time he convinced me I was imagining it, but as I got older I knew the truth."

"So your mother doesn't know?" I asked.

"Of course not, I could never hurt her that way, but I've carried this burden for years. I had to keep it to myself to protect her."

"And you never told your sister or brothers about it?"

"Never, I couldn't take the chance that they would tell her, or they wouldn't believe me and tell her anyway," he said, looking so sad, that I felt sorry for him.

"Frank, I'm so sorry to hear that," I said, but I wasn't sorry, it was exactly what Tim thought, that Sergeant Martino wasn't who he presented himself to be.

We arrived at the station and before he got out of the car, I wrote down my address and phone number for him. "Here, take this and write to me, send me your address and let's keep in touch and the next time you're in, call me."

He looked over at me and smiled, "Thanks, Kathleen, I could use a friend. Thanks for being that friend."

He turned to say goodbye to Tommy in the back seat, who had fallen asleep, and then I watched him walk into the station. On the way home, I was almost jumping out of my skin in anticipation of calling Tim.

CHAPTER 36

The night I drove Frank to the train station was a turning point in the situation Tim and I were in. He came over quickly after I called him. I filled him in on all that took place at the Martino's and all that Frank had divulged to me. In speaking about the Sergeant, I said, "Why would he be asking me about you? That you need time off; that you're up tight?"

Tim looked at me and said, "I think he's on to me, maybe he knows I've been asking questions of the guys who have been there long enough to have a ten year service pin."

I was stunned, "My God Tim. He knows he lost that pin, and if just one of the men mentioned it to him, he's—"

"Don't worry about it please, I'm not going to take a vacation, or do anything to put myself in harms way with him."

"How did you ask about their service pins? It would be so obvious that you were on to something if he found out you were asking them if they had their pins, wouldn't it?"

"I thought I was careful, I asked them one at a time, the four of them, at different times, in casual conversation."

"Like how?" I asked, "

"Well, when I was alone with Captain Jennings, I happened to bring up how I missed so many years and I would have had a ten year pin, if it weren't for Korea. He said, 'Bad luck kid, war is hell.' "Something like that, so I asked him if he ever wore his pin. He said only on special occasions. That was all. I didn't mention it again. I did the same with the other three. Why would any of them mention something so unimportant to Martino?"

"I think it's more than that," I said, "I'm afraid it might not be the pin at all, because he mentioned how up tight you are." Tim agreed with me.

"Kathleen, I have a hard time at work with him sitting there like a big shot at the front desk, barking orders, and just being around him makes me nervous. I can't help it."

I put my arm around him, "Tim, I know how you feel, I'm going through the same thing; around him I'm a mess. We think it's *his* pin but we need absolute proof, and we don't have that yet."

We were sitting together on my sofa, both worried over our next step. He couldn't comfort me, and I was sure I wasn't much help to him.

"We know he's cunning and a liar and cheater, no surprise there—that's a true psychopath, and of course his grandiose personality, charming and jovial, just a front for what he really is, and does," Tim said, "and he probably told the Sheriff 'I've got your six,' when he lured him to the place where he shot him."

"What does that mean?" I asked.

"It means, I've got your back, and he sure did—he shot him in the back of the head."

I was surprised that Tim knew so much about that kind of person. It impressed me somewhat and I asked him how he was so sure about Martino being what he called a psychopath. "Maybe he's just a rotten guy," I said.

"You can treat a mental illness Kathleen, not a true psychopath, they have no real feelings, and they are cunning predators."

"How do you know all this?" I asked, impressed by what Tim seemed to know.

"When I was in the hospital in Japan, I had a month recuperating from my injuries, I had plenty of time on my hands and one of the guys from the embassy brought me books to read. There happened to be one on that subject."

When he mentioned injuries, I was surprised, because when I first saw him after I returned, he seemed perfectly fine except for the weight loss.

"Where were you hurt?" I asked.

He looked at me like I shouldn't have asked him, "I don't like to talk about it, and it's over now isn't it? I'm home in one piece, and that's all I have to say about it!"

I thought, *Wow he must have gone through hell. Maybe that's why he has that* edge *to him, like he could snap at any moment.* I decided never to bring it up again.

We realized the only way to find out what happened to Martino's pin was resting on me. I had to spend more time with Angie, or her mother, in hopes it came up in conversation at some point. I needed to come up with a plan on how to bring up the subject at some future date.

Tim went home and I went to bed, lying awake, trying not to think of the mess I was in, but of Levi. Lucky Levi, I thought. His life was simple compared to my complicated one. I visualized Levi with his children, running carefree somewhere and enjoying nature and life. They were a real family, and I was sure they were happy; while I was barely surviving with my nerves always on edge over this malevolent man that Tim and I knew could be mendacious and we were saddled with proving it. At this time I didn't need a pushy ex-mother-in-law breathing down my neck with her plans to move close to me. I had no family of my own to turn to; to seek refuge when I was in the most despair one could be in. I knew I had to endure whatever was to come because of my son. It was *his* father's reputation I had to rescue, from the tortured man he was, into a victim and a hero, so he could be proud of the father he would never know. I could only do that by helping Tim expose his killer.

I received a phone call from Dan's mother a week after Easter. I was surprised she didn't call before Easter expecting me to spend it with her. She sounded melancholy.

"Kathleen, I was expecting you to spend Easter with me and I waited to hear from you, I have Tommy's Easter bunny and basket here for him, when can you come down?"

She caught me off guard, with all that was going on, and I forgot about her when it came to Easter Sunday. I knew there wasn't any way I would miss an opportunity to be at the Martino's. I had to come up with a good reason.

"I'm sorry, it's that Tommy had a bad cold and I thought I would stay close to home since he didn't feel well. I went over to the Martino's just long enough for him to get the basket they had for him. They don't live far."

I thought I 'd better tell her I was there, she would eventually hear about it. She apparently thought I was making it up because she said, "Well, why would you be there? They aren't family, and I could have come up if Tommy wasn't feeling well."

"You would have had to take a bus or cab, and the weather is iffy, still cool and it looked like it was going to rain up here," I said, hoping she would believe me.

"Well, when can you come down?"

"As soon as he feels better, give him a week to get over it," I said, trying to hide my annoyance of having to engage her in conversation about what I should be doing. I was torn between having to accept she is his grandmother and wishing she would disappear from our lives. If only I liked the woman, but I didn't. I knew from experience, if I gave an inch she would take a yard and as Tommy got older there would be a tug-of-war over him, just as it was with Dan. I needed her now like a bad rash with all that Tim and I were involved in.

In June, Dan's mother put her home up for sale and I nearly fell apart as I was relaying it all to Tim. "I can't let her get too close, she'll be here too often," I said, almost in tears.

He looked at me with sympathy, "Tell her she can't just barge in. Learn to say no," he said, thinking it was that easy.

"You saw how she reacted when we went down to see her after Easter. She expected me to come alone with Tommy. When she saw you, she didn't hide the fact that she was disappointed."

Tim chuckled, "Kathleen, you're a grown woman; stand up to her."

"Did you? When she asked you for the box back and wanted to know what was in it, you found excuses. I expected you to say the box belongs to Kathleen, but you told her there wasn't anything in it except some jail house notes, and when you find where you put it, she could have it back."

"I didn't know you wanted it back. It's an empty old box and if I thought you really wanted it—"

"Forget it, I said, "I don't want it. It's just that she's going to be trouble for me and I'm upset right now," I was hoping he could see how she affected me, and he did.

"Let's take your kid and go for ice cream," he said, trying to change my mood. I realized he was trying to be helpful but addressing Tommy, as 'your kid' didn't help my mood any. He was trying to warm up to me by showing my son attention at times, but if he had referred to him as just Tommy, instead of putting distance between them with the statement he made, like confirming Tommy only belonged to me, gave me pause when it came to any serious commitment between us for the future. At that moment I just didn't see it.

Summer was always a good time for children, especially my son, because he was confined to an apartment and not a real home with a back yard to play in, he was able to run around in Betty's parents back yard with her son Ricky. I had him play with Rita's kids occasionally when I picked him up from the sitter's home near Rita's. Also the park near our apartment came in handy when he needed to run off some of the energy he had stored up, where a three-room apartment wouldn't do. He was becoming more active, not a baby or toddler anymore and only six months from his fourth birthday.

In July the police department would have their annual 4th of July picnic. Tim and I planned to attend and we hoped I would be able to connect with Lottie again. I hadn't heard from either her or Angie since we got together one Saturday afternoon for lunch at Angie's. Nothing came of that visit and time was running out for Tim and me in making any progress in proving the ownership of the lost service pin. We were sure it was Martino's, it had to be, and I worried that another woman would be found murdered if we didn't do something.

Tim and I were spending more time together both consumed with the situation we found ourselves in, and any romantic feelings we had in the beginning seemed long gone between us. I liked it that way, and the goodnight kiss we exchanged was more of a friendship kiss than one of passion. The ordeal we needed to end left little room for romantic feelings on my part. I voiced my fears one night before the picnic.

"Tim, I'm worried. If I don't find out anything soon, I'm afraid another woman will be found dead."

"It's not gonna happen," he said.

"How can you be so sure? I would feel guilty for not being able to do anything to stop him. Tim, I need to do something, but what can I do? I'm not around Angie and her family often enough to find out anything."

He was standing next to me helping me clean up the supper we had just finished and he put the dishtowel down and put both hands on my shoulders making me face him. "Kathleen, listen to me, it's not gonna happen! You know why? Because I think he's on to me, and maybe even you. He may be crazy, but he's not stupid. He can see how we appear around him even if we try to hide it. He senses something and he's being real careful. The last thing he wants to do now is commit another crime."

"I hope you're right," I said.

We arrived at the fair grounds where the 4th of July picnic and fireworks would be. It was just Tim, Tommy and I. Rita wasn't interested when I asked her if she would be attending. I had hoped she would, because I needed another friend with me besides Tim. I felt lost even with Tim. I was afraid of Mr. Martino. I don't know what I was afraid of with crowds of people around, but just knowing he would be there was enough to cause me to feel fearful. I thought maybe he would come over to me, corner me in some way when Tim was off talking to one of the guys. With Rita or another woman near me, including his wife or daughter of course, I would feel safer.

We found a place at a picnic table that was unoccupied and I placed a cloth on it along with a basket of snacks. The police department and the Sheriff's department were preparing food. A couple of the young rookies and their girlfriends came up to ask if they could share the table with us. I welcomed them with a sigh of relief.

There were six of us and Tommy, sitting at the table, with Tim introducing them to me when out of the corner of my eye up close to where they were manning the grills for the food, I spotted Dan's mother with another woman I recognized as the mother of one of the Deputies from the Sheriff's department. I froze. It must have shown on my face because Tim noticed.

"What's wrong?" he asked.

Putting my hand over my eyes like a visor and looking down, I said," Don't look now, but Dan's mother is here."

He turned around and saw her. "Don't let it bother you," he said, but it did because I could see her coming over as soon as she knew I was here and taking Tommy by the hand and that would be the last I would see of him while she paraded him around for everyone to see. I was grateful that our table was filled with the young couples, but at some point they would be up and around and she would make a beeline for us, sitting herself down at our table with the other woman she came with. I didn't look forward to this day with Mr. Martino there, and now I felt I was going to have to deal with her too. I was seething inside and tried not to show it, but I wasn't good at pretending, I never was.

I changed places with Tim, so my back was to where she was, but I knew that wouldn't help much. She would eventually spot Tommy. I wished Tim was more forceful where she was concerned and maybe take over Tommy more in her presence but I couldn't rely on that ever happening. I wasn't able to see what was going on behind me so when Angie came up pushing the baby buggy, I felt somewhat relieved.

"Kathleen, why don't you come and sit at our table?" she said, "My Mom's here and so is Tony."

"That's a good idea," Tim said, winking at me.

I numbly got up grabbing Tommy and we followed Angie. Tim whispered to me,"This what you wanted, time with them, so make the most of it."

When we approached Lottie, she was alone talking with another woman. The woman left and she greeted us warmly. Tim sat for a few minutes and then got up to mingle with a few guys including John, Angie's husband. It was just Angie, Lottie, and I with Tommy, sitting together. I dreaded Mr. Martino coming to sit with us, but he was in the crowd of men somewhere.

Lottie asked, "Did you see your mother-in-law? "She's here!"

"I couldn't miss her," I said, "I'm not looking for her that's for sure. Let her find me."

Angie laughed, "She's a harmless old lady Kathleen, ignore her. Dan's gone, so what can she do? She can't ruin your life anymore."

"Oh yeah, she's selling her home, and is planning on moving back here,"

"Oh, no!" Lottie said, "Just stay cool, and don't let her get to you. Is that why you've appeared so nervous recently?"

"Well, yes," I said, knowing it wasn't Dan's mother as much as it was her own husband.

Angie said, "Mrs. Clarke's coming over."

I turned to see her coming toward us, alone and smiling.

"Kathleen! So nice to see you, and then she went to Tommy and sat next to him, and across from Lottie. We watched as she planted numerous kisses on his cheeks until he squirmed away from her and went to look into the buggy at Angie's son who was awake and cooing at some toy Angie gave him. At eight months old, he was sitting up and Tommy's attention was on him.

"Your son is so cute, congratulations," Mrs. Clarke said to Angie, and then turning to Lottie, she said, "You don't know how lucky you are that you live close to your grandson. I bet you see him often."

"Oh, not that often, Angie and John are busy with their own lives, so we don't intrude in it. When they have time they come over," Lottie said, giving me a look that said she was on to her.

"Well, I don't see Tommy much, but that will change when I move," Mrs. Clarke said.

Lottie pretended she didn't know and said, "Oh, are you moving? When?"

"Next week, I sold my home and I just closed on one on Linden Street here in Arden," she said proudly.

Angie, Lottie and I looked at each other and they could tell I was upset. This was the first I heard she bought a home already and was moving. She said nothing to me when she called the past week. She didn't mention she would be at the picnic either. There was something sneaky about her and I didn't like it.

It wasn't long before our table was filled with the guys, Tim, Tony, John and Mr. Martino. It was crowded, and Tim and John brought over my table cloth, food and drinks for us all. Mrs. Clarke was in her glory with Tommy sitting on her lap while she was helping him with his hotdog and chocolate milk. We all ate in silence with just John and Tim talking sports. My hamburger went down in lumps; I couldn't enjoy any of it. I could feel Mr. Martino's eyes on me, noticing how I appeared, nervous, edgy, and wishing I was anyplace but where I was. Angie and her mother looking at me with sympathy thinking it was the presence of Mrs. Clarke. She was the least of my problems at that table. It was the insufferable presence of the monster sitting across from us. I looked at Tim sitting next to me. His hand reached for mine on the bench we were sitting on. He tried to calm me with the pressure of his hand holding mine tightly. His face looking down at the tabletop, refusing to look up while trying to eat his hamburger with one hand, and all the while we both knew Sergeant Martino was staring at both of us. He was sitting next to Lottie across from us and the look he had on his face was one only Tim and I understood. John was speaking about something or other; I don't think Tim or I heard a word until Mrs. Clarke called loudly over to Tim.

"Tim, I'm still waiting for that box of Dan's!"

I noticed Martino, bent over the table, suddenly sat up straight, and Tim said, "I thought it belonged to Kathleen, wasn't it her box after Dan died?"

"Well, ah, I guess it was, but I just wondered about it since we couldn't get it opened. The key was lost wasn't it?" She turned to me with that question. I didn't answer and before I could, she said, "Dan kept it locked, but Tim had to take it to a locksmith."

Sergeant Martino's eyes opened wide, he looked at me, "What was in it?" he asked rather nonchalantly.

Both Tim and Mrs. Clarke started to speak at the same time and she let Tim finish.

"Just some old papers, nothing important." Tim said, trying to change the subject by mentioning the Cubs to John, but Martino wouldn't let it go.

"Why would he lock it for just some *old papers*?" he asked, mimicking Tim.

"How would I know?" Tim answered.

"If it's police business, shouldn't you have turned it over to the police or Sheriff's department?" Martino asked.

"I don't think there was anything in there like that," Tim said, his hand came back down to mine and this time it was my hand that grabbed his in reassurance, to keep him calm.

"Oh, didn't you say it was police business?" Mrs. Clarke blurted out.

"No, I think you're mistaken," Tim said.

Both Tim and I could see the wheels turning in the eyes of Sergeant Martino, the questions, the interest, the inner rage he must be feeling, not knowing what we might have found.

It was the worst day Tim and I ever spent at a picnic. We managed to stay for some of the fireworks and then Tim suggested we leave early and we waited until Mrs. Clarke walked away from Tommy for a minute while the fireworks were going on. Without looking for anyone to say goodbye to, he picked up Tommy and carried him while pulling me by the hand to his car. Once we were on the way home, we both were able to laugh about it, but it was nervous laughter. There was really nothing funny about it.

Back at my apartment with Tommy in bed, we sat together trying to make out what Martino was thinking.

"Did you notice his expression change when she mentioned police papers?" Tim said, "I think he was trying to hide his feelings, he acted indifferent, didn't ask too many questions, but as cool as he tried to appear, I noticed the twitching in his jaw."

"What must he be thinking was in the papers," I asked.

"It's not any papers he cares about, it's the license you threw away," Tim said. "I bet he thinks Dan found it and locked it in that box. Remember he questioned you about the clothing, and then questioned Dan's mother too? He knew someone had to find it in the laundry. If it wasn't you, and it wasn't her, it had to be Dan."

"Now, for sure, he's going to watch you closely," I said.

"Don't worry about me, I'm a step ahead of him."

"Tim. I'm afraid for you; don't take any chances with him," I said, feeling at that moment something I hadn't felt for him in a while. I leaned over and kissed him. I needed to feel something that night other than the terrible fear that never seemed to leave me. He kissed me back and took me in his arms and held me for a long time with neither of us speaking. We held each other long enough to calm each other down. When he got up to leave, I walked him to the door.

"Arrange a visit to their home again as soon as possible Kathleen, go when he's at work and after Tony comes home from school. Find some excuse to visit Lottie, and you said Tony enjoys Tommy, so find the time to point blank ask Tony, while he's giving Tommy his attention with or without his mother in the room, you have to find a way to engage him in conversation in a way that his father's service pin comes up." His last words to me as he went out the door were, "You can do it Kathleen, you can do it!"

CHAPTER 37

In August, Dan's mother was back in Arden, making a pest of herself. She would call at least once a week, sometimes twice and in any normal relationship, I wouldn't consider it too often, but our relationship wasn't normal, because I just did not like the woman. The less I heard from her the better. Uppermost in my mind was calling Lottie, but what excuse would I have for inviting myself to her home when we were just together in July. I had to think of a reason. It was the time of year where after the 4th of July nothing exciting would be happening, not until Labor Day. At that time maybe there would be a Labor Day picnic, or I would take Tommy trick or treating at Halloween, but October was too far off. It had to be done now. I called Tim, explaining my predicament.

"Martino brags about Tony's football accomplishments," he said, "So maybe you can try to find out when he's practicing at his school."

"Tim, it's August, he's out of school," I reminded him, "It's his last year, I think, isn't it? Do they practice in August?" I asked, not remembering much about sports.

"Yes, but maybe his mother or sister might show up to one of his practices, many parents do," he said.

"Then what am I supposed to do, if I'm there alone watching him? Wouldn't that seem strange?"

"I don't have any other suggestions," he said, "Try to think of something."

After hanging up the phone, I was left with figuring out what to do next. A visit to Tony's practice seemed contrived. I had never gone before, and what reason would I give to him for my presence, or to his mother if she happened to be there which I doubted. If I lived in walking distance to the school, maybe it would look natural, like Tommy and I went for a walk, but the school was too far from where we lived. I had to think of another way.

The idea of writing to Frank came to me. I knew he was based at Great Lakes, but wasn't sure for how long. I wanted to get him to come for a visit with his mother and me. I would ask him if he could come before he shipped out again, telling him I would be happy to pick him up at the station, and drive him home. I wrote to him and then settled down for the night, but found I couldn't sleep. My mind wandered to everything that happened over the past few years. It kept me awake. I thought of Levi, and in my mind's eye I kept seeing little Alice cuddled up against my bosom. I remembered sister Mary Louise back at the orphanage, holding me on her lap when I was very little to comfort me, but her stiff starched collar wasn't much comfort for a small child to lay its head upon. She was the only nun that was kind to the children. Maybe it was because she was young and the others seemed old and cranky and most of the younger children like me were afraid of them. I wondered what a mother felt like to a small child who was in distress. I thought of that when I held my own child. Somehow I managed to drift off to sleep; my last thought was of Levi's children, motherless, just as I was all my life.

After work Tim showed up for the usual Friday night suppers I put together for us. On most weekends we spent it together plotting our next move. Seldom did we take in a movie, we should have, but we couldn't concentrate on anything except what we were involved in. Saturdays, Tim would take us out to eat. I kept hoping there would be signs of him becoming used to Tommy, and although he made an effort to give him attention, I could see his heart wasn't in it. We were sitting at the table having just finished the pot roast he liked, when he asked me about my next move.

"Tim, going to the football practice isn't going to work, I have a better plan."

"Let's hear it," he said.

"I wrote to Frank inviting him to come for a visit while he's still nearby. He'll want to see Lottie, so I take him to her."

"Do you think he'll come?"

"Why wouldn't he, he likes me and I like him—"

"What's that supposed to mean?" he said, interrupting me.

"Oh for Gosh sakes! He's younger than me, like a younger brother, and I'm sure he thinks of me the same."

I could see Tim was jealous, it gave me reason to think he still loved me, but I wasn't sure it was the same for me. I quickly changed the subject.

"I was thinking of what you told me about how you asked the other men about their service pins, but not Sergeant Martino. In the beginning I would have thought you might have asked him first, since we didn't suspect him early on."

"Because he was the first one I was suspicious of. Remember, I knew all the personality traits of a psycho," he said, "and he has them all."

"What did you think of him when you first joined the police force? Did you think he was crazy back then?" I asked, wondering. "He didn't appear that way when I came out of the orphanage, in fact I thought he was a kind man, including me in his family; he made me feel at home."

Tim said, "Well, I didn't think anything about him when I was a brand new rookie because I didn't know him at first, until they paired me with him as his partner while I was in training. He was driving a police cruiser then, and we would go on traffic calls. Once we caught an old lady driving down a street that had a temporary one way sign put up, it had been a two way street, but they were doing road work, so they made it one way that day. Martino pulls up with the siren and red light flashing and stops the woman, laughing, and saying 'We got a hot one' so we get out and I could see the woman was old and shaking. Martino turns to me still laughing in front of her, and says 'You're breaking the law Granny, you're going down the wrong way!' then he turns to me and says,' Should we nail her with a ticket?' I said, "No, let her go." And he said, 'You're too soft kid.' I knew then there was another side to him. The way he laughed at seeing that old woman shake with fear, I figured the guy wouldn't last long on the road. A year later he was assigned to the front desk, after many complaints came in about his treatment of simple traffic violators, like the guy we had in the cell overnight for driving an overweight truck in a residential area. It was a weekend and he couldn't call his company for them to post bail. I felt sorry for the guy and wanted to bring him a cup of coffee, but Martino wouldn't let me. He said, 'Let him rot down there.'

"I'm surprised he was never reprimanded," I said.

"He was, that's why he's been at the front desk. There are a few other bullies in the department. The job attracts them."

"Tim, you're not like that," I said, wanting to compliment him.

"Well, it's hard to stay nice when all you see is the seedy side of life, but I try," he said."

I wanted to hug him but he was across the table. My feelings for Tim changed from day to day. I was a mixed up mess.

I got up and went over to him, and stood behind him putting my arms around his neck. I put my cheek against his. He pulled my hands away and stood up facing me, then pulling me toward him, kissing me like he hadn't done in a long time. I felt faint, and so confused. I thought he would want more from me so I didn't pull away, letting him make the decision for us. At that moment I thought back to the eighteen-year-old girl I was, when he made the same move that first night in Mrs. Wilkie's living room before he left. Suddenly, he broke away and with his arm around me led me to the door to the outside hall of the apartment.

"I've got to go," he said, and as I watched him going down the stairs from my doorway, my heart was pounding. Was it his strict religion? I wondered and did it still have a hold on him after all these years? I knew it no longer controlled me, I knew it the night I let Levi follow me up the stairs to my room. I fell in love with Levi that night, but I put my feelings aside because of his religion. Standing at my opened doorway, my feeling for Tim at that moment was the same as it had been years ago. It made me wonder if one could love more than one man, the same. I had regrets not being able to be intimate with Tim before he left for Korea, and here I was willing, but he wasn't. It puzzled me.

A call from Betty wanting to get together the following week, prompted me to ask her if we could get together after work the coming Saturday. I needed to talk to someone I trusted, to clear my head. She agreed, so she came over to my place after we closed up for the day. Once we settled our boys in the living room with plenty of Tommy's toys, I put a pot of coffee on. Betty could sense something was wrong.

"Kathleen, what is it? You've been looking pretty tired lately and have you lost weight?"

I didn't know where to start, so I filled our cups and sat down across from her and before I could get a word out, the tears came.

"I've been a mess lately," I said, "Because I'm not sure of my feelings for Tim, not to mention Levi, who I think of at night when I can't sleep, which is often."

"The Amish man you told me about sounds like a very kind and steady guy, but his religion would come between you, isn't that what you told me?" she said.

"Yes, but he wrote to me that he's left it. I wrote to him, and he thinks I'm coming back to him, and Tim—" I started to cry, big hacking sobs, I couldn't speak, just cry. Betty got up and came over to put her arms around me.

"Let it all out," she said.

I did, until I couldn't cry anymore, exhausted, I began to tell her how the last time Tim was with me, I thought I still loved him, and how distant he remained even though he kissed me in the way I thought he still loved me. I told her more about Levi, and that I felt guilty having been with him before Tim.

"You didn't know that Tim was alive," she said, "So don't feel guilty about that. Which one do you really love Kathleen? You must know."

"That's the problem, I don't know," I said.

She looked at me funny, and I felt she was as confused as I was.

"The way you broke down; things can't be that bad, so you have feelings for both of them, in time you'll work it out," she said, "but to fall apart like you have, Kathleen, over something like that? It's not that bad is it?"

How could I tell her of the stress I was under, the cloud of fear I've lived in since I returned. It wasn't so much about Tim, or Levi, I knew that, but I couldn't tell Betty the real cause of my total collapse. The fact that she was with me, allowed me to rid myself of all the tension I carried by letting it all out in front of her. I felt better and relieved that it didn't happen in front of Tim, or anyone else who might think I was in need of help. I settled down enough to able to share my dilemma over Tim and Levi with her rationally. By the time she went home, I felt renewed and ready to face the inevitable—seeking out information about that damn service pin.

I received a phone call from Frank, and I was happy to hear from him. I invited him to visit us next time he came in.

"Of course, I'd love to come out, I'm only going to be here another month, so anytime is ok with me," he said.

"How about this coming Sunday, I can pick you up in the morning."

" After church?"

"No, I haven't been going to church, or if you do, call that you're on the way," I said.

"I'll take the first train out at nine, meet me at the Clearidge station at ten."

"I'll be there, looking forward to seeing you Frank."

I called Tim as soon as I hung up the phone to let him know I would be picking Frank up and wondered if he wanted to come to my place to meet him before we went to his mother's.

"I'll meet you at your place," he said, "I wanna meet this guy."

"Ok Tim, but please don't say anything to him, I—"

"Do you think I'm an imbecile!" he shouted.

There it was, that edge he displayed that reminded me of Dan when he was irritated. I quickly said, "Of course not, I just meant—"

"I know what you meant! I'll be there," he said.

I wondered if it was typical of Tim to show that side when he was irritable. I'd seen that side of him before, or was it jealousy this time?

I was sitting in my car parked where I could see the train come in. Tommy loved trains and wanted to leave the car as soon as we heard the train whistle as it was nearing the station, so we got out and walked to the platform. I had to hold on to him, because he became so excited. I watched Frank jump down from the car and rush over to us. He gave me a hug that took me by surprise. He was wearing his sailor whites, since it was the end of August and pretty hot out. He didn't carry any bag because he had to go back on the night train. Tim had mentioned that Martino's weekend shift included this Sunday so I knew he wouldn't be home. Frank picked up Tommy and talked to him, laughing and showing him his sailor hat, putting it on Tommy's head until we got to the car. I thought *If only Tim could be that way with my son.*

Once we were settled in the car, Frank asked me if anything was wrong.

"Why would you ask that?" I said.

"Well, you look a little—I don't know, maybe worn out and tired. Haven't you been feeling well?"

I was surprised by his concern, if I looked that bad, and I was sure I did, why wasn't Tim worried about me? Betty could see I was under some kind of strain and telling her about my conflicted feelings about the only two men I was involved with, kept her satisfied that that was the real problem. I had to tell even myself that's what it was, but it wasn't, because to face the truth at that time might have caused me a real breakdown. I was so afraid of Martino that I knew I wouldn't be able to act like nothing was wrong in front of him, ever again. I didn't know how Tim managed, seeing him everyday at work. He had been back long enough and he wanted out of the station and back in a cruiser, with a partner again, and that's where he was, every shift. I worried something might happen to him.

"Kathleen, Kathleen!" Frank was calling me to get my attention. I looked over at him, "I'm sorry," I said, "Did you say something?"

"Yes! You almost ran a red light back there, stop and let me drive," he ordered. I didn't refuse. I pulled over and we switched seats. He followed my directions to the apartment. Once inside, I began to calm down. Tim hadn't come yet, so I offered Frank something to drink.

"I have coffee, or lemonaid," I said.

"Lemonaid would be fine," he said, watching me pour a glass full for him. I noticed he was studying me, and I was hoping he wouldn't ask me if anything was wrong, again, I was afraid I would start to cry, and how would I explain that? I walked over to the window just in time to see Tim enter the building, I ran to open the door afraid Tim might use his key. I didn't want Frank to get the wrong idea. Tim came in and I said, "Tim, I don't think you ever met Frank Martino, have you?"

"No, we haven't met," Frank, said, reaching to shake Tim's hand.

They shook hands and then I spotted the box that Tim held in his other hand. I almost lost my footing as I tried to maneuver them to sit down. I felt myself shaking inside. Tim placed the box that I thought still held Dan's notebook and the pin down on the end table. I gave him a look of—what are you doing? Without voicing my concern, he knew what I was thinking. I wondered and worried about what reason he had to bring that over. I thought, *we are going over to visit Lottie aren't we;* by *we* I figured it would just be Frank, me and my son of course.

"Would you like something to drink, Tim?" I asked, trying to remain calm, but it wasn't working. Both of them could see the state I was in.

"No, I'll take a pass," Tim said.

Tim was in uniform; that surprised me, because I thought it was his weekend off. We sat looking at each other for a moment and then Tim made small talk, asking Frank about the Navy.

"So, I hear you've made it a career, how long have you been in?" he asked.

"Seven years," Frank answered, "I intend to stay in until they kick me out."

I looked at my watch; it was almost eleven. I interrupted them to remind Frank that we needed to leave if he wanted to spend any time with his mother. Tim shook his head at me.

"Sergeant Martino isn't working today," he said, "Just thought you should know that before you go."

"Oh, no, I don't need another five minutes with *him*," Frank said, "Maybe I should call my Mother, just tell her I'm here." He hesitated, and then said, "Do you think we can get her to come over here?"

I was confused, nervous and afraid of what Tim was going to say next.

"Why are you in uniform?" I asked, looking at him with extreme bewilderment, trying to reach him with my expressions, hoping he would catch on to what I needed to say without words, especially in front of Frank.

"I was called in to work tonight's shift so I thought I could leave from here when I go," he said.

I was more confused than ever. *Why would he want to stay here when he knew* we *planned on going to the Martino's for the day*, I thought. I looked at my watch again and realized the day was half over, and Frank voiced his concern about not wanting to see his father again.

"Frank, do you want me to call Lottie?" I asked, noticing Tim was now giving me a look, shaking his head at me. Before Frank could answer, Tim interrupted.

"No!" he said, "Don't call her."

I was shocked and looked at Frank who appeared as confused as I was. Tim turned to Frank sitting next to him on the sofa. I was a shaking mess across from them, curled up in my soft worn-out Goodwill chair, afraid of what was about to come out of Tim's mouth. At that moment I wished the chair could swallow me up.

"Frank, I hear you don't get along with your father," Tim said.

"I never did, so what?" Frank answered, probably wondering why Tim would ask such a personal question.

I glanced over to the little steel box and didn't have to imagine where Tim's conversation was heading. I stood up, shaking with fear, in my head I was thinking, *he mustn't do this, not now, not in front of Frank,* but I couldn't stop him.

"Frank, I think you must know—well I have something to tell you, about your Father," Tim said, gently.

"I fell back down in my chair wanting to disappear. Frank didn't look surprised, and he shifted his position on the sofa to face Tim.

"Go ahead, tell me," he said. "Nothing you're gonna say about him will surprise me. Did you see him with some other woman? Or did you catch him in a lie?"

Tim took a deep breath, while I hardly breathed at all.

"I'm afraid it's worse than that, Frank."

Frank looked over at me, "God! How bad can it be?"

"Well, let me start by saying this; you knew Kathleen was married to Sheriff Dan Robson, didn't you?" Tim said.

"Yeah, I knew she was married, and I heard his name before, but wasn't sure when I saw her again that that was the name of who she married. I haven't been home for a few years and when I am, they talk about family stuff so I don't hear gossip about anything outside the family," Frank said.

Tim looked uncomfortable, and I was hoping he would stop right there, but of course he went on trying to explain hauntingly what would be almost impossible for Frank to believe, I was afraid.

"Her husband was killed over two years ago, and your father was alone with him; supposedly during a robbery. I looked up the entire report, and your father was the Sheriff's back up. He said he chased the robber, but he got away," Tim said, pausing before he went on.

"Did you know over the past ten years there's been many women found murdered around the Clearidge area?"

"What does that have to do with the robbery?" Frank asked, looking puzzled.

"Your father never mentioned anything about those murders to you?"

"No, I told you; I was seldom home, get to the point! Oh, once I heard my mother tell Angie to be careful when she went out at night, but my old man told her not to bring up stuff like that in front of Tony, he was only around thirteen at the time. When I first heard of a murder taking place I was a teenager, but they didn't talk much about stuff like that."

"Frank, I'm afraid that the Sheriff was investigating one of the murders and he suspected it might be someone on the Argo police department—"

"Who? Who on the police department? What are you saying?"

"I'm saying he might have thought it could be—"

Frank stood up, and cut Tim off in mid-sentence, "Are you trying to say it could be my father! Are you crazy?"

"Dan Robson was shot in the back of the head, and your father knew he suspected him. He was the only one with the Sheriff that night. In the back of the head, Frank!"

I remembered the shock I felt when I first heard he was shot in the head, I thought it was in the chest, the information was new to me when Tim told me, and it made me feel sick, and now seeing the shock on Frank's face as he stood red-faced—it looked like he was about to go for Tim, but when he saw me crying as I went to grab his arm to keep him back from Tim, he stopped.

Tim looked tense himself, but he tried to calm Frank down.

"I'm sorry," he said, "but I have proof. Did you ever see your father's ten year service pin?"

Frank paced the floor, trying to take it all in. "Yeah, I've seen his service pin, what's that got to do with it?"

"It was found under the body of one of the women," Tim said.

"How do you know it's my old man's?"

Tim went over to the box and opened it. Frank sat down and I watched as Tim showed him Dan's notebook and then the pin. Frank's face turned white, and he kept shaking his head, "My God!" he said, that's the pin Tony was playing with while riding his bike and he must have dropped it and rode over it. The tip on the bottom is bent back, and—I remember it—It's his!"

He quit talking and held the pin in his hand, and I noticed his hand shaking. I felt so sorry for him and went over to put my hand on his shoulder.

"I'm sorry," Tim said, "that I had to do this, but we've been trying to find out if this was his, and we had no luck finding out from anyone else in your family."

He took the notebook and handed it to Frank, but Frank looked like he was in shock and let it fall out of his hands. I picked it up, and both Tim and I tried to help him, I didn't know what to do for him, he was shaking so badly and then we both watched this twenty-five-year-old young man break in front of us. He sobbed into his hands. I put my arms around him and Tim went for a glass of water. We both sat on each side of him, me holding him and Tim holding the glass of water. It was some time before he was able to grasp the extent of the implications and come to terms with what he was just confronted with. His face was buried in his hands and I had my arms around him so both his face and hands were against my shoulder. I felt terrible for him. I looked at Tim, and he looked placid, like a cop doing his job, and it unnerved me a bit.

"Frank, I'm so sorry," I said, "I had no idea he was going to spring this on you today, believe me, I didn't know."

He pulled away from me, and tried to compose himself, finally speaking.

"It's not your fault Kathleen," he said, "not anyone's fault, I knew he was a bastard, but I never expected he was capable of anything like this."

Tim remained silent and offered him the water. He took it and after a few swallows, he said, "My God! My poor mother!" He looked at Tim, "What are you going to do?"

"Go to the FBI," Tim said, "I don't have a choice, certainly not the police department this time, because I fear for my own life he if found out I was—"

"You can't do anything yet!" Frank yelled, "Wait! It's my mother; Kathleen, have you noticed her looking pale lately, well five months ago she was told she needed an operation and she's put it off, not wanting it to interfere with Johnny's christening. I think she's scheduled for the first week in September."

"That's next week," Tim said, "I have to face him at work another week or two?""

"Just until my mother is back home and back on her feet. You can't do this to her while she's going through health problems," Frank pleaded.

"And if he should do something again, I'll be responsible for holding back information about him," Tim said, arguing with Frank.

His tone of voice lacked compassion and I spoke up in Frank's defense. Tim didn't like it, but I didn't care.

"Tim!" I shouted, trying to get his attention as he continued to loudly yell that he had to go to the FBI as soon as possible. "Think of what this is going to do to his family, to Lottie," I said.

He shouted back at me, "Do you have any idea the implications this will have when I'm questioned, and I have to give them a time line on the case?"

Frank yelled back at him, "Don't yell at her! She's only thinking of my mother, what if it was your mother?"

I was caught between two men yelling at each other. I took Frank's side. "Two weeks, that's all he's asking for," I said.

"Ok, suit yourselves!" Tim said, grabbing the box, and then he turned to leave. I didn't try to stop him. He went for the door and I followed, trying to placate him, trying to smooth over what had just happened, but he was angry and spurned my attempt to give him a hug before he left, and turning to me as he walked out, he said, "You don't know the law, Kathleen!"

Frank and I were alone, again, and he apologized for his part in all the shouting.

"You don't have to apologize to me," I said.

"Oh, but I do," he said, and then he went over to where Tommy was sitting on the floor in a corner of the room looking scared, and picked him up. I watched as he tried to comfort my son who had been crying. I thought, *Oh my God, Tommy,* I forgot all about my son witnessing the heated argument; he was frightened, and quietly crying in the corner. I watched as Frank held him and tried to distract him, talking to him in a soothing way.

"I'm sorry, he's upset, and *it is* my fault," he said.

Tommy quieted down, and Frank said, "There's no way I can face my mother today. I have to come back when she goes into the hospital. Do you think you can pick me up and take me there when the time comes? I want to avoid my brother or Angie driving me. Less stress."

"I understand," I said, "I'd be happy to."

He was still holding Tommy, and after walking around the room with him, he turned to me and said, "Let's get out of here today, Let me take you both someplace where we can forget all this for a few hours."

"Where would that be?" I asked.

"To the zoo, has Tommy ever been to the zoo?"

"No, I haven't had a chance to take him there yet."

Frank smiled, and said, "Well today seems like the perfect day."

CHAPTER 38

Frank received a week's leave to see his mother, and after dropping him off at the hospital, I returned home and opened my mailbox. Levi's letter leaped out at me. I hurried up the stairs with Tommy, and as soon as I could, I hastened to open it. It was short and to the point. Asking why he hasn't heard from me and informing me that he had bought a small brick ranch house with a large yard. After mentioning he and the children were fine, he included his phone number, newly installed after he moved into the house. He closed by signing off, Love, Levi.

I felt terrible and guilty for not answering his last letter, which was his first letter, the one he wrote after I wrote to him. It wasn't that I forgot him, how could I? I thought of him almost every night before I could fall asleep—I had to, to go to a place where I felt peaceful, back to that one day in the shop when our goodbyes were wordless, and our feelings acted upon. That was one of the few times I felt happy, like the day I moved back to Mrs. Wilkie's, or Frank taking Tommy and me to the zoo, and the day I met Tim as a frightened eighteen-year-old. Other than those moments, my life was always spinning beyond my control. I was encumbered by an indomitable fate. Happiness eluded me; the harder I tried to hold on, it always managed to slip away.

When Angie called to let me know her mother was going into the hospital, I pretended to be surprised. I hated not being honest, but for the greater good I had to act like I didn't know. I picked Frank up at the train station and drove him straight to the hospital. To avoid Sergeant Martino, I told Frank I would look in on his mother once she was at home and his father would hopefully be at work. Frank said he would go home with Angie and stay with her, but when it was time to go back to Great Lakes he wanted me to take him to the station. He said he would take a bus to my place. He didn't want either Angie or anyone to know we were meeting.

Tim was still upset with me, and he called to say he would wait until he got word that Mrs. Martino was home, and on the mend, but he wouldn't wait any longer than that. When Frank's leave was up, I expected him to come in time for me to take him to the station. He said he wanted to talk on the way so it was a surprise when my buzzer rang early in the morning on Saturday when he wasn't due back at Great Lakes until Sunday night.

I opened the door to a somewhat over-excited sailor, trying to thank me and apologize for coming so early at the same time. He had hailed a cab to my place and seemed out of breath and sat himself down quickly.

"I'm sorry Kathleen, I didn't think I'd make the week—it's been hell! I hope you don't mind, but I need someone to talk to."

"What's happened?" I asked, eager to know how his week went.

"Do you know how awkward it was to be in the same room with my old man, knowing what I know? Seeing my poor Ma lying there unsuspecting that her life will be turned upside down in a matter of days? Watching him fuss over her so tenderly and I can tell you for a moment there I had doubts that he was capable of killing anyone. I know it's his pin, I remember when Tony took it to play with, he wore it, among other pins, like Sal's, and mine from Boy Scouts. Tony never liked Boy Scouts, so he quit. Sal and I weren't allowed to quit, not that I would have wanted to, I liked it. The old man favored Tony, the baby of the family."

"I'm so sorry Frank," I said, it was all I could say. I tried to defend Tim by telling him he would wait.

"I thought I was going to be sick," he said, "watching my old man and Angie with her arms around him, comforting *him*. I could have slapped her, but of course I couldn't do that. They would have thought I was nuts."

I watched him pick Tommy up in his lap when my son tried to get his attention. Tommy was excited when Frank walked in. The trip to the zoo the last time Frank came in is what we all needed and it bonded my son to this handsome sailor that I really liked, but he was young and I had to tell myself, if I worried about Tommy's father having mental problems, Frank having Sergeant Martino for a father was worse.

"When is your mother going to be discharged from the hospital?" I asked, wondering if he planned to go back to Angie's tonight by cab, or if he wanted me to drive him over. I noticed when he came in he had his duffel bag with him. It now sat on the floor near the door.

He looked at me in a way that made me a little uncomfortable, but I took it that he really liked me, and was just being kind, maybe a little more than kind, but I didn't encourage him in anyway. I hoped he hadn't mistaken my affections for him as anything but an attempt to comfort him.

"Do you want me to drive you back to Angie's tonight?" I asked.

"No, if I go back there, they will wonder why I'm not at home with the rest of them. My Mom's going home today, and I can't be there—with him there?"

"You can't go back to Angie's tonight?" I asked, confused.

"How would that look? Angie is spending the night with our mother, everyone will be there, and I would be expected to be there too, in my room—it's a big empty house. How can I explain not being there my last night?"

"Where do you want me to take you?"

He looked at me sadly, "I don't want to be alone tonight, and I thought maybe I could sleep on your sofa, or the floor here, and tomorrow we could spend the day taking your son to Playland, it's an amusement park in Justice," he said, smiling.

It was the first smile he had since he arrived, and probably since Tim showed him the contents of the box. He appeared nervous and had dark circles under his eyes, a sign he hadn't slept too well since that day. I thought, *join the club I don't sleep either.* We must have looked like quite a pair. I didn't have the heart to say no, but was worried about how I would explain the setup to Tim, should he stop over unexpectedly. I had to think fast, and I didn't want Frank to think I was hiding anything from Tim. Surely he knew Tim and I were *together,* like dating. While he was busy, I phoned Tim on the kitchen wall phone, telling him I would be spending the weekend with Betty, and then I called Betty, advising her of what she should know. I told her I would explain later. I knew we had to get out of the apartment for the day, but where to go? Frank seemed to be thinking what I was, so he suggested a ride out to the Airport in Clearidge first to let Tommy watch the planes take off and then the amusement park. We would go out for supper far enough away from where anyone in his family would run into us.

"By the time we come back, it'll be dark," he said.

He sat watching television while I dressed Tommy for a day out. I then changed into another outfit, from the last minute jeans and shirt I threw on when I came out of the shower in the morning, not expecting I was going anywhere that day. By the time we were ready, it was close to lunchtime. I let him drive my car and off we went, with me in my pantsuit and Frank in his sailor blues, and Tommy in the back seat restless and excited over Frank telling him we were going to see the big airplanes fly.

After sitting in the car to watch the first plane take off on the flight path that took it right over my car, we then got out and Frank hoisted Tommy up on his shoulders to get a better view of the next plane. We spent a couple hours there mostly for my son's benefit and then we stopped at a Dog and Suds for our lunch. Watching the girl skate up to take our order caused Tommy to laugh, "Mommy, I want that," he said, pointing to her skates. Frank broke out laughing.

"He sure talks plainly for a three-year-old," he said.

"Yes, come to think of it, he does," I said, realizing how clear he spoke. With my life in constant flight, both literally, and figuratively, I hadn't paid much attention to any of my son's milestones; I took care of his physical needs— going about it like a robot, while my emotional responses where directed to the conflict that surrounded me constantly. From the day I lost Mrs. Wilkie and then married Dan, I never knew a day of real peace until the night I told Levi who I really was, his acceptance without judgment, and his gallant response to my emotional needs, gave me a glimpse into what being loved, and real contentment felt like.

We spent the rest of the afternoon at Playland, and then Frank drove us downtown to show Tommy the big ships moored at the lake, and he took us out for supper to a chicken in the basket, another outdoor drive-up.

"I hope you don't mind," he said, "I chose easy places to eat when you have a child along."

"I don't mind at all, I think it's very considerate of you to think of that," I said.

In my mind I was comparing Tim's reaction around Tommy to both Frank and Levi's. Tim fell short.

Returning home, I asked Frank to park in back of the building, where my car couldn't be seen from the street. Once in the apartment, I put a sleepy Tommy to bed, and I gave Frank the extra pillow and blanket and I threw a sheet over the sofa. I asked him if he would like some tea or coffee since it was too early for our bedtime. He accepted and sat at my kitchen table watching me as I prepared the coffee and filled a dish with an assortment of store bought cookies. As I passed close to him, he reached out and grabbed my hand.

"Kathleen, I want you to know how much I admire you, you're a great mother and a fine woman. Tim's very lucky and I hope he realizes it," he said, still holding on to my hand. I slowly pulled it away and felt a little embarrassed.

"Tim isn't the same guy he was when we met ten years ago," I said. "We are trying to make it work, but his experiences in Korea have changed him."

The minute I spoke, I knew revealing that bit of information, might have given Frank the opening he was probably looking for, and I shouldn't have said anything.

"Well, I'm usually away, but whenever I'm back in Chicago, I'll be here for you whenever you might need me," he said.

"Thanks," I said, and then there was silence as we drank our coffee. When our eyes met, I quickly looked away because I could see in his that we were not on the same page, with him thinking, *if only,* and me thinking, *impossible.*

I liked Frank, a lot, but I knew he was married to the navy, he was younger than I, and he had a father who was crazy, a barrier to any future—what ifs. If only Tim could be as caring as Frank, or as sensitive as Levi, but I knew he wasn't. I began to realize that having a physical attraction to one had nothing to do with being in love, or even liking the person. I liked Frank, could love him, maybe like one loves a close family member, but I felt no physical attraction to him, not yet. I found him easy to talk to and I knew we both needed a friend who understood what was to come—what we would soon be going through.

We talked late into the night, trying to imagine what would happen once the FBI got involved, and what could happen to his family. We both looked at our watches and realized it was almost two in the morning. I got up and wished him a good night, reminding him that I put extra towels in the bathroom.

"Go ahead," he said, "You go first, I'll sit here for awhile and finish my coffee."

As I passed his chair he reached out and touched my arm briefly. Once I was in bed, I could hear him in the bathroom and then all was quiet. I lay awake for a while thinking of how lonely I felt, and how frightened I was, and then, again, I thought of Levi.

In the morning I made a quick breakfast while Frank took a shower. I could hear the water running. When it stopped, I began to fry the bacon and eggs. Frank came into the kitchen wearing a clean white tee shirt and his blue bell-bottoms. He smelled of Lilac Vegetal after-shave. I loved that smell and I remembered Levi using it which surprised me, but that was after he left the Old Order. I liked it better than the Old Spice Tim usually wore. I felt flushed, like I might be blushing, but didn't understand why, so I kept my back to him as I tended the eggs.

After breakfast we finished dressing and Frank drove us to a park that was pretty far from Arden so Tommy could play on the swing and slide while we sat on a bench and talked. We stopped for lunch and then went to the train station where we would say our goodbyes. Tommy started to cry and Frank told him he would come back and see us again. This time I thought it would be proper to just kiss Frank on the cheek, after all he had done for us the last two days, and so I did, just as he was about to step up to enter the train. I shouldn't have done that, because he grabbed me and gave me a quick kiss on the lips. Before I could say anything, he disappeared into the train. I was left standing—surprised, unable to move holding Tommy's hand, and trying to understand why my heart was almost pounding out of my chest.

CHAPTER 39

Tim came over on Monday after I had arrived home from picking up Tommy after work. I was tired from a full day of typing up real-estate contracts, and my back hurt—not to mention my eyes needed a rest. I didn't want to read anything, or think about anything, but relax after I made supper and collapsed on my second-hand sofa. Tim appearing changed all that. He came in looking red-faced and exhausted. He was still in uniform and I noticed his gun was visible in its holster strapped to his side. He sat down slightly agitated.

"That son of a bitch!" he said, loudly, even though Tommy was in the room. I put my finger to my lips, trying to remind him of his language in front of my three-year- old.

"What's happened", I asked.

"He's following me—Martino—I looked in my rear view mirror and he was behind me after I left work. I stopped to get gas, and he parked in his car watching. Damn that Mrs. Clarke! Mentioning the box in front of him was all we needed to get his suspicions up. Is his wife out of the hospital yet?"

"She came home on Saturday," I said, "Are you going to the FBI soon?"

"Yes, tomorrow, I'll call them after I get home. I'm not driving to their headquarders because he might follow me!"

"Calm down, please,' I said, "I have to make supper so you might as well eat with us."

"Eat? I can't eat anything tonight. Do you realize all I have is the Sheriffs' notebook and that stupid service pin. What if it's not enough?"

"Well, even Frank identified the bent pin as his father's, so wouldn't that be enough?" I asked.

"If only you kept that license or better yet—you should have turned it in!" he said, like that alone would have solved the case. His tone of voice was accusatory.

"Tim, you have no idea the state of fear I was in at that time," I said, trying to defend my actions.

"How could you destroy evidence?" he said, his voice getting louder.

"I need this like a hole in the head!" he shouted.

"Don't shout, you're scaring my son," I said, "If that's all we have, I'm sure Frank will testify that it's his father's pin."

He stared at me like he discovered a third eye on my forehead, "Don't be so sure—it's *his* father we are accusing, did you ever think of that!"

"I know Frank, he's honest and he of all people realizes his father isn't who he pretends to be," I said, trying to convince him of what I wasn't sure of myself.

"Oh, so you know him? Really, you met him twice and you know him?"

"Tim, please, lower your voice," I pleaded.

He grabbed me by my shoulders forcing me to look at him, "You'll have to testify about what you found and what you did with it, and you better try to remember everything you can about what was on it, besides the victim's picture."

After that exchange between us I kept quiet. He could see I was upset, so he didn't say anything more. He stood up and said he had to go, and I nodded, thinking, *go, go,* I couldn't wait for him to leave. He went out the door without saying anything except, "I'll let you know after I make the call."

I was relieved to see him go. My insides were churning and I didn't feel like I could eat anything either, so I took the necessary steps to the kitchen, just to feed my son. That night I had never felt so alone emotionally, no shoulder to cry on, no one to confide in about the mess I found myself in, and whenever I felt that low I would think of Levi, but on this night Frank would join Levi in my thoughts. The next morning on the way to work, I decided to stop and visit Lottie before I picked up Tommy. I wanted to at least see her after she came home, and before all hell broke loose. I left work early trying to avoid her husband being there. When I arrived, Angie answered the door.

"Oh, hi Kathleen, come on in," she said, cheerfully, "Ma's upstairs."

I followed her up to Lottie's room. She was lying on the bed fully dressed, resting.

"How are you feeling?" I asked, trying to be polite and concerned.

I felt guilty for what was about to happen to her regarding her husband. Imagining how horrible the scene would be in that home when she found out about him upset me. Maybe it was betrayal what I was doing, because I knew what was about to happen and here I was trying to put on an act in front of her, like everything was normal.

She smiled and said she was a little weak, and the stairs were an obstacle, but in a few days she thought it would get better. She mentioned she wished she had a bedroom on the ground floor.

I didn't know if I should ask what kind of an operation it was, and to my relief Angie said, "Mom had needed the hysterectomy last December but she put it off waiting for the baby to be born and then she didn't want to ruin Christmas, and next it was Johnny's Christening and before we knew it, it's summer."

"You look good," I said, and she did.

"It was just a routine surgery, nothing serious," Lottie said.

I was at a loss for words and tried to make some small talk, for a few minutes, commenting on her choice of decorating. How much I liked it, but I felt like a fraud, acting like all was well when these fine people might find me testifying against their husband and father in the coming weeks.

"I wanted to stop on my way home, and see you. I would like to stay longer, but I have to pick up my son from the sitter's," I said.

"Oh, of course," Lottie answered, thanking me for coming.

On the way home all I could think of was, *what an existence I led, and how I wish I could take off and run again, but where*? I found myself, trapped in this quagmire of a life I never chose for myself. After taking care of my son for the night, I sat and pondered another letter to Levi. I wondered what I should tell him other than I was fine, but still needed time to clear up the remnants of my former life? After all this time, almost a year since I was back, it would seem ridiculous. What could possibly take a whole year? That's what he would be thinking. I felt trapped, not sure of what I wanted, and not wanting to sever my relationship to a man I might want to go back to, all the while hoping my feelings for Tim would return to what they once were. Then there was Frank, the three years between us wasn't an obstacle, it was who he was, the son of a killer. I couldn't get past that even though it wasn't his fault. I felt something for Frank, but wasn't sure what it was, or who he really was. I wasn't even sure who *I was*.

Five days after I last heard from Tim, he called, telling me I would have to either come to his apartment or the FBI would question me at mine. I chose to go to his place and drop Tommy off at Betty's. Poor Betty, she knew something was amiss, but didn't question me after I told her I would let her know what I was involved in after it was all over. She assured me to count on her to take Tommy any time I needed her. She could see the state I was in and knowing Dan was gone, she couldn't imagine what could be so bad, certainly not Mrs. Clarke, or not even Tim would have been able to cause me to break down in front of her the way I did. She had no idea, and at times would look at me like she worried about *my* mental health.

Arriving at Tim's I found two FBI Agents sitting at the table, waiting for me. I was a bundle of nerves. Tim led me into the kitchen where the men stood up to greet me.

"Hello, Kathleen," one of the men said, smiling, trying to put me at ease, "I'm Jake." I sat across from Tim and the second man, who introduced himself as Robert, got up to get something out of his briefcase. They asked me many questions and I told them as much as I could remember about Dan's behavior during that time and finding the license. They looked at me, surprised, when I had to tell them what I did with it.

"So, you threw it in your apartment buildings incinerator?" the agent named Jake asked.

"Yes, I'm afraid I did. I'm sorry, I wasn't myself at that time," I said, almost shaking with fear. My hands shook, and I interlaced my fingers to keep them still. They noticed how nervous I was. Tim looked over at me and smiled trying to relax me I'm sure, but I wanted the meeting to be over quickly.

The other agent, Robert, spoke as he held the papers he took from his case.

"We spoke with Tim here, when he called and he gave us the name of Frank Martino serving in the navy and stationed at Great Lakes at the moment. We sent a couple of Agents out to question him. He was very forthcoming with what he remembered about his father's lost service pin."

He looked at the paper he held and began to read, "It says his father lost the pin that he identified around April of 1955. Frank remembered his younger brother Tony was found playing with the pin the night the Sergeant was going out. He took it from him and must have put it in his pocket on his way out. Anyway, that's what Frank thinks he remembers. He said it was in the spring and Tony was around eleven years old. The time fits this time line the Sheriff laid out."

The Agent called Jake, looked at me. "We think the Sergeant thinks the license you disposed of is in the box Tim has here," he said, pointing to the little steel box Tim had on the table that held the notes and pin. "We'll take it with us, and put a tail on him, watch his movements. We need more than the notes and a bent service pin. Any good defense attorney could poke holes in the case as it now stands and come up with very believable reasons for their existence."

"One of which is—that the Sheriff was acting strangely just before he was killed," Robert added. "We questioned several of his deputies who could attest to that in a court of law. The guy was losing it mentally is what we were told and now trying to pin his death on the Sergeant, supposedly his good friend, would be iffy with a good defense. They mentioned arguments between the two men months before his death.

Jake added, "No, we need something more tangible, finger prints, or catching him in some aggressive act, and I hate to say this but, a very credible cop and family man is a hard case to try without more evidence against him. Without fingerprints—and there were none found on anything, in every murder we investigated, we have a flimsy case. At best it's circumstantial evidence."

I became more fearful as they spoke, "You mean, you don't believe he's guilty of committing murder?" I asked, fearful of the answer.

Agent Jake laughed a little, and realizing how upset I appeared, he took my hand and said, "It's not that we don't believe it, we do, but we need better proof. We were called in when the Sheriff was shot, we suspected him at that time, because of all the information we acquired about their relationship and all the disagreements between the two men prior to the Sheriffs death. But it was only that death we suspected him of, never the murders of a woman or maybe all the women. No, Captain O'Malley brought that to our attention."

"We need to rule out the Sheriff's—your husband, of any wrong doing by having that service pin supposedly belonging to Sergeant Martino. You finding the woman's drivers license in his clothing—"

"It was in my dirty laundry, not just in his clothing!" I said, "I told you that Sergeant Martino was at my home that morning!"

I was afraid they thought I found it in one of Dan's pockets, and even if I did, that wouldn't prove anything. Sergeant Martino could have put it there. I had to make sure they knew it was in the bag of clothing not in a certain piece of clothing of Dan's. I started to cry. Tim stood up and came over to me and put his arm around my shoulder.

"She's afraid of the Sergeant," Tim said, "The way he questioned her, and her mother-in-law about the laundry— who wouldn't be afraid, knowing he's asking because *he* planted that bit of evidence in there."

"I understand her fear," Agent Robert said with sympathy. "We'll be watching him and we need to trap him in some way—lure him would be a better word. Stay away from his home," he said, looking at me. "You said you're good friends with his daughter?"

"Yes, yes we are close friends," I said, hoping he wouldn't ask me to question Angie about anything.

"Well, I want you to be able to visit her like everything is normal, but not if her parents are there and under no circumstance should you go over to the Sergeants home again. Find any excuse for the time being," Agent Jake said, informing me on how important it was that I follow his instructions.

The Agents stood up and shook hands with both Tim and me, assuring us that they would be in constant touch and not to worry. They took my phone number and address and left with the box and its contents. I was so shook up that Tim offered to follow me safely home but I told him I needed to get Tommy from Betty's and that I would be fine. On the way to Betty's I cried the whole way and by the time she answered the door I was a mess.

"What's happened?" she asked, looking worried.

"Nothing I can tell you about Betty," I said.

She put her arms around me. "Don't worry, I don't need to know until you're ready."

I thanked her and left with my son. Once I was home, I fed him and couldn't give him my full attention, because I was so preoccupied with what was going to happen next. After I put him to bed I tried to think of what to do. I needed to write Levi, but what could I write that would make sense to him, and then I thought of writing Frank, but reasoned that would give him encouragement when it came to what he might make of it. I had feelings for him, but not the kind he might be thinking of. I had Levi's phone number and thought of calling him, *isn't that why he sent it, expecting me to call?* I thought. I needed to hear a man's voice, one that was gentle and kind without that edge to it that Dan always had and Tim came back with, a tone that kept me walking on eggs.

I reached for the phone and dialed the number.

"Hello!" the voice said, cheerfully.

My hand holding the receiver was trembling. "Levi? It's me, Kathleen," I said, sure my voice sounded shaky.

"Kathleen, I've missed you. The children miss you, and I kept talking about you to them the past year, so they would remember since we haven't any pictures," he said.

"I've missed all of you," I said, hoping he knew it included him without being specific. "I'll mail you a picture of Tommy and me soon," I promised.

"That would be great! I love you Kathleen."

I was at a loss for words and couldn't answer the same. "Levi, you didn't change your life completely because of me, did you?" I asked, afraid he might have done just that. "What about your sister, and your extended family, they will shun you. You'll be alone with the children for the rest of your life."

"I have my children and maybe you and Timmy too, I won't be alone," he said.

"I forgot to tell you, my son's name is Thomas, not Timothy. I changed it when I hid at Emma's."

"It doesn't matter to me," he said.

And it didn't matter, because all Levi thought of was being a family, but what could I tell him about what I was going through and why I was gone for so long—nothing. I longed to hear his voice and when I heard it, it brought back how kind he was, always, and how safe and comfortable I felt in his arms. We ended the conversation with me telling him I would call again, without telling him anything except a phony excuse like, I wanted Tommy to spend more time with his grandmother and that he would miss her, when we were gone—all lies, but wasn't my whole life built on a lie. I wasn't Kathleen Kelly, just Kathleen. I could only rightfully claim my first name. For the first time in a long time I began to think of my birth mother. Who was she? Was I born out of wedlock? And who was my father? Did he know about me? What was he like? Was he like a Dan, Tim, Levi, or Frank? I had to quit thinking about it all, or I would get depressed, but I couldn't help but wonder.

Chasing the Unicorn

CHAPTER 40

It was October the month of Halloween and Betty and I took the boys for new costumes. Tommy wanted a Superman costume, and Ricky chose Batman from the comics. Nothing was happening with the FBI yet, and I needed to take my son to visit his grandmother. Mrs. Clarke called almost every week, more than once, when I would answer the phone. Half of the time I didn't answer. When I didn't, I would call Tim to make sure it wasn't him. Betty, Rita and Angie were all told that if I didn't answer, to try one more time and let it ring twice for Betty, once for Rita and call again right after hanging up for Angie. It was ridicules to go through all that, but to curb Mrs. Clarke's constant calls, it was the only thing I could think of. The FBI kept their calls strictly to Tim, after he told them I wasn't able to tell them anything more and that the whole situation had me upset and nervous and it interfered with my job and the need to care for my son. I knew they had surveillance on the Sergeant and other than that, there wasn't much else going on.

Frank called, wondering if I might see him, maybe bring Tommy down to Great Lakes to meet up with him and he promised a nice day at the Zoo. I accepted his offer, to get away from all my fears. I thought I saw Martino following me one day when I was on my way home from shopping. I told Tim, and he thought I was imagining it.

"It's me he's after, not you Kathleen," he said.

It wasn't enough to quell my fear of the man. I looked forward to taking the train down to meet Frank. It was the second week of October and my birthday was on the tenth. I would be twenty-nine years old and I felt old. My twenties had been a decade of hell on earth. Having taken Latin in High School, I called it my decade of horribilis. On the way to meet up with Frank, Tommy loved the train ride, but he was more excited about seeing Frank. I wondered if it was a good idea having him become attached to Frank. The few times we were together was enough to bond my son to a man I knew would eventually disappear from his life. On one hand, Tim was with us often, and Tommy's enthusiasm over Tim wasn't anything like what

292

he displayed for Frank. I worried about what I was doing to my son by allowing him to be with Frank again. To be honest, I wondered what it was doing to me. I didn't want to be physically attracted to him, but I was afraid I was. I knew it was the kind of attraction that couldn't last.

When the train came into the station and finally stopped, Tommy sitting by the window spotted the sailor leaning against a post smiling as we came off the train, and ran to him. Frank picked him up and held him up high before letting him down. Frank was handsome, no denying that, and my heart skipped a beat. He greeted me with only a kiss on the cheek and that I was thankful for. I didn't need to feel what I would be feeling if he really kissed me. I calmed myself down, but couldn't help noticing how happy he appeared as we walked with Tommy between us, each holding his hand. He hadn't said anything to me except to smile and the kiss on the cheek and then the silence that said more than I needed to hear—what I didn't want to hear in words.

"I thought we would head for Lincoln Park Zoo first," he said, "and then maybe take a boat ride on Lake Michigan, would you like that Tommy?" he asked, addressing my son.

"That sounds great!" I said, trying not to stare at him too often, but damn, he was handsome, but for some reason I never paid attention to his looks when we first met. At age fifteen, he was still going through adolescences, so it wasn't noticeable then and he was just a young teenager beyond my radar. When I saw him again for the first time at his parents' home, he wasn't in the best of moods around his father and I was distracted by the others but here alone with him, things were different. When we were with him the weekend he stayed overnight, I was uncomfortable having him in my home, but here again with him in a safe place, my heart was beating so. I blushed easily and I was sure whenever his eyes met mine, I blushed, but Frank never let on he noticed. I was sure he was having the same feelings, and he tried to hide it by centering all his attention on my son.

Having exhausted the whole morning seeing all the animals, with Tommy's excitement causing us both to laugh, drew us closer. Walking out of the park, he held Tommy's hand on one side of him and mine on the other, and I let him. I thought, *God, what would happen if he had come to us instead, and then had to take us home at the end of the day?* I didn't want to think of it.

The boat ride was even more intimate, with Frank holding Tommy up so he could see the waves over the rail on the deck, and his other arm around me. I let him hug me; I couldn't help it. I told myself it was just for today. When we left the boat and were on our way to get something to eat, he chose a nice restaurant on Michigan Avenue. I worried about Tommy in such a fancy place, but Frank assured me he would be fine.

"I'll ask for a table in the corner," he said.

I was surprised to see my son behave so well. He would be four in January and either he was getting older, or he was so attached to Frank that he wanted to behave for him. There weren't any of his antsy movements when we were in a restaurant with Tim, and I thought, *even small children knew when they were wanted.* After the restaurant, we headed for the train station. It was early but Frank needed to be back at the base. We stood looking at each other with Tommy hugging Frank's leg and Frank hugging me. As the train approached he pulled me to him, and this time planted a passionate kiss on me. It left me feeling faint. We said our goodbyes, with Tommy waving to him as we boarded the train. On the ride home, all I could think of was Frank and his kiss, but I knew my reaction had to be because I hadn't been kissed that way in a long time, not where it made me feel good. Tim's kisses left me confused and holding back, because one minute he was irritable and the next he wanted to kiss me. It didn't work that way for me. I found myself angry during those moments when he kissed me that were becoming fewer as the weeks went by, with both of us immerged in a cesspool of crimes spanning years and a psychopath on the loose, maybe this time after Tim, or both of us.

I wondered how often the Sergeant would follow Tim around and follow him to my apartment building. He knew where I lived without Tim leading him, but if it weren't for the fact that the FBI promised they would be watching Martino, I would have been unable to sleep at night. Three days after we were with Frank, Tim decided to take me out for my birthday, on a weeknight, on my birthday. I hurried home leaving Tommy with Betty, and dressed in my new dress. Emerald green was a color I looked best in, with my red hair. It was a form-fitting dress, high collar, and long sleeves. I wore my black pumps, and black clutch purse. My earrings were small pearls and matching silver chain necklace, with one drop pearl hanging on my green dress. I knew it looked great together. I almost wished it were Frank or Levi who could see me this night. With this terrible situation hanging between us, I couldn't imagine Tim noticing how I looked. I thought he would be consumed with the case and I didn't want to hear any of it on my birthday.

He came in using his key as I went to get my coat from the closet. When I came into the living room, he was standing near the door with his mouth open in surprise.

"Wow!" was his comment, "You look great! Kathleen—that dress! You look like a million bucks."

"Thank you," was all I managed to say. I felt embarrassed for some reason, because Tim had never shown any enthusiasm over anything I wore like he did this time.

He helped me on with my coat and we left with him holding my hand all the way down to his car. He looked nice in his gray suit and I couldn't help thinking, *this looked like the Tim I remembered on our very first date.* On the way to the restaurant he chose, to surprise me, he said, so I wasn't sure where we were going, he started to tell me about Agent Jake calling to tell him that the case wasn't going to be easy to prove that Martino killed any women, but they were investigating only Dan's murder, and the one where the pin was found.

"Tim," I said, "I don't want to talk about anything having to do with Martino, or the FBI tonight, please. It's been two years and they still haven't been able to arrest him for Dan's murder. I don't want to talk about it."

He looked over and patted my arm, "You're right, tonight the subject's off limits, I'm sorry."

We went to a nice place for dinner, but it wasn't anything special, we had been there before. It was in the neighborhood and all I kept doing during the meal was comparing Frank's choice to Tim's and then I thought, maybe I was being unfair to him. Frank was based downtown and would know all the best spots where Tim very seldom left the town we lived in. I began to think I was overdressed, and wished it were Frank who had seen me in the dress I wore. It seemed there wasn't much to talk about with Tim if it wasn't police business. I brought up his mother who I hadn't seen since she invited Tommy and me over when I first returned, but that was a year ago. He seldom mentioned his parents to me. I didn't know what to make of it.

"How are your folks doing?" I asked, trying to make conversation, but really wanting to know about them also.

"Oh, they're ok," he said, and then nothing.

I changed the subject, "It must have been difficult to get through North Korea, and was it during the winter when you made your way out?"

"Yeah, it was cold the whole time."

"You said you were in a Japanese hospital for three months—why that long? Were you badly hurt?"

"Of course, we were suffering from hyperthermia, and starvation. I can't tell you how bad it was, I really don't want to talk about it," he said, his voice taking on a bit of irritation.

I changed the subject again, "Betty and I took the boys for Halloween costumes," I said, and then laughingly told him how Tommy wanted to be Superman. Tim's eyes glazed over and he made no comment. I then chased the cut up steak around my plate with the fork; I was beginning to lose my appetite.

"This steak is nice and tender," I said, trying to fill in the silence that would have been present if I didn't say something, anything, to keep a conversation going.

"I like mine a little bloody," he said.

The rest of the meal was painful for me to get through. Obviously Tim wasn't the same Tim I met years ago, or maybe he was, but we weren't able to spend enough time together for me to notice. He was only a twenty-year-old boy back then.

He drove home, with me filling in the silence—doing the talking about nothing—the weather, my work, and mentioning that I would be taking Tommy to visit his grandmother on Halloween. When we entered my apartment, he took his suit jacket off and also his tie. He looked tired, and I asked him if he would like a cup of coffee.

"I would," he said, and then nothing.

I went into the kitchen to put a pot of coffee on, then returned expecting him to be asleep on my sofa, instead he met me at the doorway between the kitchen and living room and roughly grabbed me. He kissed me and I found it hard to respond. He caught me by surprise. I pulled away from him and pretended to check the stove again where the coffee was about to perk. He followed me, coming up behind me, putting his arms around me and trying to kiss my neck. I turned to him.

"I need to change my dress," I said, trying to explain that the dress was new and I didn't want to wrinkle it.

"Let me help you," he said, smiling down at me.

"Tim, please, let me pour you a cup of coffee, and then allow me to get out of this dress, it was expensive."

"I'll buy you a new one," he said, teasingly.

I looked at him in shock. I thought, *this wasn't the same man that worried about my virtue, years ago.* His movements were aggressive and I was uncomfortable. He followed me to the table where I poured his coffee and I went to the bedroom. When I turned to close my door, he was there, entering my room.

"Tim! What are you doing?" I asked, but he didn't answer until he got me in a bear hug.

He laughed, "What am I doing? Come on Kathleen, we're not children anymore. I look at life differently after all I've been through. We're here today, and we could be gone tomorrow."

My heart was beating fast, but not because I was excited, I had in the back of my mind that I would be cheating on Levi, just like I kept Levi at bay, thinking I would be cheating on Dan. It was only after hearing that Dan had died did I allow Levi to love me.

"Tim, I can't," I said, pushing him away.

"Why not? Don't tell me that after all this time it matters to you the way it did when we were kids? You've been married, for heavens sake, or is it Frank you've been thinking of lately? Don't hide the fact that you've been with him. Tommy spilled the beans the other day when I came over and you left the room. He showed me his toy boat and said Frank gave it to him and took him on a big boat. I know you were with Frank recently, weren't you?" he asked, his voice getting louder.

"Tim, do I have to account to you for everything I do? You don't see an engagement ring on my finger, do you?"

"If that's what you want, I'll get you one," he said.

"No, I can't handle anything like that right now," I said.

"You mean you want your options open—to maybe go to Frank after all this is over?"

"Don't be ridiculous, Frank is just a friend, and we need his friendship if we want him to support us in putting an end to what his father has done to my husband—to my son's father."

He looked at me like he didn't believe me completely, and with good reason, because I didn't believe it myself. The explosive physical attraction I had with Frank put the word 'friend' out of the equation.

He left the room to allow me to get out of my dress, and I closed the door and wondered what he expected of me. Tommy was spending the night with Betty, at her suggestion, to have a sleepover with Ricky. Maybe she thought it was time for Tim and me to finally come together, instead I thought we were coming apart. Our one night alone in my apartment and I just couldn't allow myself the luxury of what I would have gladly given to him eleven years earlier. I was no longer the eighteen-year-old girl with stars in her eyes.

He waited until I came out dressed in slacks and a shirt, even though it was late, and I noticed he had put his jacked back on. He stood by the door holding his tie, ready to leave.

"I better go," he said, "until you get your head on straight, I won't expect anything from you, except your cooperation in nailing that bastard Martino."

I didn't say anything and was relieved he was leaving. I walked up to him, to thank him again for the dinner.

He looked at me trying to hide the anger I could see, in the clenched muscle of his jaw.

"You don't have to thank me, It was all in the line of duty," he said, and then he went out the door, leaving me standing there without a hug, or kiss on the cheek, or even the word, goodbye.

Angie called to wish me a happy birthday, the next evening.

"I called, last night, but then I realized you might have gone out with Tim," she said.

"Yes, he took me out to dinner."

"And then what?"

"What do you mean? There was no 'what.' Tim went home and I went to bed."

"Well, that didn't sound too exciting," she said, laughing.

"It was late, and we both had to get up for work this morning."

"When are you and Tim going to make if official? That you're a couple, isn't it time you two became engaged?"

"Angie, we are different people today, older and taking our time," I said, hoping she would get off the subject of Tim and me.

"Well, John and I thought we'd have you both over for dinner Saturday, can you make it? and bring Tommy, of course."

"I'll let you know," I said, and then we ended the call.

I thought of what she said—bring Tommy, of course? Like we were a threesome, Tim, Tommy and I. If only she knew, it wasn't even Tim and I lately. I didn't want to ask Tim to join me at Angie's, not after last night, and he might not want to go anywhere with me after my refusing him. I wasn't looking forward to seeing any of the Martinos, except for Frank. I didn't bother to ask her if her parents would be at the dinner. I knew they were never there when she invited us before, but now was different, I had to make sure. As the night wore on, my nerves got the better of me, and I decided to phone Angie after work the next day and refuse her offer, using some excuse. Tim couldn't make it, and Tommy had a cold. I just couldn't face her, knowing what I knew about her father was bad enough, but knowing I was attracted to her brother and seeing him without anyone in her family knowing? No, that was too much for me to carry, emotionally, to be in her presence.

The week before Halloween, Rita called. I hadn't heard from her in quite some time. She was busy, about to get married again, and I was preoccupied with all that I was struggling with, so we weren't in touch as often as in the past. She called to tell me that the quaint apartment above her garage would be available again. She knew how much I loved living there, but it had only one bedroom, and a bit smaller than my apartment.

"It would be ideal for you, Kathleen, so close to Tommy's sitter and my kids. My daughter is old enough to keep an eye on him for you, and we have the large back yard," she said.

"I don't know, I have a lease on this place for another three months, I would need to let you know," I said, not sure if I wanted to move.

"Well, think about it, and while you're at it, lets get together soon," she said.

I promised her we would, and thought about it the next day. After picking up my son from the sitter, I spent the evening with Betty. I wanted her take on it.

"If you think you'll be happier there, it does have a yard Tommy can play in and there's Rita's kids right there everyday," she said.

I hesitated to tell her that as much as I wanted to be there, mostly for Tommy, I was afraid I wouldn't have the safety I needed. In the apartment building one had to announce who they are outside at the speaker and then I had to buzz them in. Also, the other tenants were close by and could hear anything going on near my door. At the apartment above the garage, I wouldn't feel as safe. I didn't know how I could tell either Betty or Rita why I had to refuse.

CHAPTER 41

Mrs. Clarke opened her door and swept Tommy off his feet, before taking a look at his costume. He dropped his plastic pumpkin filled with candy all over her porch.

"Oh, dear, I'm so sorry!" she said, quickly putting him down and helping me pick up the candy we had collected from a few houses near her home before I took him to her. I was thankful that Betty and I had taken the boys earlier for trick or treating, when it was still light out. I made a trip back home to empty his treats and then left again to drive him to his grandmother's as I had promised.

"We will have to throw some of it away," I said, noticing a few had become unwrapped, and cookies fell out of a little bag one woman had given him.

"I'm so sorry, Kathleen, I guess I was so happy to see him, I wasn't careful."

"Well, he wanted to show off his Superman outfit and you grabbed him so fast—"

"I know, I'm so sorry Tommy, you look so nice, can you fly in it?" she laughed, trying to get in his good graces, because he started to cry when he dropped his treats.

We entered her home, and she apologized, again. Tommy stopped crying and she knelt down to look him over. I smiled and said, "Well we did trick or treat early so he has plenty of candy at home."

"Come into the kitchen, I have baked a nice Halloween cake and I made coffee---of course if you prefer tea—"

"No, coffee would be fine," I said.

We sat at her table while she talked to Tommy and I kept thinking, *if only she could be a gentler or nicer person I would want to bring him to her more often.*

"How are you doing Kathleen? How is your work at the Real Estate office going? If you ever need any help, you know I'm right here," she said, smiling her usual crooked smile that I liked to call her spider smile. I knew taking any help from her would be like getting caught in her web. I didn't know what to talk to her about and just sat there letting her speak to my son all she wanted, while I drank my coffee and ate the slice of cake she cut for us.

She quit giving Tommy her full attention after a while and turned to me.

"You know Kathleen, if Tim has important police department papers that belonged to Dan, he should turn them in to the police, don't you think?"

I was taken a bit by surprise, "I don't think they were anything important," I said, hoping she would change the subject.

"Well, Sergeant Martino thinks they are. I heard his wife had come home from the hospital so I thought I'd bring her a nice cake I baked, and he was home, and asked me about the papers Dan had stored in that box. He asked if I knew who had them. I told him the paper's belonged to Dan, so of course the box and papers were with you."

"Me? I don't have them, for all I know Tim might have thrown them away, and the box was old and rusty so why would I keep it. It means nothing to me. It's really nothing," I said, feeling my heart starting to race.

"Kathleen, something is going on over at the Sheriff's department, Mrs. Jenson, the wife of deputy Jensen told me the FBI has been asking questions of all the deputies."

"When were they asking questions and about what?" I asked, I was beginning to feel shaky.

Mrs. Clarke looked at me like I should have known about it. "Oh, they asked after Dan died, but she told me they started asking questions again. She said all her husband could tell her is that they were still investigating his death because they couldn't figure out how my son—"

She started to cry, and I patted her hand across the table. "What did she tell you?"

"My son was killed, and I didn't find out he was shot in the back of the head until after his funeral. You weren't here at the time; it was awful with everyone talking about it. Sergeant Martino tried to help him, but I don't know why he didn't have more cops come right away when he said Dan called him for help. Everyone said he was wearing a bulletproof vest, but the robber couldn't have known that, would he?"

She continued to cry, so I tried to change the subject again by talking about how fast Tommy was growing and how well he could hold a conversation.

"You're lucky, you have Tommy. I don't have Dan anymore. I don't understand why Sergeant Martino went alone to help him, I just don't understand it."

I was thinking, *how many others in the Sheriff's and Police departments* wondered *the same thing.* I felt sorry for her at that moment and decided to stay longer than I had planned. I wanted to find out as much as I could about anything more she knew about, that I didn't.

"I went over to visit Lottie, right after she came home from the hospital," I said, "so how was she when you went to see her?"

"She seemed to be doing ok, but she complained about how crabby her husband was becoming lately."

"Well, maybe he was under stress, you know, worried about her health."

"Yes, men aren't able to handle a lot of stress well. My Tom was a saint; he wasn't anything like Dan's father. That man's moods were difficult to live with."

When I heard that, I began to think of Dan's moods, and his mental health. Combined with the stress of the job, in the kind of profession he chose, it was a deadly combination.

"I too wondered why Mr. Martino showed up alone to help Dan," I said, "it sounds kind of suspicious, don't you think?" The minute the words came out of my mouth, I knew I said the wrong thing. I tried to backtrack, "I mean, if there were one or more cops there, they could have taken the robber down, instead of him getting away."

"Yes, you're right, but what's done is done. I'm so thankful for Tommy," she said, trying to pick him up and sit him on her lap. He didn't want to sit on her lap, so he became difficult struggling to free himself of her grasp.

I scolded him this time, because I felt sorry for her at that moment, and I found excuses for him.

"He's tired, it's almost his bedtime," I said, "so I think we should start for home."

Chasing the Unicorn

She got up from her chair and wrapped up the rest to the cake for us to take home.

"Here, take this with you," she said, "I baked it special for him, see, I decorated it with a pumpkin on it."

On the ride home, I worried about casting doubts in her mind by opening my big mouth about what I was thinking, thinking Dan's death was suspicious. Of course that's what I thought, what everyone else must have thought connected with the case, but I should have never put that thought into her mind. I hoped I changed the topic quickly and she'd forget what I said.

Two weeks after my visit with Dan's mother I received a call from Angie.

"Kathleen, what have you been saying to Mrs. Clarke?" were her first words to me when I answered the phone. She sounded upset.

"What are you talking about," I asked, knowing full well what it must be about.

"My mother's all upset over you telling Dan's mother that you are suspicious over how Dan died?"

"I think she must have misunderstood what I said, I only wondered how the criminal they were apprehending was able to shoot him in—"

"Well, my mother's upset because it sounded like you didn't believe my father, after all he was the only one there."

"Angie, she misunderstood what I said. I never mentioned your father to her at all. When did she talk to your mother?"

"Yesterday, and of course I reminded my Ma, she's a trouble maker and not to believe anything she says, that she's a busybody and if she spreads this around the department, how do you think that's gonna make my father look like—like a policeman that couldn't handle anything or worse throw suspicion on the whole situation when my father is totally alone to defend his description of what happened, since Dan isn't alive to back up his story."

"I'm sorry she called your mother over something stupid," I said.

We ended the conversation with her calming down and blaming it all on Mrs. Clarke. I thought of what she said, Dan not being here to back up her father? I had to laugh about that one. I realized I had to be careful of what I said in front of Dan's mother. She was like a loose cannon, ready to go off over the death of her son, and I like an idiot handed her the ammunition.

Thanksgiving was the time of year when families got together, and I thought of what kind of family I had of my own. I only had one small son and a former mother-in-law whom I didn't like or trust. That's when I thought of Levi. What I wouldn't give to spend it with Levi and his children. Ever since I left the orphanage, my Thanksgivings were spent with people I wasn't related to and even though I wasn't related by blood to Levi and his family, it was the closest I ever came to not feeling like an outsider. Maybe because Levi was bucking the system he lived in and wanted out of it, and I was looking for happiness and stability in my own life, and both of us were looking for a feeling of belonging and when we met, we clicked. I thought back to Levi and my thoughts and feelings when I was near him. It was the nearest I ever came to not feeling alone. It was what I thought I had with Tim before he was sent to Korea, or Dan, when we were dating.

I sat at my kitchen table going over my rent and utilities. I was just getting by and realized there wouldn't be enough money to make a trip back east to visit Levi, even if I wanted to, and I wasn't sure about seeing him just yet. I felt trapped where I was with the investigation ongoing, and some deep yearning for the excitement Frank brought into my life, it kept me from just packing up and leaving. I didn't know how much more I could contribute to Dan's case, or to the girl I identified in the picture on the license. I was called into the FBI to look over many of the victim's pictures to see if I recognized the one found in my laundry. It was frustrating because some of them looked alike, and after two years, her face faded from my memory. I could see in all the pictures that were shown to me, both colored and black and white, that all the women had dark hair, black or brown. I wasn't much help when I couldn't recall her features.

After that ordeal, Tim told me I wouldn't be needed again. I worried about Martino following us when Tim picked me up to take me to FBI headquarters, but he made sure Sergeant Martino was working at the station at the time we went. Tim never brought up what had happened the night he took me out for my birthday, but I could tell he remained cool and distant.

Looking at my two paychecks, one full time and one part time, confirmed it didn't add up to more than our basic needs, so when Frank called, asking me to come to Great Lakes again, for a full day, I jumped at the chance. I always threw my odd change in a bowl and I checked to see if there was enough for train fare. There was more than enough, so the next day, a Saturday, Tommy and I boarded the train for Chicago. The base being near the heart of Downtown Chicago was close to all the great shows and restaurants, museums and parks. Grant Park was a favorite with its Buckingham Fountain, but being November, it would be too cold for a stroll in the park.

Frank was at the station to meet us wearing his blues this time. I loved his whites because it showed off his dark hair, eyes and tan summer complexion. He greeted us with hugs and kissed both of us. I looked at him, wishing he wasn't Sergeant Martino's son. He had an arresting smile, but this time he seemed preoccupied with something and looked troubled.

"Where are we going today?" I asked, knowing we would have to go somewhere inside since it was November and although it hadn't snowed yet the wind coming off the lake drove the temperature down into the teens. I was glad I bundled Tommy up in his warmest parka and made him wear gloves and a scarf even though it was a lot warmer back home. We walked briskly toward the hotel Frank said he had a room reserved, and we could wait there until they served lunch at the hotel and then we would take a bus down Michigan Ave to the science museum for the afternoon. After that he would take us out to dinner.

"I have this weekend off, so I rented a room at the hotel for tonight. I should have told you, but I didn't think you wanted to stay overnight," he said.

I was shocked, and unable to speak for a moment. "Why didn't you tell me you had the weekend off, you could have come to Arden. I would have picked you up at the station, you could have stayed with Angie if you didn't want to go home."

He looked at me and didn't answer until we entered the hotel. He led us to the elevator and we went up to the 3rd floor. Once in the room, I stood near the door wondering what he had in mind with a three-year-old along. He saw the look on my face and smiled, "Kathleen, I only took this room so we can talk. If you choose to stay overnight or not is up to you. There are plenty of empty rooms on this floor and I can get you one if you want to stay, so we can be together tomorrow too."

I relaxed when he put it that way, but wondered why he didn't prefer coming home to see his mother and sister.

"Frank, I would have loved to stay if Tommy and I had our own room, but we don't have any change of clothing with us—you should have told us before we came," I said.

"It totally skipped my mind. All I was thinking of was seeing you again, and Tommy of course."

I began to realize that by letting him get close to me, and kiss me, he expected something from me, like me wanting him in return, but he hadn't expressed any feelings of love to me in words. He looked too serious, and I was expecting him to say he loved me and hoped he wouldn't.

"I have a dilemma on my hands," he said.

"Like what?" I asked, expecting him to tell me he loved me while thinking Tim and I were a couple.

"I called home and my mother was very upset. She thinks you don't believe a criminal trying to steal in the back of that department store, killed your husband. My God Kathleen, why would you tell his mother that? You knew it would get back to my mother."

"Frank, I never intended to say anything to her, all I said was it seemed suspicious, was all, and I never expected her to say anything to your mother. I'm sorry."

"If you could have heard how upset she was. She knows my father was the only one with him, so how did that sound to her? —Like you thought—well you know what she thought. I'm trying to believe what your husband wrote down, suspecting him, but at times I have a hard time with it."

"But the service pin he found, you were sure it belonged to him. You said Tony always played with it, and you told the FBI you remembered your father taking it away from him."

"Yes, I believe it's my fathers, unless there's a pin bent in exactly the same place belonging to someone else which is highly unlikely, but it could have been dropped there at another time—Tony rode his bike near there many times. That field is next to our town."

I was beginning to realize that Frank was having second thoughts about his father.

"Frank, are you trying to tell me, you don't believe your father could have killed Dan?" I asked, holding my breath for the answer.

"No, I believe he might have been capable of it, but my mother— My God! I can't testify about anything against my father? It would kill her."

I felt sorry for him, and I could see the quagmire he was in. I wanted to put my arms around him, but that would make things worse for both of us, so I just stood there saying I was sorry, sorry about everything. Mostly I was sorry I ever came back home. Damn that Tim, bringing the box of incriminating evidence to my place, and involving Frank in that way.

"I understand how you feel," I said, "And if you're not sure you want to testify against your father, tell the FBI you aren't sure about the pin belonging to him after all, who knows how long it was in that field. I'm sure they won't use you in any future questioning."

I wasn't sure about anything, but I said it to calm Frank down. He seemed to relax a little and he turned to Tommy, "Let's go downstairs and have some lunch, huh, Tommy," he said, smiling.

The three of us sat in the hotel restaurant trying to enjoy our time together but something had changed, apprehension and distrust hung between us like an emerging cloud on a sunny day. The rest of the afternoon all our attention was on Tommy and I could just imagine what it would have been like if I were alone with him. We went to the science museum, but I didn't see anything. All I could think of was, why, why did I say those few words of doubt to Mrs. Clarke, why did I start seeing Frank, why did I ever marry Dan, but then I would look at my son and couldn't imagine my life without him. I had so many regrets, but my regrets were all in vain. I couldn't change a thing. I was like a fallen leaf on a windy day. I had no control over my life, never had, I was sure I was never meant to be born at all. I must have looked troubled sitting there trying to eat a lunch I had no appetite for and Frank noticed.

"I'm sorry Kathleen," he said, "I didn't mean to have you look so unhappy, by what I said."

"You have nothing to feel sorry for, you did nothing wrong, Frank," I said, almost in tears. It was Tim and I who brought you to the attention of the FBI, well, not me so much, but Tim mentioned you to them, and I'm sorry about that."

He reached his hand across the table to hold mine. "Lets not talk about it anymore and try to enjoy the rest of the day, ok? For Tommy—ok?"

Frank's concern for my son touched me in the deepest way, and made my feelings for him even more complicated. I wondered what Tim would say when he heard Frank could refuse to testify against his father. I could hear his words 'I told you so!' over and over. I certainly wouldn't tell him, let him find out from the FBI later.

At the train station, there was a strain between us, or maybe it was only me who felt it. I was glad I took the train instead of trying to drive downtown because I didn't think I could drive home safely with the way I was feeling at that moment, and besides, Tommy loved riding the train. When we could hear the train approaching, I became nervous. I didn't want Frank to kiss me, and thankfully he didn't, he gave us both a hug instead. I went home feeling much worse than I did before I left home, and deep down I knew, the next time, if there would be a next time, I would refuse to meet him again, not because I didn't want to, but because I had to.

CHAPTER 42

The Thanksgiving holiday had arrived and Betty invited me to join her and her parents to Orland Park to spend it with her grandparents, but I refused. I didn't know them that well, and I found some excuse. Rita of course would be with her fiancé at his parents, and I didn't receive an invitation from the Martinos for the first time. Of course if I had, I wouldn't have gone. Tommy and I would be alone except there was Mrs. Clarke, now living so close; she would expect me to spend it with her. Spending it with Tim or his family was out of the question, and when he asked me where I was going, I said I would be spending it with Betty, but that was before she told me they were going to her grandparents. In the end, I had no choice but to take Tommy over to his grandmother.

It was the worst Thanksgiving I had ever spent with anyone. The tension I felt having to eat a meal that was supposed to be enjoyed as the highlight meal of the year, was pure torture for me. I didn't bring up what I knew about her calling Lottie. We didn't have much to say to each other and she gave Tommy all her attention, which was the real reason for spending the day with her. As soon as the meal was over, I offered to do up all her dishes so she could play with her grandson in the living room. She was happy with any time she could spend with him and my guilt over trying to keep him from her, allowed me to endure another day at her place. But while I was cleaning up in her kitchen, my thoughts were of Levi. I should have called him and wished him a Happy Thanksgiving, and I could picture him alone with his children on a day I wished I could have spent with them. By the time I was finished and ready to leave for home, I was ready to explode. It wasn't until I was safely in my car that I broke down and cried.

"Why you cryin' Mommy?" Tommy asked, looking frightened.

I quickly dried my eyes and started up the motor. "It's nothing, honey, Mommy's got something in her eye, its ok now," I said. The twenty-minute drive home seemed like an hour.

Tim and I had been seeing less of each other, sometimes a week would go by and I wouldn't hear from him, which was ok with me. He would call and keep me up on how the investigation was going. From being together every weekend except for the three times I spent with Frank, and the occasional week-night, when he would drop over after work, he started to call and say he had to work a weekend shift or something else would come up. Ever since the night I rebuffed him on my birthday, there was coolness between us. I knew if it weren't for the fact that I was supporting him in this investigation of Sergeant Martino, I wouldn't have had any reason to be with him. I needed closure concerning Dan's death, after all he was my husband, but most importantly, he was my son's father.

The month of December brought snow, and the roads became dangerous and icy. It took me longer to leave work, pick up my son and try to get safely home. When I did get home, I would get Tommy his dinner and I then pick at my food, I was losing weight and it showed. Every night with the weather bad, and Tommy and me alone most of the time, I felt lonely and abandoned. No matter how often Betty and I got together, she had her boyfriend and her own family. A few of the Saturdays I would normally work at her shop, I would take off to stay home due to exhaustion and the bad weather. She understood my needing time off. She also understood my need to meet Frank when I went downtown. I confided in her about my feelings for Frank and what was going on with my relationship with Tim, but she knew nothing else. I wasn't hearing anything from Angie since our last phone conversation about her mother being upset with me. I watched Tommy eating his supper for a few minutes and then I went into the bedroom and cried. We were truly alone in the world, my son and I. Dan's mother was useless to us, and not one I wanted around in the future to influence my son.

I decided to call Levi. I would finally give him my phone number. I was afraid to give it to him sooner because I didn't want anyone to know about him, or where I had been the year I went missing. Only Betty knew, and I let her in on the details only recently. Now that Tim wasn't showing up at my place as often, I felt more secure about him not coming over unannounced and picking up my calls in case I wasn't able to pick up the phone fast enough. I also wondered how I could ask for the copy of the key to my apartment back. I entrusted it to him when I first moved in. It made things easier when he had to deliver pieces of furniture for me, when I was at work and he wasn't working a daytime shift. I didn't want to ever feel the intense fear I felt when Frank stayed over, terrified that Tim would show up. I felt a little freer now, and I wanted my key back. I didn't know what his reaction would be if I asked for it.

I made the call and Levi answered, and when I tried to speak, I had a hard time because I was crying.

"Kathleen, what's wrong?" he asked, sounding concerned.

"Everything's wrong," I said, sobbing, unable to control it.

"Come back here, or I will come there, where you are, if you don't, because you sound like you're in some kind of trouble," he said.

"No, you can't come here," I said, "I'm just a little depressed, that's all and it's because I guess I miss all of you. It's been over a year now and I know I need to come back, and I will, just give me more time, maybe a couple more months, after the winter is over, I promise."

"Can you tell me what's wrong?"

"No, I can't explain it on the phone, I will when I see you again. It's nothing serious, so don't worry about me."

We talked for a few minutes about the children and then he told me he loved me again, as he always did when I called, or when he wrote. I said goodbye, without telling him the same, I just couldn't say the words to him that I'm sure he wanted to hear, because I wasn't sure of what I felt, I wasn't sure about anything.

Frank called again as I knew he would, and I dreaded telling him I would not be able to come up to meet him, but before I could say anything, he let me know his unit would be shipping out again and he was calling to say goodbye and asking me to write, as soon as I received a letter from him.

"I'll miss seeing you and Tommy," he said, "and I hope you won't forget me. I could use some mail after I'm gone."

"Won't your Mother and Angie write?" I asked, knowing he hadn't been in touch with them lately.

"Kathleen, they are mad at me because when I called over at Angie's she brought up what you had said about your husband's death and I defended you. They are blaming you for my old man acting crazy, and he's so angry that they are walking on eggs around him. I don't know what's going on over there, and I don't want to know. I'm glad I'm leaving."

"Frank, I'm sorry, I didn't mean to cause any problems when I miss-spoke in front of Mrs. Clarke."

"Don't give it a thought, I don't hold you responsible for my old man's moods. I think he feels the pressure around him. He's not dumb, he senses that he's being watched and talked about. Did I tell you the FBI met one last time with me, and they know I don't want to testify, but they are going to subpoena me anyway to testify to his character, and I'm so sorry I told them too much about him and now I'm not so sure of anything anymore."

"You sound like me Frank, I'm not sure either and sometimes I feel like disappearing again."

"I don't blame you if you did," he said, "I'll miss you when I'm gone. Please say goodbye to Tommy for me."

We said our goodbyes without any mention of how we felt other than we would miss each other. There wasn't anything else to say. I knew in my heart that it would be the last time we would talk. I had no intention of writing or answering his letter, if it came.

The apartment building I lived in had a large parking lot to the side of the building that was accessed from the street in front, but there was a smaller parking space behind the building that wasn't visible from the street. It's where I usually parked because it was closer to the door I used, especially when it was dark. It was where I made Frank park my car when he spent the night. Tim would park there too. It was out of view of nosey tenants who could view anyone coming in or out of the front entrance.

Tim called the night after I spoke with Frank, and said he was coming over. As usual he let himself in at the back entrance. I opened the door when I heard him on the stairs. He walked in dressed in uniform on his way home from his day shift.

"I have something to tell you," he said as he made himself comfortable on my sofa. He loosened his tie and asked for something to drink. I hurried to the kitchen and brought him a can of coke. It was all I had; I never kept beer in the house since I never drank it. I'm sure he would rather have had one, but he took the soda, popped open the can and took a deep gulp of the soda. He wiped his mouth with the back of his hand, looked at me, motioning for me to sit down.

"What is it? What's happening?" I asked, knowing by the look on his face that something was bothering him.

"What did I tell you!" he said, as if I should already know what he was about to say.

"What?"

"Your boyfriend reneged, that's what!" he said.

I didn't like him referring to Frank that way, but I knew exactly who he was referring to and I ignored it, and pretended I didn't know what he was talking about, but I knew exactly what he was about to tell me.

"Frank Martino refused to testify against his father, but the FBI will be issuing a subpoena to him if it ever comes to trial. He claims he can't be sure it's his father's pin that was found, and he won't be around much longer anyway, his ship is leaving port again."

"How do you know all this?" I asked, pretending ignorance.

"Agent Jake filled me in," he said, "and the case is going nowhere. They told me outside of Dan's written suspicions, they have nothing on him. The gun that was fired at Dan was never recovered and they said the bullets found at the scene came from Sergeant Martino's gun and an unknown gun. The Sheriff's gun was never fired. The bullet fired at the Sheriff came from the supposed robber's gun."

"This will never end, will it?" I asked.

"It doesn't look too hopeful, but they are still watching him. It's been over two years since they had their suspicions about Dan's death and the Agent said they will eventually pull back unless something significant pops up," he said, looking upset. "They said without the license you said you found, they have nothing."

"You don't think they believed me about finding it?"

"Well, it might have had fingerprints on it, and without it they can't prove anything, and your word isn't good enough. A defense attorney would have you believing you imagined it when they got through with you."

314

I began to think of all that I created by putting thoughts into Mrs. Clarke's head, and now my friendship with the Martinos, especially Angie's would soon be gone.

"Things will never be the same between Angie and me," I said, "Our friendship is lost I'm afraid. She hasn't called in weeks, and I'm afraid to call her."

Tim looked at me with sympathy. "With her father who he is, it would have come to an end anyway, don't you think? We hope the FBI thinks it happened exactly like *we* think it happened. I hope they don't think the Sheriff—Dan, your husband, was suffering from paranoia, and suspecting Martino was part of it. That's what they might think since they don't have the license, only your word on it."

"But Tim, what about his asking us about the clothes, what we did with them, and asking Mrs. Clarke about the so called papers we found in the box—what about that? And you said yourself that he could be a psychopath, didn't you say that?"

Tim was quiet for a few minutes, thinking about what I said. "This has got me going nuts," he said.

"Well, I still think he killed Dan. He asked Mrs. Clarke about the box again—"

"What! When?" Tim said loudly, "I want to know!"

"When I was at her place for Halloween,"

"Halloween? That was over a month ago, why didn't you tell me this before?"

"To be honest, I didn't think it was anything—no that's not true, I just forgot with all that's been on my mind lately,"

"So, what the hell did she tell him?"

"She said the box belonged to me and that I had it."

"Oh great! Do you realize he might try to get in here looking for it, if he's what we both think he is, and to be honest with you—I do believe he killed your husband, because I believe you Kathleen, because of the license you found. I know I keep hoping it wasn't him, but both the FBI and I haven't given up believing that there wasn't a robber present when Dan died. The only one besides me in the police department that knows about our suspicions in the case is Jerry White. I brought him in on it because he's been my partner for the past year.

He's the only one, and to be honest Kathleen, I don't like the fact that Martino thinks you have that box, and if he's after that missing license, he'll try to get it. I'm surprised he hasn't tried before this."

I started to get so upset, and afraid, that I began to cry, and instead of comforting me as Frank or Levi might have done, he yelled at me.

"How stupid can you get?" he shouted. "First you mention what you thought to the old Lady, and then you forget to tell me that she told him *you* have what we know he's looking for?"

I couldn't defend myself, I had no defense, and all I could do was cry, because I realized I wasn't safe any longer.

"I've been under so much stress, Tim," I said, between sobs. "I can't take much more, so don't yell at me, please!"

"Well, you should have known better, and now I need to notify the FBI about this so they watch this building more often. You should see how angry he is around the guys at the station, they complain about it to me, wondering what's wrong with him. I think it won't be long before he snaps. There hasn't been a murder in quite some time and if it's him, and I believe it is, he's on the edge right now. All I can say is be careful," Tim said, looking like he was angry with me.

"Is it safe for Tommy and me to be here alone?" I asked, not sure of where I would go if it wasn't.

"Don't park in the back anymore, it's too dark back there, park in front where it's well lit, and don't buzz anyone in, not anyone. If its me, I have the key. If it's a man's voice, he can mimic mine, or anyone else's, he's clever."

I knew then that I wouldn't be asking him for my key back. If ever I felt so frightened, it was exactly what I was feeling when I discovered that woman's license, and fled. This time I was frozen by fear and too afraid to make a move of any kind.

"I'll come by as often as I can when I'm on patrol, and I'm sure he won't be able to get in here, anyway, the FBI guys will be watching too, after I inform them." Tim said, getting up to leave.

He left without saying any words of comfort, and acted like he was on a routine police call. He just got up and walked out the door.

I was left feeling alone and angry, and when I felt angry, I became less frightened. I put Tommy to bed and thought of how during all that shouting he did, he never once cared about my child sitting on the floor near us, probably as afraid as I was. From the time he walked in, he never said one word to acknowledge he was there. I knew then, when this was over, if it ever was, I wouldn't wait too long to pick up and leave again. I did it once, and I could do it again, but I knew this time I had someone to go to.

The rest of the week, I tried to concentrate on my child and my work. I didn't think the Sergeant would ever try getting in here knowing my child was with me, because he had a grandchild and I didn't think even a killer of women would be capable of killing an innocent child. I did a lot of crying after Tommy went to sleep at night, I cried to release tension, and I started to call Levi more often, and he would call me. Soon, we would have long conversations and the long distant calls were adding up on my side, and I'm sure on his side too. It became expensive, so after exhausting long conversations about our future together, and the children, his and mine. We kept it to a five-minute call every night to say goodnight, with him saying he loved me, and me saying I missed him. I wanted to wait until I saw him in person to tell him that. He knew nothing about what was going on in my life. I made up nice stuff to tell him, and that was all I could do. I was really getting to know him, I knew I was falling in love with his voice, with his personality and we began to make plans. I would leave after Christmas, come snow or whatever. I would leave all this hell I was living behind. My car was old, I couldn't make a long trip in it, just give it back to Betty and take the train, just Tommy and me and whatever I could pack up of our clothes, leave everything else behind. Thinking about it gave me pleasure and it gave me strength.

Two weeks before Christmas nothing was happening, just this heavy cloud hanging over me, unable to confide in anyone. I would have broken if it weren't for Levi. Although I wouldn't burden him with what was going on in my life, just hearing his soothing voice helped me get through the last few weeks I would be here. I made plans to visit Tommy's grandmother for Christmas of course, and then I would tell Tim I was leaving for good. I would tell him I wasn't needed and didn't give a damn if Martino was ever caught, and I didn't care any longer if he killed Dan or not. Dan was dead, he wasn't coming back and as far as I was concerned, Tim wasn't coming back either, because he wasn't the same Tim I once loved.

Tommy was excited over the coming Christmas and Santa Claus, but I couldn't feel any of the holiday spirit. I would buy a small tabletop tree and have it just for him, but my heart wasn't in it, it was elsewhere. I began to think maybe I should have left before and spent Christmas with Levi, but there wasn't time and there was Mrs. Clarke to think about. I had to keep reminding myself, she was the only blood relative besides me that my son had. I didn't think beyond the last month I planned on being here, or of what to do about her, taking her grandson away for good. I was at the point where I knew, once I was gone, I wouldn't care.

Betty called, and we made plans to take the boys to Sears to see Santa on the Saturday afternoon before Christmas. The weather turned bad and they predicted a large snowfall in the beginning of the week, which would be a few days before Christmas, it being on a Wednesday. I called Mrs. Clarke, explaining that we might have to come early, maybe on Sunday because I might not be able to get out of the parking lot if the snow ended up as bad as it was predicted.

"Oh, that would be fine Kathleen," she said, "Sunday would be ok."

"See you Sunday then," I said, and hung up the phone. I knew she wouldn't be disappointed if we didn't come on Christmas Eve or Christmas day as long as she could see Tommy.

Betty and I laughed at the boys sitting on Santa's knee. Ricky was nine and asking a lot of questions about how Santa delivered his presents since they didn't have a fireplace. I doubted he really believed in Santa anymore. Tommy was too young to worry about that, all he cared about was getting what he asked for. I wondered if Tim was going to buy him anything. The first Christmas we were back, he did, and so did his mother, but after that one and only time we visited his parents, I never saw them again. The first Christmas I was back, Rita and I got together as well as Betty, but my closeness with Rita wasn't what is used to be, not because we had any problems, just that she was about to remarry after the holidays and she was spending most of her time with her future husband. If it weren't for Betty, or Mrs. Clarke,

Tommy and I would be completely alone this Christmas. Even if Tim asked us to spend it with him, I would refuse. I felt that things between us were so bad, that a day with Tommy's grandmother would be an improvement.

As we watched both boys sitting for a picture with Santa, Betty asked what I planned for Christmas Eve or day, depending on the weather.

"You know you're always welcome to be with me at my parents, for either day," she said.

"I know, and I'm grateful for the invitation, but I need to get Tommy over to see his grandmother tomorrow, before we are marooned in our apartment due to the weather. I don't know if we will be able to get out after Monday night, isn't that when they're predicting the snowfall of the century?" I said.

Betty laughed, "Yes, I think you're right, that's why Ricky and I are going to stay at my parents on Monday. My Dad's at the shop today, but we will be closed all next week."

I envied Betty, she had parents, and I had no one, except my son. We took the boys out for dinner later in the day and Betty made me promise to come over to her parents for either Christmas Eve or day if the snowfall wasn't as bad as we expected.

On Sunday, Tommy and I would go to Mrs. Clarke's. When we arrived home, I turned on the tree lights and we watched a little TV before I put him to bed. He watched a cartoon about Santa and his Elves. He would be four years old in less than a month; he was becoming the joy of my life. I could hold a conversation with him and he was a happy little boy. I baked cookies for Santa to leave with milk on Christmas Eve and then I put him to bed in the little youth size bed I put in my room, after I had Tim push my full size bed over to accommodate Tommy's bed. That was a year ago. We shared the same room and I had thought as soon as I was able to afford a two-bedroom apartment, but now I knew it didn't matter, we would be leaving. My plan was to spend his fourth birthday first with Betty and then take him over to his grandmother so she could celebrate it with us. Hopefully by then, the sixteenth of January, the roads would be clear and the snow plowed away. I would confide in Betty of my plans after

Christmas, and ask her to take us to the Train Station around the last week of January. Levi already knew of our plans and was anticipating my arrival at that time.

After Tommy was asleep, my phone rang and it was Levi. We talked for about ten minutes. He let me know the children were making something to send to Tommy for his birthday.

"I put both of the pictures you sent on my book shelf so they wouldn't forget, and after you left, I spoke of you often. Samuel remembers both of you being here, but I don't know if the other two do," he said.

"I want to wish you and the children a Merry Christmas," I said, "And I wish I had more time to send them something but—"

"Oh, don't worry about that, we might not be able to celebrate this Christmas, but there's always next year."

After we said our goodbyes I cried, but lately that was all I was doing. The time for me to leave this place couldn't come soon enough.

On Sunday, I dressed Tommy in his Christmas outfit, stopped over at Betty's for a short visit and then we left early in the afternoon. I knew Mrs. Clarke went to her church on Sunday mornings and I wanted to avoid spending an hour at Mass with her. I really never went to Mass after I left Dan. It reminded me too much of the nuns at the Orphanage. I let Tommy ring the bell at her door by lifting him up to reach it. It was something he liked to do. She greeted us with her usual big smile and reached for him. This time, he let her hug him because I told him it would be a nice thing to do, to give her a kiss, and he knew Santa had come to her house for him.

"He is getting so big," she said, and she was happy to see us.

In the back of my mind I always knew I could have been anyone, and really nothing to her, just the vehicle that gave her, her precious grandchild. Our visit went the way it always had, she was able to spend it with him and I as usual, did all the cleaning up. She did make us a nice Christmas dinner and of course, she overdid her generosity in the gift department. I felt bad because I didn't know how I was going to take all the stuff she bought Tommy to Pennsylvania with us when we left. I felt guilty knowing we would be leaving at the end of January, but planned on telling her when it got closer to the time we would leave.

On Monday morning I got ready for work, expecting I might have to leave early. The weatherman predicted snow later in the day, accumulating as the night evolved. It was expected to snow all day Tuesday and they were expecting by

Christmas Day we would have snow several feet deep ruining Christmas for everyone who needed to travel. I dropped Tommy off at the sitter's telling her I might pick him up early, maybe early in the afternoon.

When I arrived at work, my boss said, "Kathleen, you don't have to stay today. I should have called you last night, I just sent two of the agents home, I think I'll close up, I'm just waiting for Jean, she left the house before I could call her, and I tried to call you this morning but you had already left."

"Yes, I know, I had to drop off my son at the sitter's, so I leave early. Should I go home then?"

"Yes, spend it with your boy, or do some last minute shopping this morning if you need to, its going to get nasty as the day goes on," he said, looking out of the window. "It's starting already, you better go, and have a Merry Christmas, Kathleen."

I wished him a Merry Christmas and left, never having taken my coat off, and on the drive to pick up Tommy I cried. Between the light snowflakes that were beginning to fall and my tears, I had to put the windshield wipers on so I could see. The weatherman never had it right, it was already snowing at eight-thirty in the morning. I never felt so alone in my life; alone with just a four-year-old, was alone to me. I was sad, but determined to hide what I felt from my son. I would try to make it as nice a Christmas for him as I could. *I had baked the cookies and tomorrow night we will put them out for Santa. Our Christmas dinner would be a cooked ham I bought with all the trimmings.* I was thinking of all that as I drove to pick him up, trying to wipe my checks with my fingers as the tears fell.

Pulling into the driveway of the sitter's house, I checked my face in the mirror above my visor to make sure any sign I had been crying was eliminated. Tommy's sitter, a middle-aged woman, named Helen, didn't look too surprised to see me back so soon.

"I knew you might come back," she said, "It doesn't look too good out there."

"I hope this didn't inconvenience you, I should have called my office to see if they were going to be open before I left home, then you could have stayed in bed instead of getting up early for my son," I said.

"Oh, no, it wasn't any trouble. I get up early anyway," she said, "Would you like to stay for a cup of coffee?"

We both looked out at the weather, it was very overcast and gloomy. "I think I better get home before it starts to accumulate out there, it's already about an inch and it gets slippery unless it's deeper, then we get other problems, thanks, but we better leave."

She helped Tommy on with his coat and boots, and we left.

"Mommy, where we goin'" Tommy asked.

"Home, see, we are going to have a beautiful white Christmas," I said.

CHAPTER 43

Monday night couldn't come quick enough because, after Tommy and I arrived home there wasn't much to do except watch television and I tried to keep him busy. We made paper chains out of colored paper to put on the little tree sitting on top of a small table in front of the window. Tommy helped put the lights on the day before and the few ornaments were mostly homemade. He looked so cute standing on a chair as I held him, while he tried his best to decorate the tree. We watched from the window as the snowflakes became larger and more numerous. By nightfall it covered everything. Around five and after we had finished eating the phone rang. I was hoping it was Tim, checking to see if I got home ok. It was Levi, and I was happy to hear his voice. I was going to call him after I got Tommy to bed but his call brightened up my mood, and I needed something to make me feel good, and not feel so alone.

"Kathleen, I called before you did to see how you're doing out there," he said," I heard you're in for a big snowstorm."

"Oh Levi, I needed to hear your voice."

We talked for a few minutes, and he promised to call back later after we put the kids to bed.

"I'll call you about eight, my time, that's seven your time, will Tommy be in bed by then?" he asked.

"Yes, Yes, I'll be waiting for your call," I said.

When he called, we talked for two hours, Levi telling me he could afford the phone bill, "It's Christmas, and I love you Kathleen."

After we said our goodbyes he promised to call Christmas Eve. I went to bed thinking about the fact that it looked like a blizzard out there and Tim never called to see if we were ok. Although I didn't want to deal with Tim, I was hoping he cared enough to check on us. I had a hard time falling asleep. Some time late in the night or maybe it was after midnight, I thought I heard a noise, but didn't know what it could be, maybe snow plows, I thought. When I heard it again, I got up, reached for my bathrobe and went into the living room. It was dark; I turned the tree lights off when I went to bed. I stood still, listening and then I heard it again, sounding like it was near my door. My heart started beating with fear, I turned and closed my bedroom door where my son was sleeping and reached for the little key I kept in the bedroom door lock. It was one of those little keys used if a child locked himself in the bathroom or bedroom, it could be unlocked from outside the room. I locked the door to our room and stuck the key in a place where no one could find it, except me. I walked across my living room and took a few steps toward the front door to my apartment and listened again. This time there was no mistaking it, a key was in my lock and I could hear the knob turning. I turned to run back—to where, I didn't know, I was in a panic, couldn't think, and all of a sudden I felt hands around my neck, I struggled trying to free myself and couldn't see anything in the dark, I couldn't scream either because a gloved hand was covering my mouth—that's all I remembered. There were a few moments when I thought I heard loud noises but it sounded like it was far away, and then nothing.

"Kathleen, Kathleen!" It was the first thing I heard when I came to. When I opened my eyes, the room was lit up and Tim was leaning over me, where I lay on the floor. I noticed the room filled with several cops and men in overcoats. I heard Tommy crying and I tried to get up but my body felt like it weighed a ton, I couldn't move.

"Kathleen, you're going to be ok?" Tim said, "The ambulance is here to take you to the hospital." I had a hard time comprehending what had happened. All I knew was I heard my son crying. I kept calling for him, but I couldn't hear my voice; I was screaming for him inside my head.

On the ride to the hospital, I must have blacked out again, because the next thing I knew, I was lying in a hospital bed with an oxygen mask on my face, and Tim was sitting at the side of my bed holding my hand.

"What happened?" I tried to say, but I couldn't talk and knew he couldn't hear me. "Where's Tommy?" I mouthed. This time he seemed to know what I was asking. He stood up and leaned over me and close to my ear said," Don't worry about Tommy, Jerry took him over to my mother."

He patted my hand and put his finger up, like telling me to wait a

324

minute and he left the room. When he came back in, a nurse was with him. She checked my wrist and listened to my heart and then she took the mask away. I still had a hard time talking, my throat hurt, but I managed to ask him what happened in a whisper.

"Kathleen, it's a long story, but wait until you're home and I'll fill you in on everything," he said.

I mouthed, "When am I going home?"

"I hope you can get released by Friday," he said.

"Friday? What day is it?"

"It's Thursday," he said, "you've had quite a shock to your system, he tried to—" well, we tried to get to you as quick as we could, in fact we were right behind him, not expecting you to be up, but asleep in bed. He didn't have much time, but enough to cause you to lose consciousness. He tried to strangle you, like he did all the others, only this time—"

"Who? Who was it?" I tried pulling myself to a sitting position, weak as I felt.

"Martino! We got him Kathleen—we got him!"

I started to cry, and it made it difficult to breathe. Tim held me in his arms and tried his best to comfort me.

"Kathleen, I have so much to tell you, but after you're feeling better. Remember, when we first suspected him of all those murders, well we have the proof. The FBI got a search warrant and went through his entire house and garage, and—"

"Oh, no, poor Lottie, his family," I whispered, I could barely speak.

"That license you threw away—we don't need it, they found the drivers' licenses and identification of all the women he killed, those who had one, in his garage, locked in a tool box, and that's not all, — the bastard kept newspaper clippings of all the murders, and—." "I don't want to hear anymore right now," I managed to say. My throat hurt so much it was hard for me to speak. Exhausted, I lay back down and closed my eyes. "Where's my son?" I asked again.

"He's at my parents, he had a nice Christmas with us yesterday, so don't worry about him. I made sure he had extra clothes and I took them to my Mother's."

"Thank you," was all I managed to say. I felt very tired and wanted to drift off again. I thought he would be better at Tim's mothers than left with his grandmother. I think Tim kissed me on the forehead before he left, I can't be sure. I don't remember anything after that because I fell into a deep sleep.

There were so many moments I couldn't remember and all I knew is it was Saturday before I was released from the hospital. I had been in and out of sleeping away four whole days. My neck was sore and I felt like my body had been in a train wreck. Tim came in the last morning with a small duffel bag of clothing for me.

"Where did you find that?" I asked, pointing to a small cloth bag he held as he walked in.

"It's mine," he said, "I hope you don't mind but I went over to your place and gathered some clothes for you. All I could find in your closet was a large suitcase so I picked out these"—he pointed to the clothes he was removing and placing at the foot of the bed. There was a pair of slacks, a white shirt blouse, under pants and bra. I could feel my face flush as he apologized for having to raid my place as he put it. He didn't forget a pair of socks and my snow boots, not to mention my winter parka with hood.

"Thanks Tim, you thought of everything," I said, "so don't apologize for bringing my underwear," I laughed a little trying to get him to see the humor in it because he appeared embarrassed that he had to go through my personal things.

He laughed, "Well, I finally got to see them without undressing you myself."

We both laughed over the irony of the situation. He seemed so different from how he appeared before this all happened. I was confused.

"Is Tommy alright?" I asked, wondering how upset he must be.

"He's fine Kathleen, I made sure he has enough clothes, and my parents are enjoying him."

That statement really confused me because in a whole year, they never asked to see us and Tim never mentioned them much. There was so much about Tim I didn't understand and even less about his family. I had to tell myself they were there for me when it mattered and that's what was important. Tim left the room so I could get dressed and when

I was ready, we left the hospital. Once outside, I could see how deep the snowfall had been. It was cold and he started up the motor of his car to get it warm. We sat in the parking lot of the hospital waiting for the heater to warm us up for a few minutes.

"Where are we going? Are we going to get Tommy?" I asked, not sure of what was going on since I realized I was very weak and I began to worry about how I would manage with caring for my son.

"I'm taking you to my parents for now, you can't be alone for a while, just until you're back to normal," he said.

"Is it ok with them?"

"Of course, it was their idea first, but if you would rather go home and have me stay with you—." He looked at me and smiled, a mischievous smile I thought, and it unsettled me a bit.

He was so nice, so caring, that I thought, *what is this? Who is the real Tim, the one sitting next to me telling me how worried he was and how much he loved me, or the guy that acted out, yelling at me just last week.* I looked over at him and saw the old Tim of many years ago until we entered his parent's home. It sounded like his father, who I remembered as a mild-mannered man, was shouting. When he saw me his demeanor changed quickly as he greeted me with a hug and smile. Mrs. O'Malley ran up to me doing the same. Tommy ran to me as soon as he saw me and put his arms out for me. He looked like he had been crying.

"What's wrong?" I asked.

"Oh, its nothing, Barbara's son is here and you know how boys are," Mr. O'Malley said.

It was then I noticed another child bigger than Tommy. He looked a little different and I couldn't figure out what it was. The best way I could decipher in my mind at that moment was he looked unkempt, neglected, and had an angry looking face for a child so young.

"Oh, Kathleen, this is Louis, Barbara's child," Mrs. O'Malley said, "She dropped him off here for Christmas, and was supposed to pick him up yesterday, but of course typical Barbara, she can't be depended upon."

She started telling me about all their problems with their daughter and how undisciplined Lewis was.

"How old is he," I asked.

"He's six, but big for his age," she said.

I didn't ask any more questions and was beginning to have second thoughts about staying at their home.

Later, after I was settled on their sofa with Tommy on my lap, hugging me for dear life, they tried to make me feel comfortable, but I wasn't. Tim came and sat next to us and I asked him if his parents' feelings would be hurt if I went home.

"Only if I went home with you—until you're well, of course. I'm sure they would understand," he said.

I thought, of course they would, because he would make them understand since he would rather I be at home with him.

"Are Barbara's visits often?" I asked, wondering what the relationship was with her and her family. I thought they once washed their hands of her.

Tim laughed a little, looking to see if his parents were about to come back into the room. "She still uses, and they feel sorry for Louis, so they take him whenever she drops him off here. She's been in rehab at least six times and they have him when she's gone."

"Was she here for Christmas day?" I asked.

"For a little while, and then she went to her boyfriend and left him here promising to pick him up yesterday."

I wondered why Tommy had been crying when I came, but didn't need to know, all I knew is I wanted out of there. I didn't want my son around that poor boy, and especially around his mother if she came to get him, not if she was on drugs.

Tim leaned close to me and whispered so the boy who was in the room with us wouldn't hear him. "He was born drug addicted, but he's ok now, just very hyper active."

"Tim, I want to go home!" I said, with determination in my voice. He knew I meant it, so he went to his parents who were preparing dinner for us. When he returned, he said, "They understand Kathleen, but after dinner. They want us to stay for dinner, ok?"

"That's fine, Tim," I said, knowing I couldn't hurt their feelings by not at least staying for the rest of the day. I knew Tim was coming home with us and I was nervous about that. What if Levi called while he was there, how would I explain about Levi. I never mentioned Levi to him at all, and never thought I had to.

Once we were settled back in my apartment, I noticed the bedroom door was broken.

"What happened?" I asked.

"We had to break it down to get your son out, he was crying and the door was locked," Tim said, "I'm sorry about that."

"I locked him in because I was afraid when I heard noise in the hall outside."

"I'll get it fixed," he said.

We had another Christmas on Sunday morning for Tommy. All his wrapped gifts were still on the floor near the tree, and the toys from his grandmother, not to mention what Tim and his parents gave him Christmas morning. I wasn't able to do much so Tim, Tommy and I ate the leftovers that we brought from his mother's dinner. I watched as Tim gave Tommy some attention, but it was mostly me he catered to. He slept on my sofa and removed the bedding in the morning and replaced it the next night. He didn't bother me, but when he tried to kiss me, I had a hard time with it. Did I have feelings for Tim, yes of course I did, now that he appeared so kind and gentle, but I knew it was only temporary. I felt disloyal to Levi when I let Tim kiss me.

On Monday morning he stayed all day, dressing in his uniform for his night shift. I was feeling better by then, and as much as I was grateful he stayed with us at first, I couldn't wait until he left that night. As soon as he went out the door I picked up the phone and called Levi.

"Oh, my God! Kathleen, I've been so worried," were his first words.

"I've been in the hospital—"

"I know, your friend Betty, called and told me what happened."

"Betty?" Of course, I remembered I gave Betty his number in case anything happened when I was so worried the week leading up to Christmas. It was after Tim yelled at me for not telling him about what Mrs. Clarke told Martino. He was afraid he would try to get into my apartment. Poor Betty, I never thought to call her during all this; I should have called her from the hospital. I wondered if Tim called her.

He knew Betty and where I worked on some Saturdays. He must have called her, I thought.

"I'm glad she called you," I said to Levi.

"It's in all the papers Kathleen, all the major big city papers about that Chicago killer, that's terrorized the city for years. You might have been his next victim. God, Kathleen, come back, please."

I assured Levi I would be fine, that the police were always on to him and I had to assure him over and over I wasn't badly hurt. "I may have to stay here a little longer," I said, "and I'm sure I'll be needed as a witness when he's put on trial."

"I love you. Please be careful," he said.

We talked for a while and then said our goodbyes. I was crying as I hung up the phone. Hearing his voice brought back how I longed to be with him now when I was feeling most vulnerable, but there was Tim. What did I owe Tim? Was I indebted to him for saving my life? For still loving me? Of that I was sure. I thought of how caring he had been the last few days. *Did I still love him? In some way I still had feelings for him, but was it love, or something else.* I thought, *How can I break his heart if he loves me, and with all he suffered in Korea, what would it do to him if I left him?*

I felt like a real rat, caught between two men, not really committing to either or to myself on what I wanted. I thought I wanted Levi, but what would it do to Tim, and if I stayed with Tim, what would it do to Levi?

CHAPTER 44

After Tim went back to his apartment I called Betty. She came over as soon as I called. I felt terrible because Tim stayed throughout that week after Christmas. He might have stayed longer, but I asked him to go home, because of how it looked to my neighbors in the apartment building, him living with me, and thinking what ever they wanted to think. My life was a mess. Everyone now knew I was the killer's last attempt, but the only one to escape being his victim. I felt like I was living in a glass bowl, everyone knew everything about me, well not everything. Only Betty knew what I was going through. She was the only one who knew about my life the time I went missing and about Levi. We sat at my kitchen table, drinking coffee and I poured out everything I thought, and everything I was feeling to her.

"Betty, I'm in a mess and I feel trapped here with all the notoriety because of the high profile case pending with Sergeant Martino—I mean the Killer. I shouldn't give him the title Sergeant any more," I said.

She stared at me and shook her head, then after a few minutes where neither of us said anything, she said, "Kathleen, get out of here, go back to Levi and out of this mess. You'll have no anonymity staying here."

"I need to stay for the trial don't I? I'm not sure when that will be."

"That could take a year," she said, "You can't stay that long and expect Levi to just wait another year, unless you're not sure about him."

"I can't just drop Tim without an explanation," I hung my head into my hands, and if ever I felt confused, or unsure, it was then.

Betty got up and put her arms around me. "You have to tell Tim about where you've been that year, and about Levi. The sooner the better."

"Tim knows where I've been that whole year, but of course I didn't mention Levi."

"Did he call you after I was taken to the hospital?" I asked.

"No, when it came on the news that next morning, I called Levi," and then it was in all the papers."

I was disappointed that Tim didn't think of calling my best friend, and it was left to me to call Mrs. Clarke after I was home, assuring her I was fine.

She was hysterical after hearing it on the news and tried calling many times. She didn't have any of my friend's phone numbers and she said she didn't dare call over at the Martino's. She kept repeating 'Poor Lottie' several times and then offered me help. I thanked her and told her I didn't need any help and said I would bring Tommy over on his birthday. That bit of news seemed to calm her down.

After Betty went home, I made up my mind to talk to Tim. I would wait until he was in a good mood, and try to break it gently. I thought it through and tried to add up all his good qualities verses the bad, and then compared him to Levi. He came up short. I knew I was through with the life style he offered, constant worry when he was working, his moods, his drug addicted sister, a nephew with God knows what problems down the line, parents who were kind, but had an edge to them, same as Tim, when things weren't going smooth. I compared that to Levi's world. It took courage for him to leave the only life he had ever known to give his children a better education and introduce them to a more modern world. It took courage to do that, and Levi, in spite of his quiet and gentle demeanor had plenty of courage. I never once observed him lose patience with his children when he was under stress, unlike Tim. I weighed all my options and came back to realizing that the love I once felt for Tim was a teen-age girl's crush full of all the excitement that young love usually is. I had to let it go, and it reminded me of part of a William Wordsworth poem I remembered from high school— *'What through the radiance that once was so bright, be now forever taken from our sight, though nothing can bring back the hour of splendor in the grass, of glory in the flower, we will grieve not, rather find strength in what remains.'*— It made sense to me. I had to move on.

So that I wouldn't chicken out, I called Levi to tell him I was definitely returning after Tommy's birthday. I needed to let his grandmother see him for his special day and tell her news that I knew would upset her, but I needed to think of my son and my needs from now on. I could only imagine what the Martino family was going through and on both Tim and Betty's advice, I made no plans to ever see them again. I would spare them the embarrassment they must be feeling through no fault of their own. It would be bad enough to have to see me in court testifying against their husband and father, if they chose to attend his trial. Tim told me it was a cut and dried case, caught red-handed trying to kill me in my own home. His defense had nothing to defend him with, not with all the evidence against him. Not with all the murders over such a long span of time. The only case they had was an insanity plea.

I invited Tim to dinner. I knew he would take anything I said badly, if it included rejecting him. I wanted to speak with him, trying to find a way to break it gently, that I would be leaving, but I would be available to come back for the trial when they needed me. After dinner I tried to remain calm and just before I knew he was ready to leave, I asked him to hear what I had to say and to reserve judgment until I was finished explaining.

"Tim, I will be going back to Pennsylvania at the end of January, and—"

"What! Why? What's in Pennsylvania? He asked.

"You know that's where I went when I left," I said, " and that's where I want to live."

"What about us?" he asked, again, unable to hide his utter surprise.

"Tim, we have both changed, we're older, not the same kids we were when we first met. I want a different life," I said, trying to let him down easy and leaving Levi out of it until the last moment, hoping I didn't have to mention him at all.

"It's Frank, isn't it? He's based somewhere out east, is that it?" he asked, not too nicely.

"I haven't heard from Frank, I don't know where he is," I said, resenting his anger and jealousy, which only confirmed I was making the right decision.

He quieted down and tried to hug me, but I told him I had made up my mind, and that I was sorry to hurt him. I wanted to thank him for watching over me, but he cut me off by roughly grabbing me in a bear hug, trying to kiss me.

"You're feeling mixed up after all that's happened," he said, convincing himself that I would feel differently after I had time to think about it.

I pulled away from him, "You don't understand, I'm leaving, I'm not in love with you anymore, we've changed. We're not the same people we were years ago."

He looked startled, and the look on his face I will never forget. It was one of sadness, anger and shock.

"All I ever wanted was your happiness," he said, loudly, "And this is how you repay me, just walk away after you don't need me? Is that it?" I felt his stinging words as he shouted, "All I meant to you was—someone to solve your husband's murder? You used me!" he shouted, "And all the while it's been—it's that Frank, isn't it?"

"No! No, it's not Frank, you don't understand," I said, trying to explain what I really couldn't explain, not anything that he would accept. "I care about you Tim, I really do, but in the weeks leading up to this you have been so cold, uncaring, absent."

His eyes registered the shock he was feeling, "What did you expect? I've been knee deep in trying to protect you! Come on Kathleen, come to your senses, I love you, and you know you love me—don't you?"

He didn't take me seriously so I blurted out, "Tim! I met someone else when I fled to Pennsylvania. I love him, and he loves me, and more importantly, he loves my son. He's a widower with three small children. They need me and I need them."

He stood glaring at me like he didn't believe what he just heard.

"What ever happened to that beautiful eighteen-year-old girl I fell in love with the moment she walked into the station that first morning?" he said, still shouting.

"She grew up! I said, I'm not that kid anymore, too much has happened to both of us."

"I survived in that hell hole for six years, Kathleen, six years and because of you, I survived. Thinking of coming back to you helped me to survive, did you know that!"

I felt so terrible seeing him so upset, almost destroyed.

"Tim, I waited as long as I could, five years Tim, I lost all hope after five years. Wasn't that long enough?"

"I'll say, the first thing you do is marry the guy you hated, then you come back here and lead me on and all the while probably keeping your options open back in Pennsylvania?"

He was very angry, I was afraid he might strike out at me, but he didn't; red-faced, he turned, and never uttering another word, quickly walked out slamming the door so hard, it raddled the windows. I never got the chance to tell him how sorry I really was, and to thank him, or say something, anything, so he wouldn't leave so angry and broken, and leaving me with mixed feelings of guilt and extreme sadness for him and for me, both feelings of sorrow, and at the same time a sense of freedom. I was glad he didn't see me crying. After he left, the tears came, tears of regret that I had to hurt him that way, but also joy and relief that I was leaving this place with all its terrible memories. The other place that held melancholy feelings of both grief and joy was Saint Cecelia's, but it had closed down years before. I had intended to seek out Sister Mary Louise, but she had passed away. I would miss Betty and I knew we would always remain friends. I planned on keeping in touch with both her and Rita once I had gone.

The visit to Mrs. Clarke's for Tommy's birthday was the hardest goodbye I would ever have to make because she was my son's grandmother. Regardless of my feelings, she was the only blood relative my son had except for me. I think because I was raised in an orphanage, being related to someone was important to me.

Once we arrived at her home I looked at her, and didn't know how to address her, so I referred to her as Grandma in the presence of Tommy. She greeted us with such exuberance because she was so happy we were both safe.

"Oh, Kathleen, when it came on TV early that morning I was going crazy, I called Deputy Jenson's wife, but she didn't know anything more than I did. I didn't have anyone's phone number. I called the station but they wouldn't give me any information. When you called and I found out you were home from the hospital, well, I was relieved. But when you told me Tommy was with Tim's family—I don't know what that family had to do with him when I'm his grandmother, why didn't they bring him here?"

"I don't know," I said, "Remember there were police and FBI at the house that night and Tim's parents lived close by, I guess that was the reason."

I would have said anything to change the subject, so I turned the topic to the Martinos.

"He came after me for that box you told him I had," I said.

"Yes, and I'm sorry about that, who would have thought a very kind family man and a police Sergeant at that, would do what he's done," she said, "If I knew, I certainly wouldn't have said anything. I'm sorry Kathleen."

"Oh, I know it wasn't your fault, so let's forget it," I said, trying to find something else to talk to her about.

I watched her speak to Tommy, and I just sat there biding my time until I had to tell her what I dreaded telling her. She baked a cake for him, and I went through the motions with her, singing Happy Birthday to him. She picked him up and held him over the lit candles so he could blow them out.

She put him down and mentioned how heavy he was. "He's getting so big!" she exclaimed, "I missed almost two years of his growing up, those years you don't get back. They were the years where he was small enough and I could hold him," she said, with melancholy in her voice.

I thought, just wait until she hears I'm leaving and she'll miss more than a few more years. I never liked the woman, and I felt bad about it. I blamed her for Dan's problems. I knew once she got her hooks in you, it was difficult to shake her loose. Although Dan complained about her, she was his mother, and he couldn't stop her from treating him like he was a small boy instead of a man. I remembered Lottie saying once Tommy was born, that she might transfer her fixation to my son and lessen up on hers. I remembered thinking at the time, even if she did leave Dan alone, the damage was already done to him. She knew how to use the guilt card with him. Lottie had a lot of wisdom and helped me a great deal back then and I missed her and grieved for her. I could just imagine what she was going through. Although I would stay clear of the family, I made up my mind that once I was settled away from here, and some time had gone by, I would write her a kind letter, thanking her for all she had done for me since the first night I met her. I would tell her how very sorry I was about every thing that happened, that was the least I could do. I planned on doing it before I had to attend his trial. I thought it might soften things for her if we had to see each other in court. I expected her to be there, after all, he was her husband, and she might see him as a sick individual, and not the evil person he was. I was thinking of all that while Mrs. Clarke gave her full attention to my son. He was four years old and she talked baby talk to him, which I endured with clenched teeth, saying nothing.

After she served a light dinner, that I could barely eat, and with my stomach in knots, I drew her attention away from Tommy.

"We are moving soon," I said, hoping she heard me, because she didn't look at me, but still had her attention on her grandson.

"Grandma! Tommy and I are leaving for Pennsylvania on the twenty fifth," I said, loudly.

She looked startled, "What do you mean? You're going to visit someone back there?" she asked.

She knew I stayed with some people who lived there, when I left her son.

"No, I'm going to live in Pennsylvania."

"But why? I'm here, your friends are here, why do you want to go there?" she asked with her voice starting to quiver.

"I would love to have you visit us whenever you want," I said, which wasn't true, but I tried to soften the blow. She began to cry, knowing we were out of her control once we were gone. She tried to play the pity card the way she did with Dan.

"I'm old, and who knows when the good Lord will take me," she cried softly into her hankie. It was the same line she used after Dan and I were married, and trying to form a life of our own. Whenever we didn't answer the phone, or we didn't see her often enough, she would put the guilt trip on Dan, and he bought it. I could just imagine what she would try to do to Tommy, as he got older.

I explained that I had an important job waiting for me, and I had good friends there also. I told her we would come to visit often, which I knew wasn't true, but I said anything to calm her down and it wasn't easy to appease her. No matter what excuse I gave, she continued to be upset, and then she threatened me.

"I'll take you to court, so I can have Tommy during the summers when he isn't in school," she said, "I'm his grandmother and I have rights!"

"And I have a right to live where I choose!" I said, standing up and taking Tommy by the hand to put his coat on. I was through arguing with her. She continued to cry, but said nothing more as she watched me put his boots on. Just before I reached for the doorknob to let myself out of her home as quickly as I could, she realized she had lost this battle.

"Kathleen, you'll promise to call and write me, won't you?' she asked, as if the scene she just played didn't happen.

"Yes," I said, as I pulled Tommy down her porch steps.

"Wait! She yelled, running back in to get his birthday gifts.

I reached for the two boxes and put them and Tommy into the back seat of the car. She was standing on her porch as I started to pull away from her house, the last I saw of her, she was waving. I didn't wave back. I felt bad about that, but she had pushed my buttons, and I couldn't respond civilly.

CHAPTER 45

Levi talked me out of leaving everything behind and said he would have a moving company bring everything. I was happy about that, because I couldn't afford to hire one. Moving across state lines was expensive. In ten days I would prepare to move. I hadn't heard from Tim and didn't expect to. I hurt him badly and his feelings were too raw. I hoped in time he would forgive me. Betty came over to help me pack and Rita stopped by one night with her kids, to say goodbye. I made sure they had Levi's address and phone number. Against my better judgment, I gave Tommy's grandmother one last call. I wasn't comfortable with the way I left our last visit. I thought I should leave with a kinder attitude than I displayed when I left her home. Always in the back of my mind was that blood connection. Regardless of her being the person she was, I would rise above any more petty anger between us. I held my breath and dialed the number.

"Hello!" came the voice that gave me heartburn.

"Hello, it's me, Kathleen, I'm calling to say I'm leaving on an early train from union station after the mover's leave."

"What day are you leaving?" she asked.

"Tomorrow night," I lied.

"Well, have a nice trip and call me and let me know you both got there safely," she said. I could hear the sadness in her voice. All the take-charge, knows-it-all attitudes she always spoke with were gone.

"Here's Tommy, he wants to speak to you," another lie. I had to pull him away from his Lincoln logs and put the receiver in his hand.

"Talk to Grandma, say goodbye, and thank her for the birthday gifts," I urged.

He said his thank you and goodbye, and remained quiet with the receiver at his ear for quite a few minutes and I could just imagine what she was saying, so I told him to say goodbye again, and took the phone away, telling her once again that I would call.

I spent the last few days visiting Betty, or she came over with Ricky. I would never know what it would feel like to have a sister, but I imagined it would be something like what I felt for her. I would miss her, more than she would ever know. When the movers left and with the apartment empty, except for one filled suitcase, we went to spend the last night with Betty. In the morning, she drove us to the train that would take us to Union Station in Chicago. We said our goodbyes, both crying. Our boys looked at us like they didn't understand what all the drama was about. Ricky at nine years old understood we were leaving, but Tommy was too excited about the train ride to think of it as anything else.

During the long ride that would take almost a full twenty-three hours to Philadelphia, Levi would be waiting. I had plenty of time to think. I was both excited and apprehensive, not knowing how I would feel when I saw him again. It had been almost seventeen months since we left the Holsteders and Levi. I worried over what his reaction to me would be. I lost weight and wasn't as well endowed as I appeared when living with the Amish. Most of the married Amish women were anything but thin. The food they prepared was delicious, but fattening. I worried I might be too thin with my five-foot-six-inch height. Both Tim and Levi were tall men, six feet and six one respectively, so my height didn't bother me then but now I thought I looked tall and gangling, and too thin. When I first met Levi, he was kind and not bad to look at in spite of the beard that covered half of his face. He had a sweet disposition that lent itself to a constant kind expression. I could never understand how Elsa Fisher chose Jacob over Levi.

Tommy was sitting in the seat next to the window and I made a folded blanket into a cushion so he could sit up higher to see the view as we traveled. It kept him occupied and from getting antsy as he usually did when he became bored. Levi sent the fare for a sleeper car, so we would have a place to sleep, other than a train seat. I found him to be super generous and worried if his income was enough to pay for all that he insisted on. That night it didn't take long for the rhythm of the train's wheels on the track to lull us to sleep. The next day in the dining car, we shared our table with an elderly woman going to visit her daughter and grandchildren. After introducing ourselves, she gave Tommy her full attention and he ate it up. She was the kind of grandmother I wished my son could have, and I could imagine having her for a mother. She was kind and concerned about us when I told her

I was a widow. She talked about her own life, and losing her husband just several years before.

"My dear," she said, looking at me with sympathy, "Widowhood shouldn't come to one so young as you."

"He had been sick, and I guess those things happen," I said, lying again.

She didn't press for more information and I was relived, or my lying would have gotten to the point where I might have believed it myself.

"Where are you traveling to?" she asked.

"I'm visiting friends, and I often wonder, what if I hadn't any friends when my husband died, I wouldn't have survived. Friends are so important," I said, trying to make conversation.

"My dear, what if is a term I never use. It belongs in the past. It's of no use in the present or future. It means regret, and you should never regret anything you can't change now," she said, smiling. "You're young, and have a whole future ahead of you, both you and your boy."

We parted when I left the dining car and I thanked this elderly woman for her kindly advice. I thought, with age comes wisdom, and I needed her to tell me that because I was full of regret. I had to stop thinking of how I hurt Tim, and that was hard for me to do. I knew it couldn't be helped, but I often thought of all the what ifs, what if he were kinder to my son, what if he were more like Levi, what if there had never been a war and he never went to Korea, what if I had parents. I would lay awake at night over all the what if's, and meeting that kind grandmotherly woman, helped me more than she would ever know.

It was almost 7:00 pm when we pulled into the station. I carried my suitcase and took Tommy's hand as we stepped off the train. I looked around trying to spot Levi. I hoped he got there before we did. I turned around and noticed this tall blond guy, walking toward us. When he appeared closer, he smiled. It was Levi minus his beard. He no longer looked Amish. He resembled a handsome Viking, tall and blond, and my heart skipped a beat. The first thing he did was lifting my son up in his arms, and asking Tommy if he remembered him. Tommy looked confused, but smiled back at him. "I remember *you*," he said to

Tommy, before setting him down and that's when he reached for me. His hug took my breath away, looking at him I felt weak in the knees. He released me still holding me by the shoulders to get a good look at me.

"You're beautiful, Kathleen, you look great. You haven't changed at all, well, maybe a little thinner which makes you more beautiful, your cheek bones are more noticeable."

I didn't know what to say to him. I was mesmerized by how handsome he really was. The first thing I noticed was his chin, it had a dimple, and I thought back to Elsa saying he had a weak chin and the beard hid it. I found it attractive and not weak at all, just right.

He looked handsome without his beard. I found myself blushing and I could hardly speak. He took the suitcase from me and grabbed Tommy with his other hand and I followed him out to his car. Once on the road I couldn't help looking over at him as he drove. He had a handsome profile. In fact, I couldn't keep my eyes off him.

"I live near the small town of St. Johns Village," he said, "I'm in the process of selling my home. It's small, and I've been looking at a place nearby with twelve acres. It has a real nice farmhouse on it with plenty of room for all of us. I intend on remodeling it, but want your input on what you might like."

"That sounds wonderful," I said, my voice a little shaky, my heart beating at least 90 beats per minute. I had to calm down, so I looked away from him at the road in front of us. I didn't remember feeling like this when I was around him in the past. I remembered being attracted to him, but nothing like what I was feeling now.

He talked about how excited Samuel was that I was returning. He would be eight the coming August and he remembered me. Samuel was a lot like Levi except he had light brown hair, and Paul's was a darker shade of brown like their mother. Alice was blond, almost white, that was what I remembered when I had last seen them, and I was anxious to see them again.

"I can't believe Samuel is going to be eight," I said.

"Well, Alice isn't a baby anymore Kathleen, she'll be four in April," and then remembering that Tommy had a birthday recently he turned to address my son who kept saying "Mommy, where are we going?"

"Tommy, you're almost as big as Paul," he said, trying to include him in the conversation.

"Paul is six, isn't he?" I asked.

"He'll be six in June, and I guess we'll have some birthdays to celebrate soon." He turned to Tommy again and said, "We missed your birthday Tommy, but we'll have another birthday for you as soon as we get home, if it's ok with you," he said looking over at me.

I couldn't believe Levi could be so thoughtful, and I thanked him. "You don't have to, he's had two already."

"Of course we can have another birthday party for him, we just missed it by a week, so we can still celebrate, huh, Tommy?"

He asked a four-year-old—like Tommy was as important as I was, and he was one of his own children, and I couldn't help but compare him to Tim. I looked back at my son and the happy expression on his face meant everything to me, and at that moment Levi would be more than I ever wanted in life.

We arrived in the quaint little town of St. Johns Village, an hour and twenty minutes Northwest of Philadelphia. It was almost 10:00 pm and with quite a bit of snow on the ground, it took us longer. The roads glistened with snow and the trees were covered as well. It looked like a wonderful picture you might see in a painting. His home wasn't in the town, but a little outside of it, where a small settlement of homes appeared like a picture postcard one would send at Christmas.

I found the surroundings enchanting even in the dark with a half-moon barely lighting the way.

"Oh, Levi, it's lovely, so peaceful," I said, taking in the view.

"I'm glad you aren't disappointed," he said, and then he hesitated and appeared deep in thought for a few minutes. "Kathleen, I made arrangements to sleep at my neighbors, for a couple days, so you and Tommy could get some rest, but more importantly, it wouldn't look good for us to be sharing a house together and not married—not in these parts. I spoke with the preacher at the little white church in town, and he agreed to marry us. You only need to get a blood test tomorrow."

"Levi, you haven't formally asked me to marry you, have you? Did

I miss it?" I laughed nervously.

He laughed out loud, and then he said, "I thought that was a given. Will you marry me, Kathleen?"

"Yes, Levi, I certainly will."

He leaned over and gave me a peck on the cheek, and said, "That will have to do until later."

He pulled into the driveway of a small brick house, and we walked to his door in the snow that continued to fall. He carried both Tommy and the one suitcase, although my son had his boots on, and he was capable of walking. It was quite cold and he wanted to get us inside as quickly as possible. Once inside, I realized we were alone, except for a large collie that greeted us without barking.

"This is Cherokee, she's a Collie, two years old and very gentle, you can pet her," he said to Tommy.

He put Tommy and the suitcase down and turned to me, and for an instant he hesitated, and then asked my son, if he could kiss his Mommy. I thought it was so thoughtful of him and the cutest thing I ever heard. Tommy was too distracted by the dog. He began petting the dog, while Levi took me in his arms and kissed me.

"I love you, Kathleen," he said, after a long and lingering kiss.

"I love you too," it was the first time I said those words to him.

"Where are the children?" I asked, wondering, thinking he wouldn't have left them alone, asleep.

"They're with Mrs. Jenkins, the lady who takes care of Alice, when I'm at work and the boys are in school. They go to her after school— she lives just down the street. They'll come home tomorrow morning. Is it alright if they stay with you and Tommy, well, I mean would you look after them until we marry? And since it will be Sunday tomorrow, I thought we could all attend the little First Methodist for service, to meet the Pastor who is going to marry us, but of course, if you prefer some other church?"

He knew I was married in a Catholic Church the first time, and how I felt about feeling so trapped in the marriage to Dan.

"No, a marriage is a marriage, and it's your church Levi, and if you're comfortable with it, so am I."

I thought of all he had given up to be free. A religion he was born into, his sister and her family, maybe aunts, uncles, and cousins, everything he had ever known or believed in, and if he was brave enough to do it, so would I. He stayed until I unpacked our clothes and he helped me put Tommy to bed in the room his boys shared. I noticed bunk beds in the room. Tommy was tired and fell asleep quickly in the bottom bunk, then he showed me the rest of the house, the other two bedrooms, where he and Alice slept, and later we shared hot chocolate he made, to ward off the chill from being in the car for so many hours.

"I'll get an extra bed for Tommy tomorrow," he said, and put it in Alice's room temporarily until we move, hopefully in the spring."

"Oh, you don't need to, his bed is in the moving van, coming with the rest of my furniture."

I looked around at his small home and realized there wasn't any room for anything except Tommy's bed.

"Where are you going to put all my stuff? I might have to get rid of some of it," I said.

"I have a two car garage, and we'll store it there. I want you to have your things, and when we move into a bigger place, you'll be glad you kept them," he said.

"Have you bought the new place?" I asked, wondering.

"The owner is holding it until I can sell this as soon as the snow lets up. I hope to sell by spring. Homes don't move too quickly out here unless the buyer is from outside this community, but we'll manage. I can't wait to take you to see the place. If you don't like it, well, we'll find something you do like."

I was thinking, *what a contrast Levi was, to all the other men I had known.* Only Angie's John had a sort of gentleness about him, but Dan, Tim, Betty's and Tim's fathers, and even Frank—not to mention the notorious Sergeant Martino. They all had what I called an ego to protect. It was a certain defense mechanism that showed its ugly side whenever challenged. Levi was truly without guile. We sat across from each other and I felt such love for him; I thought my heart would burst.

The next morning Tommy and I were ready when Levi and the children appeared. Samuel smiled the minute he saw me. Paul hung back and paid more attention to Tommy, but Alice was so shy. She clung to Levi's leg and wouldn't come to me at first.

345

"You boys remember Timmy, I mean Tommy," Levi said, correcting himself. Turning to me, he said, "I'm sure they won't remember the difference in the name."

"Tommy doesn't remember, thank God," I said, "He's been through enough changes."

"We spent the day getting reacquainted after attending the church service, and meeting the Reverend Earl Hamilton and his wife Georgia. Mrs. Hamilton was a warm person, a middle aged woman whom Levi's children seemed to know well. I liked the couple. We arranged the wedding for the following Saturday. Levi took us for a short ride after the service to show me the farmhouse with the twelve acres. There seemed to be many trees on the property and around the house. All the branches were coated in white from the snow that finally stopped falling during the night. I fell in love with the scene before me as we sat in the car in front of it.

"Do you like it?" he asked.

"Of course I do, who wouldn't," I said.

The morning of our wedding I was nervous. I had spent the last five days getting to know Levi and the children again. We stayed together at the house, but at night Levi slept at Mr. and Mrs. Jenkins, who were the middle-aged retired couple I came to love. By the time Saturday came, we were more comfortable with each other. Tommy and Paul played together nicely, Alice followed me around and I couldn't help picking her up in my arms. In less than four months she would be four years old, and here I was doing with her what I resented Dan's mother for doing with Tommy, carrying around a four-year-old. She was the sweetest little thing, and I couldn't help enjoying having a little girl to fuss over. Samuel was an old soul, so grown up beyond his years, maybe because he took the place of a missing mother with his younger siblings. My heart went out to him, and I tried to give him as much attention as possible. Paul was a lot like Tommy, because both were high-spirited. When the moving van arrived a few days before the wedding, we stored most of it in the garage, the furniture and toys. I let

Alice help me empty a small box of items she found interesting especially the figurine of the little white unicorn. I let her hold it in her hands and then cautioned her that we needed to place it on a high shelf, so it wouldn't get broken because it was supposed to bring us happiness. She admired it and then handed it back to me. I had in mind to tell her the same story about the princess and the white unicorn that sister Mary Louise had told to me, at some later date.

Levi set up Tommy's youth bed in Alice's room. I was relieved that he didn't have to buy another bed, I worried he might be spending too much money. I wasn't sure how his finances were, being a carpenter. I didn't know what kind of work he could have in the dead of winter, and was afraid to ask. The blood test done and a copy of Dan's death certificate in the Reverend's hands, we were set to go.

It was a sparse wedding. Only the neighbors Levi was close to, the children's sitter Mrs. Jenkins and her husband attended, and a few families from the church. Levi wore a suit and tie, I wore the dress Tim tried to relieve me of the night I spurned him. It was the nicest dress I owned. The boys wore their suits, and for Alice, I bought her a dress when we went into town that week. I asked Levi if it would be ok, if I did. I used money I had saved and purchased a pretty blue dress for her. I put a large blue ribbon in her hair and she looked adorable.

We said our vows, and I didn't feel the terrible choking feeling I had, saying until death do us part during my marriage to Dan. We looked at each other while saying the words that would make us man and wife, and I could feel the love I had for him and his love for me. I had never felt anything like that before. It was the happiest day of my life. Afterwards, we went into the back room of the church where the Reverend's wife had a small wedding cake set up, and some of the ladies of the congregation put on a luncheon for the entire wedding party, about thirty people in all.

We cut the cake together and Levi whispered, "I love you, Kathleen," in my ear. I smiled up at him. "Love you too," I whispered back. Pictures were taken of us with our four children, and my first thought was of sending Betty a copy, and also Dan's mother. I hadn't mentioned Levi to her, all she knew was I wanted to move away. I thought I would write her a letter first, and maybe send the picture later. I had called her when I arrived to let her know we arrived safely and left her with Levi's phone number, but didn't have the heart to tell her I was getting married again. I saved that for the letter I would write later.

CHAPTER 46

In March we sold the house and bought our dream home. In April, Alice had her fourth birthday party on the third of April, and I discovered I was pregnant. I gave Levi the good news, and he was elated, and then I received a letter from the FBI. It was a busy month. We moved a week after Alice's birthday and the farmhouse was a wreck. Outdated, and lacking the modern conveniences of a 1961 home, I found the kitchen completely unworkable. Levi stood in the middle of the room wondering where to start.

"It's spring, I'll get started," he said, putting his arm around me, "Don't worry; I have all summer to complete the house the way you want it."

"I'm not worried at all, I know what a good carpenter you are. Mrs. Jenkin's kitchen looked wonderful," I said.

The first time she brought me into her home was when I voiced concern after we viewed the farmhouse.

"Levi is a great carpenter, he remodeled my kitchen, and so I wouldn't worry about that. He could make a silk purse out of a sow's ear," she said.

I was impressed and didn't worry after seeing the wonders he could do with wood. Every day after Levi returned from the job he had at the main lumberyard, just west of St. Johns Village, he studied for his high school diploma and worked on our home. How the children slept through all the sawing and hammering he did at night was beyond me, but having bedrooms upstairs helped to quell the noise somewhat. He tackled the kitchen first, and when he finished around the end of July we told everyone the good news that we were going to add another child to the family. Levi was so happy, that he told the children about the baby before I did. Each day I lived with him, I loved him more. There weren't any words good enough to describe Levi. The baby was expected in the middle of October, and the trial I was to be a witness at was scheduled for the following January, the worst month in the year to have to travel, and with a baby just barely three months old, it would be difficult.

When I left Illinois I left my address and phone number with one of the FBI men. I called him to notify them of my moving to another state. Betty, Rita and Dan's mother were the only people who knew where I was living. Frank had written me a letter just before his father was arrested. I never answered it. I was so happy with my little family and our emerging soon to be beautiful farmhouse that getting the letter from the FBI cast a dark cloud over all the good that was happening in our lives. During the day I was busy with the children, sending the two older boys off to school each day and taking care of two four-year-olds filled my time, but at night, lying next to my husband, I couldn't sleep. I began to have all the worries and stress I thought I had left behind. Levi knew the letter I received and the summons I expected was keeping me in a state of anxiety.

He reached over to me one night when he felt me tossing around and held me close.

"Kathleen, it's not good for the baby or you to be this upset. You're not alone anymore. I'm here and I'll be with you all the way," he said. "Try to put it out of your mind until the time comes, and then we'll handle it."

After he said that, and other words of comfort, I fell asleep in his arms. I tried to put it all away and concentrate on my family and the added joy coming to us. From that night on, my thoughts were only of our children and the little oasis Levi built for us on our farm. Paul had his sixth birthday back in June and then in July Levi started working for a building contractor who had a contract to build many homes in nearby communities. His pay was greatly increased and we added a chicken coop and some chickens on our land. The children were so excited to have the chickens to play with and feed. Levi watching them around the chickens, laughed, "Don't get too attached, just feed them," he said, and turning to me he said, "Little do they know one of them might show up on our table one of these days."

I laughed and gave him a slap on his shoulder, "Don't ruin their fun so soon,"

By August our home took on a look of wonder to me. I loved it, the only home I ever had to call my own. The farmhouse had a Victorian look to it and Levi returned it to the splendor it had been back in the

1880s when it was first built, and now with all the modern conveniences. The front porch went across the entire front of the house and wrapped around one side. We had rocking chairs, planters and a swing he built, added to the porch, and we spent many nights sitting on that swing, talking, after the children had gone to bed. He built a playhouse for Alice, and a large swing set for them. He added a small covered back porch with another swing to sit on and watch the children at play behind the house. Everything he did for our family caused me to look at him in awe. I watched Tommy playing and knew the choices I made were the best I could have ever made for both of us, and just as importantly for Levi and his children too. Not long after our wedding, Samuel and Paul called me Mommy after they heard Alice address me that way. It took Tommy a few more months to call Levi Daddy.

The church Levi attended after leaving Wilding had a small congregation so I got to know everyone quickly and liked them all. Some of them lived in town but a few were like us, living on several acres or more. I made close friends with two women my age that had children close to our children's ages. One of the girls reminded me of Betty. It helped to ease the emptiness I felt without her in my life. We continued to write to each other and she planned on coming out with Ricky for a visit before Labor Day. I looked forward to her visit.

In August Levi finished the small barn where he wanted to house the pony he bought for the children. Samuel got the pony he kept asking for in time for his birthday, on August eighth, but with the understanding that the pony was for his brothers and sister as well. He welcomed it. We added two rabbits, and some ducks to swim in the one-acre pond at the back of our property. Levi added fish and they thrived due to a natural spring on the property that fed the pond and kept the water fresh. On weekends we could be found going to horse shows or searching for antiques across the small towns that dotted the area where we lived. Our home was shaping up to what I had always dreamed of and couldn't wait for Betty's visit to our beautiful place. Levi planted corn and a large garden with plenty of vegetables to put up for the winter. I thought heaven itself couldn't improve on what we had. I was so happy— I felt afraid. I didn't know what to be afraid of, but I contribute it to not believing I could have ever been so happy. I feared I'd wake up one morning and find it was all a dream, and I was still that little girl back in the orphan home being scolded by Sister Renada.

I would look at Alice, and picture myself at her age, and with all the love I was able to give her, I was healing myself. I was giving the children the best mother they could possibly have to make up for the mother I never had. At night when Levi and I were alone, we held each other and filled the void we both carried, the loss of his mother at a young age, his cruel father, and the vacant place inside me that was supposed to be filled by having parents of my own. The doubts and fears he carried from his Old Order Amish upbringing and the same nightmares I had over the fear the nuns instilled in me, and the invisible noose I felt around my neck married to Dan, in my religion— it all began to dissipate and we healed ourselves when we were in each other's arms.

I prepared for Betty's visit, getting the guest room ready, baking and doing everything to make her visit an enjoyable one. Seven months along in my pregnancy, Levi helped me as often as he could. The children were playing in the back of the house when I heard a car coming. It was a very hot August day, a week before Labor Day, and I went out to greet Betty and Rickey. It had been over seven months since we had seen each other and Rickey had grown quite a bit for a nine year old. Betty ran up and threw her arms around me.

"I've missed you," she said, and then looking at my figure, she smiled, "Kathleen you're glowing, you look beautiful. Being pregnant becomes you."

"Oh, come on, you're just saying that, I'm as big as a house and I still have a month and a half to go," I said.

"What do you think you'll have?"

"I don't know, but as long as it's healthy, we don't care."

I gave Ricky a hug and we went into the house, and straight out again through the back door of the kitchen, with Betty following and her son right behind. I yelled for the kids, and Samuel came running first.

"Go get the kids," I said, "We have company."

He ran back and soon all four were on the porch meeting Ricky and his mother. It wasn't long before Samuel took Rickey under his wing, showing him his prize pony. Betty mentioned how mature Samuel appeared for an eight year old.

"Yes, he's a very serious boy, much like his father," I said, 'I can't wait until you meet my husband."

Later that night after dinner, Betty helped me clean up in the kitchen, leaving Levi to keep the children amused in the living room.

"Kathleen, he's handsome, and so kind too," she said.

"I knew you'd like him, he's the best thing that ever happened to me since I had Tommy."

"You look so happy and I'm happy for you," she said, "I'm glad you left when you did. You have no idea how bad the situation became back home. The newspapers and television stations were full of the sordid details of all the murders over a span of ten years or more. The FBI were able to connect them all to that policeman, Martino."

"Have you heard anything about his family?" I asked, with trepidation.

"I ran into your friend Rita at the market one day and asked her that very question. I was going to call you, but decided to tell you when we saw each other again."

"What did she tell you?"

"She talked to some of the cops' wives, and you know how rumors go, so I can't confirm what she heard is true, but she said his own son is going to testify against him, can you imagine?"

"Which one?"

"I don't know, how many sons does he have?"

"Three, and it has to be Frank—Oh, God, that will kill Lottie!" I said, feeling so sorry for her. I thought Frank wasn't going to testify. They must have issued him a subpoena and now I dreaded going to that trial more than ever after hearing that.

Betty stopped drying the dish she held and paused, looking at me with a frown, "Kathleen, his wife ended up in the hospital. I think she had some kind of nervous breakdown."

"When did that happen?"

"Once the awful details were in all the papers, Rita said, the whole family was torn apart."

Hearing that, I felt sick. I didn't want to hear anymore and did the best I could to forget what I just heard. I was sorry I asked.

The rest of the week spent with Betty and her son went well, and Levi and I took her and all the children on a sightseeing tour of our quaint town, and all it had to offer a tourist. By the time the visit was over, Samuel and Ricky formed a bond and became best pals, promising to write to each other. We stood in the driveway as we said our goodbyes. Betty left on a Saturday morning, so Levi was there with us. I was glad for that because as soon as her car was out of sight, I went into the house and had a good cry. I wasn't sure what I was crying over—seeing Betty leave, or hearing about Lottie and all that was going on back home. Levi followed me in and I couldn't hide my feelings from him as much as I wanted to. He took me in his arms and held me. He didn't ask why the tears, he just held me. It was enough to bring me out of the sad mood. That was my husband—doing the right thing at the right time. I would remember to thank God, for him, in my prayers that night.

After Labor Day, the older children went back to school, and our lives took on a predictable routine. In September Levi and I prepared to harvest our garden for putting up canned tomatoes and green beans for the winter. There was much to do to get ready for the cold weather, but most of all for the new little addition to our family. The last week of September I received a letter from Betty who was keeping in touch with Rita. She passed on all the first hand news of the Martino family. She wrote that Frank was subpoenaed to testify and granted an extended leave to spend with his family, only to be rebuffed by his mother and siblings. Their mother was in a bad way with declining health and Angie was caring for her. Rita told Betty that Tim received a commission and was now a Captain on the police force. My heart broke for both Lottie and Angie. I couldn't imagine what they were going through—what the whole family was going through.

On October 10th I turned twenty-nine years old. I got up that morning preparing to bake my own birthday cake for the children to help me celebrate, but Levi had other ideas.

"I don't want you to do anything today," he said as he was shaving while I was trying to wash Alice's face over the same bathroom sink.

"Why?" I asked, knowing exactly why.

"It's your birthday, and on the way home tonight I'm picking up a cake I ordered, and I'm going to cook dinner for us. I don't want you doing anything on your day, in your condition."

He bent over Alice's head to kiss me with his half-shaven face getting shaving cream all over my mouth.

"Happy Birthday honey," he said, "I love you."

"Love you too," I answered, as Alice and I left him to finish his shaving.

Later that evening, Levi came in with the cake and enlisted Samuel's help in bringing in a large gift-wrapped box.

After we had finished our dinner, the children and Levi sang Happy Birthday to me. Excited, Samuel and Paul carried the box and set it on the table. Both Tommy and Alice shouted, "Open it Mommy!" I couldn't imagine what it could be and let the two younger ones help me tear the paper off.

Inside was another box, and then another until we had gone through five empty boxes. I didn't have to guess what was in the last box. I opened it and it was a diamond wedding ring. Levi and I had little time to plan for our wedding and so the ring he put on my finger during the service was a plain band he bought in a hurry.

"Oh, my, Levi! Can we afford this?" I said, not believing he would buy such an expensive ring.

"I want you to have it, you deserve it Kathleen—taking on three more children, and having another one? You mean everything to me."

"You've given me this beautiful home, the first one I've ever had, and you've given me a family of my own, isn't that enough?"

He just laughed, and helped me cut the cake.

On October twelfth, labor pains began. Levi got Mrs. Jenkins to stay with the children and by that evening I was in the hospital. At 5:15 in the morning on the thirteenth, our little six-pound-five-ounce Anna Lee was born, and with red hair. Levi was beside himself with joy over the color of her hair, which for the life of me, I couldn't understand. He knew how I didn't like standing out as a kid, but he said she was a miniature of me and he loved it. She was named after Anna Wilkie, the only mother figure I ever had, but I hadn't realized it until she was gone. The middle name of Lee was for her father, Levi, and he couldn't have been more excited and pleased. We now had two girls, and with the three boys our family was complete.

Our first Thanksgiving on the farm was exciting. Both Levi and I being without any extended family in our lives, invited Mr. and Mrs. Jenkins, and her family to join ours. In December we received enough snow for Christmas to bring back the memory of my first arrival to what I thought was a magical wonderland. The children all helped with trimming the tree, and I baked enough cookies for two families. Alice helped by watching over Anna, always close by in a cradle Levi made that was easy to move from room to room downstairs. It would be the best Christmas in my entire life, and then the New Year came, and with it the dreaded month of January.

CHAPTER 47

In January I received the subpoena to appear in court on the fifteenth, not much time after New Year's to get ready for a long trip with two children. We decided to leave on the twelfth of January because on the next day I had to meet with the prosecution in order for them to do what they informed me would be a completely diligent preparation. We would bring Tommy to visit his grandmother, and of course we had to take the baby. I felt she was too young to leave behind. Thank God for Mr. and Mrs. Jenkins who would stay at our home to look after the other three children. In the dead of winter, driving would be out of the question with a baby barely three months old. A train ride taking almost a full twenty-four hours, not counting the hour-and-a-half to two-hour ride to the station in bad weather was bad enough. Levi bought three plane tickets. Betty was notified and she insisted we stay at her apartment and she would stay with her parents for the duration I needed to be there.

Going on an airplane was exciting to Tommy, but never having been on a plane before, we were a little apprehensive. Levi bought coach tickets and requested the side with three seats. I carried a bottle and formula for Anna on the plane, kept in a cool pack. The trip from Philadelphia to Chicago's Midway Airport went quicker than I expected. Levi insisted on renting a car even though Betty offered hers. I worried about the traffic, but Levi had been driving almost three years and not just around the countryside where we lived, but in the city of Philadelphia as well. We arrived at Betty's with a baby that needed to be fed, and an over-tired soon-to-be- five-year-old. Tommy's birthday was on the sixteenth and I felt bad that his birthday celebration would have to wait until we returned home. Betty made us feel welcome.

"My gosh, Tommy has grown since we last saw you," she said, as she ushered us into her living room.

"I can't thank you enough," I said, and she quickly took the baby out of my arms. Once she got the blanket off of Anna, Betty gave out a little scream.

"Oh Kathleen, she looks just like you!"

"Yes, she's a little me, I'm afraid."

She handed the baby back and gave Levi and Tommy a hug.

"Where's Ricky?" I asked, noticing he wasn't there.

"I left him at Mom and Dad's, I thought you and I could visit a little before you turn in for the night. He has to get up early for school in the morning."

After we were settled with our coats put away and the suitcase placed in her bedroom, she had a nice dinner waiting for us. Levi and Tommy went to bed early and Betty and I cleaned up the dishes. After I fed Anna and settled her in a bassinette Betty borrowed from a neighbor, we sat together in the kitchen and she filled me in on a few things.

"I was surprised that the son of that murderer was going to appear in court against his father," she said, "You are sure of which son it could be?"

"It *has* to be Frank, he'll testify to his father's character. Frank knows a side to him that his other children don't, I'm sure," I said, remembering what he had confided to me about his father. I thought he must have been subpoenaed, because at first he refused to testify due to his mother.

"You don't have to appear until the fifteenth, so what are your plans for the next two days?" She asked.

"I need to meet with the prosecution and then we plan on taking Tommy to see his grandmother."

"Does she know you're married?"

"Yes, I wrote her before Anna was born and filled her in on what my life was like. I made sure she knew I was very happy."

"Did you hear from her after that?"

"You bet, and she wasn't too pleased to hear that Tommy had a new father. In fact her first question in the letter was if I was going to change his name. At first I gave her Levi's phone number, but we had to change it to an unlisted number a month after we were married. I didn't want her calling too often and she started to call at the house often during the day, when I first got there. She didn't know I was married and I didn't tell her until I knew we had to come back here. I thought of sending a picture of our family, but I decided not to. I was angry I guess, and afraid of what she would say after the outburst I got from her when I told her I remarried."

Betty looked worried, "What are you going to do about her? Maybe you shouldn't have told her you were coming back for the trial."

"Oh, I had to, she would find out. Remember she has contact with some of the men's wives in the sheriff's department so she would know everything that was going on about the trial."

"I don't know how you're going to get through a visit with her— does she know you have another child?" Betty was concerned. "I'm afraid of how she'll treat Levi," she said.

"Betty, please don't worry, Levi can handle what ever comes along. He may appear too gentle—you know, when someone is like Levi people get the wrong impression, they think they can do or say anything, Well, let them try, they don't know him like I do, he's anything but a push over. He can handle himself and anyone else who dare to take him on. One thing he isn't lacking is courage."

Betty stayed with the children and Levi drove me over to the District Attorney's office and I spent the day being briefed on the trial and what to expect. The next day on the ride over to Mrs. Clarke's, I filled Levi in on what to expect. I wasn't too worried about her. I long ago realized she had no power over me and in the worst-case scenario, we could just leave and then she wouldn't have any time with Tommy. The closer we got to her place, I could feel my heart beat pick up slightly. I wouldn't say I was nervous, just wanted to get past the day.

Levi looked over at me. "Are you going to be ok?" he asked, half smiling. "Don't worry so much—what can she do?"

I wondered what she could possibly do or say, for that matter. I hadn't written her I was expecting a baby. I thought she didn't need to know everything about me just see her grandson, maybe this one last time. I held a grudge when it came to her, because I blamed her for Dan being the way he was. I had no intentions of ever coming back again, but always in the back of my mind was that blood connection, that made me feel guilty, keeping Tommy away. I often wondered how I would ever see Betty again unless she visited me.

We pulled into Mrs. Clarke's driveway and found her waiting at the door. I had called her before we left and I couldn't make out by the sound of her voice what she was thinking. She sounded pleasant, maybe because she only had seeing her grandchild on her mind.

Levi came over and took Anna from me. He was standing on the passenger side of the car and she didn't notice anything except Tommy as I led him by the hand up to her door. Levi followed holding Anna wrapped in a blanket.

"Tommy, Tommy," she cried, as she swooped him up into her arms. I didn't get a chance to say anything until we were inside. Levi closed the door behind him and we stood there watching her actually crying while hugging my son so tight, that he struggled to get out of her grasp, but Levi scolded him gently.

"Tommy, your grandma hasn't seen you in a long time," he said, "She wants to give you a hug."

Levi's voice seemed to snap her out of the attention to Tommy, and she stood up from where she had been on her knees hugging him, and seemed to realize my husband was there.

"Oh, I'm so sorry, I didn't see you," she said, wiping her eyes with her hankie.

"Grandma, this is my husband, Levi, and this is Mrs. Clarke," I said to him, as I introduced them. They shook hands and then she realized he had a baby in his arms. Mrs. Clarke looked uncomfortable at first and then I uncovered Anna from the pink blanket. When she looked her over a slight smile came to her face.

"I didn't know you had a baby Kathleen, why didn't you tell me?"

"I'm sorry, with all that's going on—"

"It's a girl? She looks just like you; she has your red hair. When was she born?"

"In October, she's three months old," I said, surprised at how she seemed so interested.

She offered to take our coats and seemed to relax as we made ourselves comfortable in her living room. She asked if we were going to be here for Tommy's birthday, but Levi spoke up before I had a chance to say anything.

"No, I'm afraid not, tomorrow Kathleen has to give her testimony at the trial, and our plane tickets are for the day after. I need to be back at work, but we can celebrate it today if you like."

She looked a little unsettled, and nervous, almost afraid of saying the wrong thing, which surprised me. I thought Levi intimidated her. He appeared serious, and with a sound of authority in his voice, he took charge when he answered her question. I could just imagine what she was thinking. If he had shown the least bit of weakness she would have walked right over him. He knew enough about her to know how to handle her. He was direct and truthful when he spoke in a matter of fact way. It was almost as though she sensed if she wanted to see her grandson in the future, she didn't dare cross this man. She deferred to him instead of me the rest of the afternoon. He was kind to her, and I helped her bake a cake for Tommy. We accepted her invitation to stay for dinner that evening. When I asked if I could go into her bedroom to change and feed Anna, she happily obliged, leading us in and asking if I needed anything, to let her know. I noticed whenever she looked at Anna, she smiled.

I could hear them in the kitchen as Levi filled her in on our life on the farm, and that he had three children waiting at home for us. I'm sure he told her his wife passed away, and later when we were sitting in her dining room together, she noticed how Tommy called Levi, Daddy, and how he responded lovingly to him. I wished I could have read her mind as I watched her watching them talking together. I was sure she was the same person, but maybe hiding it in front of my husband. Levi spoke kindly to her, more than I would have, but with firmness in his voice. After we finished dinner, she brought out the cake and a gift for Tommy. We sang Happy Birthday and he blew out the candles.

"If I had known about the baby, I would have gotten a gift for her," she said.

"Oh, that's alright, I'm sorry I forgot to mention her, or the other children when I wrote. I've had a lot on my mind with this trial," I said.

She turned to Levi, "That crazy man killed my son." And then she started crying again.

"I heard—I'm so sorry," he said, "That's why it's so important for Kathleen to be in court tomorrow, so they can put that guy away for a long time."

"Oh, they won't just put him away, he'll get the death penalty," she said, with conviction and anger in her voice, reminding me of the real Mrs. Clarke.

When Anna began to cry I went to where we had laid her in the middle of Mrs. Clarke's double bed. She wasn't due for a feeding and I brought her to the dining room. Mrs. Clarke reached her arms out to hold her for the first time, so I handed the baby to her. She seemed to be enjoying holding a tiny baby again.

"I'm afraid we will be leaving soon, it's past Tommy's bedtime, also Anna needs to be fed in an hour. It's almost eight," I said.

She looked at me, and I knew what was coming.

"Can you leave Tommy with me tonight? You can pick him up after you finish up at court and—"

Before she got a chance to say anything more, or I could respond, Levi spoke up.

"Mrs. Clarke, his change of clothes are at the apartment and after the trial, well, we have no guarantee when Kathleen will be called. It could be an all day thing. Our plane leaves in the afternoon the next day, we will stop by to say goodbye before we leave for the Airport, so you will see him again."

She looked stunned, his—this is the way it's going to be voice—stopped her cold.

"Well, alright, I'll be in the court room tomorrow then. I planned on staying home with Tommy, but I guess now I will go," she said.

"You should be there every day of the trial, since everyone thinks he killed your son, don't you think?" Levi said.

"Yes, I guess you're right, I'll stay home the next day to see all of you again on your way home."

We said our goodbyes and once we were in the car, I took a deep breath. Levi laughed, "That wasn't so bad, was it?" he said, "You can relax now."

"You don't know her, if I were alone I would have seen a different person."

The next morning Betty came to stay with Anna and Tommy, and Levi and I left for the courthouse.

When we entered the building, they told us we were not allowed to enter the courtroom. We could sit outside where there were benches along the wall or in a separate room next to the courtroom until I was called. When that would be was anyone's guess. I knew both Frank and Tim would be witnesses and dreaded being in the same room with them. I began to tremble with nerves, feeling like I was about to come apart. I thought, *what could I say to Frank, not answering his letter after all he did for Tommy and me, and the thought of seeing Tim again, what would he say to me, if anything, once he saw me with Levi.*

I chose to sit on the bench outside the courtroom door. Levi could see the state I was in and he took my hand to try and calm me.

"It's going to be alright," he said, "I'm sure it won't take long and before you know it, we'll be on our way."

How could Levi understand that it wasn't being on the witness stand that had me upset, It was the fear of seeing Frank and Tim again. He knew too much about Tim and nothing about Frank. We sat watching the people arrive for the trial, and when I noticed a few policemen enter the door and go to another room, I was sure Tim was one of them. I panicked and turned away facing Levi, as if that alone could make me invisible. I was shaking, and turned to Levi where my back would be to them, damn, my red hair, I couldn't hide and I wasn't sure any of them saw me. Levi leaned over to whisper to me, "A sailor just entered and followed the police into that room."

My heart was beating and I was sweating. I wondered if Angie or any of the Martinos were in the courtroom or if they hadn't arrived yet would they notice me sitting there with my back to them when they came in and I looked at Levi and whispered, "This is going to be the worst day of my life."

"Do you want me to come in with you when they call you in?" he asked.

"I don't think you should," I said.

I took the scarf I had removed from my head when we entered, and placed it back on, covering my hair as if that would render me invisible.

The longer I had to sit there, the worse it would be and if they called me last, I might have worked myself up into a frenzy—that was my main fear.

Levi nudged my shoulder, "There's Mrs. Clarke."

I watched her coming down the hall, and when she spotted us she stopped and said, "Aren't you supposed to be in there?"

"No," I said, "I'm a witness, so I'm not allowed in until they call for me."

"Oh, I didn't know," she said, and then she patted my hand. "You go tell them, and send that lunatic away for good."

"I'll do my best," I said, and then I watched her enter the courtroom.

Levi and I sat in silence while more people went in and then when the last to arrive came, the doors were shut and one policeman stood outside the door. He noticed us and smiled, but said nothing. I knew the sailor had to be Frank. I missed him with my back turned away from the door to the witness room.

I don't know how long we sat there, and I wouldn't know who was called up to testify. After what seemed like hours, but not quite that long, the doors opened and one man came out and left. I turned to Levi, "I wonder who that was," I said. The cop at the door heard me and said, "That was a reporter."

What seemed like another hour but wasn't nearly that long, the doors opened again and my worst fear happened. Tim came out and noticed us sitting there. He stopped and had a look of surprise. He took a few steps and faced us and Levi stood up. I stood up after he did. I was shaking badly.

"With my voice barely audible, I said, "Levi, this is Captain Tim O'Malley, Tim, this is my husband, Levi Yoder." They shook hands and Levi spoke first.

"I'm glad to meet you, Captain O'Malley."

"Call me Tim, nice to meet you too."

Tim could see how badly shaken up I appeared, and he chose to ease the situation.

"I want to congratulate you both on your marriage," he said,

"Kathleen's a great gal, and I wish you both every happiness."

Just then, the doors opened and I was called in. I was led into the courtroom by the cop at the door, leaving both men standing there together. I thought I was going to be sick, wondering what they could possibly say to each other. My time on the witness stand felt like what I imagined waiting for the electric chair might have felt like. I dreaded questions from the defense. I knew how Dan felt about defense attorneys. 'They ask trick question's," he'd said, "and they expect a yes or no when many times the answer is more complicated than yes or no." The prosecution did the same, but to Dan, they had a right. He figured a purely innocent man wouldn't be on trial. Dan was so rigid in his thinking, that I doubt he truly believed in innocent until proven guilty.

On the witness stand I was sworn in, and after that everything seemed to be in slow motion. I told my story and answered the prosecution's entire questions, with several objections from the defense side, which were quickly overruled by the Judge. I didn't see anything in that courtroom. It felt like I was in a daze. I kept my eyes away from the defense table; never made eye contact with Martino, never saw him sitting there where I knew he had to be. The defense questions were few, because having me up there too long would just be more damning to their client. My husband stayed outside knowing I would be more nervous if he was in the room. I realized the courtroom wasn't an environment for a man like Levi, a gentle man; he would be in a den of wolves. The comparison wasn't lost on me. He didn't belong in a place of crime, anger and revenge.

I searched for anyone in the Martino family, but there was only Frank sitting alone two rows behind the prosecutor. He must have given his testimony, and wanted to remain in the courtroom. He was in uniform and looked devastated watching me up there on the witness stand. Testifying against his father had to have been for him the most horrific thing he had to do, and I knew I had hurt him badly by never responding to his letters. I looked away. When I was finally excused from the witness stand, I walked out on legs that didn't feel like they were going to hold me up. I couldn't get out fast enough. I thought I walked out of a quagmire, expecting another one if Levi and Tim had any kind of altercation, but when I left the courtroom, Levi and Tim were just ending what looked like a pleasant conversation, with Tim turning to me saying, "Goodbye Kathleen, I know you found what you were looking for, I wish you both the best," and then he walked out.

"What happened?" I asked, wondering what Tim might of said to Levi.

"He's a nice guy who only wants the best for you," Levi said.

Whatever they talked about the whole time I was up on the witness stand, left me wondering. If something happened between them, it didn't seem to faze Levi, but I needed to know. He knew everything about Tim, because I was honest with him about my relationship and break-up with Tim. I told Levi everything that happened when I returned to him. Just as we were about to leave, Frank came through the door. He came right up to me, stopping us at the exterior door as we were about to step out, and started to loudly ask me questions about why he hadn't heard from me.

"I never heard from you again," he said, "Why didn't you write me, and at least tell me yourself? My sister had to tell me you married again."

Levi looked annoyed thinking this strange guy was bothering me.

"No, it's ok," I said to Levi, "He's a good friend," and turning to Frank, I said, "I'm sorry, I should have written to you and told you about my marriage." I was shaking and tried to introduce them, but I lost my voice. I was trying to keep from breaking down crying after all the stress I endured. Levi held out his hand to Frank who hesitated, then shook Levi's hand. Frank looked a little embarrassed as he stood staring at us. Levi spoke for both of us.

"She's been under a great deal of stress after what happened to her, and we've known each other from when she lived in Pennsylvania," he said, "and if you've been a friend to her, I'd like to thank you for being her friend."

Frank looked confused, and I felt sorry for him, he had been so kind to Tommy and me.

"I didn't answer your letter Frank, because—you have no idea what I was going through. Your father was stalking me at that time and you heard my testimony in there," I pointed to the courtroom door, "

366

I—"

"I understand," he said, "and I'm sorry for what my father put you through. When did you two marry?"

"Over a year ago, and we have had a baby girl, she's only three months old."

I don't know why I offered that information, but I was glad I did, because Frank reacted to the news with a smile, saying," Well, congratulations, on your marriage and the baby." He asked about Tommy, and then if we wanted to stop for coffee with him, but Levi declined.

"We have two children waiting for us, and tomorrow we leave for home, but thanks for asking," he said, "If you're ever in our State, look us up."

"Thanks, I might do that."

They shook hands and we said goodbye, and I watched as he walked out ahead of us. I wanted to apologize, I wanted to ask him many questions, about his relationship with his family, but I knew if we spent more time with him, Levi might get the impression we were a little more than just friends. I let it go, relieved that we parted without any of the drama I had expected from either him or Tim and I was thankful that what I feared never happened, and the dreaded ordeal was over, and we could go home. On the way to Betty's I wanted to ask Levi what really happened with Tim, but chose not to. I didn't want to spoil the good feelings I was experiencing at that moment by hearing anything negative.

Once we were back at the apartment, it was Betty who asked all the questions about the trial. I told her I was very tired, and would gladly tell her some other time about the entire day, and that I needed to get some distance from it before I could.

"I understand," she said.

We went to bed early that night, both of us emotionally exhausted. The next morning Betty came over and once we were ready to leave, our parting wasn't without a few tears. We couldn't thank her enough for all she had done for us.

"Well, one more stop, to see Dan's mother on our way to the airport, but after yesterday, its going to be the easiest thing I'll have to do," I said, once we were on our way.

"Kathleen, I'm glad you see it that way," Levi said, "she's Tommy's grandmother and you have to get over whatever you felt about her in the past. Ignore anything she might say. We don't live near her, so there is nothing to worry about anymore."

Levi had a lot of wisdom, and he never failed to pull me up whenever I felt down or defeated. Our visit to Mrs. Clarke's was short and she understood we had a plane to catch. This time she was able to control her goodbye to Tommy without tears. She wished us a safe journey home.

CHAPTER 48

When we arrived home, and by the time we reached the farm, we were ready to return to the normalcy of our lives. The children were happy to see us and both Samuel and Paul were excited to tell Tommy about the new baby rabbits in the barn. The snow was deep, but Mr. Jenkins had used our plow to clear our driveway up to the house. Later that evening after Mr. and Mrs. Jenkins had gone home and our children were put to bed, Levi lit a fire in our living room fireplace and with the hot mugs of chocolate he made, we sat together on the sofa and hardly said a word. We were savoring the quiet time we both so badly needed.

I looked over at him and he looked like he was about to fall asleep. His eyes were closed and his head was against the back of the sofa. I reached over and kissed his cheek. He opened his eyes.

"Levi," I said, "I want to know what you and Tim talked about."

"It was nothing, he was just a guy who I think was a bit sad over losing you. He didn't seem to be the type who holds a grudge, but he mentioned how he couldn't understand your marriage."

"Our marriage?"

"No, you marrying Dan. He had a hard time understanding it."

"I can't believe he would mention *that* to *you* Levi. He had no right to do that."

"I defended you, by reminding him that he wasn't around to protect you, and you were totally alone at the time without any family of your own."

"What did he have to say to that?"

"Nothing much, I think he realized you were happy. He talked about the case and then you came out of the court room."

"Yes, and when he said he knew I found what I was looking for, I guess he approved of you."

"Kathleen, I'm sure it was hard on him to lose you, and he had an ego to protect. I believe the war, and the profession he chose, created the person he is now. He might have been different had the circumstances in his life been different."

Levi was defending Tim, and at that moment I couldn't have loved him any more than I already did.

That spring of 1962, Levi completed the courses that got him his high school diploma. We celebrated by having a cookout at the farm inviting the friends we had made and Betty came out with Ricky. It was a wonderful occasion for Levi. I was so proud of him. Betty filled me in on how the monster Martino was given a death sentence. She said he was suspected of killing Dan, but all they had was circumstantial evidence because they never found the gun that was used, but they had him on all the other cases. I didn't care. He got the death penalty, but I thought it might be years before it could be carried out, and probably with the many appeals pending, his lawyers could seek to delay it indefinitely. I was beginning to think like Dan when it came to the law. That spring we also received a letter from both Mrs. Clarke and Levi's sister, Miriam. Both tried to play on our sympathy and knew how to use the guilt card. It was easy for Levi to dismiss Mrs. Clarke's letter, but his sister's letter irritated him. With me it was the opposite.

"What did Miriam have to say?" I asked, wondering, because it wasn't the first time she had written to him. He told me he received letters from her periodically telling him she's praying for his soul, and to make things right with God, he had to return to the faith.

"I don't reply to them," he said, and then he changed the subject. I could tell it bothered him, but I didn't press for any more information.

Mrs. Clarke's letter was disturbing. She informed me that Tommy's last name should remain Robson, and that she was going to speak with an attorney about visitation with Tommy. I was so upset that I wanted to call her and tell her off, but Levi stopped me.

"She can't do anything Kathleen," he assured me, "Tommy is now legally a Yoder since the adoption last year."

"What about her trying to get visitation during the summer?"

"We'll speak with an attorney, I'm sure he's too young for that to happen," he said, trying to reassure me.

In June we met with the lawyer and he thought that as long as we can prove we welcomed her to visit the boy anytime she wanted, he doubted she could get him for an entire summer, not at his age, and her advanced age. I did what I was told to do; I invited her to spend a week with us at her convenience. To my horror, she accepted. It was the week of Samuel's tenth birthday. Levi went to pick her up from the train station in Philadelphia, and I flew around the house preparing for her, making sure the guest room was neatly presented because I knew how fussy she was. I planned a nice dinner, as it would be close to dinnertime when they arrived from the ninety-minute drive. The children were dressed neatly and I told them to expect 'Grandma.' I was careful not to mention she was Tommy's grandmother, just Grandma, and I encouraged them to address her as such.

I thought of how the children could use a grandmother since none of them except Tommy would ever have one, and I only hoped Mrs. Clarke wouldn't be offended by them calling her that. I was nervous because she could be unpredictable and I never knew how she would react in any given situation. When the time was near to her arrival, I sent the children outside to the porch to wait. It was a hot sweltering day and Levi had put a fan in the window of the guestroom. The room faced east and would get the sun only in the morning so it was the coolest bedroom. I had the two windows opened to let the breeze in and there was one on the north side where the window fan was installed. When I heard Samuel call out to me that Daddy's car was coming down the road, I went out to greet her.

She stepped out of the car with a smile on her face. Of course Tommy knew who she was, so he went up to her and let her give him a hug. The other children stood with me until she came and hugged me, and then I introduced the children to her. This is Grandma Clarke," I said. She smiled at them and repeated their names as she gave each one a gentle hug. I was holding Anna, who was ten months old and not quite walking yet.

"Oh, how big the baby is," she said, and to my surprise she put her arms out to take her, but Anna was shy and turned her face away hugging me around the neck.

"She's shy, she'll warm up to you as soon as she gets used to you,"

I said, for lack of anything else to say, except to ask how the train ride was.

Levi carried her bags upstairs and I invited her to come in and make herself comfortable. I put Anna in her playpen and Mrs. Clarke followed me into the kitchen—I had to check on the beef roast I had in the oven.

"Oh, how nice your kitchen is, and your home is lovely," she said.

"Well, thank you, Levi remodeled the kitchen and I love it."

Alice followed us into the kitchen, but the boys scattered some where in the house or outdoors. I checked the roast and the silence between us for a few minutes was painful. I didn't know what to talk to her about. She sat herself down on one of the chairs at the table, so I asked if I could get her a cup of coffee or tea.

"Oh, no, that's alright. I had enough coffee on the train to keep me awake all night. You go ahead with your dinner. Is there anything I can do to help?" she asked.

"No, not right this minute," I said.

I noticed her watching Alice who had gone out of the room and came back in with her favorite doll and placed it on Mrs. Clarke's lap.

"What a nice doll!" she said, smiling at Alice.

I realized at that moment that the day couldn't be any easier for her than it was for me. Suddenly she appeared old and fragile, and I felt sorry for her. I tried to ease the strain in the visit by trying to set aside what I thought of her and took a greater effort to make her feel at home. She held a conversation with Alice, who at five could talk endlessly about anything and everything. Suddenly Paul and Tommy came running in, with Paul asking if she wanted to see their pet rabbits. To my surprise, she let Paul take her hand with Alice taking her other hand, and Tommy following, they took her to the barn. I watched them as they crossed the yard, with our Collie Cherokee, running beside them and the boys pulling her along, almost helping her. I couldn't believe she went willingly.

Later, at dinner, all the children tried to outdo each other in telling her all about their various pets. That summer we added two miniature goats, and they were Tommy's favorites. He liked how they could jump onto everything. When Paul addressed her as Grandma, I noticed her facial expression, and how happy she appeared. When each of the children called her Grandma when they wanted to tell her something, her eyes watered up. Soon all the children were vying for her attention. By the time we finished dinner she appeared tired. Levi helped me with the dishes and sent her to the living room with the children.

"You're our guest, so please, we want you to relax, I'll help Kathleen clean up," he said.

She went with the children and later when we entered the room, they were all around her as she was reading out of one of Alice's fairy tale books. Levi was holding Anna by the hands as she toddled over to her, and that's when she picked her up. This time Anna happily sat on her lap for all of five minutes. When she was ready to get off, I took her upstairs to get her ready for bed. I came back down to Mrs. Clarke and Levi having a pleasant conversation about our little farm. He promised her he would take her around to show her all the animals and the property the next day, a Saturday. That night, after the children were in bed, I showed her to her room. She couldn't have been more appreciative about the dinner, and the room.

"Kathleen! I want you to know how happy I am to see Tommy so happy. You have a fine husband, and—"

She started to cry, and I did something I thought I could never do, I put my arms around her.

Later that night I found it difficult to sleep, I needed to speak with Levi before he fell asleep. We talked late into the night.

"I can't believe the change in her, it can't be real," I said.

"Did it ever occur to you that she is just a lonely old woman—how old is she? Do you know?" he asked.

"I never gave a thought to her age, but she said she had Dan when she was in her late thirties. When I met Dan he was around thirty, and she had to be about sixty- eight at that time."

Levi took a deep breath, "Gosh, she has to be seventy-eight or more, and you're worried about her getting Tommy for a whole summer? She's too old to care for a five year old."

"Funny, she never mentioned anything about wanting him for the summer since she came," I said, hoping it never came up again.

"You know, she insisted on the name of Thomas, after her second husband, when Tommy was born. I could never understand why, and I had no say in it. Dan didn't seem to object," I said.

"Well, maybe it was because he provided well for them, and besides Thomas is a fine name, it's one of the apostles names in the Bible, same as the name, Paul," he said.

Levi could always find something good to say about anything I brought up. I admired him for that. I needed to think about Mrs. Clarke in a more positive way.

"She's having a great time with all the attention the kids are giving her, so I don't think it crossed her mind to say anything about having Tommy for a summer. I'm tired, let's get some sleep," he said, as he held me close.

The week went by all too soon, and the visit went well with Dan's mother. I was amazed that she joined us on Sunday morning in our little church, and knowing she was Catholic I expected her to say something, to object, but she didn't, and seemed to enjoy the choir and the songs. I found it hard to believe Levi wanted her to stay an extra week. He asked if it would be ok with me first, and then when he asked her, she didn't refuse. He went to exchange her return tickets, and took her along to see more of Philadelphia. The three boys went with them, to her delight. I thought about the change in Mrs. Clarke. I wasn't as accepting as Levi; I still didn't trust her motives. I thought she was putting on an act. I thought back to the past week and was sure she genuinely enjoyed Levi's children as much as she did Tommy. Realizing I might be too harsh in my assessment of her, I would reserve judgment until after she returned home, and we heard no more of her demands.

We celebrated Samuel's tenth birthday with 'Grandma' present, and I was surprised at how tolerant Levi was, taking her shopping while they were in Philadelphia, at her request. She not only bought a present for Samuel, but for all the children as well. Levi asked if she could afford it and her answer was 'Mr. Clarke left me well able to take care of all my wants and needs.'

On her last evening, after the children were in bed, the three of us sat on the porch trying to catch some of the evening breeze, cooled once the sun went down. She talked about her life, which surprised me.

"Mr. Robson wasn't a good father, " she said, sadness in her voice, "I tried to make up to my son what he didn't get from his father. A boy needs a father, and I had great hopes for Mr. Clarke taking over that role, but Danny was already ten years old and I'm afraid he became too close to me. He found it hard to accept a new man in my life. Mr. Clarke tried so hard to gain Danny's affections, but never could. He took great care of us in every other way. Danny lacked for nothing."

"Well, that's important too, isn't it," Levi said.

"Oh, but my son could have used a father in the true sense of the word. A real father—like you are, Mr. Yoder."

"Please, call me Levi."

She had referred to Levi as Mr. Yoder, throughout her stay.

"Levi, I want you to know you are a fine man, and great father to your children. Thank you for treating my grandson like one of your own."

"I wouldn't think of treating any of my children any other way," he said.

I was sitting on the swing with her and Levi was in the rocking chair. He leaned over and patted her hand. "It's getting late, I'm ready for bed," he said, "We have a long trip tomorrow, but you ladies can stay up.

"No," she said, "it's been a long day, and I'm tired."

She stood up and as we were about to enter the house, she threw her arms around me and cried. I didn't know what to say to her. She took her arms from around me and reached for her hankie. I wasn't sure if she was crying because she was leaving in the morning, or if they were tears of happiness, having spent two weeks with her grandson.

"It's alright," I said, "You're welcome to come back again."

"Thank you, Kathleen, I don't know how many more trips I'll be able to make in the future. I'll be eighty next month."

"Eighty? What day is your birthday?" I asked, kind of shocked to hear her age. She didn't appear that old, I thought, maybe in her seventies. But I never bothered to add up the years until Levi asked me.

"My birthday is on the tenth of September," she said.

I thought of her spending her eightieth birthday alone, and it bothered me. I would make sure we sent her a nice gift and call her on that day, so all the children could speak with her.

In the morning, she was in good spirits; she kissed the children goodbye equally, not spending more time with Tommy than the other children. She gave me a hug and said what I thought I would never hear out of her.

"You're the kind of daughter I wish I had," she said, and then she moved quickly into the car. I think she didn't want to cry again. We watched as the car disappeared out of view.

About four weeks after we called her on her birthday, we received a letter. I was worried it might be another demand for Tommy to visit. I still didn't trust her motives, even if Levi did. When I looked at the envelope, I decided to wait until he was home to open it because it was addressed to him. To our complete surprise, it was a request of a completely different nature. She wanted Levi to be an executor to her will. She explained that she trusted him to take care of his family. If he agreed, she would send us a copy of the will. He called her and told her he was honored to do that for her. A month later, a copy of the will did arrive. I had to sit down while I read it, because I couldn't believe it. She was leaving everything to me, not to Tommy, her grandson, but to me, with Levi acting as executor. She explained that I would have all the children's best interests at heart, and she trusted us. She said it would make her happy to know the children were in good hands. When Thanksgiving came around again, we invited her, and she came, this time for a week. She met all our friends and neighbors and seemed to enjoy the visit but we noticed she appeared somewhat tired and frail. She took a nap when Anna did each day.

At Christmas, she didn't think she could make another trip in the cold. By this time, all my doubts about her had vanished. She never mentioned wanting Tommy for a summer, or anything like it. Levi and I wondered what to do since she would be alone at Christmas, but when we voiced our concerns, she assured us she wouldn't be alone, her close friend would have her over for Christmas Day.

In the New Year, with both Tommy and Alice both turning six, all four children were in school and I had only Anna at home. At a year and a half, she was running all over the place. We checked up on Mrs. Clarke often. I asked Betty to call and check on her and she did. Mrs. Clarke knew Betty, I having mentioned her many times in the past. When we received a call that she had a bad fall and was hospitalized for a few days, Levi convinced her that it would be better for her to sell the house and come out to us, so we could keep an eye on her. She was having health problems, so we found a nice apartment complex about five miles from our place. She would have her own little apartment, but be close enough to spend a day or weekend with us whenever she wanted to come out. Levi told her it would not only be good for her, but for the children to see her as well. She agreed and came to us in June. She respected Levi's opinions a great deal.

That summer found us busy not only with the farm, our animals, and the children, but checking on Mrs. Clarke as well. She was settled in a nice first floor apartment. I worried about how it would all work out. My mind kept flashing to her constant calls in my former life, but none of that ever materialized. She was content to visit us several times a month, for a day or two. She tired easily and enjoyed her alone time. She met another elderly woman in the same building and they kept each other company.

One afternoon, with the children happily playing behind the house, Levi and I sat on our back porch swing watching them; Levi put his arm around me.

"I love you Kathleen," he said.

"Love you too," I answered.

We were watching Alice with Anna who was two months from her 2nd birthday. Alice was holding her hand as they walked across the lawn alongside our collie, Cherokee who was running around them. Levi laughed.

"Look at our rainbow kids," he said.

"What do you mean?" I asked.

"Well, no two of them have the same color hair."

I laughed, "You're right!"

Samuel had light brown hair, Paul with his darker hair, Tommy's dishwater blond, Alice's white hair and our little redheaded Anna. They were a colorful bunch.

I looked at Levi and felt such love for him. He smiled at me.

I put my head against his shoulder and said, "You are my unicorn!"

He laughed, "What does that mean?"

"My happiness," I said.

There was nothing more to say.

End

CPSIA information can be obtained
at www.ICGtesting.com
Printed in the USA
FSHW021650031020
74345FS